The Balance

The Balance

MICHAEL SELDEN

W.P.P.

WOODLAND PARK PRESS
WOODLAND PARK, COLORADO

Woodland Park Press LLC
502 Fullview Avenue
Woodland Park, Colorado 80863

Cover illustrations by Paola Sbriccoli
Cover and interior design by Jamie Kerry of Belle Étoile Studios

Front cover image: "Sunny afternoon at Norris Point" by Kenny Louie, with modification—Licensed under CC BY 2.0 https://creativecommons.org/licenses/by/2.0/

Copyediting by John Hudspith

First Edition

Printed and bound in the United States of America

ACKNOWLEDGEMENTS

I would like to acknowledge the additional contributions of the following people:

Benjamin Allen for developmental editing

Chip Cheek, proofreader

Stan Dains for his comments on early versions of the story

John Hudspith for his editing suggestions and copyediting

Paola Sbriccoli, for her contributions and discussions on the story throughout its development, and for the cover art

James Wolff, who provided a systematic read of an early version of the book

David Yoo for his developmental editing criticisms and suggestions

My Beta Readers, for providing good and timely feedback on the final plot, and for having the patience to tolerate a fairly rough draft of the actual text (in alphabetical order):

Marlene Kelleher

Katarina Rodriguez

Raul Rodriguez

Lori Stillwell

Amanda Wysocki

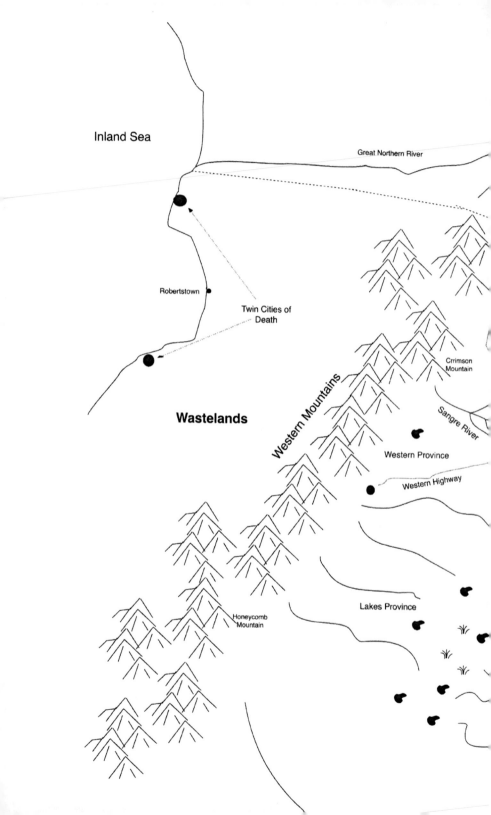

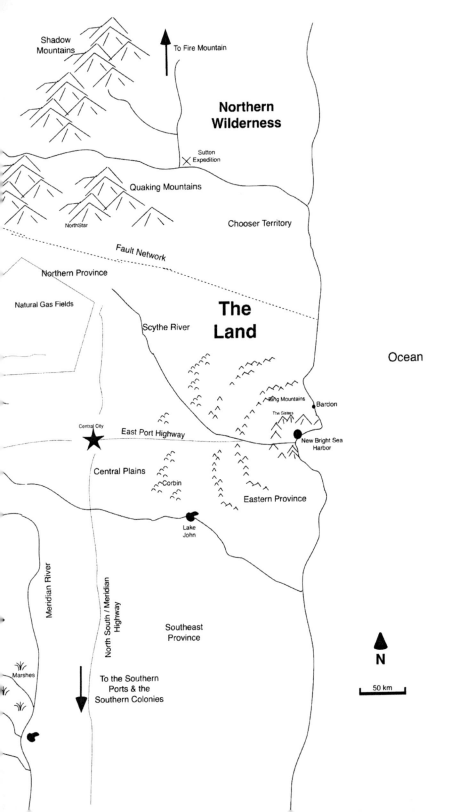

The story of *The Balance* explores the conflict between tolerance and extremism, and is not intended to either pass judgment on or to pit the concept of religion against a secular, or technological, society. This is a work of pure fiction and neither characters nor the story are based on actual people or events.

What Came Before

THE WORLD WAS CHANGING FAST. Technological advances were coming so rapidly that they severely disrupted a global economy that was unable to adjust quickly enough. Worldwide recession settled in and threatened to become permanent depression. Meanwhile, these same advances also made it possible for even the poorest nations to develop lethal weaponry.

Rising unemployment and financial uncertainty triggered a wave of nationalism that swept from country to country and continent to continent. Fear led to mistrust, which led to hostility. Political leaders—not knowing what else to do—did what they'd always done: they blamed problems on their political opponents, and on outsiders. A growing sense of helplessness combined with the proliferation of nuclear weapons to greatly escalate the danger of open conflict.

Leaders from two separate organizations independently saw where the madness was headed, and each developed a secret plan of last resort.

The Order was an ancient organization, long steeped in mysticism and alchemy, but over time it had evolved into a technological behemoth. Its tendrils were spread across borders and throughout the scientific and engineering worlds. As war approached, John Martin, head of the Order, directed vast resources to create what he called 'Sanctuaries', living time capsules intended to preserve human progress for future generations.

These Sanctuaries were constructed in secret, and geographically hidden in natural underground caverns. They were equipped and staffed with the very best tools and scientists. If war came, Sanctuaries would provide shelter from the destruction. Later, the survivors would emerge to rebuild the world.

For decades the Order had also been working on a set of clandestine genetic engineering programs, a long-term effort intended to improve human design by developing all new characteristics. In addition to their primary goal, each Sanctuary was also charged with continuing these efforts, collectively termed the Future Man project.

Separately, leaders from the three major monotheistic religions—Christianity, Judaism, and Islam—also recognized the danger of apocalypse. They met in secret, searching for a way to stop the madness. These leaders recognized that action was needed to avert war, but that their chance of success was small. The urgent threat to human existence compelled them to abandon their customary mistrust of each other and to dedicate their combined power, influence, and wealth toward a single purpose. To that end, they formed a joint hierarchy called the Council of God.

The Council ordered emergency reserves of food, water, and tools to be secreted for use after war, to save as much human life as possible. Like the Order, they hid the reserves in natural underground caverns worldwide, and assigned clergy to each location. These 'priests' would become the new leadership if the worst happened. The Council placed much of the blame for the coming war on two root causes: a loss of faith by the population, and the spread of dangerous knowledge and technologies. Besides saving as much human life as possible, the clergy was also given an additional charter: lead survivors to a simpler, faith-based life in the new world, and limit the spread of dangerous knowledge. They believed that a population rooted in faith and based in an agrarian economy would be far less likely to repeat the predicted destruction.

The war everyone feared came and billions died. Most of the world, along with almost all of the emergency food reserves, and the Order's Sanctuaries, were destroyed. Only the Land escaped the apocalypse. It was in the Land that two of the Order's Sanctuaries—always built in pairs—and one of the Council's reserves endured.

Survivors from the Sanctuaries and the new Council of God leadership only learned of each other's existence after the war, when the Order members emerged from their hiding places. The Council was suspicious of the Order, and the Order was wary of the religious hierarchy's purpose. Still, the two groups managed to form an uncomfortable partnership and penned an agreement they called The Balance. It stipulated that the Order keep its core knowledge secret. They could provide the benefits of a modern civilization, but not disclose how the underlying technologies worked. Further, the Order was to acknowledge that the Council was senior in their arrangement, and agree to not openly challenge its leadership.

The Balance forced compromise, and created a successful collaboration that lasted over 150 years. However, everything changed once the Future Man programs were accidentally revealed. These efforts had always been at the very heart of the Order's charter, and enormous progress had been made following the war. A number of the human products from Future Man's three programs were secretly living in cities and blending in with the population.

The Council considered Future Man heresy, and a direct threat to the faith. They began taking measures to expel the Order from society in what became known as the Purge. Overnight, Order members became outcasts, and were driven into hiding, or arrested. Beings created through the genetic programs were declared demons, and rounded up for public execution. The Council warned people about 'demons walking among us' and advised everyone to be on the lookout for people practicing witchcraft. The population's fear intensified when an unexpected natural catastrophe occurred.

A wayward asteroid, mislabeled the 'comet', crossed Earth's orbit, calving into many pieces as it passed too closely to the moon. These pieces rained down on the world, striking on land and in the sea, and they created widespread destruction that caused two years of winter-like weather. The threat of mass starvation created panic. Fortunately, the Council had replenished their emergency food reserve and was able to save the population, just as they had in the past. The story of The Balance begins almost eighteen years after the 'comet' struck.

Prologue

THE OLD WOMAN WATCHED BECKY settle into the seat beside her. She'd been sitting alone under the deep porch in her favorite rocking chair since before dawn, enjoying the approaching storm and waiting for the girl to wake up. It had been raining off and on since around midnight, but the lightning and strong winds had begun just a half hour before. The woman felt it when the thunder awakened her granddaughter. Becky was uneasy about the storm's violence and flinched every time a network of lightning streaked across the sky. She'd count the seconds in her head between the lightning and the thunder to see if the storm was getting closer.

"I'm glad you could come this week. You're probably wondering why your mother sent you to stay with me." The young girl nodded, looking mostly at her grandmother, but also casting an occasional furtive glance toward the clouds. "Well, I thought it was time you and I got to know one another a little better. We see each other during holidays, but it can be a little distracting when everybody's talking all at once."

Becky stared at the ground for a moment, and pushed herself up higher in the seat.

"But aren't you pretty busy?" the girl asked. "I mean, you're kind of important."

The old woman smiled, but didn't answer directly.

"It probably feels strange not to be in school, doesn't it?" Becky nodded. "A lot of things are important, especially time with family. Don't you think?" Again, the girl nodded, but didn't say anything; a small frown made its way to her face. "I think you'll see that this time we have together is important, too ... for both of us." Thunder cracked suddenly, surprising Becky. She looked even more uncomfortable now that the storm's heart was almost on top of them.

"I love the rain," the old woman said, almost to herself. "It makes everything smell so nice."

"I guess so," the girl said, her frown deepening. "But that's mostly when it stops." The old woman laughed and reached across the space between them. Her deeply veined hand closed briefly over the girl's arm.

"You're right, of course. But did you know that the water we see falling has been doing a kind of dance for millions, even billions of years?" The girl shook her head. "It's made this ... this incredible journey time and again. See that drop?" The woman pointed to a ripple just formed in a puddle near the bottom of the steps. "It might have been part of a glacier in the Western Mountains just a hundred years ago.

"Glaciers are constantly changing. They advance and retreat with the seasons, and move slowly all the time, like the thickest toffee. When the ice melts, water trickles down their slopes, collecting and forming into pools and streams. These join with other streams, until they become rivers that flow across the Land and on to the sea.

"That drop we saw was certainly part of an ocean at one time— who knows for how long. Eventually it evaporated under the sun's warmth, becoming part of a cloud that drifted through the sky—it may even have gone all the way around the world. Later, cool air caused it to condense into the drop we saw, and today it fell to give us something interesting to talk about.

"Everything and everyone we see is connected in one way or another—and they're all constantly changing, too. It's amazing when you think about it. That such a small thing—a drop of water— can go through so many changes, be part of so many different things, so many times. And yet somehow, it always manages to come back as a drop of water." Becky's frown faded while she listened. "A lot of people think *we* go through something like this, too—they say we return repeatedly as one person or another. I don't know if that's true, but it's interesting to think about while you watch the rain fall."

The woman knew that the girl was more relaxed now, and no longer paying attention to the flashes in the sky.

"You probably know something about my life, and at least a few of the things that happened to me." The abrupt shift in subject startled Becky. She could see the surprise in her eyes.

"Yeah." Becky looked down, and her voice was almost a whisper.

"One reason you're here this week is so that I can share something with you. It'll be just the two of us."

"Will it hurt?" Becky asked unexpectedly. The old woman tried hard not to laugh, but a tiny smile escaped her control anyway. "Because I've heard some of the stories about you," the girl clarified.

"No," the woman said, trying to put as much reassurance into her voice as possible. "Not at all. There'll probably be times when you'll feel afraid, and there'll be things that you'll find confusing—you may not understand them right away. But your mother and I waited until we both thought you were old enough for this." The woman touched the girl's mind with a thought, and then paused before asking the next question. She wanted to give her time to absorb everything.

"Is that all right with you—do you want to go on?" she asked. It was important to her that Becky be given the choice, but the old woman also knew that the girl's time was running out. Before long things would begin to happen to her—terrifying things that no one should have to face alone.

Becky thought a little longer. "Okay." And then she asked, "What will it be like?"

The old woman took a deep breath, and let it out as a long sigh. "Like a dream, one that will seem very, very real. But you should know that I'll be with you all the time."

Becky swallowed, and then stared directly into the old woman's gray eyes for several seconds.

"Okay, I'm ready."

CHAPTER 1

Is This Real?

PHOEBE STUMBLED AND FELL. HER hands were already bleeding from before, but now they had all new stones and dirt embedded into them. She lay on the ground coughing, trying to decide whether to get up, or just give up. But then something flared in her chest—a toughness, or maybe just plain stubbornness. She gathered herself together and pushed forward. One quick look over her shoulder was all she could spare. It wasn't possible to see who was chasing her, but what she did see made her gasp—the sky was burning.

Thick clouds hung over the valley where she lived, and beyond the surrounding mountains. Dark columns of smoke rose up to meet this dense canopy, like giant pillars, and at the base of each one was an enormous fire. Light from the flames was reflected in the clouds, painting everything in a dim red cast.

Phoebe's legs ached from climbing, every step hurt more than the one before—she prayed her legs wouldn't cramp up and make her fall again.

Need to stop, she thought, coughing, *just for a minute.*

She'd been climbing a long time, but still didn't know exactly where she was. The trail zigged and zagged its way up the mountain, following the hill's contours. It was hard to spot anything through the smoke, let alone a clear landmark, or to even see where the city was.

A horrible smell filled the air—the odor of rotting fish. Millions of them had been washing up on the shores of the harbor for weeks, and the east wind carried the odor inland. But without the breeze, her eyes would have been burning from all the smoke, and it would have been hard to breathe.

How did I know that—about the fish? Phoebe wondered. She felt dizzy, and it was so hard to think clearly. *Where am I? Why the hell are those people chasing me? Is this real?* Phoebe wasn't sure it was happening at all. The last thing she remembered was going to bed, but that hadn't always meant she was just dreaming. Lots of horrible things happened to her while she slept, but never anything quite like this.

This has got to be someone's dream! she thought. *But it doesn't make sense. It's too real—even the people.*

Anger poured out from the mob of people behind her, fear and hatred—all directed at her. The men and women in dreams she shared had never been like this before, with emotions so strong that they caused her pain. Dream people usually lacked presence, and they didn't have thoughts. These people were real. But there was no time to stop and think about why she was here—it was run, or die.

For now, Phoebe concentrated on the path, and on each step. The trail was barely visible in the darkness. The only illumination came from the firelight reflected in the clouds. The path was badly damaged, its edge crumbled, and sometimes half of the trail was missing altogether. One wrong step could mean a very long fall.

Rocks in the soil helped to hold the soil together, but they were a problem, too. Wherever the dirt had washed away, these same rocks became dangerous trip hazards. She overlooked one, her foot caught on it, and she fell face-first into the ground. The salty, metallic taste in her mouth triggered a memory of the bright copper pennies her father used to give her for ice cream on Saturdays. Phoebe swore out loud and got back up, confused, but angry, too.

Why is this happening? she wondered, stumbling forward again.

As if to answer her question, familiar images and sensations—like a lost memory—flooded into her mind. Everything around her changed all at once. Time on the trail slowed to a crawl as her mind raced ahead—whole minutes were experienced in the moment between two footsteps.

♎

Now Phoebe was standing on a hill, just under one of the torches that ringed a little hollow, and she was looking down into a crowd. Hundreds of people had gathered and were kneeling around a hooded man. He stood inside a small circle of torches speaking passionately, his arms spread out wide, gesturing as he spoke. Other figures, also wearing robes but with bare heads, moved among the kneeling people. Each carried a torch in one hand and what looked like a coil of rope in the other. The kneeling people were dressed in ordinary street clothes, but many had dark streaks on their backs.

The speaker's face was hidden in the shadow of the hood. His head turned side to side as he looked around, slowly rotating to face different parts of the crowd, but then the man abruptly stopped to stare in Phoebe's direction. He pointed a finger at her, issuing some sort of command. Everyone turned to look at her and, after a shocked pause, picked up his words, repeating them. Phoebe could feel the fear spreading through the crowd. A few individuals sprang to their feet and rushed toward her, the rest followed more slowly. Everyone was yelling the same words over and over. After a moment, she understood what they were saying: "Kill the demon!"

The memory ended as suddenly as it had begun and she was back on the hill, climbing again.

♎

What was that? she thought. The abrupt shift in time made her stumble and almost fall again. She paused for a moment to get her bearings, and finally saw two landmarks that she recognized: a glint of steel high above her in one direction, and the muted glow of the town in another. She knew where she was now, and the trail took on an all-too-familiar look. She'd climbed here with her father years before. The town's shape was more obvious when she zigged west at the next turn—it was across the harbor. She couldn't escape this way—the trail was a dead end!

She was heading east along a peninsula—the rocky appendage of a mountain to the north of town. This trail ended at the top of tall cliffs overlooking the sea. *Crap,* she thought, almost ready to cry. But the others were getting close, and she had to go on.

After a while, the path ended and the ground opened onto a broad shelf facing the east. A sharp line of rock was at her feet and nothing but a vast emptiness beyond it. She could hear waves breaking on the rocks far below, but it was too dark to see much detail.

Individual voices were beginning to emerge from behind now—they'd reach her soon. She looked west and saw the torches they carried, a line of fire snaking its way up the hill toward her. Ominously, the sound of several hundred feet pounding on the earth was getting louder, too.

"Crap!" Phoebe breathed again.

All at once, a new sensation ignited from deep inside of her. It started as an icy chill in her stomach and then changed, tearing across her chest and to her arms and legs and fingertips. A blistering heat and unearthly cold passed through her all at the same time—intense, and getting stronger.

"What's happening to me?" she yelled.

The pain seemed to double every second and she fell to her knees screaming in agony. The mob was forgotten, the smoke and the fires and the smell of rotten fish all faded away. But the pain kept on building higher and higher until Phoebe was sure she'd pass out. Then everything changed again. A strong presence touched her from inside—a woman. It felt as though warm arms were holding her, and helping to keep her mind and body together. Finally, the burning dissipated, slowly at first, but soon she was free of the pain.

What the hell was that? she thought, weaker than before. She managed to climb back to her feet, and almost fell over the lip of rock before catching herself. But now her executioners were arriving.

The hooded man was in the lead, just cresting that last rise. He'd have her in a second or two. Desperate, her mind raced ahead, evaluating and choosing in an instant. And as his hand reached toward her, she leaned out over the cliff and jumped.

Phoebe looked up as she fell, her arms flailing. She stared back into the shadow of the hood where the man's eyes *must* be. Just then, a woman's voice spoke into her mind.

I love you, Phoebe.

CHAPTER 2
Burnt Toast

THE SUN HAD BEEN TRYING to peer through the window but was frustrated until a helpful breeze started playing with the curtains. Each time they parted, light splashed on Phoebe's face. The alternating bright and dark pattern reached into a different, more pleasant dream, stirring her consciousness. Not fully awake, her mind strayed to that curious place we all sometimes go, a world between dream and reality where our senses and imagination blend. It was natural for her thoughts to wander back to the cliffs high above the sea, and to the moment when she'd decided to jump to her death. Phoebe awoke with a start. Her eyes were drawn to the familiar pictures on her walls, anchors that always brought her back to the safety of her own bed.

Her room was simply furnished. A narrow bed was centered on the north wall, with a wooden nightstand to her right. It held an oil lamp, still lit, but turned down very low. This way she could have light quickly, without struggling to find a match in the darkness. A tiny flame was still visible, but only when the curtains met to block the sunlight. A battered but sturdy wardrobe was set against the west wall. Dresses hung in its left-hand side, and there was room below for shoes. The right-hand door hid a column of different-sized drawers and shelves. Phoebe kept folded clothes, linens, and her personal belongings there. The wardrobe had originally belonged to her uncle before he left for Central City, some twenty-five years ago.

It was difficult to tell what color the walls might originally have been. Every available surface was covered with pictures—charcoal and pencil drawings, watercolor and oil paintings. They hung without apparent plan or order, and the pages were many layers deep in most places. Each morning her eyes sought out these familiar images—reminders of a thousand nights of terror. But for Phoebe they were strangely comforting, a record of the many things she'd survived.

Her father, Daniel, was asleep in the old rocking chair near the window, his head rested on his chest, and he was snoring softly. The sound of his breathing had let her know he was there through the night, and helped her sleep again. Daniel had come when he'd heard her screaming—just as he always had.

The rocker stood sentry in a triangular niche attached to the east side of the room, where the walls came together in an unusual mixture of oblique and sharp angles. To Phoebe, the area had always seemed an afterthought, an eccentricity added to an otherwise normal space. She thought that it made for an odd room and was well suited for her—an odd room for an odd girl.

She watched her father sleep, wondering—not for the first time—how much better his life might have been without her. Phoebe noticed how thin his hair had gotten, and how much it had changed. No longer the brown she remembered so well, it had faded to an indeterminate color, one that most people call gray, even though it really isn't.

The sound of hooves on stone and the creaking of wooden wheels under load came through the open window. It was late. That was probably the sound of the milkman finishing his rounds.

Phoebe climbed from the bed with a deep sigh, hating to get up, not wanting to disturb her father, but they had to get moving. Her legs were like rubber, as though she'd actually climbed the trail last night, but phantom feelings were nothing new to her. Phoebe moved in her sleep, tensing muscles and reacting, as though physically experiencing what happened to whomever she touched telepathically. If that person experienced trauma, she felt it, too. She could remember a beating shared with a woman from the neighborhood, and awakening with blood on her face and pillow. At the time, her father guessed that she'd hit her own nose, thrashing around while asleep, but she wasn't 100 percent sure that pain was the only thing that could be transferred through her mind.

A loose floorboard protested as she crossed the room. Phoebe froze and gently removed the offending foot to sidestep the board and kneel beside her father's chair. "Dad, wake up." Her voice was just above a whisper. She gently put one hand on his shoulder and his eyes opened, but his head moved up much more slowly. An expression of pain and confusion gradually changed to recognition and then concern.

Morning, Princess, he said in their silent language.

Why didn't you go back to bed? she scolded silently.

I slept, he thought at her, yawning. "What time is it?" aloud.

"About six-thirty," Phoebe admitted, trying to avoid his stare. She knew how much he hated to rush in the morning.

Her father closed his eyes and pushed up from the chair. His teeth were tightly clenched, trying to hide the pain he felt, but a tiny groan escaped anyway. "Okay, I'm up," he said, taking a breath to recover. "Can you make coffee while I get ready?" Phoebe stood, too, nodding. The guilty look on her face made her father swallow.

"Sorry, Dad," she mumbled, looking at the floor. He put a hand on her shoulder, and a twisted half smile made its way to his face as he put his forehead against hers.

"Hey, kiddo. You know, I'd almost forgotten how comfortable that chair could be. Let's get ready, okay?" Phoebe tried unsuccessfully to smile back, and nodded again.

Phoebe walked unsteadily through the apartment's main room to the front door, her muscles still stiff. Outside, on the landing, was a wood and metal box, from which she retrieved milk and butter. The glass bottle was still ice-cold; condensation had formed on its surface and drops of water ran over her hand. She handled it gently, not wanting to disturb the cream on top. Back in the kitchen, she stood on her toes to retrieve two matches from a can on the shelf above the stove then used one to light the gas lamp. The other one would be used to light the stove's burners. Next, she poured out half of the cream that had collected at the top of the bottle into a small jar for their coffee, and then mixed the rest back in with the milk.

The percolator was in pieces; its parts had been left upside down on the counter beside the stove to dry. She hadn't put things away after washing up last night, but at least everything was clean. Once the coffee was on, she started breakfast.

Yesterday's bread was in its box. The dark, heavy loaf gave off a nutty aroma, but she'd forgotten to wrap the end again and it had hardened overnight. *Oh well,* she thought, picking up an oversized bread knife. *Toast is supposed to be hard.* Three thick slices went onto a metal plate that covered two of the stove's burners.

While the water was heating, Phoebe set the table. Their dishes, the table, and pretty much everything they owned were old. Most things dated from the pre-comet era and bore the unmistakable uniformity of industrially manufactured products. There used to be twelve plates, but time had taken its toll and now there were only five. This established a limit to their guest lists, but that had never been a problem since only her grandfather, Jacob, ever visited anyway. Not paying attention, Phoebe burned one side of the toast. *Well, it isn't really-really burned…besides, the butter will spread better this way,* she told herself, nodding. Once everything was ready, she called for her father.

Her coffee was strong but not bitter. Phoebe had added a pinch of salt to the grounds—a trick her grandfather taught her. As she stirred the first mug of coffee, her mind drifted back to the strange dream again, and to the presence of the woman she'd felt at its end.

The woman was just as confusing as the dream. Phoebe had connected with countless people before, especially when she was asleep and her mind wide open. She'd shared people's waking thoughts, their dreams, their experiences, and much more. But none she'd touched in this way had ever been aware of her. And no one besides her father and grandfather had ever told her that they loved her.

Last night was very different from the other experiences she'd shared. The Land and everything in it was so strange—and far too real. It felt much closer to how things were when she lived through them firsthand.

Most people don't notice everything they see, and remember even less. They don't pick up on the little things around them, details and subtle variations in surfaces. Then, when something draws their attention, they forget everything else—like how the air is moving or the scent it carries. When Phoebe connected with someone, she could only perceive what that person's mind noticed. But the Land in last night's dream was absolutely complete and incredibly detailed—as real as the kitchen was right now.

She'd seen bits and pieces of what the Land had been like just after the comet, fuzzy images of chaos still present in older people's dreams. But last night's vision of the Land was as though she'd been there herself. It was all stored in her flawless memory now, seductive and inviting—and easy to slide back into without conscious thought. Even now, Phoebe's mind drifted back—she'd just stepped up to the edge of the cliff and could feel the humid breeze from the sea blowing her hair. The sound of a door closing brought her back.

Her father came out wearing his court robes. He had an early case today. The robes were black, of course, with blue piping on the sleeves and at the neck. The color identified his role in court, and this exact shade of blue had always been Phoebe's favorite color.

Everyone in court wore black robes. Blue piping was reserved for the defenders; red piping meant you were a prosecutor; gold signified that you were a judge. The Justice Keepers wore white piping. They were the police, the soldiers, and the executioners. Only Council elders, the eight members of the Inner Circle, were permitted to wear the solid red robes. These had been adopted from the distant past, from a church or order that no longer existed.

After sitting down, her father frowned at the toast and glanced at Phoebe, but didn't say anything. She pretended not to see his look, and smiled to herself. Neither mentioned the previous night's drama. This was one of the things Phoebe really loved about her dad—he respected her feelings and her privacy, even though the privacy of his own thoughts was under constant threat. But she always did her best to stay out of his mind, and had never, ever, probed his deeper, more painful memories.

After her father left for work, Phoebe cleaned up the mess and then got ready for school. She brushed out her dark hair, working to constrain its disorder into a simple loose braid. It really needed to be cut, but she hated doing it and, somehow, always found one reason or another to procrastinate.

The girl in the bathroom mirror was shaking her head at what she saw this morning. The long black hair and gray eyes were familiar enough, but Phoebe was still getting used to the new school uniform. It was mandatory, and reflected the classic Council fashion elements: dark, shapeless, and uncomfortable. But its uniformity helped her to blend in better. Stepping out of the bathroom, she put on the Council-approved shoes, grabbed the lunch she'd made last night, picked up her books from the table near the fireplace, and left for school.

"At least it's Friday," Phoebe sighed as she closed the door.

CHAPTER 3

The Steel Tower

THE TOWN OF NEW BRIGHT SEA HARBOR rests on a shelf of land created over millions of years. One by one, mountain-sized slabs of rock had broken off from vertical slopes and tumbled into what was once a much larger harbor. These fallen cliffs formed the valley's foundation. Over time, the Scythe River carved a path back through the mountains from the west, and its regular flooding had covered the bare rock with soil.

The Ring Mountains had been created long before. They stood like ripples in the earth's crust, as though some enormous object had been thrown down into the sea, causing the land to liquefy, buckle, and flow, creating waves of rock that had frozen in place. But as soon as they formed, the mountains began to tilt, splinter, and fall into the ocean. Peaks closest to the town were tallest. Subsequent rings were farther from the epicenter and gradually lost height until they blended with the central plains, farther west. Valleys formed between the concentric heights and collected soil over the millennia, nurturing trees and creating rich farmland.

$$\Omega$$

Phoebe walked toward school on the west side of the street, the sunny side for now. The air was cooler than it had been for days, but there was no breeze between the buildings. The sun felt warm on her face. Later today, the air would grow hot and sticky. She paused a moment to look back toward the hills she'd climbed in her dream. Tree-covered slopes rose up sharply just north of town giving way to fractured bare rock about two thirds of the way up.

The hills where she'd been last night were farther east, an extension of the large mountain directly to the north. It was a part of the semicircle of mountains that hedged the town against the sea. The mountain's extension stabbed out into the ocean, creating a peninsula that formed the north side of the harbor. As she climbed, Phoebe had run back and forth along its slopes, and then out toward the cliffs overlooking the sea.

Directly north of town stood the highest point of that same mountain. She could make out the tall metal structure that rose from its peak and gleamed in the morning sun. Phoebe had often stared at the tower, thinking about the mother she never knew.

Becky had been a member of the Order, the organization that built the tower, and other towers like it. Most had been removed or destroyed by the Council, as a part of their effort to erase all trace of the Order's existence, but this one had frustrated them. Years before, it had served as a communications link to other parts of the Land. The Order had lifted the entire structure whole, and planted it deep into the rocky peak. They'd used technologies that the Council never possessed. But the Order destroyed their more advanced tools and machines as they fled the Purge, leaving only older technologies from before the war. This lone monument to the past was a landmark she'd spotted last night. Phoebe sighed and then turned south, toward school.

Daniel and Phoebe Lambert lived in a two-bedroom apartment at the north end of town, along East Third Street—and three blocks east of Main Street. By tradition traffic on odd-numbered streets flowed one way, north. A number of private carts passed by as she was walking south, toward the town's center. The sound of hooves on stone pavement was somehow reassuring. These carts were mostly single-horse affairs, often used by well-to-do citizens, but the ones going by were making deliveries. Street sweepers were already busy collecting manure left by the horses, moving quickly before it had a chance to mature in the afternoon heat. But it was the smell of fresh bread that filled the neighborhood now. The sound and feel of the town waking up were helping to put last night's dream behind her.

As she reached the second corner below her building, the seven-thirty trolley made its turn from Fourth Street, to head over to Second and turn south again. A team of horses strained against the streetcar's weight and its metal wheels, rolling on iron rails, made a thumping sound every time they hit a seam. The bell rang to announce that the trolley would stop at the corner, but Phoebe didn't hurry. She'd decided to walk to school today, preferring open space to being crammed into a trolley with everyone else.

Wading through people boarding, she turned west to make the one-block jog over to Second Street. The town was wrapped around the curve of the harbor's shoreline, as were most streets close to the water. But here, near the center of town, the streets lost most of their bend and she could see all the way downtown to the park.

It was the first of September and summer vacation had already faded to little more than a memory. Phoebe read somewhere that students in country schools didn't start classes until October; their hands were needed at home for the fall harvest. Here in the city, they didn't have a good excuse to delay classes. She complained to her father that he should have been a farmer so she could skip a month of school, too.

"You could always go with your grandfather on the September fishing run—it's the last of the season and I'm sure they'd understand," he offered, trying not to grin, but the look on Phoebe's face was too much, and he sprayed coffee all over the table. Her father chuckled every time he looked at her that night, remembering the expression of horror.

As Phoebe drew close to the school, other students were visible; she could see them up ahead, in groups of twos and threes—all part of the same sad march, and each one dressed in the same drab garb. She kept a good distance from them, not wanting to speak with anyone. It was easy enough to hear their thoughts—if she wanted. Most of the time Phoebe struggled to *not* hear their endless chatter. She was far from perfect, but being able to silence the voices had been essential for survival.

The Land was a very dangerous place for Phoebe. People would notice her if she wasn't careful—if she made too many mistakes. They would think she was different or strange, and being different or strange in the Land could cost you your life. But Phoebe was used to it; she lived with the threat of death every day. Her biggest challenge had been blocking the continuous stream of images and feelings and fears and words—they never stopped. But she was much stronger now, stronger than the little girl who screamed in terror when surrounded by crowds. Last night's unwelcome connection had been a big setback, and one she couldn't explain.

Still, strength alone couldn't keep her safe, and it had never been a reliable defense. So Phoebe practiced the Discipline, a way of life that didn't depend on her being perfect all the time. The Discipline had been drummed into her day after day, year after year, until it was second nature. But it imposed severe restrictions. There were a lot of things Phoebe couldn't do that other people her age took for granted. Most of the Discipline could be summarized in just a few phrases: Go slow. Make sure. When in doubt, remain silent. But the most important, and heaviest to bear, was: Avoid other people as much as possible. The Discipline had kept her alive and out of the hands of the Inquisition for years, but she paid a heavy price.

A familiar mind was approaching. Phoebe felt the girl's presence long before hearing her footsteps, or her greeting.

"Morning, Phoebe." She turned, making sure she'd actually heard a voice before replying. The expectant look in Sarah's eyes meant that she was waiting for her to say something.

"Hey Sarah. You ready?" she asked quickly—questions kept other people talking and minimized other questions they might ask.

"I think so," Sarah replied. "My father...*helped* me." Phoebe didn't see, but felt Sarah's eyes roll. "The interrogation lasted more than two hours! How 'bout you? Ready?" She didn't turn to look at the girl this time, but nodded slightly, which she might have done anyway, even if she was just thinking.

In school, Phoebe was 'the quiet, slow girl'. People made jokes about her, but she pretended, for her father's sake, that she didn't mind anymore. He'd held her many times while she cried about the names they called her that first year.

"Sorry, Princess," he'd say. "I wish there was something else we could do." But the ridicule was a small price to pay to avoid being killed.

Sarah was pretty and thin, although in the shapeless robes it was hard to tell. Her hair was somewhere between brown and red—auburn. Sometimes Phoebe wished her eyes were like Sarah's, an ultra-clear blue that reminded her of shallow water over the sandbars in the harbor. But it wasn't her eyes, or her looks, that Phoebe really envied—Sarah was normal.

They walked side by side the rest of the way to school. Sarah prattled about the other girls in class. Phoebe listened, nodding now and then to keep Sarah talking. She'd tell herself that she didn't care what the others were up to—who was with which boy, or if there was a get-together this weekend. None of that would ever apply to her anyway. It had never bothered her much before, but lately she'd been feeling more and more lonely—another fact she tried to hide for her father's sake.

CHAPTER 4

Classes

THEY REACHED THE SCHOOL'S GATES at first bell. Everyone hurried to pass through the narrow portal, and they pressed in around her. It was times like this that Phoebe felt the most vulnerable and likely to make a mistake, so she looked down and clamped her mouth shut. It was an unnecessary measure. The others had long since been ignoring her. It made her feel almost invisible, but a little safer, too. They made it to the church before last bell, and Mistress Judith shot Sarah and her a warning glance for cutting it so closely.

♎︎

The school was originally built as a monastery, centuries before the war. It had once been famous for its extensive library and for the music skills of its monks, but over time the role of the church in people's lives declined, and with this loss the ranks of monks also dwindled. Eventually, the bishops felt that they could no longer justify the expense of the monastery's maintenance and closed it down. An industrialist bought the property just a few years before the war and donated it to the town, to be used as a library and fine arts center. In the aftermath of war it was converted into a high school, jointly staffed by the Council and the Order. Following the Purge, the Council severely restricted the school's curriculum, removing many of its books and other teaching materials, especially those related to the sciences or engineering. It remained a school, but with these changes the campus began to echo the feel of a monastery again.

The school had offered morning services since it was founded. A renaissance of faith and trust in the church for its leadership in the aftermath of the war increased attendance. But as the Council grew more authoritarian in its approach, attendance became mandatory. Now there were severe penalties for students who failed to participate.

The Council maintained separate schools and churches for each of its three founding faiths: Christianity, Judaism, and Islam. People of similar belief tended to collect into separate enclaves. It was not unusual to find a town that was predominantly populated by people of one religion—the population in Southport, for example, was mostly Muslim, while a village just to its north was overwhelmingly Jewish. New Bright Sea Harbor was primarily a Christian city, and Phoebe's school was one of three Christian high schools in town.

♎︎

Throughout morning prayers, Phoebe's mind kept drifting back to the dream, and to the overwhelming surge of pain during its final moments. She wondered about the woman with whom she'd shared the experience—a consciousness that Phoebe had not directly touched before, still there was something vaguely familiar about her feel. These thoughts distracted her throughout the service. A short night with little sleep added to her exhaustion making it difficult to stay awake.

The students moved to their first class once the service ended. Phoebe and Sarah were assigned to Mistress Judith's room for the twice-daily Council announcements. She tried to listen, but soon found herself back on the cliffs.

The stream of imagery and sensations was as sharp and detailed as it had been last night. Her vision kept jumping from place to place. Once again, Phoebe could see the sky glowing red behind a man's hooded face as he reached the shelf, and she could feel the intense anger of the mob. It was all so clear to her. A humid breeze from the sea stirred her hair, and brought the odor of rotting fish. The ache in her legs and palms had returned, too, along with wetness, as blood trickled from cuts on her knees. Her memory jumped in time again, to the point where she was turning away from the ocean to see the torches making their way up the hill. That strange cold sensation began to form in her stomach, as if triggered by the memory...

"...Miss Lambert. Phoebe!" Judith's voice was angry, urgent—it brought Phoebe back to the present, breaking the spell.

"Huh?" Phoebe muttered in a voice that was brittle and frail. But even in her confused state of mind, she was able to probe what Judith was seeing. The teacher was standing directly over her, glaring—a mixture of anger and worry. Phoebe had been very close to losing control, right in front of everyone. *Crap, what's the matter with me?*

"Are you with us, or sleeping?"

From Judith's mind, Phoebe saw that the teacher had been thinking to speak with the headmistress about her, but—somehow—couldn't bring herself to add to Phoebe's problems. Judith was especially nervous today. There was a Council observer in class and she couldn't show tolerance for misbehavior.

"Sorry," Phoebe said wiping a hand across her face, still unable to meet Judith's eyes.

"I'll see you in detention," Judith snapped, before returning to the announcements. Phoebe acknowledged the punishment with a stiff nod, and quietly sighed. Judith went on with the day's announcements.

Ω

Phoebe's first regular subject was art. It was the only class that always went by too quickly. She thought of time as an enemy, one who conspired to slow down when she was stuck in classes she hated, but rushed by when she was having fun. Art had always been therapy for Phoebe, and drawing a way to explore and disarm the more terrifying things she'd been through. Somehow, drawing reduced the power fear had over her.

She worked on two drawings today—things she'd seen that morning. She would put off the images from last night's dream for later, when she could be alone. This was the agreement made with her father after that time she'd made a big mistake in school.

♎

When Phoebe was a little girl, her mind was completely defenseless, and her consciousness would wander outward from her body as she slept. People who broadcast strong emotions attracted her, like a moth drawn to the brightest lights. Strong feelings of fear, pain, and sometimes love could lure her in, and she'd be trapped inside of someone, sharing his or her life, a part of them. An incident happened one night when she was almost nine years old; the event had terrified and revolted her. She'd been so embarrassed by what happened that she even hid it from her father.

Phoebe had recently been forced to attend regular school with other children. She understood what was happening to her during the telepathic connection—it wasn't her first exposure to that kind of thing—but she'd been unprepared for the level of violence and pain that accompanied it, and how it had made her feel. The next day, any little reminder brought tears, and she'd just experienced a flashback before art class.

Still shaking as she sat down, Phoebe felt compelled to draw what she'd been through right away. She began a sketch of one of the more disturbing parts of the experience. She'd been looking through an older woman's eyes, and feeling everything the woman felt—they'd both struggled to escape, but couldn't move. Phoebe believed that if only she could draw what the man was doing to her, it would help a little bit—even if she couldn't see his face clearly.

The woman knew who the man was, but wouldn't look directly at him, as if avoiding his eyes would help. She lay helpless, bleeding, and stunned from the many blows she'd already sustained just before he started to rape them.

Phoebe drew quickly, adding detail, highlights, and shadows—almost without thinking. Everything was so clear now. She had to keep going, to exorcise the experience from her mind. A teacher was walking around the classroom and paused to look over her shoulder, wondering what the girl was working on so frantically. She turned pale and her hand latched onto Phoebe's shoulder so tightly that it hurt, but the girl kept on drawing, unable to stop now. Finally, the teacher snatched the paper from the table and dragged Phoebe by one arm, toward the headmistress's office. It was too soon! She needed to finish, and kept screaming: "No! Not yet!" Her cries echoed in the hallway, and the despair in her voice frightened the other children.

The detail of the drawing was exceptional—near photographic quality—but the violent and sexually explicit image shocked the teachers. It was especially unnerving having come from such a young girl. The Keepers brought her father from his office after they'd been summoned to investigate. Daniel couldn't explain why or how his daughter could have drawn such a thing. The man's face in the image was just a blur and the Keepers assumed it must have been him.

Phoebe quickly realized her mistake. She'd drawn from fear and a sense of violation. It occurred to her, too late, that whatever she drew in school could never be private—so she told a lie. Phoebe told them that she'd found a photograph that looked just like that lying in the street on her way home the previous day. She was taken to the hospital and forced to submit to an uncomfortable and embarrassing medical examination. There, different people kept coming into the room and looking at her with pity in their eyes—she hated it. Afterward, she showed the Keepers exactly where she'd seen the picture.

It was a place she'd noticed trash being dumped in the past, a little out of the way from her path home, but not unreasonably so.

The photograph was not there, of course, but after that day the site was always kept clean. A sign warned people against leaving trash there. Eventually, the Keepers let her go home with her dad.

That night, her father spoke with her about the kinds of things she should and shouldn't draw at school, explaining that other girls couldn't see things the way she did, that her visions frightened people. Then he tried to engage her about what happened to her.

"Why didn't you tell me about this? You always talk to me about things that bother you." But she was still upset from the day's ordeal and didn't want to talk about it. She wouldn't look him in the eye, and kept staring down at the table, gripping her small hands into tight fists. He noticed she was drawing blood.

"Not all the time," Phoebe said in a whisper he could barely hear. She stood in front of him as tears streamed down her face.

Phoebe knew that her dad never fully appreciated how intense the connections were—that they weren't just visions, but experiences she lived through. It was a hard thing to explain; how do you describe the sky to someone who's never seen light?

"It's all right, kiddo," he said, gently bumping and resting his forehead against hers.

There were a lot of incidents like this that she wasn't able to share, not even with her father, but she'd found a way to cope. He'd see her working on a drawing, so dark and disturbing that he had to leave the room. From that day on, she made sure these images stayed at home. They hung on the walls of her bedroom and greeted her every morning.

♎

Phoebe wasn't considered slow in art class, and her silence was accepted. Instead, people thought of her strange behavior as a kind of artistic quirkiness. Although she restricted her work to inconsequential subjects, its quality was breathtaking. Her teacher, Grace, often praised her drawings and paintings, and several examples of her work hung in the Council's offices. Phoebe didn't seek the added exposure, but since it made Grace happy, and her own life in school easier, she tolerated the visibility in exchange for a little peace.

She sat at the table with Sarah. Her friend had never been very interested in art and was easily distracted. Lately, she'd been obsessing over one of the boys in their class, Caleb. Sarah wasn't the only girl who found him interesting. A number of the others seemed to find one reason or another to wander by his table, or to accidentally bump into him in the hallway. Phoebe suspected that Caleb might be interested in Sarah, too. He visited with her now and then, but Phoebe didn't care much for his type—Caleb was from a Council family.

Certain families had strong connections with the authorities. Following the Purge, many of these had gained a tangible benefit from the alliance. Their wealth had increased significantly over the intervening years. Phoebe was frequently forced to interact with children from Council families. Whenever the Curia of Law—the Council office responsible for the courts—had their little get-togethers, her father and she went. Technically, they were invited, but attendance wasn't actually voluntary. She also met Council kids at church, which was equally mandatory. Most seemed rather superficial and arrogant, not the kind of people she wanted to be around.

To be fair, Phoebe had never seen Caleb behave like a jerk, and had never directly probed his mind. She didn't normally do that sort of thing. Deliberately intruding on a person's mind didn't feel right, and staying out of their heads was a part of the Discipline— it was safer that way. Besides, Phoebe liked to learn about people the ordinary way; it made her feel a little less like a freak and more like a normal person.

She watched Caleb leaning on their table from the corner of her eye. He was asking Sarah about the best way to mix a shade of yellow for a sunrise—not that Sarah would know. But Phoebe wasn't really focused on what he was saying as much as how he was treating her. She could see what the other girls liked about him; he *seemed* nice enough. Phoebe peeked at him just as Caleb looked her way. She barely had time to look down again, pretending to be engrossed in a drawing, but she thought he'd been smiling at her.

Once he'd gone back to his own table, Sarah reached over to lift Phoebe's drawing to reveal what she'd been hiding underneath it. The picture of a trolley was just camouflage for what she'd wanted to draw: a fully rendered image of Judith's hostile face from that morning. The eyes were intense, with just a touch of fear, and they glared out of the picture. But Phoebe had also included a hint of softness behind the angry look. She knew Judith had protected her—still, the angry look had stuck in her mind.

"That's a great drawing! Are you going to show it to Judith?" Sarah asked, snickering. Phoebe paused for a long time, looking between Sarah and the drawing several times before answering.

"I don't think so." The blank expression on her face was too much. Sarah couldn't help laughing, and when she snorted, Phoebe started to laugh, too. They both lost control for a while, only stopping to gasp for breath. Grace started walking toward them, frowning. Phoebe quickly hid Judith's picture under the sketch of the trolley, realizing how reckless she was being. Still, it was hard not to chuckle at Sarah's red face a few more times. Other students in the class looked at Phoebe with confused expressions. Most had never heard her laugh before.

Their next class was history—there was a test today. The exam was on the origins of the Council's formation. Phoebe made sure to miss just enough questions to maintain her reputation for mediocrity. She wanted to be considered an average student, even a little slow—but not too slow.

It was imperative that she stay in 'regular' school; Phoebe would receive far too much attention in the 'special' school for slow learners, and it would be much harder to hide her strangeness. The opposite was true as well. Top students might well wind up in an advanced program where—once again—there was a lot of individual attention. Blend in. Don't stand out. All part of the Discipline.

CHAPTER 5

Lunch With Sarah

MORNING CLASSES FINALLY ENDED. THE day had begun with a shaky start, but Phoebe had recovered well and was quietly proud that she'd made it through the morning without accidentally overhearing anyone's thoughts. Other than the strange connection with the woman in the dream, Phoebe felt she'd been doing pretty well at suppressing unwanted intrusions. It hadn't always been that way.

Blocking out thoughts had never been easy. As a young child she had no idea how to do it at all. She may as well have tried to stop her own heart at will—how would you even begin to do that? The first glimmer of an idea had come by accident when she tried to draw. The concentration needed to get a picture just right seemed to numb her senses a little—it was a start.

She tried to copy that same degree of mental focus during everyday situations and it worked—a little. But she found herself tripping over objects and missing things when people spoke with her. Plus, it wasn't possible to maintain that same level of concentration all the time. Even after she'd finally come up with a crude but usable technique, based on the same principle, the effort of holding multiple people out at the same time consumed more and more of her attention. Phoebe told her father that it was like trying to balance a tall stack of books in each hand and another on top of her head while trying to do everything else. When she was very young, it seemed impossible. And the greater the number of people she had to block, the harder it was to do.

40

In the Land, every child is required by law to attend a Council school. Her father managed to get her a delay of almost three years. He told the authorities that Phoebe was slow and needed more time at home to grasp the basic skills that other children took for granted. They didn't want to listen, but he pulled in favors through his connections at court and secured the delay. Still, the Curia of Truth, the office responsible for the education of the young—and for the Inquisition—made it clear that 'more time' didn't mean an indefinite time. They demanded a plan and regular progress reports. A representative from their office even visited their home every six weeks or so, and at the end of each visit, he'd remind them that there were special schools for the very slow. They were in a race against time; it forced Phoebe's father to push her very hard, much harder than he wanted.

He and Phoebe used the extra time to discover and develop different techniques to control, or at least numb, her senses. It was a slow, painful process, especially at first. Her father had no idea about where to begin and felt helpless. The tiny bit he'd gleaned from conversations with Phoebe's mother weren't of much use. Back then the subject hadn't seemed important since it was assumed that Becky would be there for her. Worse, nothing could have prepared him for the agony Phoebe went through. He often felt that they were wasting time, but there weren't a lot of alternatives available.

Phoebe first began sensing other people's feelings when she was just two years old; deeper connections started just a few months later. Her father tried isolating her from people as much as possible, but her rapidly growing sensitivity soon made that impossible. Instead, he began exposing her to others in controlled ways, hoping that her mind would find a way to cope on its own. He worked relentlessly every day, letting her gradually adapt to thoughts from different people. He started with his own mind first, but soon began inviting one or another of their neighbors to their home for short visits. It was surprising to see how well Phoebe did—she was able to function even when two or three people were present. But he soon learned it was a false progress.

Phoebe had always been tough, and able to tolerate a lot of pressure. She wanted to make him happy. She knew what he wanted to see. But then he took her to the crowded market near the center of town, and it was a much different story. She bore the pressure for as long as possible, but the prolonged assault from the voices and images, emotions and fears of so many people were too much. After a while, she closed her eyes and covered her ears, hoping that would help, but before long she was screaming.

"What's it like, Princess?" he asked after they'd returned home that first day.

"Daddy. It's like the whole world is inside of me. Everyone is there. It hurts and...and there are scary things, too."

"Scary?"

"Please don't make me remember!" Her thoughts and awareness had returned to the market. She was reliving something that terrified her, and was unable to break free. Phoebe rubbed her eyes and then started digging into the skin on her face. Her father grabbed ahold of her hands to stop her.

"Why do you do that, why do you hurt yourself?" he demanded.

"I don't know," Phoebe said closing her eyes tightly and crying. "Just to make it stop."

They worked hard, but it was almost a year before she could be around large groups of people for more than a few minutes at a time. The immersion test at the market was the best tool her father had to measure Phoebe's progress. She could fool him sometimes, pretending to be doing better than she really was, but large crowds were his test of truth.

Just before her ninth birthday, the inspector from the Curia of Truth let them know that Phoebe's extra time at home was coming to an end. By then, her father had gained confidence that she could be among crowds without becoming catatonic. She could do better, but they'd run out of time. The authorities demanded that she attend regular school within one week, or enroll in a special program—one where students stayed overnight during the week. To help her survive, her father began compiling a set of rules to guide her, which he called the Discipline.

♎︎

Phoebe headed to lunch carrying a book and the sandwich she'd made the night before. The school's main building had been constructed around a central courtyard, which served as a lunch area during good weather. A portico ran along three sides of the open quadrangle and provided cover when it rained. Phoebe ate alone, but liked to be in the open area, too. Her favorite spot was in the northwest corner of the courtyard. Lonely and exposed to the sun, Phoebe shared the location with what she thought of as a steadfast, silent friend—an exposed fragment of a large underground boulder. The rock had been so deeply rooted that the builders chose to incorporate it as part of the monastery's foundation rather than dig it out. Phoebe normally perched on 'her rock' with a sandwich and a book, and was headed there when Sarah intercepted her.

"Phoebe, would you sit with me today?" Sarah spoke quickly, her eyes darting nervously toward the east door. She pointed toward a place at the table that ran along the north portico.

Why? Phoebe thought unhappily. Sarah knew that she didn't like big groups of people, and usually left her alone for lunch, but something was different today. Sarah oozed anxiety, biting her lip and almost bouncing with impatience as she waited for an answer. Sitting with Sarah would mean having to interact with a lot of people at the same time. The confusion might cause her to make a mistake. But Sarah was the closest thing Phoebe had to a friend. "All right," she agreed, sighing.

"Don't listen to everything I say today, okay?" Sarah advised, as she hurried them both along. Phoebe frowned, but nodded, trying to steel herself for the coming hour.

They took a place about three-fourths of the way down the table, near its east end. People were still trickling into the courtyard and gradually filling the tables. Phoebe looked down as the others took seats nearby, trying not to make eye contact with anyone. A few girls looked at her strangely, their eyebrows were raised in surprise.

One girl stood on the other side of her table, frowning; Phoebe was in the seat she usually used.

Sarah had chosen their spots with care, near a group of boys who always sat near the end. One by one, their minds occupied the empty spaces to Phoebe's right, and on the other side of Sarah. Boys had a different mental feel than girls and Phoebe usually avoided them.

She had come to accept that she'd always be alone, unable to date, or even to let herself fantasize about it. It was better that way, less painful, and far easier if she just pretended that those kinds of relationships didn't apply to her. Phoebe knew what love meant through other people. Not all of her experiences had been like that horrible rape incident. She'd lived numerous lives through surrogates already—experienced love and loss, passion and companionship, everything that men and women go through. But she couldn't allow false hope for herself—love was for other people, not her.

Who the hell wants to be with a freak? she thought bitterly. Sarah interrupted her thoughts, speaking more loudly than necessary, and directing a question at Phoebe.

"I maxed out the test, even the essay. How'd you do, Pheebs?"

"I…uh…I did okay." She was taken aback by the new nickname, but didn't complain. Sarah wasn't acting like…Sarah, exactly. Phoebe listened to her hash out every detail and nuance of the test before moving on to the other things that had happened that morning. When she started to describe the incident with Judith, Sarah noticed her flinch and stopped.

As she'd been talking, Sarah had also been stealing glances at someone near the end of the table, across from them and to the right. Phoebe recognized the boy's feel right away. It was Caleb, the boy from art class. *I should have known.* She glanced his way quickly, making a show of turning in her seat as if to be more comfortable. They locked eyes for a moment—his were a deep blue. The moment passed so quickly that she didn't have time to feel self-conscious, but her heart was beating faster. *Sarah really likes him,* she reminded herself. *Anyway, it's impossible.*

By the time she realized that Caleb was the boy Sarah was so nervous about, her friend had launched into her family's plans for winter break. Phoebe brought a hand up, releasing her braid as she masked a second surreptitious glance his way. Caleb was talking to someone next to him. Meanwhile Sarah, still agitated, was babbling even more than usual. Phoebe peeked in Caleb's direction a third time, and again their eyes met before she could look away.

She took a deep breath and tried to feign interest in what Sarah was saying, but she couldn't help thinking about the boy. She wondered what Caleb thought about Sarah—and if he was listening to her. Movement from the corner of her eye made her think that he had looked in their direction again.

Would it be so bad if I connected to him? she wondered. *Just a little?* Phoebe debated the matter for several more moments, and made a snap decision.

She concentrated on narrowing her senses in his direction and opened her mind a tiny bit, ever so slightly and for just a fraction of a second. It was like taking a drink from a fire hydrant; she might hope for a small sip but had to take whatever came through. A stream of thoughts and feelings flashed through her mind—including how hard Caleb was struggling to not look at her. Phoebe's eyes widened, and she looked at him again, trying not to stare.

She'd blocked many of his thoughts, but had a sense that he was focused on her. Was it possible that he'd seen her make a mistake? Worried and confused, she decided to connect with him again.

Phoebe tensed her body in anticipation, ready to stop the flow if it became too much, and touched Caleb's mind—this time for a whole second. Her face burned and she slammed the door on the connection, self-consciously slouching down beside Sarah. *Idiot,* she thought, knowing what these feelings could do to her.

Phoebe had seen fantasies like his play out before, but they had always been about someone else—and always sensed through another person. No one had felt that way about her, and she was lost, unsure of what to do or think, so she put her head down. Her long hair was free now and formed a curtain, covering her face. She wanted to leave, and maybe find a classroom where she could hide.

"What's wrong, Phoebe?" Sarah wanted to know.

"Nothing, I don't feel well." She could see Caleb looking at her now; his eyes unsuccessfully tried to peer through her hair.

Phoebe kept her face hidden the rest of the period, and put her elbows on the table. Her heart was beating fast again—part of her desperately wanted something that could never happen. Whatever may have remained of her appetite vanished as that reality sank back in. *No one will ever want to be with me,* she thought, biting her lip hard. She wanted to cry, but didn't of course—part of the Discipline.

CHAPTER 6

Al Sutton

D ANIEL LEFT FOR WORK. HIS neck was just a little stiff, but his back really ached; he could still feel a ghost imprint from the rocker's slats. But Daniel would never willingly admit any of this to Phoebe; she had enough to worry about. Her coffee had partially revived him, but it looked as though this was going to be a very long day. The thought of sitting in a cramped streetcar didn't seem appetizing, so he walked to the office.

Phoebe was back to her normal self this morning, but last night had been a real setback. Daniel hadn't heard her scream like that for years. He couldn't help still thinking of her as his little girl, and seeing her like that had really affected him and it made him wonder if she'd ever be free of the nightmares. It had taken her a long time to stop shaking, and even longer to get back to sleep. His mind drifted back.

Ω

He'd been dreaming about the sea again, when the waves of pain and terror started. The thoughts she was broadcasting were so intense that they caused physical discomfort—and then the screaming came.

Daniel rolled out of bed fast—too fast. The floor was much closer than expected and he landed on his knees, which made him bend forward, causing him to bang his head on the nightstand.

After swearing out loud, Daniel reached for the matches on his nightstand, and hit the can that held them with the back of his hand, almost knocking them over. Finally, lamp in hand and a little more awake, Daniel made his way through the apartment. He knocked on Phoebe's door out of habit, but didn't wait for an answer before swinging it open, lifting the lamp up high so he could see.

He'd made this trip to her room countless times before, and had spent more nights in that damned rocking chair than he cared to remember, but that was years ago, when Phoebe was still a little girl. She was seventeen now, and he'd hoped that the midnight horror shows had finally ended. What he saw in the room scared him. Maybe it was just because she *was* so grown-up, but seeing her like that shook him up.

Phoebe was still in the grip of whatever had taken hold of her mind; her consciousness wasn't really in the room. Half sitting, with her arms held out wide, Phoebe was making circles in the air as though she was falling. But it was her face that shocked him more than anything: a frozen mask of horror, eyes that stared unseeing through the ceiling, as if focused on someone or something above her—they held a dead, vacant look. She screamed again; Daniel started across the floor, determined to shake her out of it.

He only made it halfway to the bed before everything changed. She'd been released. Awareness and recognition returned to her face and she looked around at the walls, before starting to cry. That wasn't like her at all. Phoebe was the strongest person Daniel had ever met. She had to be to survive.

He didn't ask questions, he didn't say anything at all, but perched on the small space she made for him at the edge of the bed, and he held her for as long as she'd let him—it was all he could do for her. When it was obvious that she was starting to feel awkward about the embrace, he let go, but still kept ahold of one hand.

Phoebe surprised him by sharing how she felt, speaking emotionally and rapidly. "I don't know what happened," she said, shaking her head. "I thought I had this under control." She was panting, as though she'd just been through an extreme physical exertion; her voice quivered as she went on. "Remember when

I managed to go a whole week without…without something happening?" Phoebe looked up cautiously, as though unsure about saying more. He nodded once and saw her eyes slide past him to one of the pictures on the wall. Daniel hated the drawings, but he knew how much they meant to her.

"Well." Phoebe paused again. "I learned how to do something back then, a…a kind of trick." She swallowed, taking a breath—less shaky now. "It's how I control these connections, at least I thought I was."

Phoebe looked down and closed her eyes, afraid to look at him, unsure of how he'd react. He squeezed her hand, very gently, she took a deep breath. The hair fell from behind her ear and blocked Daniel's view of her face; she didn't push it back out of the way.

"I keep a little piece of myself awake at night—all the time," she said. "That way most of me can sleep." Her voice dropped to a whisper. "It's like…I divide myself into two people. No, that's not right. It's still me," she corrected, her voice was stronger again. "I divide my mind into two parts, but the pieces aren't even. One part is tiny and doesn't require a lot of attention—like when you tap a finger on the table while mostly thinking about something else. I set this little bit of myself on guard. It blocks the other thoughts out, or maybe it just keeps me from wandering off to find the other people—I don't know which."

Daniel squeezed her hand again, and gently touched his forehead against hers briefly.

After sighing, she swept the hair back out of the way and tucked it behind her ear. A faint smile made its way to her face as she lay back into her pillow, staring into Daniel's eyes.

♎

Daniel reached the courthouse with just enough time to review his notes. His morning was filled with appearances today. Most cases amounted to minor infractions: adolescent curfew violations, repeated failures to attend church, and a few instances of public swearing, but one more serious offense was possession of a forbidden artifact.

A ten-year-old boy found an ancient radio buried among the odds and ends that had belonged to his great uncle and was stopped while carrying it in the street. Possession of anything related to electricity was strictly forbidden, but Daniel was confident he could get his client off. The boy's age was in his favor, and he hadn't known what the radio was.

In court, Daniel summarized the case for the judge. "This is really just a case of poor timing. The boy would certainly have brought this thing to his father, who in turn would have turned it over to the Keepers right away. He didn't even have a chance to learn what it was he'd found before being arrested."

The boy's father corroborated the story, and Daniel pointed out that the family regularly volunteered at church. The case was dismissed with a warning about handling strange, unfamiliar objects.

"The next time you see something you don't recognize, or understand," the judge said, "let it lay where it is, and report it to the Keepers." The boy, almost too scared to speak, managed to nod that he understood.

Another case involved a young woman, not much older than Phoebe. She was accused of stealing fabric from a dry goods store. Theft was not tolerated in the Land, but it was the young woman's first offense, and she came from a well-connected family. She received a thirty-day sentence in the custody of the local Keepers, and she would also be required to work twenty hours each weekend for six months, after release. Overall, nothing terribly traumatic happened; no one was sent to the Inquisition, no one faced serious punishment—a good day.

Daniel ate the sandwich Phoebe had prepared for him at his desk. He was by a window on the third floor of the courthouse that overlooked the park's west side; it was just across the street. His desk was covered with folders and stacks of paper. Numerous seashells he'd collected as a boy lined one edge of the desk. Several of the larger shells held down stacks of paper to keep them from being blown across the room by a draught from the window. Daniel also kept a small collection of worry stones in his top drawer—round, smooth pebbles from a stream where another defender fished. When Daniel was especially concerned about something he'd keep one in his pocket, trying to improve on what the water had done over the years. He'd begun carrying one when Phoebe first started hearing thoughts from other people.

After lunch, a rumor made its way through the office that a member of the Order had been captured and was being held in Central City, rare if true. The Order had been effectively wiped out of existence almost eighteen years before. Some stragglers were known to remain at large, most living under false identities. The Council had decided not to actively pursue those who blended in— there was no reason to do so, as long as they didn't make trouble.

Daniel had paled when he heard the rumor, his lunch felt like lead sitting in his stomach, and a sense of dread hovered over his head the rest of the day. Intellectually, he knew that Becky was gone; he'd read the testimony of those who'd witnessed her death. But somehow he could never completely let go.

Active members from the outlawed Order were considered a threat, and only an active member would have been arrested. If this prisoner knew about Phoebe then she might be in danger. Daniel's emotions alternated between worry and misplaced hope all afternoon. *Who was captured? Did they know Becky gave birth to a daughter? Would they talk?* He knew the answer to this last question: of course they'd talk, sooner or later everyone talks to the Inquisitor. The Council had reconstituted this ancient institution for the explicit purpose of seeking out the last members of the Order, just after the Purge. No name had been mentioned with the rumor, but in the late afternoon Daniel heard one of the Keepers refer to the prisoner as a 'he'. At least it wasn't Becky.

Idiot! he thought. *Becky's dead.* The likelihood that anyone captured would know about Phoebe was microscopic, and only a few people had ever known about her birth. Becky's contacts had managed to secure fake documents for Phoebe, even before she was born. He sighed again, and tried to refocus on the day's work.

In the late afternoon, Daniel normally met with clients, those just arrested, and those nearing trial. He sometimes met with them in the defenders' office, but more often at the prison. Today he was scheduled to meet with a new client in the man's jail cell.

The prisoner had not offered identification when the Keepers found him floating on what one of them described as a 'strange rubber boat'. He'd been picked up just off the coast to the north, and had been in possession of a functioning electric flashlight. The prisoner referred to it as a 'magic light stick' and claimed to have traded food for the boat and the wondrous object. A separate note from the arresting Keeper said that the prisoner didn't seem very bright. His main concern was in getting the magic light stick back. Daniel laughed aloud; the other defenders looked up from their desks at his outburst.

This man clearly has not yet grasped the gravity of his 'sin', he thought—wondering if he was really as thick as the report implied? The case was scheduled for a first hearing Monday morning.

Ω

Daniel stood outside the client's cell; he'd been escorted by one of the Keepers. The prisoner was lying on the cell's lone cot, staring at the ceiling, and hadn't reacted to the sound of the door being opened. He was dressed in the standard black-and-white prison garb. The cartoonlike stripes were supposed to make prisoners easy to spot, and Daniel always had to suppress a grin when he saw them.

"Hello," he said politely. "I'm Daniel Lambert, your defender." He was still standing in front of the open cell door, waiting to be invited in. The Keeper accompanying him was responsible for Daniel's safety, but didn't seem concerned. This prisoner wasn't considered much of a threat.

Finally, the man turned his head and stared at Daniel. "Who says so?" There was a strong accent that Daniel couldn't quite place.

"The defenders' office says so, with approval from the judge for your case. My job is to help get you out of this mess." The man seemed to find something amusing in what he'd said. He sat up and gestured toward a chair beside the cot.

The Keeper locked eyes with Daniel, raising an eyebrow. Daniel nodded, dismissing the guard.

When they were alone, the prisoner's face took on a more serious expression, looking at and then through Daniel.

Daniel was shuffling through his notes, trying to decide how best to start, when the man interrupted.

"I'm Al, short for Albert. Al Sutton. Can't exactly say I'm pleased to meet you, but at least you don't look like a stooge." His accent was stronger for certain words.

"Uh, thanks—I think." Daniel grinned. "Do you mind if I ask a few questions?"

"Go-on." The two words blended together into a single syllable.

"Where did you tell the Keepers you lived?"

"I didn't, mate. I'm from Robertstown. It's a long way from here, that's for sure, 'bout five hundred kilometers west." Al pointed in the direction of the Keepers' office, but was still looking into his defender's eyes, a test. Daniel frowned; the report said that the prisoner was from the north. Al saw his confusion. "I told them I'd come from the area where the Northern River dumps into the ocean. That's why they brought me here—the closest big port, I guess."

Daniel thought a moment, looking at his client more closely. He'd been surprised by the man's sudden trust, and by his coherence. Al didn't sound like the person described in the report at all. *An act?* Daniel also understood where Al claimed his real home was.

The direction and distance he'd described was outside of the Land, and that just wasn't possible, not in the direction he'd indicated. Five hundred kilometers west would put him beyond the Western Mountains—and into the Wastelands. Everyone knew that people couldn't survive there; the Wastelands meant radiation and certain death. For now, Daniel decided to ignore this ridiculous assertion; he wanted to hear what else Al had to say.

"Okay, how did you get here—to the coast of the Eastern Province—without learning something about the Council, and its general distrust of things…modern? You had a flashlight, didn't you? Anything that uses electricity is banned here; you must have known that, especially if you traveled across the Land on foot," he said, probing deeper.

"I didn't walk here, mate," Al said laughing. "I flew in an airplane." The statement was made so matter-of-factly that he believed Al right away.

"Ah," Daniel said, thinking of the implications. The two men stared at each other for a minute, Al with a half smile on his face.

"How do you know you can trust me?" Daniel asked abruptly.

Al laughed. "I don't, but it isn't like I have a choice, and you seem like a decent enough bloke."

Daniel laughed, too, shaking his head at what the judge might say if he were listening. "Are there many airplanes in this Robertstown, where you claim to come from?"

"Nope. But don't worry, the ones *we* have aren't all that evil." Both men laughed again.

"So, where is the airplane now?" Daniel asked, shifting on the hard wooden chair.

Al made a face, and shook his head. "I had to ditch off the coast, so it wouldn't be spotted."

"But why fly *here*? The Council doesn't exactly roll out the welcome mat for pilots."

"Hmm. Well, I didn't actually plan to come here. My brother and some of his mates formed up an expedition to the lands north of the Great Northern River. Back in May, they chartered a boat and sailed north, along the coast of the inland sea, and then east along the river to a place on its northern banks. They had plenty of supplies, horses, and mules to help carry everything.

"They were supposed to return in mid-August, but didn't show up. The boat went back again at the end of August, just in case, but they still weren't there. So I borrowed an airplane—a long-range craft with extra fuel—to fly up and look for them.

"I knew more or less where they were heading and followed the route they'd planned—up and back—but without success. I went as far north as Fire Mountain, a volcano, and then I tried heading east along the river, all the way to the ocean. If they were in trouble, James could have built a raft to float downstream. One of your villages is at the river's mouth and they might have been able to get help there. But I didn't see anything along the way, or at the village—no raft, just more trees, the river, and the ocean. As a last resort I flew farther east, out over sea. They might have been swept out too fast to make landfall, a raft was always the last resort and they're not very controllable.

"My fuel was getting low, but I still had enough to get back home. I decided to go south and check out the area along the east coast. I was alone, and mostly looking down. Guess I must have looked down too much, because I hit something, a flock of birds, maybe. I didn't see 'em, but it sure did make a mess. One engine was gone, and the other was sputtering—I was going down. I took advantage of the wind, to get a little farther out, into deep water but still close enough to make it ashore. The engine lasted about ten more minutes. It went down east of that village just to the north, far enough out to hide the wreckage." Al gave Daniel a grim smile. "Imagine what would happen if they'd found me with a whole airplane and not just a bloody torch—I forgot it was in the kit.

"Your police—you call 'em Keepers—picked me up and found the 'unholy thing' right away. Instead of denying it, I just pretended it was some kind of treasure beyond my understanding and demanded it back." Al laughed again, but of course he was in jail.

"So you don't want your flashlight back?" Daniel asked, a deadpan look on his face. Al laughed again, slapping his leg.

"What was your brother doing in the north?" Daniel asked, but Al shook his head.

"Can't say. That's their business."

"The place described, this Robertstown, sounds like it's in what we call the Wastelands. It's not supposed to be a very inviting place. Do a lot of people live there? How do you deal with the radiation?"

Al snorted. "Well, we don't consider them wastelands. There aren't as many people beyond the mountains as live in the Land. Robertstown is on the coast. It's pretty big for the Westlands, that's what we call the area. About a thousand people live in

Robertstown, but there are other towns just like it scattered along the coast and to the east. A lot of us left the provinces around the time the Council started banning things. We didn't like being dictated to by a bunch of priests. Things are different in the Westlands. We still use electricity—when you can find fuel, or if you're lucky enough to have a reactor.

"We Westlanders weren't any happier with the Order, slapping the Council's face with that 'we don't need a God anymore' stuff was just stupid. They were asking for trouble. We don't take sides. We just want to be left alone."

"And the radiation?" Daniel prodded.

"It's safe enough. Radiation levels are a bit higher than here, but not lethal. It's not safe near the old cities, of course, but the whole place isn't hot. Just stay away from the big holes in the ground."

Daniel decided he liked Al, and he had an idea.

"Well, you did the right thing pretending the magic light stick was something special. It kept them from thinking that you were from the Order—stick to that. The story about how you traded food for the 'magic light stick' and the strange boat is a good one, but we need something more.

"There was a group of penitents that settled in the north called the Choosers. Are you familiar with them?" Al nodded, a look of disgust on his face. "Good, that saves a long explanation. The Council doesn't care much for them either, but they mostly leave them alone. If you tell the judge that you want a Chooser confessor, he'll probably draw his own conclusions and find a way to let you go. He's not a bad guy, but if he thinks you're lying, things could get ugly. Don't act smart. Keep it simple. And don't mention the Wastelands."

"Thanks, you're not a bad guy, for a Council man," Al said, grinning.

Daniel stared at Al without expression. "I'm your defender, not a Council man," he pointed out sharply. The two shook hands, and Daniel stood to leave.

"How are you getting home?" Daniel asked. He was waving at the Keeper to come open the door.

"I'm not sure yet. The boat's supposed to return at the end of September. It's maybe, what, a hundred fifty kilometers to the river versus three hundred to reach the Western Mountains—and I'd have to cross those in winter."

"Yeah, about a hundred fifty to the Great River—hard terrain." Daniel thought another moment. "The village of Bardon is just north of here, you saw it before you crashed. I'll speak with my father about picking you up there in his boat. He can drop you off at the mouth of the river, or even a little inland. That'll save a lot of walking. Dad's getting ready to make one last fishing run this year, before the big storms come."

"I'd appreciate that. And if you ever make it to Robertstown, look me up."

"If I ever do, count on it. I'll see you in court Monday." The Keeper arrived and Daniel left.

CHAPTER 7

The Promise

I T WAS TIME TO START the evening meal. Phoebe's dad
would be home in a few hours; tonight they'd have lamb stew.
She went to the fireplace to take money from the bowl on the
mantel, but stopped to look at an early drawing she'd done of her
father, one he'd had framed. She stared at the image, looking into
his eyes and wondering what he'd been thinking at the time. What
had he imagined their life would be like today—ten years later?
She sighed before taking some of the money and heading out.

Too many things were happening at once. The dream, with
its unusual connection, had shaken her confidence. Phoebe had
believed that the nightmares were over. Then there was the way
she'd felt during lunch. Caleb was awakening feelings inside that
she'd been trying hard to suppress. It was difficult enough to
imagine having a real friend, someone she could trust with her
secrets, but envisioning more seemed utterly impossible. What
was going to happen in the long run, beyond just surviving?
Everything around Phoebe kept reminding her that she didn't fit
in. The future was starting to look pretty bleak—a future she'd be
facing alone someday.

Once on the street, she walked as though in a trance, not really
seeing the people around her. She hardly noticed it when a horse
sharply veered to avoid hitting her while crossing the street.

What's the point? Why do I try so hard to fit in? she wondered
numbly. It had been a long time since she'd let herself surrender
to this much self-pity; she knew how dangerous it could be when

she lost focus. But today, the risks didn't seem to matter. Only the thought of her father, and what it would do to him should something happen to her, made her stop and think more about what she was doing. *I need to talk to Dad.*

Once back home, Phoebe began preparing dinner. It helped to have something to do. She worked mechanically, cutting the lamb, potatoes, and carrots into uniform pieces, and then she browned the meat in a heavy cast-iron pot, before adding the vegetables, water, and spices. Most of the work was done now; the stew would more or less look after itself for a while.

There was still a lot of time before her father got home—time she had to fill somehow. Phoebe shocked Monday's homework by starting early—at least she tried. After thirty minutes of staring at the same page in her schoolbook, she gave up. *I could always clean,* she thought glancing around the apartment. By the time her father walked through the front door, their home was sparkling— he knew something was wrong.

"Uh, what's up, Princess?" The half smile he'd been wearing was gone.

Phoebe was stuck, not sure how to start. These past few years, she'd been avoiding uncomfortable conversations, and it had become her habit to pretend nothing was wrong. But now she realized that ignoring the future didn't make it go away.

There were so many things to worry about every day—school, cooking, cleaning, shopping, the laundry, and, of course, trying to survive without being arrested. The future had taken a back seat and become a kind of mythological concept, so far removed from her daily life that it may as well not even exist. But time keeps moving; before long another ten years would have gone by—the picture she'd stared at on the mantel reminded her of that.

Phoebe wasn't a little girl anymore, and the way she felt about herself was changing, too. She wanted to spend more time with people her own age—and she wanted to meet boys, but didn't know how to start, or if she could handle it. Phoebe didn't have the luxury of being moody and slamming doors when she wasn't happy. The line between life and death was too sharp for her and her father. Moping would make her dad think something dangerous had happened; it was better to talk things through with him, even if the subject was uncomfortable.

"Well," she said, putting both hands on her lap, and not looking directly at him. *How do I start?* She gripped her thighs under the table, her nails digging into them. Pain always helped to hold back strong emotions; she'd used pain a lot since she was very young. Phoebe described what she'd felt today and what Caleb had been thinking, leaving out embarrassing specifics. "You know, I can tell exactly what's on a boy's mind." *Not much of a mystery there,* she thought. "What should I do if a boy actually wants to act on his feelings, and maybe even ask me out?" Phoebe looked up to see her father's reaction, her cheeks warm. "If anyone ever does," she added. "I know it's impossible," she admitted, looking down at the table, and gripping her legs even harder to hold back the tears.

Her father put his hand on one of the chairs. "W—well," he began, sitting down heavily. "I knew this would come up, sooner or later." One of his eyebrows went up. "I guess I was hoping for later." He took a breath and stared at the table between them for a moment. "There isn't...Phoebe, there isn't some magic formula," he said, shaking his head. "I think..." He paused a moment. "For now I think you should find a way to put him off, if a boy seems to be interested in you—as a girl, I mean. Sorry, kiddo, but I don't think you're ready yet. These feelings are a lot to handle, probably more than you realize."

After another long silence, he spoke again, struggling to keep his voice even. "This doesn't mean you'll always be alone."

Phoebe couldn't speak for a while. "How do you *know for sure* this isn't permanent?" she asked, her voice just above a whisper.

"I know. You're going to have to trust me on this one. I keep forgetting how much you've grown up already." Phoebe rolled her eyes. "But I do have a pretty good idea of what you're going through. Becky..." His voice broke. "Your mother had to go through this, too. I guarantee you that things will get better. It's just going to take a little more time."

She was blocking his thoughts, but felt him flinch inside and knew that his mind was somewhere in the past, probably back with her mother. She tried to avoid saying things that would remind him of her, but that wasn't always possible. His eyes took on that familiar glazed look they sometimes got. Phoebe knew better than anyone what it was like to be lost in a memory.

I should trust him, she decided, and started to get up.

"Phoebe, sometimes boys can be fairly…umm…aggressive, even if not in a physical way. If you ever feel uncomfortable—even a little bit—don't wait. Call me. You've done it before and I'm sure your range is a lot more now."

The last time she'd felt real danger had been when a strange man in the park had come up to her—he was a little too friendly. Her father was more than two blocks away at the time, but had gotten to her so fast that she'd wondered if he'd flown.

"Okay, Dad," Phoebe said, trying to smile. "Let's eat," but the smile didn't extend to her eyes.

During dinner, her father described an unusual man he'd met at work that day, someone named Al who had a funny accent and who lived a long way away. It seemed as though he was going to say more, but he changed his mind. Phoebe guessed her father thought that saying too much might violate the man's trust. The meeting had obviously affected him.

She spent the rest of the evening doing chores, cleaning the dishes and mending their clothes under gaslight in the main room, before going to bed early.

Once asleep, the presence she'd felt the night before returned—it was the woman from the dream. Something about her felt…familiar, an impression rather than the clear memory of a person's feel. It was like a memory from before she'd started to change, but that didn't seem possible.

Suddenly, Phoebe was swept away to that strange version of the Land she'd visited the night before—and she was falling.

♎

The frigid water hits her from behind like a locomotive, and she goes down, down, deep under the water. The shock from the impact knocks her breath out and the enormous pressure from the water squeezes until she sees a gray tunnel form in her vision. Somehow she's able to stay conscious.

It takes a lifetime to surface and she gasps in lungfuls of cold air again and again, coughing. The salt water burns her throat, nose, and eyes, and it feels as though someone just beat her up. Still gasping, Phoebe glances up at the top of the cliff.

High above in the darkness a line of tiny torches is waving, just where the darkness of the rock transitions to the glow from the clouds. She can't see individuals, just the flames. At this distance and in this light she doubts they can see one small head bobbing above the waves, but she's still careful not to splash a lot. She assesses her situation. Not good. She isn't far from the base of the cliff, but the tide's pulling her out. Waves are breaking on the sharp rocks between where she is and the shore. Although exhausted, whomever she's connected with is a strong swimmer—of course rocks don't care about that.

She notices a slightly less dangerous path between the rocks and a narrow ledge at the base of the cliff and strikes out for the shore, fighting the tide and the waves that try to throw her onto the rocks. One hits her side, but not hard enough to break a rib, and miraculously, she makes it to the ledge.

With barely any strength left, she crawls out of the water and drops onto her stomach, dizzy from the battle with the tide. Her legs are numb, but they ache, too. It's cold and windy, and she's soaked.

A shadow on the wall of the cliff stands out in front of her, a deeper blackness in the face of the rock. She squirms toward it, crawling on torn hands and knees, hoping to find a refuge from the wind.

The shadow turns into a recess—it's less than a cave but more than a crack. The ground angles up, gradually flattening out a meter or two above the high-tide mark—it's all she can do to keep crawling forward. Inside, the floor is lined with a soft layer of soil that hurts less than the rock.

She's shivering so hard that her teeth chatter uncontrollably, but manages to burrow her way down into the soil, curling up into a ball for warmth—finally ready to let go. Just as she's beginning to lose consciousness, she hears the woman's voice again. It's clear and strong, almost as though the woman is standing above her, speaking aloud in the darkness.

Phoebe, I'm coming for you.

CHAPTER 8

The Sisters' Eyes

"**D**ID YOU TOUCH HER?" THE voice asked in a deep rumble. The woman took a breath, releasing it slowly to give herself more time to answer.

"Yes," she said, pausing. "But it was just as difficult as last night." Her voice was like fractured glass. "She's *so* strong."

The woman was in her early forties. Long black hair framed a regular face, pale with exertion. Her hands were shaking, so she put them in her lap. This had been a long week for Rebecca: first the trip from Corbin, and now two nights of struggle against the toughest resistance she'd ever met. Rebecca was trying hard to hide her exhaustion.

"She'd have to be, to have survived this long." The bass voice came from a large man seated to her left. His face was partially hidden by thick hair and a full beard. Both were black but streaked with silver. A pair of intense dark eyes peered out at Rebecca's face, as if measuring her.

The room was dark. Its only light came from a stone fire pit that protruded more than two meters into the room. The fire had long since died down to a steady red glow, and random strands of the gray ash that coated its embers formed interesting patterns on the walls. There were three people in the room. Matthew, who had just spoken, was at one end of the fire pit, sitting in an oversized chair that seemed too small for him. Another man, his skin almost black and who was more compact in size, sat beside the woman on a sofa made from animal hides stretched across a wooden frame. This was Gabriel, the Scout who'd guided Rebecca from the Sanctuary. He watched the others, trying to learn what he could from their exchange. It would be his job to lead the follow-on mission, if Matthew decided it was viable.

The building had been constructed of whole rough-hewn logs that had been covered with earth and plants to hide it from view, and the entire site was further hidden within a wooded copse, just below the tree line. They were a little more than ten kilometers northwest of town, two-thirds of the way up the mountain. The cabin had been built near an important trail, one of just a few paths north through the Ring Mountains.

Above the cabin a saddle spanned the space between two sharp peaks. Because of their similarity in size and shape, they were known as the Sisters, and the cabin took its name from them. Among the scattered members of the Order this place was called the Sisters' Eyes. It had originally been set up as a way station along the difficult trail over the pass—a stopover for refugees fleeing the Purge. But over the years, it had become an important outpost for the Order, a place from which to watch over the harbor and the comings and goings of Council ships.

The room was quiet for several minutes as Matthew stared, unseeing, into the fire. He was the Guide—head of the Order. It was a job requiring the very best skills of a leader, but also an ability to see into the future. Matthew was a genetically created Prescient. As Guide, he was responsible for plotting a course forward to fulfill the Order's goals and to keep its members safe.

He remained frozen in place for several more minutes, staring through time. The others waited in silence, trying not to disturb him. Noise from the wind outside was the only sound in the cabin. It rushed through the pass above, and then cascaded down the slopes and toward the town below. As it passed, the wind brushed through trees that surrounded the cabin, causing branches to sway and creak and rub against one another. Finally, Matthew's eyes returned to the present and focused, once again, on Rebecca's face.

She'd arrived the previous evening, having received the Guide's urgent message to come. Gabriel had brought her on foot, along unmarked trails in the wilderness that he knew by heart. They'd taken an indirect route to avoid being recognized by people on the East Port Highway, and had scaled the outer rings of the mountains and traversed the valleys in between. The final stage had taken them up and over the pass between the Sisters. Gabriel and Rebecca traveled fast and with little rest through the late August heat in order to arrive in time for the meeting. Ten hard days through the wild and Rebecca's face showed it.

She was wearing one of two sets of clothing she'd brought. The standard-issue pants and tunic were the same as used by the Scouts when they traveled. A weathered poncho was draped over the back of the sofa, and a pack that contained the rest of her things leaned against the wall on the other side of the fire, its contents had been scattered across the floor to dry.

"Are you *certain* that you'll be able to make the connection again? Is it possible that she'll strengthen to the point where you can't penetrate her defenses?"

"Yes, I'm sure of it." Rebecca put the palms of her hands flat on her legs as she spoke; it was a position intended to project calmness and objectivity. "She's strong, but it'll be years before she'll be able to stop me completely." The confidence in her voice reassured him.

"And the guardian, Daniel?" The question seemed an afterthought, but Matthew's eyes still watched her intently.

"I can connect with him, of course," she answered. Unconsciously, the ghost of a smile appeared on her face. "He'll cooperate. I'll make sure tonight by planting seeds of worry in his subconscious while he's sleeping—a vague fear of impending danger. The doubt will nag at him and break any sense of complacency he may be feeling. Phoebe will probably be thinking about these last two nights, too. If they speak about what they've seen or felt, they may begin to suspect that I'm still alive, but there won't be tangible evidence, just a few unusual dreams."

"How long will you need, when it's time to move them?"

"Two or three days at most, no more. I don't want them to panic. If they act in an unusual way, it'll draw attention." Rebecca stared back into Matthew's eyes. She wanted—no, she *needed* him to understand that she was committed to this path, and that she was ready to do anything he asked. She held her breath, willing her eyes to stay calm and waiting for what Matthew had to say.

Although a Sensitive, Rebecca didn't know what the Guide could see with his strange vision. She'd once tried connecting with him as he looked into the future, but hadn't been able to interpret the wild, chaotic things she'd seen. Even that one brief glance had given her a headache that lasted days.

"Okay," he said, staring at her, an uncharacteristically soft expression on his face. "We'll move ahead."

Rebecca let her breath out slowly to mask the tension she'd been hiding. When she started to say something Matthew held up a hand.

"But not right away—I'm sorry, Becky," he said using the name she reserved for friends. "We can't just walk in and take her. There are records from her past that could be traced back to our agent in Central City. We need to destroy that evidence and cover his tracks first. For now, I want you both back at Corbin," he said, looking at Gabriel. "I'll get things moving right away. Becky, you can help, too. Since you know the guardian and his family so well, can you put together a credible story for their departure, some excuse about where they're going and why they'd need to take an extended trip? It needs to seem reasonable. We don't want to raise suspicions too quickly—when they don't return." Rebecca nodded.

"Now for the mechanics of the operation," he said, looking at Gabriel again. "We'll need primary and backup teams, and at least one alternate route out of the valley, just in case they're being watched. There's no reason to think this is the case, but there's something strange happening with the girl. It's difficult to see the threads of her future clearly—I'm not sure why. I see one image of Phoebe together with a Council elder, one of the eight from the Inner Circle. It's not the Inquisitor, nor any of his people, but one of the spiritual leaders. The two of them were alone in my vision, somewhere outside in the dark, just speaking with each other. It may be nothing, or it may be a phantom future that will never happen, but for her sake we need to be extra careful. Nothing is as clear as it should be, but I know it's not safe to act right now—I can see that much.

"We can't wait too long." Mathew stared into the distance again. "No more than four or five months. Trying to see into Phoebe's future is like looking through muddy water. Still, everything tells me that the risk for her increases exponentially next year. I wish I could definitively say what the threat to her life is, but I can't."

"Let's set a tentative date for mid-December. That'll give us a little margin, just in case. I'll let you know if there's a change in plan." Matthew shook his head. "Things are too fluid for me to be confident—fluid and unpredictable. It almost seems as though she's doing things that would deliberately change the future herself. I don't know how that could be—she's not a Prescient." A perplexed expression on the Guide's face stayed for a moment and then he looked at Rebecca again, his black eyes back to being as inscrutable as ever. "I know how much you want this to happen quickly, but be patient. It'll just be a little while longer." Rebecca nodded again.

Matthew stood, preparing to leave. His imposing frame seemed to fill the room as he collected the few things he'd brought with him, a simple backpack and a waterproof poncho to go over his coat. Before leaving, he addressed the Scout.

"Gabriel. You should delay leaving until tomorrow night to avoid the patrols. It'll be safe to set out after that, but you'll only have a one-day window before they start snooping around the pass again—they'll be using old-style drones. The Council seems to know something's going on, but not what," he added, looking meaningfully at Gabriel. "Travel by dark for the first two days, and without fire." The Scout nodded and stood to grasp Matthew's forearm.

"Be safe," Gabriel said, staring into the large man's eyes. His own habitual look of worry had returned. Matthew smiled at the expression. Gabriel had been his traveling companion and protector for the past five years; it probably felt strange to watch Matthew leave alone. But the Guide had insisted that Gabriel be assigned to protect Rebecca, at least until the operation was complete.

"I'll see you both at Corbin in two weeks," Matthew said, ducking through the doorway. He planned to climb the pass and then travel through the night to reach another important meeting in the village of Bardon.

After Matthew left, tension faded from Rebecca, and her shoulders relaxed ever so slightly. Just two weeks earlier—had it only been two weeks?—a message had come from Matthew saying that Phoebe was in danger. The communiqué said that her daughter's fate was narrowing, her potential futures disappearing one by one. Phoebe was being erased! He'd explained in the note that this happened when some event, or set of events, consumed multiple timelines, eliminating choice. When choice disappeared completely, it meant death. The message hinted that they might be able to intervene, but warned that he needed a test first— something that could touch Phoebe directly and disturb the future, just a little bit. That faint touch would send out small waves into the flow of time, like the tiny ripples from a pebble thrown into water. By looking at how these waves behaved around her, he could see if there was a path forward, but he needed her help to do this.

Rebecca had wanted to immediately run to her daughter, panic overcoming her—an all-consuming fear. Members of the Guard had been forced to restrain her, to keep her from rushing out of the Sanctuary that night. Matthew's message assured her that he would help, but warned that blindly running to Phoebe would probably only get them both killed. The message said that Gabriel was on his way to guide her; she would leave as soon as he arrived. For Rebecca, that small wait had seemed an eternity. But now the test was done, and it had been a success—Phoebe had a chance to survive.

Just one more thing to do tonight, she thought, trying to summon more energy from her depleted strength.

"I wonder how the girl and Daniel will react," Gabriel mused, interrupting. "And how do you think she survived while staying in town this long?"

"I don't know, but it must have been a living hell for her," Becky said, biting her lower lip, gripping her hands into tight fists, trying to hold back the fears for her daughter. "She's had to deal with these senses all by herself. I had help, special teachers—people like me—who knew what I was going through. They're all dead now of course, but they helped me get through the early years in one piece. Except for Daniel, she's been alone—it's a miracle she's sane.

"I was sure he'd be forced to leave, to get her away from people so she wouldn't be discovered. He must have decided that their best chance was to stay put and, somehow, they found a way. What I can't understand is how she developed such powerful defenses on her own. If you could have felt her strength—the raw power inside of her." Rebecca took another deep breath, shaking her head. "I doubt that anyone else could have penetrated her mind, and it wasn't easy, even for me. If I didn't know better, I'd have guessed she was at least twice her age."

"What has age got to do with strength?"

"We Sensitives get stronger over time."

Becky closed her eyes in concentration again, directing her thoughts toward the town, to Daniel this time. "Incredible," she said afterward, shaking her head.

$$\underline{\Omega}$$

Gabriel stepped out of the cabin to clear his head. He wanted to check on their security before resting. This discipline was so ingrained into his routine that he did it without thinking. The Scout was in his early thirties: still young enough for the physical challenges of the job, but experienced far beyond his years. His knowledge of the Land and its wilderness, his ability to move swiftly and with stealth, and his skill at protecting others were considered phenomenal. He was a Scout and a member of the Guard, trained to fight and ready to die in his charge's defense, should it prove necessary. Unlike Rebecca and Matthew, his talents were not the product of genetic engineering but of training and tradition. Gabriel's family had been important members of the Order for generations. His loyalty was beyond question, and his skills considered the very best in the Guard.

The journey between the Sisters and Corbin Sanctuary should take ten days with Rebecca along, and that at an aggressive pace—for her. He'd brought her from Corbin at Matthew's request and had used the time to study her physical capabilities, and limitations. Gabriel knew that he could make it to Corbin in five days on his own, but that Rebecca would not be able to keep up that pace, nor would she be able to use his favorite shortcuts—shortcuts passable only by a skilled climber. Still, he'd noted that she was in reasonable condition and that she didn't complain when he pressed on late into the night.

Matthew's information about the drones meant that they would have to travel by night—and more slowly—for at least the first two days. *Okay, maybe it'll take eleven days,* he thought.

The Scout was impressed with Rebecca's stoicism. He'd led other people on journeys like this before, people much younger than her. Some never seemed to shut up about how uncomfortable they were, or how tired they felt, or that they were hungry, or thirsty, or whatever. Rebecca didn't complain once.

CHAPTER 9

Daniel

DANIEL SAT UP QUICKLY AND threw off the covers. His pillow and sheets were soaked with sweat, despite the cool temperature, and he was shaking. Sleep had come to him unwillingly and then refused to stay quietly. At first he'd been bothered by the discussion with Phoebe, but then, once he was asleep, a vague feeling of danger had overcome him. It was a fear that he couldn't pin down—something was creeping up on her. He couldn't put the feeling out of his mind—dream after restless dream—it kept coming back. He almost got up to check on her, but this was different than Thursday night. This sense of unease wasn't coming from her—it originated inside of him.

The air drifting through the window didn't feel right, either— it felt early, much too early to be getting up. There was no hint of dawn, and no glint of light reflecting from the windows across the street. Daniel often woke before the sun rose. Sometimes it was noise from the bakery next door that awakened him—maybe a baker's helper lighting the oven's fires at three thirty. More often it was something else that pulled him out of sleep—the quality of the air, as it changed just before first light, or the taste of salt carried in from the sea. The wind could shift before dawn, driven by rising temperatures out over the ocean. People who make their living on the water tend to develop a sense of the weather and of time, but this morning something else had awakened him.

It felt as though someone was touching his mind, just as Phoebe did when she needed help. *Who?* he asked. It felt as though he should be doing something. *What? What am I supposed to do?* More sleep simply wasn't in the cards. 2:50 a.m.

The discussion with Al was an eye-opener. The Wastelands had always been a foreboding place, filled with death, and hot with radiation. The Western Mountains were more than three hundred kilometers away; their high, rocky peaks had sheltered the Land from the worst effects of the war. Beyond them lay the western plains that gradually sloped eastward to a large bay, which then opened to an inland sea. A city had stood at the southern end of that bay, a metropolis with towering skyscrapers. One hundred kilometers north of it, just south of where the great northern river opened the path between the inland sea and the ocean, was its sister city. The old children's nursery rhyme came to him without effort:

Twin cities on the shore, reaching for the sky,
Twin cities, turned to ash, no one can say why.

Daniel couldn't remember the original names of these cities—something to do with... no, even that was lost. For almost two centuries, they'd simply been known as the Twin Cities of Death and the nursery rhyme was taught to children, a warning to stay away.

The Council had forbidden travel to the Wastelands since the war. Everyone was told that you couldn't survive the radiation there, but now he'd heard differently. Apparently, whole communities thrived in the Wastelands. If they could do it, so could he and Phoebe.

As she'd matured, she reminded Daniel more and more of Becky. It wasn't just the way she looked—Becky was in her voice, her eyes, and even her mannerisms, especially when she was angry. She was just as stubborn, and could also be just as reasonable as her mother, too. And they shared something else—something far more important.

The nightmare Friday, followed by last night's disturbing talk, and now this ominous feeling of danger all reminded him of how much Phoebe was changing, growing up. Someday she'd have a chance at a life of her own, maybe even a family—but not here; the Land was just too dangerous for her. The look of despair in her eyes last night was what had kept him awake. She couldn't see that things could get better for her. All she'd ever known was fear and isolation—watching other children play and make friends—never knowing why she was so different. Phoebe needed to know who and what she was, and she needed to see that it was possible to have a future.

Becky had been taken from them too early and, for better or worse, Daniel had not told Phoebe everything about her mother, or what had been done to them both. He glanced at the locked wardrobe, standing in the corner of his room, and shivered. He'd left it exactly as it had been the last time he saw Becky. It contained memories and material legacies, things that he'd kept for Phoebe. But she carried an even more vital legacy in her blood. It was time they had that talk he'd been putting off for so long.

CHAPTER 10

The Healer

H E WAS BORN DURING THE first Jubilee, celebrating the rebirth of humanity and commemorating a decade of leadership by the Council of God—just ten years after the war. Decades before, the idea to develop him had emerged, and work began on the Healer program, the first of the genetic engineering efforts. And with Samuel's generation, the Order had finally achieved a major success.

There were three programs all told, but the Healers had come first, and earlier than expected. A surprise leap forward in the bloodlines had accelerated progress and put the team decades ahead of schedule. Random chance brought success, but it also brought unwanted consequences.

Ten Healers were created and, although they each exhibited the superficial physical traits of gender, none were completely male or completely female. The program had produced genetic eunuchs, beings incapable of reproduction—a very successful dead end. An inability to breed was a huge disappointment for the geneticists. It meant that they would have to try again, go back to an earlier stage in the program to tap older genetic material. The DNA of every generation had been stored in cryogenic tanks for exactly this kind of eventuality. The scientists would work to find, recreate, and then repair the flawed gene sequences, all without losing the desirable features they'd managed to create.

The second surprise was much worse: five of the ten Healers exhibited mirrored—reversed—traits. Just as the quadratic equation produces both positive and negative roots, the program had produced positive and negative beings.

The five reflected Healers, called the deadly five, were quickly destroyed. Rather than fighting illness, their bodies had begun creating new lethal and highly contagious viruses. Somewhere along the bloodlines, among carefully controlled generations of engineered beings, a fatal flaw had crept in. The genetic twist that produced the deadly five would take years to understand, and it would be decades before the scientists tried to produce a next-generation Healer. But the Order had always been a patient organization, and the program would continue to be funded. In the meantime, the five true Healers matured and began their work.

♎

Samuel awoke just as the first light of day formed a glow along the horizon. It would be an hour before the sun rose, but he refused to use a lamp. This was his habit. The precise time he got up varied throughout the year, but he liked to see the first color of day and detested waking to artificial light. Over the many decades of his life, he had evolved into a creature of habit, at least in the small matters.

His favorite morning tea waited on the deck, just through the open doors of his bedroom. One of the Scouts assigned to his protection had set out a spartan breakfast for him. He'd be able to watch the sun rise over the ocean while sipping tea. The fresh air might even stir his fickle appetite.

Samuel noted that the water was unusually still this morning; it looked more like the surface of a lake than an ocean. There had been little wind to disturb its slumber through the night. He often thought of the sea as a living creature, wild and capricious, warm at times, and prone to anger at others. Today it was resting, and its waves were arriving in even, shallow breaths. Samuel closed his eyes to appreciate the moment.

The patio he was using contained a rough-hewn table and an old chair made from wood and bone and thick leather. The tea had been steeped in his own primitive ceramic pot, its glaze was uneven, and the design irregular and faded with time.

The house, like the chair, had been loaned to the Order. It was a cleverly constructed wood-frame structure made from weathered materials that blended in with the environment. Although close to the sea, it was high on a large stone, an erratic swept here from some distant place. The rock was obviously not part of the local geology, but a granite traveler deposited onto the surface of the limestone, and here to stay. Samuel felt a sense of kinship with the rock, and just as out of place. *Well,* he thought, *we all wind up somewhere.*

His mind drifted through memories of the many people he'd met and known during his long life as the sun crested the horizon. When it had risen completely, he shifted to business.

Later today, Samuel would treat a young man in his early twenties. The boy suffered from an illness that the Council physicians had been unable to subdue with the usual drugs and treatments. Yesterday, he'd received a unit of the young man's blood and, using his own unique senses, had detected traces of disease in the blood. He knew its essence if not its pedigree.

After analyzing it, Samuel transfused the blood into himself, and his powerful immune system had been working on a cure for the past day. He suspected the disease was a soft-tissue tumor, one that had metastasized and spread throughout the young man's body. There was also evidence of secondary infection—a putrid background tone that was unmistakable. His unique senses had been designed to isolate and categorize disease in this way. It was a part of what he was: a Blood Healer, although he used more than just his blood when treating people.

Each time Samuel helped someone, he put himself in danger, but not from illness—his immune system was far too potent to be subdued by a mere disease. The danger lay in exposure. The Council knew of him and had been desperate to capture him since the Purge. If successful, they would either carry out a very public execution or—more likely—secretly exploit his abilities for their own benefit.

Healing meant taking risks, but Samuel had no choice. He was driven to help people by a compulsion rooted in his DNA. Healing fulfilled a primal need, and helping others served the Plan.

The Order wanted safety for its members, and they wanted to resume fulfilling their original charter. Ultimately, their safety depended on achieving broad acceptance among the population. Being a member of the Order carried an automatic death sentence, and an excruciating execution, if caught. The Council's extreme political wing had resurrected many of the practices used in the distant past, practices that were every bit as brutal as the Inquisition. Exposing Samuel to outsiders increased the risk that he would be caught, and left a trail of information that could be exploited to predict his future movements. The Scouts protected him with their skill and their lives, but without the Guide's foresight he would have been captured years ago.

Samuel finished breakfast. He wouldn't eat again until tonight, preferring to be a little hungry as he worked. It was a part of the routine that helped keep him mentally alert all day. The Scouts who cared for him often worried that he didn't get enough food or rest, but he'd already survived one hundred sixty years this way.

There was a soft knock at the door. It was Jonathan, the lead Scout. He was young, maybe twenty-five, and dressed in what looked like Council robes.

"Samuel," he said. "I've confirmed that the patient is back at the inn."

"Thank you. We'll leave after I've had a chance to speak with Matthew. Has he arrived?"

"He's here…having breakfast." Jonathan paused, frowning as he looked over his shoulder. "He seems to know your habits very well."

"He should. We've been friends since before your father was born."

Jonathan shifted his weight from one foot to the other. "Well, he's a little strange to be around." His voice was low now, almost a whisper.

"So am I," Samuel said, looking into the Scout's eyes. Jonathan should have been used to the way the Guide looked through people by now. *Maybe it's just the reputation,* he thought. "How will I be dressing today, and what's our story?" Samuel asked.

Jonathan grinned. "I'm your 'older brother', here to keep you out of trouble." He waved his hand at the robe. "We copied the new seminary uniforms. Nice, aren't they? By the way, the Guide brought us new documents. He said we needed to change names again."

"Let me know when he's finished eating. I want to be ready to leave by dark, if possible. We need to get to Central City before long. There's a patient waiting, and I'm afraid we may already be too late." Samuel was thinking that he'd also like to see the cathedral again, but didn't want to get into another security argument with Jonathan. The Scout nodded and left.

CHAPTER 11

An Overdue Talk

I T WAS ALMOST TEN O'CLOCK. Phoebe could hear her father moving around in the next room, probably trying to be quiet, but the smell of fresh coffee and biscuits had filled the apartment and was sneaking under her door. She decided it was time to get up. He was taking a batch of biscuits from the oven when she drifted into the space that served as a combination kitchen, dining room, and living room.

"Mm—I'm glad *someone* likes to get up early."

"Morning, Princess. How'd you sleep?"

"Fine," she said, yawning, as she covertly grabbed a biscuit from the counter, trying not to burn herself. Her other hand was reaching for her favorite mug, the gaudy one with the tiny chip on the handle. It had been a birthday gift from her grandfather, something he'd picked up trading in the south. She nibbled carefully, while stirring cream and a little honey into her coffee.

Her father pretended not to see the missing biscuit. Food had a difficult time making it all the way to the table when Phoebe was hungry. Her eyes were already darting around the kitchen even now, trying to see what else might be available. She noticed that his weekend face was missing, and that there was an odd weekday feel to the room.

After they'd eaten, he began clearing the table, and Phoebe started thinking about the best way to spend the rest of the morning—maybe a walk along the waterfront. She wanted to make sketches of the boats moored at the docks, and it was sunny today—it wouldn't be right to spend the whole day cooped up inside. The painting she'd planned—an image from the cliffs in the dream from last week—could wait for bad weather. She ducked into her room, grabbed her sketchpad, and started toward the door.

"Phoebe, can you wait awhile? I'd like to talk to you about something." Her father was wiping down the table and didn't look up when he spoke. She sensed tension in his voice and was picking up waves of anxiety.

She wondered if it had something to do with last night's little chat. If so, this wasn't going to be pleasant. Uncomfortable, and potentially embarrassing, talks with Dad weren't high on Phoebe's list of fun things to do on a Saturday. But she put the sketchpad away, and plopped down into one of the overstuffed chairs that faced the fireplace, then she draped one leg over an arm of the chair, as if to say: "Okay then, talk."

If it was going to be as awkward as she suspected, the living room was the best place to be. That way, she wouldn't have to look him directly in the eyes if he blushed. Her father didn't seem to be in a hurry, and was taking more time than usual in the kitchen. *Uh-oh, he's stalling. It must be worse than I thought.*

"So," he said, settling into one of the other two chairs. "We haven't talked a lot about your mom, and I've been thinking that was a mistake." A slight widening of her eyes was all Phoebe allowed. Her father paused, probably expecting more of a reaction from her. "The thing is, I think you need to know more about her."

"What brought this on?" Everything about Becky, even her name, was taboo. Her grandfather was the only reliable source of information about her, and even he was pretty tight-lipped on the subject. Of course Phoebe *could* have learned anything she wanted to know without asking, but she refused to intrude on the people closest to her.

"A lot of things brought this on. For one, you're getting older, and there are things you need to know—and, your future isn't quite as bad as you've probably been imagining. Other people like you—people with gifts—have been through this before. The problem is you've never had a real role model, someone like yourself to learn from. That would have been Becky's job." Phoebe heard the hesitation in his voice when he said her mother's name, and knew what it must be costing him to talk. "Secondly, you deserve…actually you *need* to know what she was like, and why you have these abilities.

"You're not so different from her, except in how you were raised. She lived with other people like herself for years, and they helped guide her through the problems of growing up with extra senses. You never had that. She could have helped you with the voices, and showed you how to deal with other people, too. Believe me, things will get better, and you'll have a more normal life eventually. Becky managed to do that.

"Your problems are different from hers in another way, too. It's never been safe for you here. I've tried to convince myself that things would settle down and we'd all get back to the world we knew before, but right now I don't see how that'll happen. And, I'm not sure it'll ever be safe for you here." He paused a moment. "I think the time is coming, not long from now, when you'll need to leave." Phoebe's eyes narrowed, and her mouth opened to say something, but her father wasn't done. "I recently learned that there might be a place where you could be safe—safer than here, anyway."

"I'm not going anywhere without you," she snapped.

"You won't have to. I'm only saying that this may not be the best place for us in the long run."

Phoebe took a breath to calm down. "Okay, okay. Sorry. Tell me more about Becky, and about this idea of leaving." An awkward silence developed. Her father seemed to be trying to decide where to start.

While he was thinking, Phoebe looked around the room, to distract herself from the thought of leaving the only home she'd ever known. The wooden floor in front of the fireplace was covered with the same carpet they'd had since she was born. She noticed a stain at its edge from one of her early attempts at painting, probably finger-painting at the time. The fireplace itself was small, and the masonry above it had darkened from smoke that leaked back into the room. The chimney had always smoked—you just needed to crack the window open a little to help overcome the pressure.

A small desk was wedged in the corner, crammed into a nook by the window that overlooked the street. The gas lamp on the wall above it had a broken shade, but she'd never minded, it was where she did her homework. Phoebe knew every corner of this place, every mark on every wall—she'd made most of them herself. She looked down now, trying to imagine never seeing her home again. A lock of hair fell forward. She pushed it back out of her face, tucking it behind one ear.

Her head was still tilted down when her father started to speak again. His voice was low at first, more hesitant than normal, but still steady. "I met your mother when I was about your age—maybe a year younger. I didn't know anything about her at the time. It wasn't until much later that I learned what she could do. But I think you knew that much." He glanced at her briefly.

"I liked her right away, but she was so shy." He shifted in the chair. "I thought that maybe she had a problem speaking, since she almost never said anything—even when people said hello. Becky arrived during the middle of the school year. That wasn't so strange back then, since people moved around more than they do now. It was a lot easier to change jobs and cities at the time.

"I'd been assigned as her sponsor. That wasn't a big deal, mainly it meant you were supposed to show the new person around, and make sure they had someone to go to when they had a question. But she didn't seem happy, or very comfortable with me. She never looked me in the eye, and always answered questions with one-syllable replies. I figured she'd do better with a girl as sponsor, and didn't take it personally. I decided to ask the teacher to assign someone else, and mentioned it to her; I thought she'd be relieved."

♎

"No, no. I'm sorry, I didn't mean to be rude." Becky frowned, as if not sure of what to say. "You're fine ... I mean you're a good sponsor,

Daniel. It's me. I don't say a lot, even at home." She tried to smile but didn't quite manage to finish, as if distracted, thinking about something that was bothering her.

Maybe she's worried that I'll be a problem, he thought. Daniel stared at the wall, trying to decide how to make her feel more at ease. "Tell you what. I'll do most of the talking today, and I won't ask a lot of questions. I'll just show you where everything is, and then—if you have questions of your own or *want* to talk—you'll know where to find me. I can even introduce you to some of the girls in our class. Of course you're welcome to sit with me at lunch— or not—it's up to you. And it's all a part of the Daniel Lambert sponsor package, no extra charge. Now, I can give you the full tour, or the abbreviated one."

He smiled nervously at Becky, entranced by the look in her eyes. A strange expression passed across her face and then she actually smiled back at him—a real smile.

"Okay, it's a deal. I'll take the full tour, please."

♎

"From that day on, we were friends. Years later, she told me that I was the first friend she'd ever made outside of the Order, and that she was amazed by how easy I was to be around. I was unusual to her, because I didn't hide my feelings, or think one thing and say something else.

"As she matured, Becky grew stronger—much stronger. When we first met she had trouble hiding her mistakes. That's why she was so quiet. A few people wondered if she could speak at all, but she'd learned a lot from her 'family' at the Order. That's what she called the people who raised her. This was her first time out, all by herself—just like when you went to school that first day.

"The Order made everyone use titles with members who raised them, like Mother, Father, Grandmother, and so forth. But I doubt that Becky ever really knew for sure who her biological parents were. One older woman in particular spent a lot of time teaching her how to control her senses—she showed Becky techniques that you've had to learn on your own. My biggest fear when she died was that I wouldn't be able to help you. I'm afraid I wasn't very useful, but you did pretty well, anyway."

Phoebe shook her head, looking down to hide the tears she felt forming. "I'm not sure how much more she could have done."

"I don't know. But Becky said that having someone like herself to lean on was very important. If she'd been here you probably would have been spared a lot of pain, but that's in the past at this point.

"She spent her early life in a compound, like a monastery. The Order was always very secretive and kept to itself. She'd been kept isolated, except from the other special people, like herself. We didn't talk about the Order much back in those early days. She wasn't allowed to discuss it with outsiders, but little things slipped out now and then. I learned that she'd been given opportunities to mix with people in town, but always under supervision. Her time at school was supposed to be a kind of final exam, to see if she could fit in and survive on her own. If she passed, she'd be allowed to live in the city and work for the Order. They still supervised her, but not during the day. I'd tell you more about the short leash they kept her on, and how we were almost not allowed to be friends, but it's a long story and we'll have to save it for another day.

"We spent time together *outside* of school, too. She was even allowed to come home with me on a regular basis, but I never got to meet her family, nor was I ever allowed on the Order's compound. It had a high fence and tons of security.

"After we'd been seeing each other for a few weeks, I started noticing little things. Becky always seemed to know what other people wanted, or what they were trying to say, even better than they did. I thought she was just very intuitive, but she was quiet around new people—especially when we were in groups. It seemed strange that she could be so shy sometimes but so talkative at others. Her people smarts didn't appear to be consistent.

"Eventually I began to suspect there was something more than intuition at work—something beyond normal. For example: she'd sometimes answer a question before I'd even asked it. But I didn't *want* to think there was anything wrong with her. I liked her a lot, probably too much, so I intentionally didn't notice the little mistakes. I told myself that she just knew me very well, and could guess where my mind was going—I've seen couples like that." Her father stopped for a moment, his voice had been getting higher and tighter as he talked. This wasn't easy for him, so she asked a question to help him along.

"When did you know for sure?" She tried to keep her voice casual. "What did she say or do that made you think she was a fre…that she knew what you were thinking?" Her father's eyes flashed at what she'd almost said.

"She wasn't a freak! Sorry, I didn't mean to snap at you, Princess, but she wasn't, and neither are you. You're both gifted, that's all.

"When did I know for sure? Years later, I'd had a fight with your grandfather. It had been coming for a while, so I was pretty mad. I wanted to go to sea, just like him, but he'd decided I was going to school. We'd sparred over this off and on all year—my last year in high school—but the fights hadn't really been serious. Now it was time to decide—I needed to apply to a university soon.

"Anyway, I was supposed to meet up with Becky that night. I sent her a message that I'd be late, but lost track of time and showed up even later than I'd promised. We met at the park and were supposed to have dinner downtown. I was in a terrible mood and snapped at practically everything. The things I *should* have said to your grandfather kept running through my mind; I went back and forth with arguments all night.

"She'd had enough. I guess it must have been pretty bad listening to me rant inside, and she blew up. It was as if I'd been saying everything out loud. First she told me to grow up, and then shot down—word for word—every argument I'd made. She called me an ass, and a few other things besides. Boy, was she angry." He shook his head and then almost smiled. "It was supposed to be our anniversary; we'd been going out for two years. After yelling at me, she stormed off—didn't even say good-bye, or go to hell." Her father stopped talking again and stared at the wall above the fireplace.

Phoebe could feel his mind drifting away—and into the past. She knew all too well what that felt like. For her, the past and the present were pretty much the same thing. She remembered everything she'd ever seen, everything she'd ever felt or tasted, and everything she'd ever thought. It would have been nice to be able to delete a few things.

"What did you do?" she asked in a low voice.

"Me? I tried calling. I tried sending messages. I even tried to visit her at that place she called home, and she disappeared from school, too. I didn't see or hear from her for almost a month. Obviously, we got back together again—later.

"I was an idiot, of course. But you know, she didn't leave because of the fight; she was taken away because she'd made such a huge mistake and then reported it. Everything about the programs was still a big secret back then. Somehow she managed to convince them to let her come back, but, as I said before, I'll tell you that story another time."

"Programs? What was the big secret? What exactly was she— what am I? How did I get this way? Was it something the Order did to Becky that accidentally affected me, too?" Phoebe was firing questions at him quickly.

"I'm sorry, I let myself get sidetracked; I forgot *why* we were having this conversation. Becky wasn't just an employee of the Order; she came out of the genetic programs. She was what they called a Sensitive, and a potent one.

"Becky had come from a long line of Sensitives. The Order wanted to develop telepathic abilities in people. There were a number of parallel genetic chains within the program, like branches of an experimental family tree. They wanted to be sure which genetic change caused which improvement, so they introduced them one at a time along each of the branches. By the time Becky was born, most of these branches had been combined; there were just two left. Each one was called a bloodline, and members within a bloodline were all closely related. Many traits from bloodline to bloodline were similar, but she said that there were significant differences, too. They'd kept the last two Sensitive bloodlines separate for some reason. I don't know why.

"All of the programs started long before the war. The Order wanted to develop new abilities in people—things that no one had thought possible before. They created genes and encoded them into the DNA of human test subjects. But it was more than just DNA that they changed inside of Becky. The scientists had also begun controlling how genes expressed themselves. They manipulated her cells during conception and gestation, and they used machines that Becky said belonged more in a physics lab than as part of a biological experiment. It's all pretty much beyond me, but I know that the Order had long since pushed the envelope on what they could accomplish through genetic manipulation alone. You were a part of that program, too, and your senses are definitely not an accident.

"The Order believed that the characteristics they were developing were important for the future. But no matter what the reasons were, they deliberately made you the way you are, and it took the Order more than two hundred years to develop your senses. Eventually, they planned to combine the abilities from the programs. It was all part of some project they called 'Future Man', intended to make war impossible."

Phoebe blinked. She didn't know what to think, or say—this was much more complicated than she'd ever imagined. She'd always suspected that her weird brain was some kind of runaway experiment, but had believed it was an accident—something they did to Becky that bled through. But they actually planned it this way, and they'd even done something to her, fabricating her brain in a lab. It was too much. She wanted to rant and stomp through the house, but there was no one to rant against. This wasn't her father's fault, and the jerks who'd done this to her were all dead.

"I know it's a lot to take in. But you need to know a little more." Her father wasn't looking directly at her any longer.

"More? You mean there's more than being a genetic monster, partially bred and partially manufactured—like a machine? I don't know how much *more* I can take today."

"I'm afraid so—no holding back today, kiddo." Her father's hand started toward her, but stopped halfway.

"Tell me," Phoebe said, hunching down in the chair and gripping her hands into fists.

"Princess, most of the things I just told you, I learned after the comet hit. By then, Becky was just trying to survive. I think she was scared that something might happen to her, and she wanted me to know as much as possible, just in case. I'm sorry. I should have had this discussion with you before—and maybe a little at a time rather than all at once, huh?" Phoebe couldn't help smiling.

"Yeah, maybe."

"Okay, Becky said that you'll continue to develop as you grow, and that new abilities might be activated at different stages of your life, probably triggered by hormones, or strong emotion. All of the important ones should have started already, but it's possible that more could come as late as your twenties, or after childbirth." He looked away again when he mentioned her having a baby. "Anyway, you may realize one day that you can do something new that you couldn't do before. She also said that you'll grow stronger as you get older, and keep getting stronger your whole life."

"Great! Just what I need—more sensitivity." Phoebe closed her eyes and banged her fists on the arms of the chair, trying not to cry.

"Sorry, kiddo, but there's one more thing I need to tell you—a big one."

She let out a sigh and put her head in her hands, elbows on her knees, and looked at the floor. "Go ahead."

"She seemed to believe that you might develop abilities she didn't have. The geneticists told her that they'd tried something new with you, an experiment." Phoebe rolled her eyes at this. "They crossed the last two remaining genetic bloodlines when you were conceived. They'd always kept them separate, but you are the end product of both Sensitive bloodlines. Becky didn't know what kinds of abilities the other line might bring.

"Most Sensitives start developing when they're two—that's when things started for you, as well. In her case, they used a drug to delay the onset of changes—for a while. When girls reached about seven or eight years old, the drug stopped working and they'd be paired with another Sensitive who would act as a guide. By the time they were twenty or so, most things had already started—so you might be out of the woods—they may never come."

"Is that all of it?"

"That's all I know about your senses. But I learned something new yesterday that gave me a little hope. I started to tell you about it last night and I just mentioned going away a little while ago."

"Good news? I'm not sure I'd know how to handle that." She sat back in the chair and played with a lamp on the table between them using one hand. There was blood in her palm.

"I met someone in jail yesterday, a client. He lives in…he lives outside of the Land—outside the control of the Council. No Inquisition. No executions. We might be able to start over there—both of us. You'd be safe and your gifts would probably be accepted, or at least tolerated. Think about it. I have a strange feeling we may need to act sooner rather than later. Call it intuition; call it whatever you like."

"Well, I'd be the last person to have a problem with intuition. But there's one thing I *would* like to know more about. How exactly did Becky die?" Her father opened his mouth, and looked at her, unable to say anything for a moment.

"It was after the comet. She was on her way back home, trying to sneak into town for a visit—it was late, and she probably thought no one would notice, but luck wasn't with her that night. A man named Michael Johnson identified her. He'd been with the Order, and even worked with Becky for a while, but he'd recanted and become a leader with the penitents—fanatics who wandered from town to town stirring up trouble. Johnson and his followers chased her into the hills and out along the peninsula, north of the harbor. They cornered her on the cliffs, and…" Her father stopped talking for a moment again. "And then she jumped to her death." He took a deep breath and added, "At least it was quick."

"When was that?"

"Months after the comet. She'd gone into hiding before it hit, just before you were born. You were born almost as the comet struck."

"What was it like back then?"

"Terrible, chaotic, and there were fires everywhere. It was hard to take a breath half the time. People were afraid to go out because of the penitents, and the stores were closed. The crops died, or burned up in the fires, and so many fish were killed that your grandfather had to give up working for two years—the smell was awful."

Phoebe didn't say anything for a minute, thinking back to the dream. There was no point in speculating about it being similar to what had happened to Becky. It may have just been a coincidence.

"Your grandfather could probably tell you more about the time she was in hiding."

"Why?"

"Because she hid on his boat until you were born."

CHAPTER 12

A New Friend

P HOEBE RESUMED HER USUAL PRACTICE of eating lunch alone. When the weather was good, she'd sit on her rock, and when it was less cooperative, she'd find an out-of-the-way staircase or an empty classroom. It would be a while before she risked having lunch with Sarah again.

She'd brought a book today. Books were silent, undemanding companions. They let people know that you were busy—and that they should stay away. But she was only pretending to read this afternoon. Saturday's conversation with her father kept running through her mind. She was playing it over and over—quietly fuming about what the Order had done to her—and failed to notice that someone was approaching until she was in his shadow.

"Hey!" Phoebe was ready to complain about anything today. *I'm reading here!* she thought angrily. But when she looked up, Caleb Addison was standing in front of her rock. She could tell it was him by the way the sun outlined his hair. Whatever she'd thought to say next stuck in her throat. He noticed that she was squinting into the sun and shifted over to squat down beside her.

"Sorry," he said. "I didn't mean to sneak up on you."

Phoebe's book was in one hand, the lunch bag on her lap, and a sandwich in her other hand. She lost track of what she was doing for a moment and the bag slipped to the ground. "What?" she asked.

Caleb scooped the bag up and set it on the rock beside her. "I said I didn't mean to sneak up on you. That must be some book—you haven't looked up once. I've been trying to get your attention."

Phoebe had gotten over her initial surprise, but still avoided Caleb's eyes. They were the exact color of the piping on her father's robe—she'd never noticed before.

"W-why? What did you want?" she asked.

"I just wanted to talk," he said.

"About what?"

Caleb sighed and she misread this as impatience with her. "I'm sorry. Was that question too hard?" But she'd spoken more harshly than intended. Caleb was looking around, obviously uncomfortable, and probably wishing he'd stayed away at this point. "No, really—I *am* sorry. I shouldn't have said that." She was shaking her head. "I don't deal with people very well." Phoebe wondered if she'd actually said that last part out loud. Caleb looked as though he was thinking of how to respond and Phoebe's eyes slid past him, to a table under the portico. Sarah was glowering at her across the courtyard, so she looked back at him.

"Well, you do spend a lot of time by yourself," he noted. There was a long pause as he shifted his weight from one foot to the other. "I just wanted to tell you how much I liked your drawings. The one with the old guys playing cards on the dock was incredibly...incredibly real. Maybe you don't know how to deal with people, but you sure know how they tick inside."

Phoebe felt her face getting warm, but couldn't think of what to say. She was still unsettled by the fantasies she'd seen in his mind on Friday, but those kinds of thoughts weren't so unusual. *He is a guy after all,* she thought, *they don't seem to be able to help themselves.* A few of his immediate thoughts were leaking through even now. *He likes me—God knows why—but he thinks I want him to leave.* Phoebe tried to decide if he was right.

"I...umm, thanks." That didn't sound coherent, even in her own ears, so she took a breath to calm down. "Look, I really am sorry for snapping at you. I've had something on my mind all day. I *do* like to draw; it helps me to relax, and I appreciate the compliment. But I'm not so sure that I know people." She didn't look directly at him, but gazed back at Sarah again. Caleb turned his head to see where she was looking and Sarah waved, pretending that she'd just noticed them.

"I was surprised to see you at our table on Friday," he said. "And happy." Phoebe had been doing her best to forget Friday. "But then I figured it out. Sarah talked you into coming. It didn't look like you wanted to be there." He stopped to allow her to say something, but didn't wait for another long silence. "You know, sometimes Sarah has a reason for the things she does…"

Phoebe gave him a cold look, and made him stop. "Sarah's my friend," she pointed out.

Caleb held up his palms. "Peace—I wasn't being critical. I like her, too. I was trying to say that Sarah usually has a motive, or plan for the things she does—sometimes they work out, and sometimes they don't. I figured she was trying to get you more involved with people—to help. You know, since you're so quiet."

"Yeah, maybe."

"Anyway," he went on. "I'm glad she brought you last Friday. I've been looking for an excuse to talk to you, but that lunch was one of the things that didn't seem to work out so well—did it?" Phoebe bit her upper lip, shaking her head. "So, I thought it might be better to try by myself, just one-on-one. Is that okay? Or am I just being a pest?" His mouth was drawn into a tight line, as though he was waiting for Phoebe's axe to fall on his neck.

She sensed that his vulnerability was genuine—that wasn't something she'd expect from someone like him. "It's fine, really. I don't mind. I'm just not in the best mood today—a family thing." Phoebe was baffled about something. Why was he singling her out? She was trying to think of a question to ask—something that would make him feel more comfortable and keep him talking—when she saw that the mistress was getting ready to ring the bell that ended lunch. "Maybe we should try this again some other time."

He looked confused until the bell rang, then his face cleared. "It's a deal. How about lunch tomorrow?" She managed a quick nod, before heading to class, thinking that her decision to avoid boys hadn't lasted very long.

"Phoebe, we're going to be late." Sarah was waiting by the door. "What did Caleb want?" she asked.

"He wanted to tell me he liked my drawings."

"It looked like he was flirting with you."

"Did it?" Phoebe had a puzzled look on her face. "I don't flirt—I don't know how."

"*You* may not, but I'm pretty sure *he* does," Sarah said sharply. "Well, let's get going or Judith will be impossible!"

CHAPTER 13

Jacob

I T WAS MONDAY, THE MOLLY was in port, and that meant
that Jacob Lambert would be at home cooking. Mondays were
when Daniel and Phoebe came to dinner every week. They used to
come on weekends, but getting together on Monday seemed like
a better idea, since it gave everyone something to look forward to
on the worst day of the week. This evening, they'd have Jacob's
famous spicy ragout, made with chunks of beef, hot chilies, onion,
tomato, and an odd assortment of herbs and spices. The day had
started early—cooking ragout took a while. It needed time to
braise properly, so that collagen in the meat would soften, and
dissolve into the sauce. He'd also baked a crusty bread, and had
even made a special dessert for Phoebe. He loved to cook for them.

At sea, Jacob left the cooking to his crew. There, it was fish
yesterday, fish today, and—no doubt—fish tomorrow. He carried
preserved foods, of course, and these helped to provide the illusion
of variety in their diet, but the main protein for every meal was
from the sea. Now he was ashore, and here Jacob avoided seafood
in favor of what he called 'land food'.

His boat, the Molly, was undergoing routine maintenance, and
being readied for the last run of the season. It had been a good year
already, and Jacob had squirreled away a decent profit already. This
run would add to that financial cushion.

Late fall and winter were the times for intense storms in the
ocean. They'd come up on you quickly and could snatch the lives
of the crew and the boat in a flash—the Molly would stay in port

through the winter. It was dangerous to venture out into deep waters this time of year. The fishing grounds where Jacob hunted were already a graveyard for hundreds of boats where crews had tempted fate.

Before the Purge, life at sea had been better—easier. Jacob could count on a powerful engine and accurate weather forecasts. There had even been an onboard icemaker to keep the fish fresh during long cruises. Now they were slaves to the wind. The Molly had always been a dual-powered boat, equipped with both engine and sail, and that had made the transition to pure sailboat easier, once the bans started. Other Captains had not fared as well. He'd also learned to depend on his own nose to predict the weather, and now the Molly carried all the ice they would need when she set out. Blocks of it were cut from frozen lakes and rivers every year through the winter, and then packed into sawdust deep underground to keep it from melting quickly. At sea, fish gradually replaced the volume left behind by melting ice until the ice-to-fish ratio reached a critical point, then they knew it was time to hurry back. *Oh well,* he told himself, thinking about the past, *no point in crying over what can't be changed.*

The treat he'd made for Phoebe was tucked away into the corner cabinet: a double chocolate cake, not yet frosted. Chocolate was precious now, expensive, and damned hard to find. But Jacob traded with boat owners from the colonies for it whenever he could. It didn't help that chocolate was his granddaughter's favorite treat. He looked at the clock—still three hours before they were due, just enough time for a quick nap. He opened a bottle of the dark-red, almost black wine Daniel and he favored, to allow it time to breathe.

Jacob had an agenda tonight, beyond enjoying their regular get-together. He was determined to broach the subject of Phoebe's future, but didn't want a fight. She'd be graduating after next year and, thus far, there'd been no mention of what she might do afterward. More school? Work? One thing for sure, Phoebe wasn't going to sea. He chuckled at the memory of her last voyage. "Poor girl." But she still needed to maintain a low profile—just like her mother.

There didn't seem to be much of Daniel in Phoebe's features, not that *that* mattered—and there was definitely something unusual about her—but he knew better than to pry. He had other grandchildren, all boys. They lived in Central City, too far away to see often, but even if they'd lived next door, Jacob was sure that Phoebe would still be his favorite. He wondered if that was because she was a girl, or because of some other, more mysterious quality she'd inherited from her mother.

A knock at the door surprised him. At first he assumed it was one of the crew, although he'd made it clear that they were not to disturb him on Mondays. Not unless the Molly was on fire, or sinking. It was Phoebe.

"You're early," he said, not minding.

"I know. Sorry—I probably interrupted naptime, but I need to talk to you—privately."

"Okay," he said, drawing the word out. "Make yourself comfortable and tell me how I can help." She walked into the small living room and settled onto the sofa.

"Is that chocolate I smell?" Her eyes had brightened. He didn't say anything, but scowled—some surprise.

Jacob perched on a chair across a low table from his granddaughter. "This has to do with my mother. It's okay," she added when he pursed his lips. "Dad and I had a talk about her on Saturday. I know where she came from—and other things, too."

"I probably know a lot less about that than your father," Jacob warned.

"That's not what I wanted to ask you about. I need to know more about her personally, and about what happened."

He closed his eyes; it had been close to eighteen years now, and he was trying to imagine the sorts of things that she might want to hear about. "Your mom was real smart, and real pretty, but she had a problem." He rubbed the side of his neck as he looked toward the windows. "The Purge was starting up and she was in danger. I had the impression that she was fairly high up in ... well, you know who she worked for—and she was pregnant with you."

"It was just a matter of weeks before the comet hit, and people had already begun to protest in the streets, they were angry about what they'd heard the Order was doing. A few of your mother's colleagues had been caught and were roughed up pretty badly. The Order had shut down their offices and retreated to the compound west of town. Everyone could see that something big was coming, but the Council was quiet, and the Order still pretended that everything was going to be all right—Becky wasn't so sure. She was scared, for herself, and for you and your father, so I hid her."

"How?"

"She went to sea with me, we traded up and down the coast rather than fishing that season. I told the crew her name was Hanna, and they assumed the baby was mine. Back then I changed crews pretty regularly. None of them had actually met her before— she was a natural on the water, even as pregnant as she was." Jacob smiled at Phoebe.

"Are you sure she was *my* mother?" Phoebe asked, grinning.

"'Fraid so—I delivered you myself." Her eyes opened wide.

"And then the comet hit?" she asked.

"Yeah. Later, Becky said it was really an asteroid, but I don't think anyone really cared what it was called. It created a lot of problems. If it hadn't broken up beforehand, I don't know what might have happened. Some of the pieces hit on land and some hit the water. Wherever it landed in the sea, the water vaporized, and tremendous waves formed. On land, there were fires all over the place and we had terrible weather for a long time."

"Tell me about afterward, I mean when she died."

Jacob took a deep breath and let it out slowly. "Someone saw her. It was several months after you were born—maybe four. The Council was circulating photos of Becky early on, but the first pictures were old, from when she was still in school. Her hair was different, too, and that made her hard to identify, but she was still afraid of being recognized—because they'd find you. Her biggest fear was always that you'd get hurt. Just after you were born, she decided to leave."

"Where did she go?"

"A number of her people were hiding in towns, all over the Land. She wanted to find where they were, hoping for a safe haven, and then she'd come back for you two. Everyone hoped that things would calm down after a while, but they never did.

"More recent pictures started appearing on wanted posters, and officials came by asking questions. They knew Becky had lived with your father and suspected him of being involved with her work, but they backed off after a while. He didn't have any other connection to the Order, and being a defender meant he worked for the Council. Our family's been in the Land a long time, ever since people lived here. There's Bardon blood in us Lamberts."

"Bardon? Bloody Bardon? The guy who made drums out of his enemies' bones and skin?" Phoebe was having a hard time imagining her father being related to the ancient hero of the Land.

"One of our more bloodthirsty ancestors. Getting back to Becky, she didn't have much luck finding help, but did manage to find odd jobs on boats trading with the colonies. They weren't looking for her that far south. She came back to see you guys—I know she wanted to be here for you as you grew up—she felt it was important that you two be close to each other. Mother-daughter stuff, I guess." Jacob looked at Phoebe to gauge her reaction.

"And someone recognized her, right?"

"Yeah, this guy Johnson. He'd worked as a lab technician, and recognized her. What a kook! He and a bunch of other kooks were going around bullying people. They were here the night she came back for some kind of prayer meeting. She stumbled into them. They chased her up north and then out to the cliffs until she couldn't run any farther and had to jump to get away. Believe me, it was a much better death than the one she'd have had otherwise."

"Did anyone look for her body?"

"We all did. I knew your father *had* to know for sure if she was gone, and the Council obviously wanted to see her body. We searched and searched, but it was damned hard getting close to the point."

"Can you show me where she jumped—on a map?"

"Why?"

"I don't know, but I need to see." The look on her face was too much for him. Jacob had never been able to say no when she looked at him like that.

They stepped over to a map of the coastline, it hung on the dining room wall. She looked at where he pointed. "And they never found her body?"

"No. Never. I searched for a week, but the sea wasn't herself yet. A lot of silt was stirred up, and of course the fish were still floating everywhere, too."

"I don't remember anything about her. I'd like to ask Dad more, but…You knew her, though. What did she sound like—I mean what was her voice like, and how did she speak? Did she have an accent?"

"Yeah, I don't mention her name around him, either. But I can do better than tell you what she sounded like. I have an old recording from my fiftieth birthday—a gift she had someone make for me."

Jacob secured the door, and looked out the windows, shutting the curtains as he went by. He gave Phoebe a glance that made it clear she wasn't to say anything, not even to her father, and went to the back of the house. After a few minutes, he returned to the living room with a small cube in his hand. It was shiny, and seemed to be made of metal and glass.

"I used to wonder if the battery on this thing would run out, but it's Order technology. The battery is as amazing as what it does."

Jacob sat beside her and placed the cube on the table. Then he put his finger on one side of it until they heard a click. At first nothing happened, but after a short time, three beautifully pure colored lights appeared on the ceiling above it. They danced around and then combined into a single white spot, which fluctuated—changing from white to red to blue to green and back to white before going dark. Next, a haze—shaped like a hollow vertical cylinder—formed in the air above the cube, partially obscuring light from the other room. It seemed to sparkle with colors before changing again. Phoebe leaned forward and her hair stood up.

"Be careful, don't get too close," Jacob warned.

Light appeared from inside the cube again, and then a face materialized within the cylindrical cloud. It was a woman and she was smiling at them. To Jacob, Phoebe looked like a younger version of Becky, now that he could see their faces side by side. Then her mother spoke. The sound seemed to come from all around the cube. "Happy Birthday, Dad! I wanted to give you something really special. One of my friends made this for me—it's a secret." A finger appeared in front of Becky's mouth, a warning to be quiet. "Don't tell anyone," she whispered. Then she started to sing—it was a traditional birthday song. Phoebe's eyes kept getting wider and wider and her mouth stayed open, but she didn't say anything—it looked as though she couldn't. After the song ended, the recording stopped, the haze disappeared, and the cube's lights went out with a second click.

Jacob could tell something was wrong—something more than the surprise of seeing such a strange object for the first time. He started to say something, but Phoebe interrupted him.

"Please don't tell Dad I came here."

"What is it? What's wrong?" Obviously she was in distress, even pain.

"I'm not…I mean, I don't know what to think—but I've heard that voice before."

CHAPTER 14

New Feelings

PHOEBE HEADED TO LUNCH WITH an uneasy stomach, definitely not hungry. Apparently she'd filled up on butterflies for breakfast. She'd never thought of herself as exciting, at least not in a way that she could share with others, not without making them run away. *If Caleb knew the real me, he'd be terrified.*

The night before, Phoebe lay in bed, unable to sleep, wondering if it was really such a good idea to encourage this new friendship—and, if she did, how to do it safely. After several sleepless hours, she decided it would only work if she interacted with him as a normal girl. There could be no deliberate probing of his mind, and she'd need to shut out his feelings as much as possible—then ignore whatever bled through. If she could pretend, even to herself, to be normal then it might be possible to have a real friend, one who was a boy.

Phoebe's knees were shaking when she entered the courtyard. Caleb was waiting, and politely, but firmly, herded her to a small table near the edge of the quad—just under a small tree. She eyeballed her rock in its corner as they walked, but submitted without comment.

Sarah looked at her in a way that could have made icicles form when they passed her. She'd been uncharacteristically quiet all morning, watching her and watching him during art class, as if expecting to see hidden signals being sent back and forth.

Caleb brushed a seat off for her. *There's nothing wrong with my hands,* she thought, but her mouth stayed closed.

Phoebe looked across the little stone table at him, not knowing what to say, and so she methodically unpacked her lunch for something to do. He'd only brought an apple for lunch. *That was a good idea.*

A question might make him talk first. Questions were useful as offensive weapons, when you wanted to hide what you were. "Tell me something about yourself," she said.

"I'd hoped *you'd* talk a little this time," Caleb said, grinning. Phoebe swallowed, and her eyes drifted around the courtyard while she chewed on her lower lip.

"Okay," he said, "I'll go first, but you're not off the hook." She quickly nodded.

It was obvious that he was trying to maintain eye contact with her, but she wasn't cooperating. *At least he's focusing on my face today*, she thought.

"My family's been in New Bright Sea as far back as anyone can remember. Our first ancestor was probably a local witch doctor; we always seem to wind up being involved in medicine, one way or another. My father, my uncle, and my grandfather—all physicians—but not me."

"Why not?"

"I don't know. Maybe I'm just not Addison material, or maybe it's because the world seems to be going backwards. Take my dad, for example. He's a cardiologist; at least he used to be. But everything changed after I was born, and the comet hit. Since then, he's become more of a politician. I doubt he even treats patients any longer. He's a spokesperson for the other doctors, and constantly protecting the hospital from…well, the Council." The last two words were said in a whisper. "They don't bend, even when it comes to saving lives. But Dad keeps pushing.

"Things really started to change in a big way once the new rules came. Most of the doctors saw what happened to—you know who they were." Caleb looked around and lowered his voice again. "The Order. That scared them. It made them reluctant to stand up for what was in the interest of their patients. They believed the same thing would happen to them next, so they kept their mouths shut—but not my father. Uncle John says that he was sure they'd arrest Dad. He pushed hard, and was embarrassing the Council. Instead, they made him director of the hospital—go figure. But the new rules kept coming."

"New rules?"

"Oh, you know. For almost a year things stayed more or less normal, at least at the hospital—and by normal I mean modern. The bans focused on other things first: cars, airplanes, boats, but then they banned the use of electricity and anything electrical in nature. That's when things really started to go downhill." Phoebe's eyes narrowed. She was surprised that Caleb would be so openly critical of the Council. After all, he barely knew her. She tried to keep her face blank, but inside she was starting to like him more.

"How exactly did they start?"

"Well, I don't remember all the details myself, but Dad told me that electric power for housing was cut first. He thought they'd exempt the hospital, but a couple of months later they cut its power, too. The hospital had its own backup generator, but it was never designed to run all the time, and anyway, the Council shut it down before long.

"Most modern medical equipment depends on electricity. Without that, the diagnostic tools, the refrigeration units, the automatic pumps, the oxygen machines—lots of stuff I don't know about—all stopped working. That made it a lot harder for the doctors to treat their patients. Even if the generator hadn't been confiscated, it wouldn't have mattered for very long, because they took the equipment next. Anything supplied by the Order was first to go, 'tools of the devil', they called them." He seemed ready to launch into a longer speech, but stopped. Phoebe bit her lower lip again, sighing.

"I know," he said. "My mother was one of the first they killed."

"What do you mean? How'd they do that?" she asked.

"My sister was born after the bans, and there were complications. Dad said it would have been easy to save them before, but she died during the birth, and my sister went a day later."

"That's terrible!"

"Yeah." Caleb was quiet for several moments. "Every year Dad goes to Central City and makes a big push, trying to convince them to let hospitals use electricity. And every year he comes back empty-handed. Uncle John calls it a big waste of time. Like I said, the Council doesn't bend." Phoebe looked at his face and took a bite from her sandwich. He was absentmindedly playing with his apple on the table, apparently not very hungry.

"Sorry, I didn't plan to talk about that kind of stuff." He looked around again, as if to make sure they hadn't been overheard, and then shrugged. "No harm done."

Phoebe wanted to change the subject. Everything had gotten too serious, and so quickly. "What do you like to do?" she asked. "I mean when you're not at school, or making speeches about the Council."

Caleb laughed, and his frown vanished. "I like to climb."

"Climb? You mean, like, with ropes? On cliffs?"

He laughed again. "You're looking at me as though I murder puppies for fun."

She shook her head. "Is there anything else you like to do?"

"I like being out on the water—sailing—that is, when I get an invitation from someone with a boat…Hey, are you okay?"

"*That's* supposed to be better than climbing?"

"What's wrong with sailing? You know, you look like you aren't feeling well."

"I'm…okay." She was trying hard not to slide into a flashback from the last time she'd been out on the Molly. "I get seasick."

"But I just mentioned the word s…"

Phoebe held her hand up. "I know—I know. Sometimes that's enough. I have this really, really good memory, especially when it comes to unpleasant things." She took a breath to calm the queasiness. "So, do you do anything normal people do?" *There's got to be something we have in common.*

Caleb scratched the back of his neck and took a bite from the apple. "Uh, sure I do."

"That's good to hear," she said, smiling. "Okay, tell me about this climbing insanity." Caleb chuckled again.

"Well. I'll bet you could travel pretty far and never find a place as good as right here for climbing. We have incredibly challenging cliffs less than an hour's walk out of town. But I guess you don't climb."

"Not really," she said. Jumping off a cliff to kill herself in a dream probably didn't count. "I've done that other thing, though—the water thing. The last time was pretty bad. The sea was rough and I started throwing up right away, but my grandfather wasn't able to turn around."

Caleb rolled his eyes. "I thought girls didn't get seasick."

"I don't know who told you that. Maybe I'm just abnormal," she added, staring bleakly at the table. "Anyway, I'm an extreme case. Well, at least I had that one extreme experience, and I've been afraid to try again ever since." Phoebe was feeling a little queasy again—the memory was trying to return, so she placed one hand under the table and made a tight fist to keep her mind in the present. "I thought I'd better not press my luck."

"That's no fun. Maybe you've outgrown it. You'll never know until you try again." There was silence for several moments. Phoebe closed her eyes, still not past the aftereffects of the memory. "Are you feeling better?"

"I'll be fine. It's just my quirky memory. Once it gets started, it can be hard to stop." *Stop, Phoebe!* she thought, digging her nails in even harder. The pain was helping a little.

"Hmm. That memory problem sounds pretty inconvenient."

"Yeah."

"So, without thinking about that last time, do you think you might be willing to try the s-word again sometime—maybe together?"

"Maybe." Phoebe shrugged. She realized now that the color of his eyes also reminded her of the sea. She'd never made that connection before. The sea, Caleb's eyes, and her father's robes all had that same dark blue hue. "I'll think about it."

"Okay," Caleb said. "I did my part—now it's your turn. Tell me something about yourself. What do you like to do? And what's your family like?" He smiled at her.

She'd been so engrossed, listening to his voice and watching his face, that she wasn't ready. Phoebe looked down at the table, searching for something to say, but then she let herself get distracted.

She moved a finger across the table's surface. It was old, and made of formed concrete with flattened, smooth pebbles that had been embedded into its top. She looked for inconsistency in the size of the pebbles, or randomness in their pattern—it was too regular to have been made by hand. There were no signs of the asymmetry she expected in newer tables. This had to be from before the comet. *I wonder how many survived?*

The silence had become uncomfortably long, and Caleb was shifting in his seat, and clearing his throat. "Phoebe," he prodded gently.

"All right, I was stalling," she admitted. "I really don't like to talk about myself."

"No kidding!" Caleb settled back in his chair, laughing. "At least you're honest—that shows in your work, too."

She looked up into his eyes, not smiling. Even without hearing his thoughts, she could tell a lot about him. Caleb would always say exactly what was on his mind.

"You don't like compliments, do you?" he asked.

"Only when I deserve them," she said, biting her lip again.

"Can you at least tell me a little about your family?"

She hesitated; these were exactly the kinds of questions she was most afraid of. "My mother died the year the comet hit. I don't remember meeting her, and I'm pretty sure my biological father died that year, too."

"Where did they live?" he asked.

Phoebe didn't want to lie to him any more than absolutely necessary. "I think they both lived in Central City, but I don't know much more than that." The uncertainty made her feel slightly better about the white lie. "My real family is from here. My dad adopted me when I was just a baby, and I have two uncles—although they moved to Central City a long time ago. But my grandfather still lives here. You'd like him. He fishes for a living." Caleb's eyes brightened, probably imagining potential invitations to sail.

"It's pretty unusual for a single man to adopt a baby girl, isn't it?"

"Yeah, maybe so, but it's the best thing that ever happened to me. He's a wonderful father." This was an emotional subject for her and Phoebe was afraid she'd been too intense. "Sorry."

"No," he said, his voice just above a whisper. "It's very personal, you obviously feel strongly about him, and I feel a little less like an interrogator when you talk like that. What's he like?" With her view of the courtyard, Phoebe could see that the mistress was getting ready to ring the bell to end lunch again.

"Maybe later," she said.

Caleb frowned until he heard the bell. "Saved again," he teased. But there was something else in his eyes—a look that made her heart beat faster. "Tomorrow?" he asked. Phoebe nodded, unable to speak.

Sarah didn't bother asking about Caleb this time—she was too busy pretending Phoebe didn't exist. His fascination with her had surprised them both, and had hurt Sarah, but Phoebe had no idea what to do to make things better. *I wonder how long this is going to last?*

A few of the other girls in class looked at her with odd expressions after lunch. She imagined their whispers were about her. *Or maybe I'm just paranoid.*

♎

The next day was easier. She knew what to expect. Caleb met her as she entered the courtyard and, once again, led her to the same small table. She watched without comment as he cleaned the seat.

"You started to tell me something about your father yesterday." He was focused on her eyes.

"Dad's a defender in the Council court. It's a frustrating job, but he likes being able to help people, especially the innocent who get caught up by the flood of rules. Only a handful of people seem to know them all. But I think he really wanted to fish for a living, like my grandfather." Caleb frowned; it looked as though he was going to say something but didn't, so she raised an eyebrow to encourage him.

"I can't say I blame him, but why fishing?"

"Like your family, the Lamberts have been around here for a long time. Before my dad's generation, they were all fishermen. I guess Jacob will be the last—unless one of my cousins goes crazy. Both uncles work in a tool factory, and they have boys, but no one seems interested in fishing—at least that I know of."

"Maybe you could take over the business and become the town's first female fish tycoon." He was grinning.

Phoebe shook her head, working hard to keep the revulsion off her face. "No. I think I'll be a professional cliff climber instead," she laughed.

"Sorry, didn't mean to tease," Caleb said.

"Sure you did, but that's all right. I need to be able to talk about things without going overboard—no pun intended." After a few moments, she asked: "Do people really get over being seasick?"

"I hope we can try sometime."

Despite his strange idea of fun things to do, Phoebe liked that Caleb was thinking about them doing something together. *He's got to have other interests.*

At Caleb's prodding, Phoebe described what it was like growing up as the only girl in a family. She talked about looking after her father. "Since it was just the two of us, I grew up pretty fast." She didn't mention the other things that had matured her. They'd only frighten, and probably disgust him. Where could she safely steer the conversation next?

"When did you start drawing?" he asked.

This was a good subject, even if it brought back memories of those painful early years.

"When I was very young, I used to stare at things: shapes and patterns, and the way light seems to change how everything looks. I remember watching clouds for a whole day one time. And the trees! Trees are incredibly complex objects. Most people don't think about them that way. We pass them every day, but have you ever really looked at one? Try looking today, at a tree, or you can choose anything you like. Look at it as though this was the first time you'd ever seen it. I see everything like that, shapes and even subtle differences in the surface of the street. I know I sometimes concentrate too much on minutia, but it's the quirky little variations in life that make the world interesting—not just with trees, with everything. Thinking about and seeing the world that way helped me relax when I was younger, especially if I had to plan how I would draw what I was seeing. The process of drawing also let me show my dad the world as I saw it. Clouds and trees and horses and people and buildings, and…and other things—things I only see in dreams." Phoebe shuddered.

"Were you upset a lot when you were young?"

Phoebe stared at him for a moment, wondering how much of herself she could share without actually telling him too much— and without lying. Her instincts told her that lying to him, more than absolutely necessary, would destroy the way she was starting to feel around him.

Her mouth twisted into a half smile. "I had a problem when I was younger, like an illness. You see, I was…" Phoebe shook her head. "No, I *am* strange." Phoebe looked up to see if there was a reaction from him, but he simply nodded. "I'm a lot better now. I learned how to deal with who I am. The way my mind works is helpful at times, but it can also cause emotional issues—more so when I was younger. That's why I stayed at home for so long."

"Did you go to school at home?"

"Yeah, for almost three years. My dad was my teacher." She felt warmth building behind her eyes. Thinking about everything her father had done for her always affected her this way.

Caleb's expression changed again, especially in his eyes. It was the same look as yesterday. She was unconsciously picking up on his emotions, even though she was trying hard not to. *He likes me…What the hell's wrong with him? Maybe he's a freak, too.* But her heart was beating faster again, even more than yesterday.

"You were telling me about when you started drawing."

"Oh yeah." Phoebe took a breath. "Looking at the world that way—and I still do—makes me want to capture everything so I can show people how I feel. They're more than just drawings to me. They're therapy."

"Painting, too?" he asked. Phoebe couldn't help grinning when she thought back to her discovery of color.

"A few years ago I started experimenting with paints. I tried watercolors first. It's hard to get a lot of detail using them, but they're really great for certain kinds of pictures. Then I discovered oils. Oh my God! They're the best. They let me do things I never dreamed possible. You can blend oils so many different ways. They can be thickened, or thinned, to get just the right consistency. You can spread the paint down in layers, and then manipulate it on the canvas to make complex textures, like clouds and trees and other shapes that I can imagine, but are hard to describe in words.

"I just learned a new trick. I started weaving the layers with different kinds of tools to create these amazing hatchings. You can make textures that are subtle and it's hard to nail down exactly what the color is. They also change with the light, and as you move in front of the painting."

Phoebe was speaking fast, and saying more than she'd ever said in school before. It was as if a bottle had finally been uncorked, and his eyes were glowing—that same expression that had made her heart race was back again. She wanted to open her senses up so badly that it hurt. But there was no way she was giving up now— there was no way she was going to stop trying to feel normal. That's when she realized how much she'd been talking, and stopped.

"Sorry. You got me going." She'd almost launched into a narrative on the images in her room, but those pictures could never be seen, or even described to other people. Phoebe took a deep breath and looked down. "I still like to draw, but painting is fun, too." She'd never felt as exposed as she did right now. Caleb didn't say anything, but he was still staring at her.

"What's wrong?" she asked.

"Sorry. I was taking it all in."

The mistress rang the bell and lunch ended.

♎

They met for lunch every day that week. To Phoebe, this was different than anything she'd known before; she wasn't sure what to do next. She thought about how she felt around him. Their time together never seemed to be long enough, and she was afraid that, maybe, she was starting to like him more than was good for her. But it was a relief, getting to know him this way, a little bit at a time. And it felt good—weird—to have someone else know her this well. New feelings had been growing inside of her all week. They were different than she'd expected—different and confusing. Phoebe didn't understand them all just yet, but she knew one thing for sure—she didn't want them to stop.

CHAPTER 15

An Eye in the Sky

REBECCA SLID DOWN THE HILL, tearing her pants and scraping her thigh on a rock. A sudden intake of breath and a short-lived grimace were all that betrayed her pain.

"Sorry," she said.

"Sorry for what?" the Scout asked, with a perplexed look on his face.

"For being a nuisance, a klutz, and for making so much noise."

"Don't apologize," the Scout said. They'd been traveling in silence since sunrise, but Gabriel didn't chat while he walked; his thoughts were usually enough to keep him occupied. He stopped to take a sip of water from the bladder hung across his shoulders, and she copied him. Neither took more than was necessary, but Gabriel also wanted to check on Rebecca's leg. He shrugged off his pack and removed a small parcel, the medkit.

"Let me see your leg," he demanded. At his direction, Rebecca removed her outer pants and lay on her back, elevating the wound with her knee bent, but still modestly covered by a pair of shorts she wore underneath for warm weather.

The wound was deep, and dirt from the rock had been crushed into her skin, so he cleaned and sanitized it using alcohol. She didn't flinch, or make a sound. *Of course not,* he thought. After cleaning the scrape, he applied pressure to stop the bleeding, and then wrapped a clean bandage over the wound to protect it. Finally, he removed another small kit from his pack and sewed a patch over the tear in her pants. This would help protect the injury, too.

"Thank you," she said, getting up and putting her pants back on. He nodded with a grunt.

"Do you feel well enough to push on, or should we stop?" Gabriel already knew what she would say, but wanted to hear it, anyway.

"Let's keep moving," Rebecca said.

Gabriel turned to hide the smile on his face. He admired Rebecca's grit, but wouldn't admit it out loud. He hoped Phoebe had inherited some of her mother's toughness.

They'd been traveling four days now. The first two had been the hardest, walking in the darkness and sleeping during the day. The paths he chose offered good cover, but cover also meant there were more obstacles: roots to trip over, and branches to grab at their clothing and faces. The clear, easy trails were tempting, but the Scout was wary of the sky. Matthew said the drones were a threat. These were surveillance vehicles armed with sensors, which the Order had left behind when they fled, autonomous spies that were effective both day and night. But the darkness offered Rebecca and him a slight advantage. The high-resolution camera contained in its nose wasn't sensitive in the dark, and the drone wouldn't be able to identify their faces. Its infrared sensors could still find them, but it would be unable to classify them as being members of the Order. As a precaution, they hadn't used fire those first nights, and ate only cold rations. Matthew had been right, as usual.

♎

It happened during their second night of travel. Rebecca was stumbling along, having difficulty seeing where to step. Her night vision was probably not what it had been when she was younger, so she stayed close to him, trying to step where he stepped. As they were moving through a cluster of pines, he heard a buzzing sound in the distance, like a large insect, but its tone was much deeper.

"Stop," Gabriel hissed. Rebecca heard him fumbling in his pack, as if he were looking for something. "Come closer," he ordered, urgency in his voice. She obeyed without asking why. As she stepped to his side, Gabriel swung an arm up and over them. A deeper darkness followed the sweep of his arm, blocking out the few stars that had been visible between the branches of the trees, and a lightweight material descended over their heads. It was thin and film-like—almost weightless. Gabriel pulled her down, low to the ground, allowing the material to cover them completely and to make contact with the soil. As it touched the ground, they felt a small shock, like a static discharge, pass through the material.

"Keep very still," he whispered.

"What is it?" Rebecca asked.

"A drone, we need to be quiet," he whispered.

The buzzing changed several times, increasing and decreasing in volume as the machine followed a search pattern over the area. After around fifteen minutes, the sound faded into the distance. When it had gone, the Scout stood up and refolded the thin material into a small packet; this time he put it into a pocket of his vest.

"Matthew said the trails would be watched, but I didn't really believe they'd waste a drone on us."

"What does it do?"

"It's an eye in the sky, looking for us. A drone, equipped with sensors—visible and infrared cameras. It has a sensitive directional microphone to pick up sound, as well."

"I've heard of them, but never seen one in action."

"The Council doesn't have many. Some of our equipment was still functioning when we abandoned the facilities. The really dangerous stuff was all destroyed, but we couldn't get everything. I'm pretty sure they won't be able to fix one if it fails, so when they use a drone, you know they mean business."

"How do you think they knew we'd be here?"

"Matthew thinks there's an informer. We were investigating rumors when I was sent to guide you. It's possible that someone knew that an important person would be traveling through the area this week."

"Do you think they know about Phoebe?" she asked. He could see her chewing her lower lip in the moonlight, and knew how nervous she was about her daughter's safety.

"No, absolutely not. The details of this mission were kept very close. Besides you and me, just three other people know what we're up to. But we had to make arrangements to use the cabin, and communications leave a trail. Maybe the timing of tonight's flyover will help us identify the traitor."

Rebecca couldn't see Gabriel's face, but could sense his emotions. They'd catch the traitors soon enough, and then she, or someone like her, would interrogate them. Once they'd gotten everything they wanted from the traitor, he or she would become an example for other would-be informers.

"What was that thing we hid under?"

"A special kind of blanket. It hides our heat signature, and matches what the drone sees to the ground around us—anything it touches—both visible and infrared. We call it the Chameleon, old military technology that the Order improved on—useful.

"I'm pretty sure they were just looking for heat signatures, a campfire or warm bodies moving in the darkness. To the drone's sensors, hot things, like our bodies or fire, show as bright objects, and cool things look dark. They scan for bright things—especially if they're moving, or have a human shape."

"But we're safe now?"

"We're safe, *for* now," he corrected. "It's interesting how the Council uses the very things they call evil when it suits them, isn't it?" Rebecca nodded. "They just say: 'It's being used in the service of God', and everything's okay. Matthew told me that it isn't so much the modern equipment that they distrust—they're afraid that knowledge of how to build things that might threaten them will spread."

"How much of the equipment do they still have?"

"We left quite a bit behind, mostly pre-war technology. It'll all fail, or run out of power, or rust…eventually. They didn't get our quantum batteries, although rumors indicate they may have found a portable reactor. The Order has a model to predict what's probably still working, but no one really knows for sure.

"Anyway, the drone's gone, let's move. We should keep going until midday—if you think you can manage it." Gabriel looked at her and Rebecca nodded. "Tomorrow, we'll shift back to a daytime schedule. I don't like to travel in the dark, too many opportunities for a mistake."

♎

It was late. The shadows of hills to the southwest had already covered the valley and were touching the base of the ones to the northeast. They reached the small stream where Gabriel planned to stop for the night. Becky was feeling especially tired, more so than she'd felt since they first set out on the mission. The almost constant walking combined with her age amplified her fatigue, and everything ached.

They each had one of the Scout's traveling rations, supplemented by a little meat from a rather thin rabbit that he'd trapped the previous night. It was roasted over a tiny smokeless fire along with an herbal tea that Gabriel blended himself. It wasn't long before Rebecca was asleep.

They were up and moving again early the next morning. "Tell me something about Daniel and Phoebe," Gabriel asked. "At least what you know. I understand she was fairly young when you fled." Rebecca swallowed before answering. Thoughts of having abandoned Phoebe didn't sit well with her. But she knew what the Scout really wanted to know; she'd overheard him thinking about the next mission during breakfast.

"Daniel will do his best to protect Phoebe," she said. "And he'll work hard to do what we want, at least once I've had a chance to speak with him. I can't say that I know Phoebe all that well. As you said, she was young when I left, but I learned something about her those two nights we connected—and from Daniel when I connected with him. Phoebe is very disciplined. If you could have felt her mind and understood how...how incredibly difficult it was for someone like her to survive, you'd respect her strength. She's tough. I doubt I could have done as well." The Scout didn't argue.

♎

They were following an unmarked path, more a deer trail than anything else. It ran through a deep valley between two ridges. This forest had been spared the fires eighteen years before, and the trees here were older and taller. Two days north of them, a road followed the channel cut through the hills and mountains by the Scythe River. It went from Central City to New Bright Sea Harbor. Gabriel and Rebecca could have saved time by using the road, but it would have been very dangerous.

Beneath the soil they walked on, the sedimentary rock was riddled with deep cavern networks that formed when the limestone dissolved. It was the caverns that had brought both the Order and the Council to the Land two hundred years before. Rebecca and Gabriel were headed for a specific cavern. Corbin was one of the original Sanctuaries built before the war, and the Order had kept its location a secret, even after establishing the Balance. Beyond Corbin, another fifty kilometers northwest, was Central City, capital of the Land and seat of power for the Council of God.

♎

As she walked, Rebecca focused on the little things, keeping under trees when possible, avoiding a branch that was about to hit her in the face, and trying not to trip on a rock or fall, as she had before. This was how the Scout lived most of his life, and he seemed at home.

It was their last stop before reaching Corbin, and Gabriel chose a campsite near a cold spring fed from an underground river. They were close to the Sanctuary now, too close to risk a fire.

Tomorrow night, I'll sleep in my own bed, Rebecca thought. She closed her eyes momentarily, glad that the journey was almost over. Familiar stars peered through the branches above her as she lay on the ground, looking up with her head pillowed on her arms.

"How many places like this do you know about?" she asked, indicating the spring.

"Lots," he answered. "I've never counted them all, but I suppose hundreds."

So many, she wondered. "Do you use a map, or remember where they are?"

"I've made maps in the past, but I know most of the places pretty well now. I travel a lot, especially with Matthew. After a while, the campsites become old friends. I'm not as familiar with the areas near the Western Mountains, so I keep a journal to remind me about where I've been. It's a lot like the navigation records sailors used to keep—logbooks containing detailed observations whenever they sailed through uncharted waters. My logbook is in code, of course. It wouldn't mean much to anyone else."

"In case you lose it, or in case you're captured?"

"Only if I lost it," he said. "If you're captured, the Inquisitor will get what he wants sooner or later, you need to be ready to kill yourself to protect everyone." The matter-of-fact way he said it reminded Rebecca of how interconnected they all were. *We're at risk, no matter who's captured,* she thought, shivering.

"How did you learn to live like this? Did you have a teacher?"

"My father was a member of the Guard and he became a Scout, later. Of course we both had a lot to learn together. Things were much easier before the Purge. You don't always think about how you'll manage without the tools you're used to—until there's no choice. We had all the things a modern civilization offered. Why learn to make a fire using sticks if you've got matches or a lighter—or if you don't need fire at all?"

"The Scouts existed as an organization before the comet." It wasn't exactly a question, but Rebecca was curious about their origin.

"Sort of, the Guard has always provided security for the Order, but the number of Guard members who were Scouts faded over time after the war. I'm a member of the Guard and a Scout, but everyone has different skills, not many Scouts wander alone, or guide people, as I do."

He paused before changing the subject. "Rebecca, it's not really my business, but what can you tell me about being a Sensitive? I know you can read minds, but I've always wondered what it was like."

"My close friends call me Becky," she said, deciding that she liked and trusted Gabriel a lot. He was the kind of person anyone would want as a friend. "I was … engineered—maybe *manufactured* is as good a word as any—to be what I am," she laughed. "Well, not exactly. Those of us who came from the programs are people, too. We're born, like anyone else, but we each have extra abilities of one kind or another. In my case, I can connect with people, their thoughts, feelings, and more. When we're young it's hard on us— we can't turn it off. Imagine what it would be like with all of those thoughts coming from everyone around you, and all the time. As we get older, our abilities get stronger, so the circle of people we hear at any one time keeps getting bigger. It takes a while to learn how to not listen."

She was quiet for a few minutes, thinking about the choices she'd made. "I can't change who I am. Sometimes I wish I could have." The Scout frowned, and she felt his unease. "I'm not resentful," she added. "The Order has been good to me, but I would have been just as happy to settle down with Daniel and raise my family without all the intrigue. Still, there are advantages to being a Sensitive. I know the work I do helps the Order, and it keeps my friends safe, too."

"Your daughter is a Sensitive," he reminded her. Rebecca's face fell.

"Yeah. And I just threw her into the world without help—it was a horrible thing to do. Thank God Daniel understood what she needed, and thank God he's the kind of man he is."

"Will he come? Does he have other family?"

"His father's still alive, and he's got two brothers, but Phoebe is his family, and his daughter in every way that counts. I can't see him letting her go. He'll insist on coming, even if only to look after her. Anyway, it won't be safe for him to stay once she disappears."

"What will he do?"

"He's smart, and he knows about sailing and fishing, and he's a lawyer."

"There isn't much for a lawyer to do out here," the Scout observed.

"True." Daniel's happiness was another one of the things she worried about.

Rebecca had been mulling something over for days now, ever since her first connection with Phoebe from the Sisters' Eyes. Near the end of that first encounter, while Becky was sharing her experience of that night on the cliffs, something strange had happened. A painful surge of energy had run through Phoebe, unlike anything Rebecca had ever felt before. Its raw power had frightened her, and she wasn't sure what it implied. But she'd decided, at the time, to keep the incident to herself.

The travelers fell silent. It took Rebecca a long time to fall asleep—there were too many things on her mind.

They slept in the next day, delaying their departure by several hours. Gabriel wanted to arrive after dark.

Once on the trail, they followed the stream for a while, and then the Scout led her along an unmarked, serpentine path through the darkness. Rebecca walked close behind him, just as she had those first two nights. She would have been lost among the various turns on her own.

The cave appeared as no more than an overhang with a pile of rubble at its base. Behind the rubble was a switching mechanism disguised as yet another rock. Gabriel lifted the cover to expose a control, and released the latch. A large rock at the back of the overhang moved downward revealing a low entrance and a carved stairway that descended into the cave behind it. Once inside, the door was lifted back into place, and a wooden rack just inside held flashlights for navigating down the rocky stairway.

They stopped at the bottom of the stairs and waited. A door on the opposite wall opened, flooding a room-sized area with bright light. The Guardsman on duty identified the two visitors before disarming traps hidden within the floor. They'd arrived at Corbin Sanctuary, a base for more than fifty permanent residents, and a variable number of transient guests. Rebecca was home.

CHAPTER 16

Invitation

THERE'S A COMFORT WE GAIN in knowing our own little piece of the world. We get used to things the way they are and find it disturbing when they change, even little things that don't affect us directly. So it was at New Bright Sea Harbor's Central High School. The girls in Phoebe's class noticed changes in her, and this made them uncomfortable. They were being forced to look at her in a different light. She had always been the strange, quiet girl who seldom spoke, rarely smiled, and never laughed. In fact, many people never noticed her at all, but that was changing, too.

Girls tended to hang around in cliques. Phoebe likened them to packs of dogs, each of a common breed, and she'd classify a pack based on the things its members had in common. There was the 'rich pack'. For them, having to wear the new Council uniform was pure torture. Many were from Council families, and wondered why special dispensation hadn't been granted to those who deserved it. Another pack contained the most devout girls, those who arrived early to service every morning, and were always the last to leave church. Phoebe referred to them as the 'pious pack'. Some of its members believed that Phoebe was one of their own. They assumed that her reluctance to speak was really a vow of silence. Then there was the group Phoebe called 'best in show'. It was populated by the school's beauty queens. The best-in-show girls often paraded in front of the school before service, displaying their wares. There were lots of packs, several loose associations, and mixed in here and there a few loners, like her. These characterizations may have been unfair, but as the school's leading pariah—and a victim of ridicule for many years—she felt entitled to make fun of them.

Phoebe had never been very popular with the packs, but she'd also never been considered a competitor, at least not where boys were concerned. But things were changing here as well. Her recent friendship with the most popular boy in the junior class had altered their fundamental perspective—she was being reassessed.

♎

For weeks now, it had been her habit to spend lunch with Caleb every day. He waited outside the school in the morning to meet her. She'd see him standing by the front gate, smiling, and her heart would lift. At times, it was a little scary to think about how much she'd come to depend on seeing him every day. When she was with him nothing else seemed important.

Her father noticed the changes in her, too. She was different at breakfast, eager to get to school. He no longer struggled to get her up in the morning, and she'd begun to pay more attention to things like her hair. Phoebe caught him looking at her several times. There was a speculative expression in his eyes, as if he was unsure about what to think. She sensed his feelings, too: Should he be worried that she was doing something dangerous, or relieved that she was happy?

For Phoebe, it wasn't her, but life that had changed. She no longer struggled to survive from day to day. She liked life now. It was strange to have someone like Caleb as a friend, not family, but she shared so much of herself with him that it felt like he was. New feelings had begun to grow inside of her, and they were stronger than anything she'd ever imagined—they scared her, too.

Several times each week, after school, they'd walk through downtown together, and then wander into the park. There was a special place near its center, with a bench and a statue that was not far from a small bridge. She knew that the park was close to where he lived, but wasn't ready to meet his family yet. He seemed to understand this intuitively, and never pressed.

Every morning she'd get up early, anxious to get to school. Classes were no longer tedious, and the crowded hallways less of a challenge. Even Sarah was talking to her again—she'd forgiven Phoebe. Her teachers also looked at her differently. They'd stopped thinking of her as the strange girl, but she sensed the question in their minds, wondering if the rumors about Caleb and her were true.

One day—it was at the end of their third week together—Caleb hinted that he wanted to talk about something important. She didn't know what it was, but had sensed a tension in him all day—he wanted to ask her something, but was hesitant. They were in the park, milling around their favorite bench.

♎

"All right, you've been dying to say something all day. What is it?" she demanded.

"Phoebe…" Caleb started to say something, but laughed instead.

"What?" She reached up with one hand to make sure there wasn't something on her face. "You're not supposed to laugh at me. What's so funny?"

"You. The way you looked at me. You'd think I was going to ask you to go climbing…or sailing." She pretended to be offended, crossing her arms and gazing around the park as though he wasn't there.

"I think I heard Sarah likes to sail," she offered, taking a few steps toward the north gate.

"Stop. Wait. Look, I'm sorry, but that isn't it. Yeah, I kinda wanted to ask you to do something, but it's not climbing, and it definitely has nothing to do with boats."

"I *might* listen," she said, still not looking at him.

"Come on. Be serious."

Phoebe turned around and grinned at him. "All right, what is it?"

"My father's having a... get-together in a few weeks. I know you're not big on crowds, but it's an opportunity for my family to get to know you—and I don't want to spend the whole night talking to my aunt. She's got loads of advice, hours of it. Can you help me out?" He was watching her face closely. She sat down on the bench to think. "Don't make me ask Sarah," he added with a grin. Phoebe looked up at him from the corner of her eye, and he shut up.

"What kind of get-together?" she wanted to know. "Who'll be there? How many people? And how do I have to dress?" The questions came at him too quickly.

"Wait, wait! Slow down a little—one at a time. This is a dinner party; my father has them now and then. He'll be there, of course, and my grandmother, too, if she's feeling well enough. My Uncle John, and his wife, Aunt Lydia, along with their daughter, Mary, and her boyfriend, Ian, will be there, as well. Ian's sister, Elizabeth, will probably show up." He looked uncomfortable when he mentioned her. "Liz is Mary's best friend. But there'll be a few unrelated guests invited—doctors from the hospital, their husbands and wives, and maybe..." Caleb glanced at her—it was a guilty look.

"And maybe what?" she demanded.

"There may be someone from the Council there." He was no longer looking at her. Phoebe stared at him, with her mouth open.

"You don't have to talk to him," he added quickly. "He's just in town for a few weeks and my father's *expected* to entertain the Elders when they visit."

"Hmmm. So why am I there?"

"You're *my* friend—I'm entitled, too." Phoebe bit her lip, still thinking his offer over.

"What about the dress?" she wanted to know. Her closet held a total of three dresses suitable for church, but there was nothing at all for formal events hiding in its corners.

"Come any way you like. You can even wear that—what you're wearing now," he said, pointing at the school uniform. She rolled her eyes and huffed.

"Guys! You just don't get it, do you? It's easy for *you*. Put on the standard man uniform and the more alike you look, the better."

Phoebe was quiet for several minutes. Caleb had obviously begun to understand her better, because he kept quiet, too. She was thinking that she might be able to make something. "This sounds pretty formal," she mumbled, wondering how much money was under her bottom drawer. She'd saved a little bit of her allowance every week over the past several years, but it probably wouldn't buy much.

"Please, please come, Phoebe. You don't know how miserable I get when Aunt Lydia corners me. I'd sit by Mary, but she spends all her time with Ian now, and Liz is getting kinda clingy—and weird." She took a deep breath, not sure how to solve the clothing problem, but Caleb wanted her there pretty badly. She wondered if Aunt Lydia was really as terrible as he described, but she definitely didn't like the sound of Liz.

"Okay," she said. "I'll come. But you're going to owe me."

"Thanks, I knew I could count on you."

♎

Aside from how relaxed she had become, and how much easier it was to interact with people, Phoebe sensed even bigger changes happening inside—something she couldn't put her finger on at first. Then it hit her. After seventeen and a half years of thinking about herself as a freak, she had begun to feel like a normal girl.

Another, even more incredible thing had happened. It was something she hadn't expected, or noticed until it was over. Being with Caleb—being careful around him, but at the same time not feeling that she had to hide who she was—had strengthened her a great deal. Somewhere during the process of pretending that she was normal, Phoebe had gained control of her senses. The unwanted thoughts and feelings emanating from other people had stopped intruding—and there were no more uninvited connections when she was asleep. She began allowing herself to feel a tiny bit of hope about the future. Hope was something she'd never had before.

CHAPTER 17

A Healing

TO SURVIVING MEMBERS OF THE Order, Matthew was the Guide, the leader and oracle who had foreseen coming danger, and led them through the catastrophic Purge. He'd warned the Directors of the coming upheaval, more than a year before it happened. But a disagreement among the Prescients delayed action until it was too late, and their hesitation to act led to thousands of unnecessary deaths. A few people, like Rebecca, listened to him and had gone into hiding at the first signs of trouble. They managed to escape the initial wave of violence that followed, although many were eventually captured.

Those closest to Matthew knew him as a complex person, a study in opposites: calm and steady, yet volcanic when angry. He could be funny and entertaining when he wanted, but was serious by nature, and a trustworthy, reliable friend.

As with Rebecca and Samuel, Matthew was the product of a special program. A Prescient, he could peer into the future and, when he chose to act on what he saw, could avoid the problems he'd seen coming. But Matthew knew the limitations of foresight all too well. There were always unintended consequences when you manipulated events to change the future, and sometimes the consequence was even worse than what would have happened. Trying to change the future was always a gamble.

This morning he was in the library of a safe house in Bardon, waiting to meet with Samuel. His few things had been taken to a bedroom, where he would sleep after the meeting. Matthew's days and nights were often reversed—that is when he had time to sleep at all.

The physicians had supplied him with pills that allowed him to extend his waking hours. The drug had originally been developed for combat soldiers who needed to fight through days of battle without sleep; it had been three days since Matthew last rested—this morning he'd skipped a dose. The drug didn't eliminate the need to sleep. It only delayed the effects of exhaustion, and allowed him to accumulate a sleep debt, one that must eventually be repaid.

As he waited, Matthew stared through the window toward the horizon. His eyes were unfocused, and his mind elsewhere. He'd charted a path forward for Samuel several weeks before, and was making sure that the town was still safe.

He maintained a watch over a growing number of key individuals, all of whom were essential to the Order's goals. These vigils demanded a lot of his time, and were in addition to his primary mission: to lead the Order and restore the Balance.

The Balance had originally taken months to negotiate, and had led to a successful collaboration for more than one hundred fifty years. The agreement enabled both the Order and the Council to fulfill their goals, while compromising in ways that didn't conflict with their core values. The Council had agreed to let the Order bring technology from the past into the new world, a concession that seemed to contradict its own mission, but they'd imposed a number of conditions. Unfortunately, the Order violated the agreement first when its leader began questioning the need for a God and then provided an excuse for retaliation when the programs were revealed. But the Council's overreaction had both dishonored the spirit of the agreement and ignored the built-in mechanisms specified to resolve conflict. Matthew knew that restoring the Balance would be unbelievably difficult, but he'd accepted the mission along with his job.

The members depended on him to find a way forward, and to give them hope and a purpose for their lives. To that end he'd developed the Plan. It depended on achieving a basic level of grassroots acceptance among the population. Without this, no agreement with the Council would last. It also depended on building trust through incremental demonstrations of goodwill—small actions that proved their worth, both to ordinary folks and key influencers throughout the Land.

The Order was surreptitiously providing both technical and financial assistance to micro-projects in towns and villages, and to small farms. Whenever possible, they gained the confidence of important people, leaders in the small and mid-sized communities who hadn't been able to find alternative ways to solve their problems. The Order had difficulty gaining access to leaders of the larger cities, but they did what they could to save businesses and lives. Little by little the Plan was starting to work, but it would be a long, slow process, requiring patience.

Still, goodwill alone wouldn't be enough to achieve the goal. There could be no real agreement without approval of the Council, and that wouldn't happen unless there was a change at its top. Some of the Elders were reasonable and sympathetic, but they didn't hold real power. If the more extremist members of the Council's Inner Circle were to be replaced, and conditions among the people supported change, the spiritual Elders—more conciliatory by nature—could be reasoned with, and a path to the Balance might open up.

After leaving Rebecca and Gabriel the previous evening, Matthew had descended the mountain to where his horse and new traveling companion awaited. They'd ridden through the night, reaching the safe house just as the sun was starting to rise.

The house belonged to an Order sympathizer, and was situated at the southern edge of Bardon, nestled on a spit of land between the sea and the mountains. Bardon was the oldest community in the Land, and was isolated from New Bright Sea Harbor by the first ring of mountains to its south.

Today, his vision was showing him that the threats to Samuel hadn't changed—there was nothing new to fear. The lone risk came from the innkeeper where the patient was staying—a man who could never be trusted. But risks were a part of every visit, the key was knowing where they were. Matthew had agreed that this healing was worth the exposure, not that Samuel would have listened, anyway. The Healer was stubborn and had his own way of deciding what was important and what was not.

The patient was the son of the mayor of an important town in the south. He'd been referred to them by a trusted connection. This mayor had close ties with the Council, and was in a good position to betray Samuel. But even if Matthew had seen that as a major risk, the Order would have found some way to help the boy. Opportunities like this, to open a crack in the Council's hold on a larger town, were tempting, and Samuel was their very best ambassador. The Guide made a mental note to speak with Jonathan about specific precautions to take.

Matthew was tired, his fatigue more noticeable today, and deeper than the loss of just a few days' sleep. He always had to be right. The consequences of a mistake were often fatal. It felt as though he was in a fight all the time, but there were no physical enemies he could confront and strike down once and for all, his real enemies were the constantly shifting currents of time.

As Guide, Matthew made life and death decisions every day, too much rested on his ability to see the future, and on every decision. But there'd been no training for this job, and no user's manual for his prescient abilities, and there was no one with whom he could consult.

Only one other Prescient—an infant at the time of the Purge— had survived. The Order had spirited him away, to hide the boy in a secret location—secret even from Matthew. This was done as a precaution to protect the boy should Matthew's own vision ever fail and he be captured. Prescients had the natural ability to shield themselves and those around them from each other's vision. In theory, Matthew shouldn't know where the boy was hiding, but he'd noticed aberrations—inconsistencies in the way time unfolded in certain places. Anomalies appeared when someone deliberately acted to change a future event and distorted the natural flow of time—a systematic skew in the statistical distribution of improbable outcomes.

There had been several instances where obvious deliberate changes had occurred. They appeared as non-random outcomes, like having the same person win the lottery ten times in a row. He couldn't see the boy directly, but he could see where he'd touched the world around him. Matthew created traces like this himself, and knew that another Prescient could find him this way, too.

♎

Matthew's visions weren't strictly intuitive—most didn't come as recognizable imagery at all. Interpreting what he perceived required grounding in mathematics and physics, and an artificially augmented mind—enhanced through both genetic engineering, and by physical means. These changes to his brain allowed him to visualize and understand multiple dimensions simultaneously, and helped him detect subtle variations in future outcomes. His brain had also been engineered to increase its capacity to store and correlate billions of pieces of information quickly. Without these enhancements, he would not have been able to make sense of most of what he saw.

Prescient vision worked in three very different ways: Linear Mode, Statistical Mode, and Stream of Chaos Mode. These three ways of looking at the way time moved were closely aligned with the three different ways physics describes the motion of objects through space.

In physics, there are at least three approaches to describe and predict the position and motion of things. Which is used depends on a number of factors, like the size of the objects, the forces involved, how fast the objects are moving, and how many are present and interacting with each other at any one time.

Classical Mechanics deals with the position, motion, and forces involving a limited number of objects. It's the easiest method to understand, and uses Newton's three laws as a foundation. It's useful to describe things like cars in a parking lot, how they accelerate and move, and where they will all be at any one time.

Quantum Mechanics deals with large numbers of tiny objects, impossible to accurately track individually. Here, the position of objects are expressed in terms of their energy levels and probabilities. The objects still follow predictable rules, but, since their number is large, how much can be known about any one object at a time is limited.

Relativistic Physics deals with very large objects—like black holes—and things that travel very fast—near the speed of light. These are situations where behavior may be less predictable and the ordinary rules, or forces, are distorted, or highly non-linear.

As with Classical Mechanics, Matthew used Linear Mode vision to predict the passage through time of a limited number of people. Each person he tracked was free to make choices over the interval of time he visualized for their future. Every time that person made a choice, a new thread—a path through time—was created. Just one person, if presented with just one choice each day, would spawn over a billion threads in one month, and people often made multiple important choices every day. The need to keep track of so many threads for each person limited how many people could be tracked this way, and how long of a period that his predictions would remain accurate. He could compute the likelihood of any one future, based on the number of threads, how they crossed, and his best guess about which choices that person would make.

When the number of people or the length of time increased, Matthew depended on Statistical Mode. This mode didn't predict specific events for each individual, but could be used to see larger trends, and estimate the probability of where individuals or a society would wind up over a long period of time. But Statistical Mode also depended on predictable forces being at work. If time was distorted by a chaotic, non-linear event, all bets were off.

The Stream of Chaos Mode was a much different way of looking at the future, and offered visions that were out-of-focus snapshots in time. These left a lot to the interpretation of the Prescient involved. It showed him when massive catastrophic events would come, and there were random scattered bits of information he could see, like a jigsaw puzzle with most of its pieces gone. It was up to the Prescient to fill in the gaps. This was the vision Matthew had used to see the comet coming. Other Prescients at the time didn't interpret it correctly, and ignored its impact. Without the comet, the world would have returned to normal within two years.

It was very important that a Prescient employ the right mode for each situation, otherwise the accuracy of his prediction failed, and his ability to look at the same event a second time, using a different mode, was degraded, too.

Matthew was using Linear Mode to watch over Samuel. He could see and project events along different paths, using the choices Samuel would likely make. The projection for the people on his watch list was updated each week.

♎

The Guide closed his eyes, trying not to strain or look directly at his goal. Shadows could form and mask events if you focused too hard. He emptied his mind, waiting for information to come—it was a repeat of last night's vision, and his newest problem, Phoebe.

The future hinted that, somehow, she was key to the Balance. Other timelines—trillions of threads and event outcome probabilities—were all starting to bend around her, and yet she remained out of focus. It was as though he was looking at her through swirls of water—standing in the center of the future— but she had been fading all year. Detail was impossible to see, and when he tried to look farther ahead, she disappeared completely, as though swallowed up by time itself.

Her immediate future, using Linear Mode, was just as uncertain as that distant mirage—only vague possibilities were visible. There were countless threads for her, all twisted together, knotted in some places, disappearing and reappearing, as though going in and out of a tapestry. Along most threads he saw her dead. His best guess was that she would develop some sort of disease, but there were many visions of her broken body covered in blood, and in one future, drowned. He saw her in a Council prison, captured and sent to the Inquisitor for prolonged questioning before a public execution. Hers was a fragile future, and, like the comet, portended chaos.

But there was hope, too. Phoebe brought an opportunity that couldn't be ignored, and this was one reason why he was willing to risk his life and the lives of others to save her. Somehow, she could create a path to the Balance. However, acting too quickly would be a mistake, even a simple operation brought enormous risk. It wouldn't take very much to get her killed. Then, her death would be just another one of those unintended consequences that often happened when he intervened.

Jonathan knocked at the door to let him know Samuel was coming. A few minutes later, the Healer arrived and took a seat opposite him.

"Thank you for coming," Samuel said.

Matthew snorted, shaking his head. "As if I'd let you recklessly expose yourself without a last look."

"You should let me replenish your strength. It doesn't help to drive your body with no rest." Matthew benefitted from regular treatments to maintain his health and these had also prolonged his youthful vigor by decades.

"You'll be safe as long as you follow the directions I give the Scouts. Stay away from the innkeeper—don't even meet him." Matthew looked into Samuel's eyes to make sure he was listening. "I'd prefer that you pretend to be the assistant, but it doesn't dramatically change the risk if you don't." He watched Samuel nod. *Good, at least he's paying attention.* "It'll be safe to travel. By the way, I know where you plan to go next." Matthew was shaking his head in disapproval. "Right into the lion's den." Samuel shrugged.

"There's another matter I wanted to discuss with you." The Healer raised his eyebrows. "A girl in her late teens, very gifted, maybe the only stage-four Sensitive ever created, although that's not been tested yet."

"You must mean Becky's daughter, Phoebe."

Matthew nodded. "She's in danger. I think she might become gravely ill soon. I'm not absolutely certain about that—well,

I'm not *absolutely* certain about anything—but her future is particularly murky. Can you be available to help? There won't be much warning, and I suspect everything will happen, one way or another, within months—it could be sooner. She's important to our Plan—I can see that much. I've seen one vision of her leaving the Land…" The Guide stopped abruptly. "Well, I'd better leave that for another time."

"Of course I'll help her," Samuel said, frowning. "Where do you plan to take her?" His voice was just above a whisper now.

"Corbin. I'll send a message. Please make an effort to check in wherever you go, and keep security advised about your plans."

"I will."

♎︎

Samuel entered the room just behind Jonathan. Two other members of the Guard were keeping watch from positions across the street, and another was in the inn's tiny dining room downstairs, eating lunch for now, but he was really keeping track of the hotel staff.

A young man lay on a narrow bed against the window. His face was pale, and there was an unhealthy feel in the room. Samuel was sure that only he noticed it. Curtains had been drawn across the window to shade the room, and two oil lamps were lit. Gas for the room lights wouldn't be turned on until dusk.

Samuel strode over to the bed, his senses focused on the young man's signs. An older woman sat in a chair near the window. Worry was etched into her face. He guessed she was the young man's mother, she looked almost as bad as the patient—worn out, but healthy.

"Hello," he said. "I'm the Healer sent by the Order." He said almost the same thing every time he arrived for a case. Surprise and hope played across the woman's face but disappeared quickly. She'd undoubtedly had false hopes before.

"You seem young to be a famous Healer," she said. It wasn't quite a question; there was doubt in her voice.

Samuel smiled at the all-too-familiar comment. "I'm a little older than I look," he admitted. It was hard for most people to grasp the concept of ageless youth. "What are your names?" he asked politely.

"I'm Anne, and this is my son, John." Her eyes softened when she looked toward her child.

"I'm very pleased to meet both of you. Now," he said addressing John, "tell me how you feel. Is there pain, nausea, are you able to eat and drink without difficulty?" The Healer asked questions for some fifteen minutes. He'd already made a diagnosis, but their answers would confirm it. He also knew that it helped the family to be a part of the effort. They needed to know that their observations were important. He guessed that the cancer had originated in either the lungs or the liver, but it might have started somewhere else—it didn't matter. He could help.

"Okay," he said, nodding. "The symptoms you're describing sound like what I was expecting, but it's good to know that I'm on the right track. My treatment is probably a little different than the ones you've experienced before, but it works. Yesterday, a member of my team took your blood." John nodded. "Well, that blood is going to heal you. I'm going to give it back now. My body used your blood to develop a kind of medicine precisely targeted at the illnesses you have. I've done this many times. It won't hurt—well, maybe just a slight sting, but less than a mosquito bite." Samuel removed the medical kit from his bag. He could donate as much as two units of blood safely—almost a liter. His immune system had already created powerful antibodies and other agents at the cellular level, which would attack the tumor, and the infection, as well. The treatment would give John permanent immunity to this specific cancer.

It took time to transfuse blood back into John, and Samuel stayed afterward to observe him for several more hours. The change started almost at once, although it would be days before anyone else in the room would be able to tell. He liked being with the patients until he could detect the treatment's effects; it eased his mind to see things working before he left.

Samuel stayed until well after dark, chatting with John and his mother, and learning something about their lives. John was in training in his uncle's business, selling fabrics. He wasn't interested in politics. They had traveled by coach from their home, changing carriers in Central City, and well away from the prying eyes of their neighbors.

"Things will begin to improve now. We've given you just enough help to let your body heal itself. It may take a week before you feel well again, but you'll be much better in just a few days. A month from now, this'll just seem like a bad dream." John closed his eyes, sobbing; the months of illness and ineffective treatments, the stress of constantly getting weaker and weaker, and watching his parents suffer with him had all been too much.

Anne put a hand on Samuel's arm. "Thank you," she said, tears were already running down her face, and he hugged her.

"It's our privilege to help where we can."

He gave Jonathan a look, and the Scout stepped out of the room to check on security, and was back in a few minutes, nodding that it was safe to leave. With a last look at mother and son, Samuel left the inn and headed back to the safe house. The other Scouts shadowed their route, ready to spring into action, if necessary.

"That went well," Jonathan commented. Samuel nodded. It had been a good day, but he was tired. His high-powered immune system drew more energy as it reacted to disease. He'd planned to leave tonight, but it was later than expected, so he changed his mind, and decided to sleep first. They would set out first thing the next morning.

CHAPTER 18

Explorations

AFTER PHOEBE REALIZED THAT SHE'D finally stopped the constant invasion of thoughts, she began to question her attitude about the senses she'd always considered a curse, and wondered if she might be able to make use of them instead.

There were good reasons to learn more about her senses. If new capabilities were going to come along, then exploring the ones she already had would provide valuable experience. According to her father, anything could happen.

Phoebe was the last Sensitive ever created, the culmination of development along two separate bloodlines. Even Becky hadn't known what might happen to her. Testing her limits and practicing control seemed a better strategy than just waiting around for the next shoe to drop, especially if she was also going to keep getting stronger over time.

How much control do I really have? she wondered. *And what are my limits?* The thought of all new senses appearing, unannounced, made her shiver, but she'd learned something valuable from Caleb, and the way he tackled life. It was better to face your fears head-on than to constantly fret over what might happen.

Of course, experimenting presented her with another dilemma. She'd have to intrude into the minds of other people on a regular basis—there was no getting around that. And that was something she'd never been comfortable doing. It was one thing to connect accidentally, or for an emergency, but quite another to routinely, and deliberately, invade other minds. Regularly intruding into the very core of other people would feel like a step backward, and she'd just begun to feel a little bit more normal, and less like a freak. Connecting always affected her in one way or another—none of them made her feel good about herself.

Phoebe spent a restless night thinking everything over, going back and forth on whether the whole idea was really worth it, but in the end she decided it was the right thing to do. She had to control her senses, both now and in the future. And she wanted to be able to protect her family, including Caleb, if something bad happened. Her senses, as hard as they'd been to live with, offered an advantage in looking out for trouble. She decided that the people she cared about were more important than a little discomfort.

When she'd first learned to draw, and later to paint, Phoebe had found that mastering new skills was easier to do if she broke them down into simpler, more basic steps first. Later, she could systematically add the complexity back in until she was comfortable using all of the tools available to her.

She set up a schedule, allocating time each day, and began practice after getting home from school, working until it was time to start dinner. That gave her at least two hours each day—she'd improvise on weekends. No one was around during late afternoons, and her schoolwork waited until after dinner. Of course she'd had to put up with gas lighting for homework, but that was a small sacrifice to make. There were plenty of subject people around, neighbors, strangers passing by, and people working in shops—it wasn't even necessary to leave the house.

Phoebe started with the most basic skill, the one with which she was most familiar: blocking and unblocking her senses. Switching them on and off was a little like opening and shutting her eyes—harder to do—but she was better at it now.

Initially, the flood of information seemed overwhelming, but as she practiced, Phoebe learned how to pick out exactly what she wanted to know from the flow of others' thoughts. It was a subtle technique that she'd only tried a few times before. She selected and isolated individuals and then filtered out everyone else.

There were other aspects to this concept of 'flow control'. For example, she varied how long her senses were open, and then tried to close them as quickly and cleanly as possible. What she wanted was a crisp switch, like the shutter of a camera opening and closing just long enough to capture an image, without letting excess light in. Initially, it was more like she was opening and closing blinds in a window, but after a short time, she improved.

Phoebe also explored how many different people she could connect with simultaneously, and then practiced a variation of focusing on one person by changing her subject, jumping from one person to another quickly. When the first exercises seemed easy, it was time to move on to something more difficult.

During that first week of practice, she'd enhanced her skill of listening to multiple people at the same time as well. This meant splitting her consciousness, much as she'd fragmented her mind into two parts to sleep. She connected with two people, then with three, and four at a time. After a couple of days, she was connecting with a dozen different people concurrently. It wasn't always easy to keep track of everyone, but she'd improve with more practice.

One unexpected skill she discovered was an ability to accurately gauge distance and direction to individual minds around her. She tested its accuracy by estimating where someone was, and then counting the steps to reach them. *This could be useful.*

As she worked, Phoebe gradually began delving more deeply into the minds of those she touched, noting the different levels of connection possible. The most basic level was how a person was feeling, a simple awareness of their emotional state. Phoebe classified this as a level zero connection, because she couldn't turn it off. Individuals radiated feelings of happiness, or sadness, or anger, and she picked up on these without trying.

When she penetrated more deeply—call it level one—Phoebe tapped into what was on a person's mind at that moment, their immediate conscious thoughts. It was still a relatively superficial level of connection, since the person needed to be actively thinking about what she learned.

When she delved just a little more—level two—she began experiencing what they were receiving through their senses, seeing what they saw, hearing what they heard, or tasted or felt with their sense of touch. Of course what she was really sampling was what a person's mind noticed, she couldn't directly connect to their eyes or ears.

Phoebe tried connecting to multiple people this way, shifting from person to person, and noting how different people perceived the same things at the same time. There were always little variations in what each person perceived, and it was hard to predict in advance how any one person would visualize a thing. This contrast was even more pronounced between men and women.

Later, looking at the world from several people simultaneously, fragmenting herself, felt very strange, but she was able to understand and remember everything everyone registered. It made her feel a little schizophrenic, but with every step, she was learning more about how her own mind worked.

The next level of difficulty was in varying the types of connections she maintained with different people at the same time. She tried listening to one person's immediate thoughts, while looking at the world through another's senses, thinking *I really am a freak*. But the bitterness long associated with this word was gone. She was learning to accept that her differences were simply a part of who she was.

Another challenge was determining her effective range and endurance. She'd discovered a way to narrow her focus with pinpoint precision. It enabled her to isolate individuals within a large crowd all the way across town, and beyond.

Up to this point, she'd hesitated to dive more deeply. Not so much from fear of what she'd learn, but because it would affect her more strongly. Ultra-deep connections were very intimate experiences and, in the past, they had only happened accidentally. They were dangerous, and reminded her of the worst nightmares she'd shared. These kinds of connections could affect her for days, and in the past she'd felt trapped as they happened. But if she was going to learn more, and truly master her senses, then this was where she would gain the most knowledge. Reluctantly, she began this new stage, joining with Lorna, a woman from the neighborhood. This time Phoebe was determined that she would be in control.

It was fascinating to descend through the different levels of consciousness within Lorna's mind—levels three, four, and five—and to be able to stop at any depth she chose, and then back out. Initially, she worked to gain experience in regulating the depth and duration of each connection. She wanted to be sure that she had a failsafe method to exit, should the experience become too intense.

Each day, she penetrated Lorna's mind a little more, diving through memories and feelings, and burrowing down into the very core of her essence, to where her innermost fears were imprisoned. Lorna wasn't aware of what caused many of her anxieties, but they were rooted in early experiences stored deep in her mind. All were laid bare for Phoebe to examine.

She noted, with some surprise, that she could see the physical location of different thoughts and memories that were stored in Lorna's brain, automatically creating a map of where everything resided. She was tempted to manipulate some of the information, thinking that she'd be able to free her of the more troubling phobias. One of these—the fear of being in close spaces—originated from an early childhood experience, one that Lorna couldn't remember. But Phoebe stopped herself. It was one thing to probe into the heart of a person's being, and quite another to play God.

Lorna held intense, frightening images in her mind, some were real and some imaginary—monsters that were really an echo of actual events. These were deeply rooted in her psyche, and had become a hybrid mixture of real and superstitious fears. Phoebe could hold these inner monsters at bay now, and isolate herself emotionally from what she saw. If she'd been able to do this earlier, it would have spared her a lot of trauma.

Ultimately, Phoebe successfully connected completely with Lorna, integrating herself until it felt as though she was putting her on like a suit. She *was* Lorna. The main difference between this connection and the ones associated with her worst nightmares was that Phoebe was in control, and could disconnect any time she chose.

When she was connected this way, the boundary between herself and Lorna began to fade; she had to remind herself who she was. Had she chosen, Phoebe could have taken control of Lorna, like a puppet master—literally possessing her. But again, she stopped. This was yet another threshold she wouldn't willingly cross.

Over the weeks of practice, Phoebe had gotten to know a number of her female neighbors pretty well. In some cases it would be uncomfortable looking them in the eye. She only made these deep connections with women, but knew her reluctance to join with men was just a silly aversion. The world of human relations held no mystery for Phoebe. She'd experienced everything adults did in private from the time she was a little girl. Excluding men from her practice was mostly driven by her sense of self, wanting to maintain her newfound feeling of quasi-normalcy.

As a final test of her skills, she followed Lorna's friend Amy around town for hours. Amy worked at the bakery on the corner and was a good choice for a long excursion.

One afternoon Phoebe telepathically went along with Amy for a ride. First, they took the trolley to visit Amy's sister at the southern edge of town, and then stayed for an hour before returning to her home on the west side. At maximum distance, they were physically separated by several kilometers, but it still felt as though Amy was at the bakery next door, just meters from her home, all without a reduction in the quality of the connection.

One thing Phoebe had never done through the weeks of practice was to delve into Caleb's mind. She could sense him, and knew his feel—his flavor, as she thought of it—almost as well as her father's. It felt so good to gently touch him, just on the surface, and know that he was close. But she refused to listen to his thoughts. Of course, with Caleb, there was no need; he always said exactly what he was thinking, no ambiguity or schism existed between his feelings and what he presented to the world—just like her father.

If Daniel had provided the foundation that made Phoebe into who she was as a person, then Caleb was rapidly becoming her anchor to normalcy. She depended on being near him for her sense of well-being. School days and weekends had been reversed in her mind. She only saw him on weekdays, so school was now like her home, and she looked forward to going every day. Weekends were like being in exile, she wouldn't see him for days. The week he unexpectedly disappeared made her realize just how addicted to him she'd become.

CHAPTER 19

Missing

IT WAS FRIDAY, AND CALEB had been missing from school all week. Each morning this week, she left the house, wondering—hoping that he'd be at school. She'd walk slowly with her eyes down, willing herself not to search ahead with her senses, and nervously chewing on her lip. Each day, she prayed he'd be standing outside waiting for her. The tension would build as she got closer to school, and every day, the spot where he normally waited was empty.

He might be hurt? Climbing! she thought bitterly. *Why can't he do something normal?*

Phoebe moved through the day as though in a trance. She'd been sitting with her old friend, the rock, through lunch this week, but the food had no flavor today—she didn't even *pretend* to read. Sarah tried to console her during art class.

"Don't worry. I'm sure he's fine. There's a cold going around; he's probably just lying on the sofa at home, reading." Phoebe didn't say anything.

After school, she took a circuitous route home, wandering along streets near the park, just south of the hospital—and well out of her way.

It's a nice day for a walk, she told herself.

As she marched through the neighborhood near Caleb's home, Phoebe opened her senses and began to methodically scan houses along the street. She was probing both to the left and the right, maintaining a constant focus. It was like walking along a path in the dark, searching with two narrow beams of light, one to either side, and looking for a special splash of color. If he were in one of these homes, she'd feel his presence right away. She touched the minds in each home, softly, just to sample their feel.

For her, each mind exhibited a unique pattern. When she met someone, her mind automatically cataloged it, storing that person's unique mental fingerprint forever. But it was more complex than the simple whorls of a fingerprint, as if it contained multiple dimensions or characteristics, like colors, and shapes, and flavors, and textures.

Phoebe thought of this pattern as a person's 'feel', and she'd be able to recognize anyone she'd ever met for as long as she lived. A person's feel never changed, no matter how old they got, or how much their physical appearance was altered.

Caleb's feel was so familiar to her now that it was never far from her mind. He was like a drug, one that she was finding increasingly difficult to be without.

She could have searched from home—her experiments had proven that she could touch any part of town as easily from her own room. But walking the city street by street and neighborhood by neighborhood was far more satisfying, and besides, Phoebe couldn't sit still today. *Fresh air and exercise are good for me.*

Searching for him was surprisingly easy to do, it took only a tiny part of her attention, and registering an individual required the smallest fraction of a second. *Where is he?* she asked, growing more frustrated and opening up her mental search area to increase the number of people she touched at a time. Now she could cover multiple city blocks using a single pass along one street. Her nervous energy had been building up, making her more and more impatient, even angry. Then she found him.

Phoebe closed her eyes, sighing. She'd been imagining all sorts of things. It was a relief to know he was safe, and that she'd be able to find him again—until she realized that he was in the hospital.

Now what do I do? she wondered. *I'm not allowed to probe his mind.* Phoebe also knew that she couldn't physically go into the hospital to check on him, there was no reasonable excuse for her to be there, nor any earthly explanation as to how she would know that *he* was. What would she say when he asked how she'd found him? *"Hey, Caleb. Well, I was just mentally sweeping through the neighborhood when I noticed you were in the hospital—so, what's up?"*

She was stuck. Maybe it hadn't been such a good idea to be so rigid about peeking into his mind. What if this had been an emergency? She probably wouldn't be able to sleep tonight if she didn't know for sure that he was okay. Worry and uncertainty plagued every weekend. The southern cliffs were very dangerous, and anything could happen. For some reason, Caleb seemed to like, or even need, this danger. It wasn't easy being his friend. *Maybe if I limited it to just his immediate thoughts,* she argued. *I have to do something!* She couldn't go three whole nights without knowing if he'd been hurt, and if he was in pain. She had to know now.

She took a deep breath and held it. The precise control she'd gained over the past weeks would come in useful. The connection to Caleb's thoughts was formed gently, with the minimum connection necessary, but one that would let her find out what she needed to know. Her heart was thumping and her knees shaking as she looked. *He's fine!* Phoebe let her breath out. She'd been prepared for anything, but now she knew that he was okay. He was just sitting with his grandmother, who was definitely *not* okay.

Caleb was thinking that his grandmother would never leave the hospital, and he was trying to make her comfortable. She didn't seem to be in pain at the moment, but was very thirsty. For some reason the doctors wouldn't let her drink water the usual way, from a cup, so he was putting little squares of wet sponge into her mouth to keep her hydrated. This wasn't a visit. It was a deathwatch.

Now she felt like an intruder—but one who couldn't seem to help herself and let go. She remained connected for a few more minutes, feeling increasingly guilty as each second ticked by. *I shouldn't be here,* she thought. *Why can't I let go?* already knowing the answer. *Because I want to be with him.*

She stared at the front door of the hospital, most of her was desperate to go in to do whatever she could to help him. At the very least, she wanted him to know that he didn't *need* to be alone—he had a choice. But her feet were anchored to the pavement.

What would happen if I did go in?

She stayed balanced between two forces: the need to be with him was pushing her toward the door, and another force was pulling her back—the fear of being discovered. She was touching his thoughts as she wavered, but the Discipline that was so closely associated with fear was winning, and she had to admit the truth: *I-Can-Not-Enter-the-Hospital.*

Caleb could never know about her...strangeness. For weeks, she'd deluded herself into thinking that somehow she could be almost normal, but now that was all melting away and, along with it, her confidence in finding a real life. Phoebe felt herself sliding back toward that dark place where she'd lived before Caleb. But even as she was getting ready to let go of the connection to leave—she heard him think about her, and all of the hope came rushing back, making her feel soft and warm inside. *He misses me.*

The impulse to go inside was overwhelming again, and she started moving toward the door without realizing it. Only the thought of her father's safety made her stop. Phoebe was willing to take a chance with herself, but she couldn't put her dad at risk, too, so she let go, closed her eyes, and turned to walk home.

CHAPTER 20

The Hospital

"**W**HAT'S THE MATTER, PRINCESS?" THEY were having dinner. Phoebe had been unusually quiet since her father had gotten home, and was picking at her food.

"It's nothing," she said, knowing that he would worry if she told him.

"Phoebe, something's wrong. You know I'll just imagine the worst. Whatever's bothering you probably isn't one-tenth as bad as what I'll make up."

"It's Caleb." The name obviously didn't do anything to relieve his concern.

"Did he say or do something to upset you?"

She grimaced, rolling her eyes in frustration. "No, no. It's nothing like that. It's just...that he wasn't at school all week. I've been worried about him. He takes a lot of crazy risks. Why do people go out of their way looking for dangerous thrills?" She paused, debating whether to tell him what she'd done. He had his defender's face on, so she couldn't tell what he was thinking unless she cheated. "I was afraid something had happened to him. It wouldn't take much for him to get hurt, climbing. And so...and so I went looking for him after school." She held her breath, waiting for a reaction.

Her father sat forward in his chair and frowned. His look reminded her of the time, when she was six years old, that she told a neighbor about how her sister and husband played funny games in the house every other afternoon.

"Umm, how exactly did you do that?" There was *some* curiosity in his voice, but mostly alarm.

"Well," she said, "you know, there've been a few changes these past few weeks—with me, I mean. It's kind of hard to believe." She tried to smile at him, but his expression didn't change. "But I think I finally learned how to control my senses—how to shut them down—and I've been practicing." Phoebe noticed that the last part of what she said hadn't helped.

"Practicing?"

Tension was rolling off of him now. She wasn't telling it right. "Dad, it's okay. I've got this under control. I finally know how to shut it off." Her father opened his mouth, as if he was going to say something, but nothing came out.

"I started learning how to do more things with them, too, like tracking people, and even listening to someone all the way across town. But it's controlled." She saw that he still wasn't buying it. "Dad, it's fine. I really do have it under control. I doubt I'll ever make a mistake again.

"I needed to see what I *could* do. I wanted to know how far I could push myself. Remember you told me that more of these freaky senses might come any day?" Her father didn't nod, but his eyes narrowed a bit and he blinked. "I decided that I needed to get ready, so I'd be prepared if something new started."

"What has that got to do with Caleb?"

"Well, I think he's the reason I've been able to do this. I think I was going about it all wrong. You know, fighting my senses instead of going with what I am. Being around him helped me figure it out. It's really been great these past weeks, and I think he's the reason I'm better."

"Is that why you're so anxious about him missing a few days of school?"

Phoebe decided to be completely honest. "No," she breathed, half closing her eyes. "I'm anxious because when I found him, he was in pain…and I." She had to stop to take a breath. Her hand closed onto her leg under the table, and she worked to keep her voice even, but it broke when she spoke again, anyway. "I couldn't help. I couldn't even go see him." She took a few more seconds and another breath to calm down a little. "He wouldn't have understood how I found him." Her face felt very warm and she had to grip her leg really hard to hold back the tears.

"This is the same boy who was thinking embarrassing things about you just weeks ago, right? Your sort-of lunch partner at school now." They weren't really questions. Her father seemed to be trying to get the facts straight in his head.

"I don't think he thinks that way about me now," she said.

Her father laughed. "I doubt that's changed, but what he thinks is less important than what he does. Where did you find him?"

"At the hospital. He was with his grandmother, who's *really* sick." Her father looked calmer now that he understood everything.

"What is your relationship with Caleb? I thought he was just a friend."

"I don't know. We *are* friends, but it feels like...more than that. Except for you and granddad, he's the only person I can trust."

"I see," he said, staring toward the front window. Phoebe suspected that he didn't really see, but didn't argue.

"I was standing outside the hospital today, and I could feel how upset he was inside, and how terrible things were for him. He was alone, and I wanted to...I really, really wanted to go inside, just to be with him, and keep him company. But I couldn't." She looked down at the table to hide her face. "And I won't get to see him until next week—maybe not even then. I don't think his grandmother's going to make it." Her father settled back into the chair again, trying not to stare at her; she'd lost the battle with the tears. After a minute he put his elbows on the table and his head on his hands.

"I guess I've been pretending that everything was normal, when I should have been paying more attention. I should have found out why you've been so different lately. It's obvious that you feel strongly about him.

"Princess, I'm really proud of you—and of the way you handled this. I only wish there was something I could do right now to make you feel better. Do you think he suspects anything?" Phoebe rolled her eyes and shook her head at the same time, but didn't get upset.

"No. He doesn't know I'm a ..." She stopped.

They sat at the table not talking for several minutes, both staring at the table. Finally, Phoebe got up to clear the dishes. Doing something, anything, was better than just sitting there. Her father didn't move.

Once the kitchen was spotless, she picked up the unfinished sewing from a couple of nights before. Her father still hadn't moved.

"I have a client," he finally said. "She's in the security wing of the hospital and just had a baby. I wasn't going to see her until next week, but sometimes I meet with people on weekends, even in the hospital. If you like, we could go there in the morning.

"But you should understand that Caleb's grandmother may not make it through the night, and there's no guarantee he'll be there the same time we are. Anyway, you're not allowed in the confinement area, so at least you'd have an excuse for being there, and a little time to look around."

Phoebe put the sewing down, her hands were shaking, but her father wasn't finished. "I want you to understand that I'm not completely comfortable with all of this, but I trust you, kiddo, and I can see how important he is to you. You have to promise that you'll still be careful."

She nodded, unable to speak, so she crossed to give him one of her infrequent hugs. Tears had started running down her face again, but this time she didn't care. He patted her on the back, without saying more, and then she went to bed early.

♎

It was still a couple of hours before sunrise when Phoebe got up the next morning. Even her father was still asleep, so she decided to prepare a weekend-style breakfast for him. He must have smelled coffee or bacon in his sleep, because he showed up just as she was thinking about how she'd cook the eggs.

"Trouble sleeping?" he asked.

"Not really. I went to bed early, so I woke up early." The first glow of dawn was already in the eastern sky. They sat and enjoyed a leisurely breakfast together. Afterward, her dad read through notes while Phoebe cleaned up.

Their house rule was: whoever cooked also cleaned. This was established just after Phoebe first learned to cook. She was messy, and it usually looked as though a riot had happened in the kitchen when she was done.

Once the dishes were clean, Phoebe took longer than normal getting ready. Her father had to knock on her door several times before she came out.

As they walked down the steps to the ground floor her father broke the silence. "I'd like to meet your friend Caleb." Phoebe didn't say anything at first, mulling over his request—it sounded more like a demand. "Did you hear me?"

"I heard you, I'm just thinking."

"What's there to think about?" he asked a little too quickly.

"Nothing. I don't have a big problem with your meeting him; I'm just thinking about Caleb. I don't want him subjected to an extensive cross-examination." He looked hurt, so she softened what she'd said, "But I know you'll be polite, you always are."

It was a nice day, and the morning air was a little cooler—cooler and soft, like velvet. Summer's humidity was gone and fall had finally arrived, although it still wasn't cold enough for a jacket. Phoebe spread her hands out to her sides, letting air flow between her fingers. *How do you show that air is soft in a drawing?* Her mind was wandering, trying not to think about how nervous she was.

Her father was dressed in street clothes today, his robes were only for court appearances and formal meetings. Phoebe was wearing her very best dress. Her dad's eyebrows had gone up when he'd first seen her come out of the room, but he hadn't said anything.

Once at the hospital, he strode up to the reception desk and presented his credentials. The woman on duty scrutinized the papers longer than necessary, squinting and clearing her throat, before giving him a pass. It was on a cord that he hung around his neck. She looked at Phoebe, who felt about as welcome as a cockroach in a fine restaurant, but her father told the woman that his daughter was with him.

"She's not allowed in the security wing."

"I know. She'll stay in the waiting area," he assured her. Phoebe's pass was a different color than her father's, and pinned to her lapel instead of being on a cord. He walked her a few meters deeper into the hospital, to where the main corridors intersected, and then gave her directions, loud enough for the receptionist to hear.

"The waiting area is in that direction," he said pointing down the center hallway. She nodded and started toward the back of the hospital, searching as she walked. It turned out that his grandmother's room was also along the central corridor, just past the waiting room ahead.

The hallway opened up into a large space, where people were seated in groups, mostly two or three together. There were a couple of loners like her sprinkled here and there, so she didn't feel overly awkward. Almost forty people were in the room, some reading, while others spoke together in hushed voices. Phoebe didn't see anyone she knew, but decided it would be better to sit down for a few minutes before wandering back to the patient rooms.

The chairs were aligned in rows, some around the perimeter and against the walls, while others were set back-to-back in the middle, creating aisles. Phoebe took a seat along the wall that faced Caleb's direction. She left a couple of empty seats between herself and the next group to avoid being drawn into a conversation.

The waiting room, and the four hallways that radiated from it, were all painted a sickly green. *Why green?* she wondered. *Any color would be better than that—well, maybe not black.* There were pictures on the walls, a mixture of poorly done landscapes and better-quality portraits of Council members dressed in their red robes, but there were no windows, so the gas lamps were kept lit, even in the daytime.

She'd just settled into the chair when Caleb walked in. At first he didn't notice her, so she raised a hand and waved. When he did see her, his mouth fell open. She stood up to greet him as he walked over.

"Why are you here?" he asked. "Is your dad sick?"

"No, I'm with him, but he's here on business, and visiting a client in the security area. We were on our way downtown," she added. "Why are you here?" she asked innocently.

"It's my grandmother. She's been sick for a while, but she got a lot worse last weekend. We found her on the floor Sunday night." Caleb's grin had vanished and his shoulders seemed to sag.

"Will she be okay?" Phoebe asked.

Caleb tried to say something, but was having trouble speaking. She could feel him struggling, and felt guilty for putting him through an unnecessary explanation. "I don't think so." He was looking at the floor and seemed so emotional that her hand moved toward him by itself—she stopped it partway. But it felt as though she should do something, so she took a deep breath and reached for him.

"I'm sorry," she said, squeezing, and felt his hand close tightly over hers. He didn't let go as they sat down together, and his heartbeat pulsed through her fingers. The calmness that had eluded her all week spread through her whole body.

"It's really weird, you being here," he said.

"Why?"

"I was just thinking about you, and suddenly here you are."

"I can stay."

He looked up, surprised at her offer, but then frowned, shaking his head. "It isn't very nice here." His voice was low, and hard to hear. She pretended he hadn't said anything.

"Anyway," he added in a normal voice, "I'm taking a break. In fact that's why I came out. My cousin, Mary, is due to spell me for a while. We've been taking turns."

As he was speaking, a girl with brown hair, who looked to be a few years older than them, stepped in from the entrance hallway. She stopped for a moment, looking around, and spotted them. Phoebe saw her eyes zero in on their hands and noticed a fleeting look of disapproval cross the girl's face before she walked over to where they were seated.

"Caleb, I thought you were with Grandma." It sounded like an accusation.

"Uh…I just came out a minute ago, in fact to meet you, but saw someone I knew." He smiled at her and they stood up together. "Mary, this is my friend Phoebe, from school." Caleb let go of her hand.

"Nice to meet you," she said with a guarded smile. Mary shook her hand, but kept her mouth in a tight line—something was wrong. *Maybe this isn't the best time to meet*, Phoebe thought.

"It's always nice to meet one of my cousin's friends." The shallow smile didn't extend to her eyes. "I don't remember seeing you before. How long have you known Caleb?"

"Just a few weeks, but we've attended the same school for years." Some of her hair had escaped from the barrette she'd put on, so Phoebe pushed it back behind one ear.

"That's great." There was an oily tone in Mary's voice; Phoebe's instincts were warning her to be careful. "And why are *you* here?"

"I'm waiting for my father. He's meeting with a client."

"A client?"

"My father's a defender with the Council court."

"He meets with *criminals*? Here in the *hospital*?"

Phoebe's face was suddenly warm, and she counted to five before answering. "He meets with people *accused* of crimes in a lot of places," she said coolly. "We were on our way to have lunch and stopped by—I don't mind." Phoebe didn't know why she felt the need to explain, but something about Mary was making the hairs on her neck stand up.

"How nice," she said, stepping between them and turning her back on Phoebe. "Can we go somewhere to talk about our grandmother?"

"What's wrong with here?" Caleb asked.

Mary turned her head to look at Phoebe for less than a moment. "This is family business. You don't mind, do you?"

"N—no, of course not." Even Caleb looked confused. She guessed Mary didn't usually act this way, but didn't want to create a problem between them—especially now. "It's fine, Caleb. Maybe—

if you have time—you can join us for lunch." Mary glanced over her shoulder again, not even pretending to smile this time. "I don't think my father will be long. He just had a few questions for his client."

"That'd be great," he said. Mary started pulling on Caleb's arm, trying to steer him away. Phoebe fought the temptation to do something petty. *Maybe Mary would like a little bout of confusion*, she mused, but took a breath instead. *Be good, Phoebe. She's his cousin.*

She sat back down again to wait, second-guessing her own irritation at Mary, and reminded herself that their grandmother was very sick. She tried putting herself in Mary's place. If her grandfather were that sick and some strange woman was holding hands with her father in the waiting area, how would she feel? She didn't know, but this was a bad time to meet her. Still, Phoebe was curious, and wondered what Mary really thought about her. She bit her lip and, with a guilty glance around the room, connected with Mary's mind.

Mary didn't like her—at all. They were in the hallway, just outside of their grandmother's room, and she was giving Caleb her opinion about 'that girl', although not quite as bluntly as she wanted. The words in her head were much stronger than what she was saying. Out loud, she questioned him about letting some girl flirt with him just outside the room where their grandmother lay dying. But inside, other words were passing through her head: 'low class trash' and 'bitch' were a couple of the milder terms.

Phoebe squirmed in her chair, embarrassed and confused. *What the hell did I do to her? We just met!* She probed more deeply, trying to see what the real problem was.

Mary had plans for Caleb, and they didn't include Phoebe. She was involved with a guy named Ian, her best friend's brother. To call him a 'boyfriend' would be generous. Ian was cold, and ignored her most of the time—except when he wanted something from her. Mary's feelings for him were very intense—intense and a little strange. It was a one-sided relationship, but Mary believed that if Caleb and her friend, Liz, got together, things might improve between her and Ian. *That's just crazy!*

In a bizarre way, she was relieved. At least it wasn't something with her personally. Phoebe closed her eyes, shaking her head, and wondered how much more complicated being Caleb's friend would become. There was still a lot for her to learn about boys, and she had no idea what to do about Mary. *I'm not backing off!* she told herself. *No matter what his cousin thinks.*

While Mary was giving Caleb a list of reasons to avoid her, Phoebe's father sat down next to her.

"Are you ready?" he asked, looking around.

"Umm. In a minute," she said, holding up a finger. "If we wait, Caleb can join us today. Is that okay?" she asked.

He nodded.

CHAPTER 21

Spark

PHOEBE'S FATHER AND CALEB TALKED all through lunch. Afterward, they all walked around town together, he and her dad chatted about the buildings they passed and the people who owned them. He seemed to know almost as much about the city as her father.

As director of the hospital, Caleb's own father hosted a number of official functions at their home every year. He'd been able to rub elbows with some of the most important people in town, including the mayor and even visiting members of the Council. Caleb seemed comfortable with her father, and was probably using some of the experience he'd gained.

They had lunch at a pub on Harbor Drive—fish and chips. Caleb loved listening to her father's fishing stories, especially the one where the boat almost capsized in a storm. Her father invited him to go sailing with them the next time he and Phoebe's granddad went out on a two-day cruise. Phoebe did her best to not be irritated—there was no way she'd be going, but it *would* be a good chance for all of the guys to get some of that all-important male bonding time. Her dad had glanced at her when he made the offer, but she pretended not to care.

After lunch, they walked around the park for a half hour. Her father excused himself, telling them that he needed to see a friend before leaving them alone. Caleb told her dad that he would walk Phoebe back home.

The sun was setting and they took a meandering route, trying to prolong their time together. Caleb was quiet, and they were walking close together. After their fingers touched a few times, he took her hand.

"I'm sorry about Mary. She's…well, she wasn't exactly herself today."

Phoebe pretended not to understand, and was glad that he didn't know the real extent of Mary's disapproval.

Caleb's mouth twisted into a grin. "Come on, I know you better than that. She was rude, but in her defense…" His voice trailed off.

Phoebe looked at him. "But in her defense?"

Caleb took a deep breath and let it out slowly. "Look, I'm not defending the way she acted today, but that wasn't Mary. She's not *officially* my sister, but we're just as close, and she can be a little protective."

Great—like a sister! but Phoebe kept her face blank. "Don't worry about it. Bad timing, that's all."

They reached home too soon. Phoebe didn't want to invite him upstairs since the apartment was a mess, so they lingered outside at the bottom of the front stoop. Mrs. Tailor, a neighbor, looked at them as she passed, the surprise was clear on her face. Phoebe ignored her.

"I can't tell you how great it was to see you today," he offered. "It's been a bad week, but seeing you really helped." She could feel him withdrawing, and his mind returning to his problems. It was time for him to go back to the hospital.

"Can I see you again this weekend?" she asked, hoping she didn't sound too desperate. His eyes had a hopeful look for a moment, but then it faded.

"I'd really like that, Phoebe. But I'm going back now, and I'm just not sure what might happen. I don't want to make a promise I can't keep."

"Don't worry. If you get a chance, I'll be here. Try to get some sleep, if you can."

"Hmm," he exhaled, and leaned toward her. She was sure he was going to kiss her, but then the moment passed.

Damn!

Caleb turned to leave, but she didn't let go of his hand, and pulled him back. That's when he kissed her.

The close physical contact amplified the emotions she felt coming from him. She tightened her grip, using all of her strength, and wrapped an arm around his shoulder, inadvertently sending some of what she felt into him through the physical connection. He flinched as a little of her energy hit him, nearly falling over.

"Wow!" he breathed, unable to speak for a moment.

Of course, that's when her father walked by, quickly climbing the stoop to enter the building.

Damn! At least he didn't stop, or say something. There'd just been a slight clearing of his throat as he went by.

"Good night, Caleb," she said. He was still a little unsteady, and she smiled to herself.

"Huh?" It looked like he was trying to remember where he was going. "Good night, Phoebe."

Inside, her father was sitting in his favorite chair. The sun was gone, but there was still enough light coming through the window to see his head shaking.

"Don't worry, Dad," she said.

"As if that were possible," he mused. "You know I trust you, Princess. I *want* to trust Caleb, too, but I don't know him yet."

"That's okay, I do," she said. "And the kiss was my idea," she added.

"Just be careful."

Phoebe looked at him, smiling. "I'm a little tired. I think I'll go read in my room for a while. Good night."

CHAPTER 22

Search for the Past

CALEB'S GRANDMOTHER DIED EARLY SUNDAY
morning. Phoebe awoke with a start, thinking that she'd heard him calling to her, and reached out toward the hospital, finding him easily. His mind was a sea of sadness and loss. She looked through his eyes, unable to stop herself, and saw that his grandmother's face was gray and her fingers blue—she was past the pain forever.

The image blurred as she watched, so she let go. Phoebe cried, too. Going back to sleep was unthinkable. She would sit up with him for the rest of the day to mourn his loss, even if she didn't connect with him directly. The shared vigil would make her feel closer to him.

Phoebe moved from her bed to the rocking chair, turning it to face the sea, and looked toward the horizon, thinking. Their apartment was on the fourth floor, and land to the east sloped down toward the ocean. She could see boats moored in the harbor, and the open water beyond it. The faintest blush of light was visible, a ghostly red line glowing along the horizon. It faded to violet and then black high in the sky. The red color reminded her of the dream she'd had more than a month ago now, and made her think about her mother.

She still had questions about the dreams, and about what she'd learned since. Had Becky really survived all this time? And, if so, where was she? Why hadn't she come back? Maybe she was awake even now, looking east toward this same sky.

The dreams might have been Rebecca's way of communicating. If so, then she'd learned something of value through their connection. She thought back to the feel of the woman in the dream. If that had really been her mother, then it might be possible to find her using the feel.

Phoebe's memory was perfect. It held the pattern of everyone she'd ever touched, even those encountered through dreams. She'd come to believe that her freakish memory had been designed this way—it had a purpose. Maybe she'd been engineered so that she could catalog and store patterns for a reason. But the *why* didn't matter today. Phoebe was sure that if she located the pattern—the one from the woman—then she would find her mother as well.

Where should she start? Obviously, searching to the east, toward the ocean, would be a waste of time. That cut her job in half. While it was possible that she lived along the coast, most of the coastline was treacherous and rocky, and not many people lived there. New Bright Sea Harbor was one of the few communities on the northeast coast. Much farther to the south were the large harbor towns that traded with the colonies, but Rebecca's face was known now, and Council agents would probably identify her.

She would most likely be within an arc that began in the southwest and swept north, probably in a smaller, isolated community—maybe even on a farm. That still left a large area to search, but she had to start somewhere.

The lands immediately west were sparsely populated, until you reached Central City. That should make searching easier. Of course Rebecca could be even farther west, past the capital, or living in the Lakes Province, somewhere along the Meridian Road. Phoebe still had no idea what her maximum range might be, she'd never yet been seriously challenged.

Phoebe had discovered that restricting the area she touched seemed to increase the strength of the thoughts she received from people, as though focusing on a small spot amplified the signal. That seemed logical and it would increase her effective range in the same way that a powerful telescope gathers and concentrates light, allowing you to see farther away.

She turned her chair to face west. In the past, her physical orientation had never seemed to matter, but she'd never tried to sense someone this far away. It made her feel better—and it seemed right—to face the direction she was going to look. She closed her eyes and instinctively stretched her arms out wide, before reaching out with her mind.

Phoebe created an imaginary three-dimensional search box into which she focused her awareness. She would move the box around to search small areas in different places, just like pointing a telescope. Directly ahead of her was west. If she shifted the box left, she'd be looking southwest, and if she shifted it right, she'd be looking northwest. The virtual box could be moved out—farther away—or brought in close to town. The search area was about three kilometers on each of its sides, and one kilometer tall.

To ensure that she didn't miss something, Phoebe formed an imaginary grid pattern, and projected it out over the Land. This would provide a reference to help her search more methodically. The grid spacing matched the size of the search box.

Her search began in the south. She systematically moved the box from close in—just past the first ring of mountains—to farther out, before shifting the box a little to the right—north—to start over again. When the box was close, she was touching points just outside of the valley where she lived, and at its farthest point, she was just beyond the last circle of the Ring Mountains.

If Rebecca were alive, it seemed likely she'd either be to the southwest or directly west. The northern provinces were rocky and less inviting, and that was also where many of the Penitents had settled over the years. She would definitely want to avoid them.

This is fantastic! Phoebe could sense, and even sample, the life within an area her search box covered at any one time. People appeared to her as tiny sparks of life in the darkness. She differentiated between male and female sparks easily, like different colors. Animals had sparks, too, but theirs were very different—and distinctly non-human. Filtering out animal sparks was simple— she ignored them altogether. It was like looking through the rain for someone or something you knew, while ignoring the raindrops.

Phoebe was only interested in sensing the female sparks, so she ignored the male sparks in the same way that she ignored animals. The human brain is great at this kind of signal processing, suppressing irrelevant information and highlighting what's important. In Phoebe this ability was even more pronounced.

Just as when she'd searched for Caleb, Phoebe found she could sample an individual spark in the tiniest fraction of a second. Valleys between the mountain rings mostly contained farms, but much of the land lay fallow, too. More empty space meant she could search faster. A farm took less than a second to scan, while a settlement or village could take a few minutes, say five minutes for a medium sized village. A town the size of New Bright Sea Harbor would have taken her most of the day.

The process was tedious, and Phoebe wasn't sure how long it would take. Just when she'd almost decided to stop for the day, her mind touched a familiar pattern—it felt like the woman.

She was far away, more than one hundred kilometers. *Can that be right?* She touched her again to be sure. *Yes, that's her!* The woman was living in a small community—maybe seventy people. Phoebe focused on her feel, probing one last time to make sure it matched the pattern in her memory, and then tried to penetrate the woman's mind, intending to connect with her senses.

It was much harder than it had been for anyone else before, as though the woman's mind was protected—she had defenses. But Phoebe's strength had grown over the past weeks, more so than in the years before, and she was stronger than the woman's defenses.

At first she saw a blur of light, but then, slowly, an image came into focus. She peered through the woman's eyes first, and then joined more fully.

♎

A washbasin, filled with water—warm water. Our hands submerge, dipping into the basin to rinse our face. The image flickers, going dark as our eyes close. There's a soap dispenser at the edge of the basin, walls covered in textured fabric, the smell of lavender and honeysuckle, and pain. Our—my—her—our back hurts, we strained it in the gym. We look up into the mirror to see our face. A familiar, but older, image stares back at us, we sigh at what we see: dark circles and lines that weren't there just a few weeks ago. And the eyes, sad, worried eyes look back at us... Phoebe recognized echoes of her own face in the reflection now. The same gray eyes, the same chaotic black hair and high cheekbones. Only the nose was a little different. And now she is aware of us.

Our eyes widen and our mouth gapes open, and we begin to lose some of the deeper connection, becoming more distinct again— Phoebe. Still connected, still seeing, but now separate—apart.

♎

"Phoebe?" She saw the mouth form a word and heard her mother's voice—the voice from the dreams, and from her grandfather's recording.

Yes I'm Phoebe. Rebecca—mother? The last word sounded like an accusation, with just a hint of anger.

Rebecca blinked—darkness and light again. Regret and pain filled her thoughts, and the connection began to fade. Maybe her mind was waking up, and more fully asserting its defenses, and Rebecca had questions. *Where are you? How did you find me?*

Phoebe was only able to answer the first question in time—one thought, one word, before the connection broke—but she knew Rebecca heard.

She began to reestablish the connection, standing with her arms still out wide. This helped to increase the link's intensity—she didn't know why—and standing helped, too. Just then her father knocked on the door.

"Phoebe? Are you ever going to get up? I've already been out to get the paper, and we need to get ready for church."

"C-coming," she said, as the impact of what had just happened hit her. *That was my mother!* A confirmation of her suspicions, and a slap in the face at the same time. *What do I do now?*

Even more confused than before the connection, she'd learned something new: Rebecca had been surprised she could reach out so far, and was shocked that her own mind had been penetrated. It made Phoebe wonder how her own abilities compared with her mother's. She needed time to think—but not now. Caleb would need her. His pain was real and more urgent than her own needs—he was becoming more important to her every day.

She thought about telling her father what had happened, but decided it was better to wait. She didn't want to hurt him, and didn't know enough not to. How would it feel, knowing that someone you loved more than yourself had so casually cast you aside?

It took Phoebe a few minutes to compose herself, but she was surprisingly hungry. *I hope he didn't eat all the food,* she thought. *And I'm really going to need some coffee.*

"It looks like you didn't sleep at all," her father said.

"Ouch! So I look haggard and ugly, huh?"

Her father rolled his eyes. "That's not what I said."

"That's okay. I probably do." Phoebe took a breath and then explained about Caleb's grandmother. "I felt his pain when she was gone."

Her dad was quiet for a moment. "You seem to be pretty tightly connected to him."

"I am who I am, and I didn't plan this, but I'm going to the funeral one way or another." Her father didn't argue.

"All right. The funeral won't be until tomorrow, or even the next day. I'll try to 'learn' about what happened. Maybe the Keepers from work heard something."

Ω

Pretense turned out to be unnecessary. The priest announced the death during his sermon—the funeral would be early Monday afternoon.

Phoebe stood beside her father as members of the defender's office collected outside the church. He volunteered to represent the office at the funeral. She saw relief on the faces of the other defenders. They were happy to let him represent them, and everyone agreed that Phoebe should go, too, especially since she was a friend of the family.

She shook her head as they were walking home. That was too easy—she'd been ready to help her father find the right person to speak with, if necessary.

CHAPTER 23

Corbin

P HOEBE'S LAST WORD TO REBECCA had been 'home'. That meant that she was in New Bright Sea Harbor, more than one hundred kilometers away. Rebecca stared openmouthed at her reflection, trying to imagine the power it must have taken to reach out that far, and then to penetrate the mind of a powerful Sensitive hiding deep within the earth. The implications were unbelievable. What would it take to do that? Even if Rebecca could stretch her senses out that far, how would she go about finding one person among the entire population of the Land—someone she'd never met? Rebecca was in awe of her daughter.

Years ago, the program lead told Rebecca that developing a Sensitive with this kind of power was almost impossible. Ten times Rebecca's maximum range implied a power of at least one hundred times her own—and maybe much more.

Her first thought was to get word to Matthew. *He needs to know what happened.* But after a moment she wondered if, maybe, he already did. What had he really seen in her future? He was always so close-mouthed about the details of his visions. You never knew if what he was telling you was everything, or just everything he thought you needed to know. Was Phoebe's power the real reason he was willing to risk so much to help? Rebecca shook her head. She felt guilty just thinking that way, betraying the trust he'd earned, and after all the things he'd done for her.

Matthew had proven himself many times, and kept on proving his loyalty to his friends every day. It was Matthew who'd rescued her from life as a homeless refugee, and given her safety and a purpose to keep on living after she'd lost so much. Rebecca took a breath to compartmentalize her new knowledge for future meditation. Then another thought occurred to her: *Why did Phoebe contact me? Was it just curiosity, or is she in trouble?* Rebecca finished dressing and left for the security office. She wanted to see if Matthew had sent her a message.

Rebecca's apartment would have been enviable in any era. It boasted all the conveniences of a modern civilization, combined with sumptuous luxuries only found in the residences of wealthy people prior to the war. Her walls were covered in rich fabrics, and the home's overall finish was one of comfort and elegance.

One wall looked out of place. Dark and smooth, it could be programmed to simulate the view from almost any place in the world—a virtual window into the past. Rebecca had spent many hours gazing at gardens and cityscapes, and panoramic natural scenery. All were contained within Corbin's extensive holographic library. She used the window to escape to Paris, Rome, or the New York of more than two hundred years before. And, for a little while, she'd forget that she was buried under hundreds of meters of rock, and the losses she'd suffered to serve the Order. The dynamic screen created a three-dimensional illusion so real that it was impossible to distinguish it from a real window. Even the sounds and smells of wherever she looked were simulated.

Corbin boasted many such quarters. There were also offices, recreational facilities, and everything else a large group of people might want as they waited belowground to escape the effects of a global thermonuclear war. The team originally stationed here had been hesitant to leave at first, afraid of the radiation and chaos they imagined were above ground. But they'd emerged from their underground cocoon after just one year.

The hallway outside of her door was carpeted, and its walls were finished in wood paneling. Decorative lighting fixtures simulated the changing light outside, strengthening the illusion of normalcy. Where the hallway ended, was a heavy steel door—it opened into a much different space: the unfinished areas, natural rock altered just enough to make walking through the semi-darkness safe.

Corbin had been built within an existing cavern network. As she passed through the dimly lighted tunnel, and toward the main offices, Rebecca's hand reached out to touch the rough limestone walls. She found their primitive feel reassuring and, together with the damp air, they often triggered memories of her first day at Corbin—sixteen years ago. It had been the first time in more than a year that she'd felt safe enough to relax.

♎

"How big is this place?" she asked Matthew.

"Big. Large enough to shelter more than a thousand people in comfort."

"How long has it been here?"

"The Order started building Sanctuaries about ten years before the war. But it's more than just a shelter." Matthew gestured as he spoke. "They built in everything we'd need to modernize what was left of the world. Beneath us—below the residential levels— are laboratories, workshops, and enormous stores of material. There are even underground farms. We have warehouses filled with the best, most advanced equipment the old world had to offer. The people who lived here knew that they might have to stay underground permanently, should conditions aboveground require it." It sounded as though he'd given this tour before.

"Did they dig the tunnels, too?"

"No, these are natural caverns, but they've been adapted to our needs. In fact, the sanctuary only fills a small portion of the available space. We've never explored all of it; the tunnels go on for kilometers in every direction. But we did carve out new access points, in case the main entrance is found, some can only be reached using boats we keep on an underground lake."

"Where does the power come from?"

"It's nuclear. We have three fusion reactors about a kilometer below the surface; any one of them can power the entire complex. Plus we've got portable reactors, but we've only used those a few times for special projects outside."

"How do you keep everything hidden? I know that the surface doesn't show what's down here, but how do you hide the radiation and electronic signatures?"

"The equipment is all shielded."

"Amazing! Why didn't I know about this place? I was born to the Order and was even an associate advisor to the executive board." Rebecca had been identified early in life as a future board member.

"You didn't need to know, Becky. We've always kept our secrets close—I only wish we could have kept the programs a secret, too."

"Are there more places like this?" Matthew paused for a moment before answering.

"I suppose you *do* need to know now. There are two surviving Sanctuaries, Corbin and North Star. As far as we know these are the only two that survived. My ancestor built the Sanctuaries, and he always located them in pairs. Close to each other, but not too close. Unfortunately, no one knew for sure where the warheads might fall."

"You mean John Martin was…"

"I thought maybe the name would have made you guess."

"Can you communicate with the other facility?"

"Yes. There's an entangled link to North Star—untraceable and of extremely high quality. But we had to set up a more primitive communications network elsewhere. It's based on older technology—invisible lasers. We tied it in to cameras and other sensors we managed to put in parts of the Land. In fact, that's how we found you. A camera recorded your face and another sensor picked up your voice. Once I was sure you were alive, we used them to track you down.

"We need you, Becky. You're the best there is. My vision is only so good—and far from perfect. You can help save lives and, together, we can rebuild the world."

Rebecca closed her eyes and whispered, "Thank you." After a moment, she added, "I'd like to speak with you about my daughter, Phoebe—when you have time, of course." Matthew nodded.

♎

Rebecca paused in front of a large hover-style flying machine that was stored in an unlighted alcove. The machine of war, equipped with deadly weapons systems and a sophisticated optical subsystem that could render it nearly invisible, had been permanently mounted onto a platform. It looked as though it was poised to lift off high above the surface, but to Rebecca's knowledge it had never been activated. The Order eschewed the use of most military technology and had refused to consider violence, even after the comet. The 'Stalker' would never leave Corbin, and was already fulfilling its only real purpose: a museum exhibit.

Once in the security zone, she looked for Jürgen Zimmer, head of the Guard. He was examining data extracted from the perimeter sensors and comparing it with older data gathered in the region. Jürgen was looking for discrepancies that might have been missed.

♎

Each of the sensors scattered throughout the Land was shielded, just like certain equipment in Corbin was. Shielding helped reduce the energy radiated that might identify its location. There was always a slim possibility that trace electromagnetic energy could be detected, so the Order also employed an operational security measure to keep them hidden. One of these was called random sequence duty cycle, or RSDC.

RSDC is best explained through the analogy of the ringed seal, a mammal that spends much of its time swimming under the ice in Polar Regions. But the ringed seal has a weakness. It needs to pop up from time to time through a hole in the ice to breathe. When that happens, it's vulnerable to the hunter. Polar bears, a ringed seal predator, know about this weakness and wait patiently by a hole, ready to pounce. To confuse the polar bear, a ringed seal makes dozens of holes in the ice and then changes where it surfaces to breathe each time. This frustrates the polar bear, who's been waiting by an unused hole—most of the time.

The same principle described the RSDC strategy. The Order hid many sensors, but only one or a few at a time popped on, and only for a short duration—just long enough to record what was going on around it. Random sequencing, coupled with short power cycles, kept the network quiet.

Data accumulated by the sensors was collected and automatically routed by the laser communications network to camouflaged collection points. These points were made deliberately hard to reach. The final journey to the Sanctuary was always done by hand—data was downloaded using a handheld device and then carried in. The network also connected security offices, secreted throughout the Land. Members were able to send coded messages covertly and securely over vast distances using multiple short line-of-sight hops.

♎︎

"Jürgen," Rebecca said, interrupting the security chief. "I'd like to get a message to Matthew as soon as possible."

"I'll do my best, but can't guarantee it will reach him quickly. We'll put it out on the network. Matthew's hard to keep track of."

"That'll do," Rebecca answered. "I'll encode it now."

"All right," he said.

His eyes narrowed. "Is there anything I need to know?"

Rebecca thought for a moment, wondering what she should tell Jürgen. "Not quite yet. It's just a hunch I want to check out."

"I'll send a courier out to load it onto the network right away."

"Thank you."

After entering her message, Rebecca left for the canteen. She had a kitchen in the apartment, but liked to eat with everyone else. It helped her feel more a part of the community. As she was finishing breakfast, Jürgen rejoined her.

"Coincidentally, a courier arrived with a message for you from Matthew. It was marked 'Urgent', so I decoded it."

Rebecca opened the paper and read:

Rebecca:

Things are changing fast in New Bright Sea Harbor, but I don't think it's safe for you to travel. We need to extract Phoebe early. The risks have changed and accelerated. I believe that the danger I saw to her before was from illness, but something new is emerging—a Council threat.

We need to start right away. I've already got an armed team moving—a Scout contingent—they'll take a while to get there, but I'm telling Gabriel to go now. The team will be his backup. I also see a danger for you, should you go. It's likely you won't return.

I sent a separate message to Jürgen. Everything needs to happen within three weeks, four at the very outside.

—Matthew

PS: If you go, you may find yourself trapped in a small cave, some place you'll be hiding. Stay in the cave! If you leave, you'll probably die.

—M

Jürgen watched her face as she read. Matthew warned him to make sure she didn't do something foolish. He recognized a look of resolve settle into place and knew what she would do.

"I'm going," she said, a fierce look in her eyes.

"I thought as much. Gabriel will take you with him. You should pack now and then rest. You leave after dark."

CHAPTER 24

Funeral

MORE THAN FIVE HUNDRED NOTABLES attended the funeral. Although the Addison family fortune had declined over the years, their name was still important, and closely linked with the Council of God.

An Elder from the Council's Inner Circle was in attendance. His presence provided added incentive for people to express their condolences in person—the church was packed. This was the Arch Bishop Primate of the Christian faith, and he'd be in town for at least another week.

From the moment she entered the church, Phoebe looked for Caleb. She didn't pay attention to the crowd, nor did she let herself be distracted by the famous works of art, but zeroed in on the red robes, certain that the Elder would be near the family. She stretched up on her toes, trying to see Caleb, but hordes of people—most, taller than herself—kept moving about and blocking her view, so she cheated. He was in the front row. Now, all she had to do was to find a way to get to him.

There was no way through the crowd, a solid wall of people blocked the aisle, but *that* wasn't going to stop her. She poked the man ahead of her on his left side, and when he turned to see who it was, she slipped by on his right. She repeated different variations of this trick and started making her way toward the front of the church. Her father, seeing what she was up to, followed closely behind.

Caleb's father was on the right side of the central aisle, standing half in and half out of the pew, and facing the back of the church. Caleb was to his left, helping his father greet people as they passed by to express their condolences. At the moment Dr. Addison was speaking with the Council Elder. Others in the queue were keeping a respectful distance and the line had stopped.

Where Dr. Addison's face was unreadable, Caleb was obviously grieving. Phoebe could feel his exhaustion and the effort it was taking him to stand there. She bit her lip, feeling powerless to help.

The men were generally dressed in black suits, without adornment. Mary was to Caleb's right, and her face was even paler than his. She seemed less haughty today, her pride suffering from the loss—*death can be a humbling affair,* Phoebe thought.

A young blond man stood beside her—Phoebe guessed this was Ian. Mary was clinging possessively to his arm with one hand, her other was on Caleb's shoulder. A blond girl, resembling Ian, leaned over from the pew behind, and was speaking with Mary. *That must be Elizabeth.*

Once the Elder moved on, the line started up again and before long they were up front. She saw a change in Caleb's face when he recognized her—he even smiled a little. Her father handed a card to a man standing behind Caleb's dad. "Court Defender Daniel Lambert and his daughter, Phoebe," he read.

Mary stiffened at the names and then glared at her. It looked as though she had been about to say something to Liz. Phoebe smiled, nodding to her. Mary didn't acknowledge the pleasantry, but sent out a cold look of hostility. She whispered something to Liz, who also looked at her, seeming more curious than anything else.

Against her better judgment, Phoebe briefly touched Ian's mind, wanting to see what he was like inside. The kindest thing she could say about him was that he was detached from the world around him, and this extended to Mary, too—there was a total lack of feeling for her. She stared at him for a few more seconds, tempted to probe further, but then she was distracted by her father.

"We are so sorry for your loss," he told Dr. Addison. Phoebe dropped her eyes and curtsied, as her father had advised on the way to the church.

"Dad," Caleb said touching his father's arm. "This is Phoebe—I told you about her?"

A light went on in his eyes. "Ah! Thank you, Mr. Lambert, and Phoebe," he added, with a smile. "I'm sorry we had to meet this way for the first time." Then he addressed her father again. "I'd be pleased if you both could join us for a late lunch at our home after the funeral."

Her dad bowed his head. "We'd be honored."

The people behind them were getting impatient. One man even cleared his throat, so they moved on. Caleb's grandmother was in an open casket at the front of the church. They paid their respects before finding seats.

Once the service was over, everyone filed out, passing the family in a line by the door. Dr. Addison was thanking everyone for coming. Caleb reached out to hug her rather than just touching her hand, as was customary. Phoebe didn't look at Mary this time—there was no need.

As they were leaving, she looked back over her shoulder, wanting to see Caleb one more time, and met Liz's eyes. She touched her mind, and shuddered. Liz shared something of her brother's inner coldness, a sense of ruthless self-interest that seemed out of place with her innocent looks, and with the venue. *I'm not going to make a lot of friends there*, Phoebe thought with a sigh.

Outside, they lingered near the front doors. Her father was exchanging words with his colleagues. Phoebe had met them before, the lead prosecutor, one of the judges, and their spouses. Everyone told her how grown-up she looked today. She just smiled, pretending to be shy.

After twenty or thirty minutes, a procession made its way from the church to the small cemetery behind it, where an open grave awaited. Phoebe and her father followed the small group of people who had stayed for the burial. Caleb, his father, and several other men had carried the casket to an awaiting carriage and then followed it along the streets to the cemetery's gated entrance. Afterward, they carried his grandmother on her final journey.

The burial itself was brief, with Caleb's father leading the family to throw a handful of earth into the grave.

After the burial, it took less than ten minutes to reach the Addison home, a large manor house set back from the road, and within a private garden.

"Welcome to our home," Dr. Addison told her.

"Wow!" Phoebe said. Caleb leaned in to whisper something.

"I'll tell you a secret: it's a nice house, but we just live here. All the Addison properties are owned in trust. But don't let Mary know I told you."

More loudly, "At least now you know where to find me—no more excuses not to visit."

"Aren't you the…quiet girl from school?" Elizabeth asked with a saccharine smile on her face. She didn't *say* the word, 'slow'.

"That's me," Phoebe said, winking. Elizabeth's smile vanished.

For lunch, they were served foods that Phoebe had only heard of before, like rice, a rare commodity imported from the colonies. The meal was catered, but Caleb's father provided wine from his own cellar.

Phoebe would have enjoyed the afternoon more if she hadn't felt like an ant being roasted under the dual magnifying glasses of Mary and Liz. Her only solace was being close to both her dad and Caleb. Whenever she felt the resentment build, she'd lean into one of them to absorb their feelings for her.

By the time lunch ended, Dr. Addison had invited her dad to attend the dinner with her next weekend. He scolded Caleb for not thinking to invite him before.

CHAPTER 25

Legacy

"IT FEELS SO WEIRD ... EVEN DISRESPECTFUL, to be
having a party so soon after my grandmother's death. What
are we thinking?" It was Wednesday, and they were sitting on their
favorite bench in the park, near the monument.

"Come on, your dad didn't know that was going to happen. And
you said it was kind of an official dinner—doesn't sound like much
of a party to me." Phoebe was not happy about Saturday night
either, but had agreed to attend. She was looking at the ground,
biting her lip and thinking about spending a whole evening with
Mary and Liz.

"Yeah. Sorry, I know Mary's being kind of a pain, but I don't
think I'd go if you weren't coming."

She shook her head. "You've got to be there ... for your dad. But
don't worry, I'm coming." Her voice had dropped when she spoke,
and Caleb squeezed her hand.

"Oh well, I'd better get home," she said. "Time to start dinner.
See ya." Phoebe leaned over and kissed him quickly. They were still
holding hands as she left, their fingers separating as she moved
away.

♎

Twenty-four hours earlier, Phoebe had been frantic, struggling
with a problem she'd put off for too long. At first, the dinner had

seemed remote, comfortably off in the future, giving her time to find an answer to her clothing problem. Later, she was distracted by the week Caleb had been missing, the discovery of her mother, and then the funeral. But there was no more putting it off—the dinner was in four days and she still had no idea what to wear.

Her father kept glancing at her throughout the evening meal. She was picking at her food.

"Okay, what is it, Princess? What's bothering you tonight?" he asked.

"Umm…Well, I've been procrastinating about something for a while. I should have talked to you earlier, but…"

"Talked to me about what?" He started rubbing the back of his neck, as he often did when she'd done something stupid.

"It's the dinner—I don't have anything to wear."

"What do you mean? What do you need to wear?"

"I don't know, fancy stuff. This dinner's kind of formal." She stood up and then pulled him into her room. The wardrobe had already been opened and half of its contents thrown across the bed. "Look! What am I supposed to wear?" She felt guilty even as the words were leaving her mouth—they had a very limited budget. Infuriatingly, her dad was smiling, and he'd even put an arm around her.

"Don't you think this is important?" Phoebe asked.

"Of course it is." Her father chuckled, and then continued. "Kiddo, you should have said something sooner."

He led her into his own bedroom and pointed to the mysterious-looking wardrobe in the corner, the one that was always locked. Phoebe assumed that it had been her mother's, but had been afraid to ask, or even mention it. Her father retrieved a key from his desk and gave it to her.

"Why don't you open it," he suggested.

Inside, the wardrobe was full. In addition to loads of everyday clothing, there were a number of garment bags hanging to one side. Below them, on a shelf, was a large wooden box and a number of shoeboxes, all neatly stacked.

"What are those?" Phoebe asked, pointing at the bags and the box.

"They were your mother's ... umm, work things. Well, technically, they belong to the Order, but no one submitted a claim, so I kept them for you." He choked on the last words and, after a brief pause, added, "Why don't you look through everything? I'll be in the other room."

Phoebe stared at the bags for a moment then started opening them, one at a time, until their contents had all been carefully draped across her father's bed. Her eyes had gotten bigger with every garment bag.

Each one contained a formal gown, and Rebecca was almost exactly the same size as her. The dresses were made of high-quality silk that almost seemed to float in her hands. Silk was virtually unheard of in the Land, very rare and extremely expensive. With each gown was a matching wrap, made from some soft woven material she couldn't identify. Phoebe counted a dozen outfits altogether, every one of them was better than anything she'd ever seen before.

The shoeboxes contained dangerous-looking shoes. It looked as though they could be mixed and matched with the gowns. She lost track of time, looking through everything, and began to wonder exactly what kind of work her mother had done.

Finally, she lifted the heavy cask from the wardrobe. It was made of a dark wood, with a hinged top that closed with a hasp. Even the box 'felt' expensive. She placed it on the desk, handling it very gently. The hasp was made of a heavy gold-colored metal, and she carefully twisted the mechanism to unlock it. Inside were stacked four velvet-covered boxes with sturdy fabric handles attached to their sides, to make them easy to lift out. The boxes were each about the size of a school notebook on top, and about as deep as the width of three of her fingers. There was a crystal recessed within the top of each box. Four boxes and four crystals: red, blue, green, and the last one clear. She opened the one with the blue stone first—her favorite color.

Inside, resting on more velvet and held in place using display forms, was a suite of matching jewelry: earrings, a necklace with a stone pendent, and an elaborate bracelet. Each piece was set with blue stones.

Holy crap! she thought, quickly opening the other boxes. They were all the same. The stone on top indicated the color of the jewels inside, and she assumed they were real. That meant the green stones were emeralds. *So these are sapphires, and the clear ones are probably diamonds.*

Phoebe couldn't believe her eyes and stared at everything. Her father found her this way, frozen in place, still looking down at the open boxes.

"How?" she asked.

"I told you, they were Becky's. She attended diplomatic functions, and represented the Order. They gave her these things to use. I wish I had more to give you. They're not much of a substitute for a mother, but they're yours now."

Phoebe didn't know what to say. She'd known her mother was an important member of the Order, but seeing everything here made her realize that she would have been close to serving on the Order's version of the Council's Inner Circle. She had no idea what they were worth, but her respect for her dad went up several more notches. Any one of these sets was probably worth more than a normal person could afford, and yet he'd never even thought to sell them. She was afraid to talk because she might cry, and crossed the room to hug him.

She knew what this would cost him, not in a material sense, but it meant that he was finally letting go of hope.

Should I tell him she's alive? It was the right thing to do, but she still didn't know *why* Becky had stayed away. It didn't seem fair to put him through pain when she couldn't tell him what happened. Phoebe wasn't looking forward to *that* conversation with her dad, but knew one thing for sure: she'd have to speak with Rebecca about everything first. For now, she'd consider the dresses and the jewelry to be on loan, and forced herself to put the subject of her mother on the back burner.

Time to focus on what her grandfather called 'the now'—today, this week. What did she need to do first? She needed to get through the dinner, and to do that she'd have to decide which dress to wear and make whatever alterations were necessary.

The blue dress, she thought, *and the sapphires.* The gown would be more revealing than anything she'd ever worn. She smiled, imagining what Caleb's reaction would be.

CHAPTER 26

The Dinner

D ANIEL KEPT LOOKING AT THE clock over the
fireplace, and then at Phoebe's door. *How long does it take
to put on a dress?* he wondered. But when she came out he forgot
everything. With her hair up like that, and dressed as she was,
Phoebe looked so much like Becky that he couldn't speak.

"Are you ready?" she asked, stopping in the bathroom to adjust
her hair in the mirror. He nodded, still unable to say anything.
"You look great in that old suit, Dad. I didn't even have to let it
out"...*much,* she added to herself. "Okay, I'm ready. Let's go."

Her father had arranged for a taxi to pick them up. The single-
horse coach was just turning onto their street when they reached
the walkway.

♎

The formal dining room had been emptied of furniture for the night.
Instead, it was left open for guests to mingle. Trays containing
unusual appetizers were sprinkled throughout the room and the
first floor. The doors to a glass-encased patio, adjacent to the dining
room, had been opened. This was where the guests would be seated
to provide the illusion of dining under the stars.

Rather than having everyone sit at one long table, Dr. Addison
had placed five round tables in the house's former attached
greenhouse. This would provide a less formal, more intimate

experience. Gas lamps, stationed around its perimeter, were turned down low. Their flickering light would blend with the natural illumination from the full moon. There were heaters, too, but they weren't lit. The weather was mild tonight, and some of the window panels were tilted open to let in fresh air.

When Caleb first saw Phoebe, he froze, staring at her and looking more like a well-dressed mannequin than her date for the evening. He mumbled something, but she couldn't hear what he said.

"And you were worried about what to wear?" he finally managed.

"What, this old thing?" she said with a shrug, laughing.

Although this was ostensibly an official function, Dr. Addison wanted to keep the atmosphere as informal as possible. Caterers were dressed as guests, rather than in uniforms, and the seating arrangements were to be a surprise. The main course would be followed by an intermission, to allow everyone time to wander through the house and the gardens before dessert.

The Council Elder from the funeral was there. Dr. Addison took him from room to room, introducing him to small groups. Phoebe and her father were talking with Caleb and two other guests when they approached.

"I'd like to present His Grace, the Most Reverend Excellency Frances James, Archbishop Primate of the Christian Faith." Up close, the Bishop looked younger than Phoebe had noticed. He was about her father's age, maybe a few years older. The priest who followed him around was dressed in traditional black attire. The title of Archbishop Primate meant that he was the spiritual leader of the Christian church within the Council. He served the role for Christianity that the Pope, or another head of church, would have filled in a different era. However, unlike the Pope, the Archbishop Primate was subject to the will of the Council.

Less than an hour after the Archbishop arrived, Caleb's father announced that it was time to be seated for dinner. Each table would be hosted by someone from the Addison family. Caleb's father was at one table and Caleb another. Mary, her mother, and her father each hosted their own tables, too. The surprise about

the seating was in keeping with the spirit of the evening. People
wouldn't have assigned places. Instead, where they sat would be
determined by a draw. This way, guests would dine with people
they may not have otherwise met. The draw was not mandatory,
and didn't apply to spouses or 'best friends', like Phoebe.

In addition to Caleb and herself, there were four others at their
table: Dr. Klaus, a cardiologist from the hospital, along with her
husband, Don; the Council member; and—for some reason—
Elizabeth. She'd 'risked' the draw rather than taking advantage
of the 'best friend exception' to sit with Ian and Mary. Phoebe
guessed that they'd managed to rig the process. Liz was seated to
Caleb's right, and the red-clad Council Elder, who had insisted on
participating, was seated to Phoebe's left. He'd been glancing at her
from time to time, as though he recognized her. But Phoebe was
determined not to pay him any attention, or even to be nice. She
deliberately tilted her chair away from him, and toward Caleb. This
meant she'd be partially facing Elizabeth all night. *Oh well*, she
thought gloomily—*could be worse, I could be between her and Mary.*

The Archbishop was listening to Dr. Klaus discuss a patient.
"He's been in and out of the hospital over the past several years,
always with the same issue—chest pains caused by angina. There
used to be a treatment…uh, but, I'm not certain if anything could
help him for sure. Did you try the fish appetizer? It's got a funny
sounding name. I found it just inside the front door." This was
probably the first time Dr. Klaus had been so close to an important
Council member.

Liz put a hand on Caleb's arm to get his attention—and left it
there. "What's for dinner, Caleb?" she asked.

Calm down, Phoebe told herself, but pointedly stared at Liz's
hand until she took it away. Liz half smiled at Phoebe.

"You know, I'm not sure, Liz. It'll be a surprise for me, too,"
Caleb said.

"Weren't you involved in the planning process?" she asked.

"No. And that's a good thing." Caleb had witnessed the
exchange between them, and shifted his chair a little closer to
Phoebe. "Are you allowed to have wine tonight?" he asked.

"My dad won't mind, as long as it's *good* wine." She picked up a stem, pretended to evaluate its bouquet then held it up to the light to check for color before finally taking a sip. "No. He won't mind me drinking this at all." *And the alcohol might keep me from punching Liz's lights out.* She took another drink with that idea in mind.

The Archbishop was laughing. "I'm sorry," he said, "it's nice to meet such a beautiful young lady with a great sense of humor, too." Phoebe gave him a half smile, but didn't look directly at him.

"Did I hear that your name was Phoebe?" he asked politely.

She sighed quietly, obviously the cold-shoulder approach wasn't working. "Umm, yes," she said, at a loss. Phoebe didn't want to spend a lot of time talking with him, but she also didn't want to be rude. "I'm sorry," she said, frowning. "I'm not exactly sure how I'm supposed to address you."

"Ah yes, titles. Let's keep it simple, shall we? It'll save a lot of time. Just for tonight, please call me Father James, or just plain Father. It's a lot shorter than His Most Reverend Excellency and so forth, and in this setting 'Your Grace' is a bit much."

Phoebe couldn't help grinning. "Okay, Father James it is—just for tonight." She held out a hand, while probing, too—just the surface tenor of his mind. He didn't feel evil, or even hostile. "Pleased to meet you. How long has it been since you actually *were* just plain Father James?"

"A while, I'm afraid, and I miss it." She had a sense of his character now, but hadn't fully connected. He was surprisingly open, even honest, not at all what she'd expected. "Of course it's a great honor to be entrusted with the responsibility, but a lot of what I do now isn't why I originally joined the church—but enough of my complaints. Do you still attend school?"

"I do. I graduate after next year."

"You look so grown-up." There was a puzzled look on his face. "And that's a beautiful dress you're wearing." Phoebe felt her face get warm, hoping it was the wine.

"Thank you, Father. It was my mother's." The confusion in his eyes faded, along with his smile. But before Phoebe could check on what that meant, she was interrupted.

"Your mother's?" Liz asked. "Sorry, but I couldn't help overhearing."

"Uh-huh, that's what my dad told me."

"It looks…expensive—silk, if I'm not mistaken. The jewelry looks real, too. Is it?" The intense look on her face contrasted with the casual tone of her question.

Phoebe shrugged. "I don't know. It's one of the few things I have from her. Of course I'd rather have a mother than a dress, but no one said life was fair." She looked past Caleb, and toward her father, the good humor she'd begun to feel was passing away.

Father James touched her arm. "I'm sure your mother would have been proud of you tonight. May I ask what happened to her?" The question was asked without inflection and sounded odd.

"She was killed when the comet hit."

"Ah," he said, nodding, "there were so many losses that year. I'm sorry if I brought up a painful subject." She sensed a deeper feeling behind his words, something more than mere politeness—a sadness that seemed to wrap around her. There was something even more odd about him. Father James felt protective toward her. *Weird,* she thought. Against her better judgment, Phoebe was beginning to like him.

She looked around to see if anyone was listening, knowing that she'd probably never get this kind of opportunity again: the chance to talk with someone in power who knew everything that had happened around the time of the Purge. A hundred questions ran through her mind, but she hesitated to ask.

Phoebe stared at the table, biting her lip, trying to decide if she should say anything. "Can I ask you about some of the things that happened—when the comet hit?"

Father James paused. "Phoebe, a lot of things happened back then. It was a pretty chaotic time. Maybe we can discuss it somewhere a little more private, perhaps after dinner? I wouldn't want to bring the mood of the table down." It was a reminder that they weren't alone.

She smiled an apology. "I'd like that, Father. Let's drink a toast to…uh, Caleb, what exactly is this dinner for?" Dr. Klaus gasped, choking on the water she'd been drinking, but Father James was laughing out loud.

"His…I mean the Father is here to set the cornerstone for a new cathedral. New Bright Sea Harbor is getting its own Bishop. Isn't that right?" Caleb said.

"Yes, it is—at last. I've been trying to find the resources to do this for years. This town holds a special place in my heart—I was born here, you know."

Dinner carts were arriving now, and each guest was offered a choice between locally caught fish, or corn-fed beef from the Central Plains. Phoebe chose the fish out of loyalty to Jacob.

Throughout dinner, Liz seemed to be trying to irritate her. Every now and then she'd make a not-so-subtle comment, warning her not to spill something on her dress, or pointedly apologizing when she mentioned her own mother. Phoebe stoically bore it all. More than once, Father James gently prodded Liz about a particularly rude comment. Whenever he'd raise an eyebrow, she'd retreat—for a while.

Why is he so protective of me? Phoebe could have found out her own way, of course. But once she'd started to know him a little, she felt it would be wrong, and sensed a new, unlikely friend in him. This was so unexpected—she'd always assumed he'd be an enemy.

After the main course, guests were invited to wander through the house and the garden. Dessert would be served later.

"It's a nice party, and I like the house," she told Caleb when they were alone. Liz had wandered over to chat with Mary and her brother.

"Yeah, it's nice. Dad's older than Uncle John, so he has the right to live here. I'm next in line, and I like it, but I'm not so sure I want to stay after I graduate."

"Why? Where would you go?"

"I don't know. I'd kind of like to see more of the world. I love this area, but there's a lot out there still waiting to be discovered. Someday we'll need to explore the rest of the planet, to learn what survived, and what's recovering."

As he was speaking, Mary approached and asked him to accompany her, putting a hand on his arm. "Ian wants to know if you can show him the famous Addison wine collection."

"Hello, Mary. I like your dress. You look great tonight." Phoebe thought she'd try being polite and see how far it got.

"Thank you, Phoebe." She didn't return the compliment, but tugged harder on Caleb's arm. "Come on, Caleb, please?"

He pressed his lips together, looking at Phoebe. Clearly, he didn't want to leave, but she tilted her head in the direction Mary was pulling as a reminder that he was still a host.

"Do you mind?" he asked, looking as though he hoped she would.

"It's okay, Caleb. I promised to have a talk with Father James." He pointed toward the garden, ignoring Mary's continued protests, and winked at her.

"I'll be back soon," he promised.

CHAPTER 27
Warning from a Friend

PHOEBE WANDERED OUT THROUGH THE doors at the back of the crystal patio and into the garden. It was cooler outside, so she put the wrap around her shoulders.

The garden was as cozy and inviting as the Addison home. Scattered gas lamps illuminated intimate spaces where people could linger for a while. Oil lamps, also turned down low, hung along footpaths, so that visitors could see where they were stepping without being overwhelmed by light.

Phoebe heard voices coming from somewhere beyond the shrubs in one direction, and getting stronger. She recognized Father James' baritone, and Dr. Addison's voice among them. The Father was speaking now, arguing, or trying to make some point. Shadows moved across light, revealing four figures together. Besides Father James and Dr. Addison, the town's mayor and the priest, who seemed to follow Father James around, were in their company—presumably, the priest was an assistant. The black vestments hid his body, making it seem as though his head was floating through the garden.

"I'll do what I can, Dr. Addison," Father James said, "but you know that it's not up to just me, and the Council is divided on the matter. His Holiness hasn't said what his advice will be yet. Please, try to be patient—I know it's difficult."

"It's been almost eighteen years now, Your Grace. A lot of people died who might otherwise have been saved."

"I'm sure His Holiness will weigh all factors, doctor. We know your motives are good, but he has other pressures to consider as well. I'll speak with him again, but I can't make promises about a particular outcome."

"Your Grace, you've heard Dr. Addison's arguments through, but we need to be careful. Discussing these kinds of things openly could be misconstrued..." It was the priest who'd spoken.

"It's all right, Robert. We're all friends here." He turned toward the house, and noticed her. "Ah, Phoebe. I'm glad you remembered. Gentlemen, I have a promise to keep. Dr. Addison, do you know Phoebe?"

"Absolutely," Caleb's father said, with just a trace of agitation still in his voice. He gave her a friendly nod. "We've had the pleasure of meeting, Your Grace. My son seems very attached to her."

Phoebe smiled at Caleb's father and shook hands with Father Robert and the Mayor. "It's nice to see you again, Father James," she said. A sudden intake of breath from the Mayor caused him to hold a hand up. "It's perfectly fine, Mayor. That's what I asked her to call me tonight. Will you gentlemen please excuse us?" The three men nodded and then left.

"I hope you weren't disturbed by the spirited discussion we were having."

"I don't know what it was about, and it's none of my business anyway."

He pointed toward the path he'd just come from. "Shall we take a stroll?" She followed him along the path, passing shrubs and trees along the way. Father James seemed upset about something. Phoebe guessed it was whatever he and the others had been discussing.

The path was wider than she'd thought. They walked side by side, until they found a bench set into a small cove. He invited her to sit while they talked.

"Now. We were discussing the time when the comet hit, and you wanted to know more about what happened."

"I was wondering…It's hard to understand why people acted so—hostile back then, and why so many new rules were created."

"A lot of things were happening at the time. You probably know most of it, but memories and perspectives are things we gather over years and they have a tendency to evolve. I may be able to help clarify a few things, and I'll share what I know—but you'll have to decide what to believe. This isn't something I talk about very often, but I'll make an exception for you—and I'll tell you why, later."

Phoebe nodded, hoping he wouldn't change his mind. "I'd like that."

"Of course, you've heard most of the history in school," he began.

"I heard some things," she said, interrupting, "I think the teachers believe that they're telling us the whole truth—everything they know, anyway. But sometimes I'm not sure which parts are factual, and which parts propaganda. My dad saw some of what happened, and my grandfather, too. I've been trying to put it all together, but some things just don't make a lot of sense."

Father James took a deep breath and let it out slowly. "A lot of events came together at one time—the Order, the Purge, the comet, and the chaos that followed. Times were bad, but things might have turned out much, much worse."

"I didn't mean to be rude, Father. Sorry for interrupting."

"You weren't being rude, just young. How much do you know about the Council's organization? And what do you know about the Order?"

"I know that the Council is led by His Holiness, the Supreme Elder, and that there are seven additional Elders within the Inner Circle: three Archbishops—one for each faith—and the four Elders who head the Curiae. The Curiae are responsible for different aspects of society, and every member of the Inner Circle must have been a priest, or the equivalent from one of the other faiths. I know that the Council was founded before the war to save humanity, and that, without the Council, none of us would be here. I don't know much about the Order."

"All true. The Council of God was the first true ecumenical organization, created by leaders from the three major religions that all worship the same one God. You probably don't appreciate now how hard that must have been to accomplish back then. Just getting the different Christian sects to join together was an enormous challenge. Everyone was required to submit to a new, unified hierarchy, for the collective good. That was thought impossible. You can imagine how much harder it was to bring so many different faiths together, too."

"Father, I can understand that creating the Council was a hard job, but...what did that have to do with the Purge, and making up laws that dragged everyone back into the past? We had it all before, peace, and the best of both worlds—the Council changed all that. What I want to know is...Why?" She was afraid that maybe she'd gone too far.

"Phoebe, I had a pretty good idea of what you wanted to know. But for now, just listen, even if some of what I tell you is familiar. It's important that you understand the roots of what happened, because they drove the decisions made during the Purge." She took a deep breath and nodded, wondering how he could possibly have known what she was after. She felt a momentary chill and almost decided to probe his mind. But still he felt so...so good that she couldn't bring herself to do it. Even as she was speaking, there'd been no sign of impatience on his part.

"First, we have to go back to the emergence of the postwar Council, almost two hundred years ago. They witnessed the war, and every one of them blamed it on the spread of dangerous knowledge, not just the actual machines of war, but the knowledge that allowed people to build such catastrophic weapons, as well.

"The Council believed that dangerous information had become too easily available, and the tools used to create weapons were everywhere. The knowledge and tools together gave individuals the power to kill millions. So they made a choice: the core knowledge and technologies, even more than any one specific political position, were the problems."

"But, how did medical equipment in the hospital threaten anyone? How did powered boats and ships, or even communications equipment, like the ones the tower on the mountain gave us, harm anyone?"

"You're right, Phoebe, technologies bring a lot of benefits to the people. All I can say is that—like most times when people overreact—fear was the driver. On the one hand, knowledge brings prosperity and health, but on the other we've seen it bring the apocalypse.

"Let's go back, again, to the time just after the war. You need to understand this, because when we try to separate decisions made during the Purge from what drove the decisions—experiences from the past—nothing makes sense.

"At that time, some of the most respected theologians of the day believed that there was a relationship between unrestrained technological knowledge and original sin—the knowledge of good and evil. These scholars believed that destruction was an inevitable consequence of too much knowledge being made available, and that, sooner or later, war would happen again. Remember, billions of people had just been killed, and the majority of the Earth's surface turned into a radioactive wasteland—their fears were understandable, even if their actions were extreme. One problem was that they had difficulty separating the good knowledge from the bad."

"What do you believe?" Phoebe asked.

"Well, I don't believe they were correct but, personally, I think there is a grain of truth in their thinking somewhere. People are people, and there'll always be a certain element not satisfied with living their own lives. Instead they're compelled to control others by force—they're bullies. Bullies have always existed, and we humans have a long history of conquest to prove it. But, historically, most bullies lacked the means to cause such widespread destruction. The damage they could do was limited by the amount of raw energy they could manipulate and direct. Advances in science and engineering changed all that—it democratized destruction."

"I still don't understand." Phoebe crossed her arms, frowning. "Why were they so heavy-handed? Weren't they being bullies, too?"

"Phoebe, there are a number of things that were happening at the time, and I'll get to them as soon as I can, but without understanding how the leadership was thinking, it's hard to see how it would act. Please be patient."

"Sorry, Father. I'm not blaming you."

"I know." Father James smiled and briefly placed a hand on her shoulder. "This distrust of knowledge, and how it would inevitably be abused, was a cornerstone of the Council's original charter. The members who survived the war were charged with a mission to save as many people as possible, but also to prevent a future recurrence of the war. The original pre-war Council never intended that advanced knowledge of the physical sciences would survive the destruction."

"Really?" Father James nodded.

"You can imagine how shocked everyone was when the Order first emerged from their hidden cocoons, offering to make available the very thing believed to be at the root of the apocalypse. The Order had a mission, too, and it was almost the exact opposite of what the Council was trying to achieve. I say almost, because of subtle differences between what was feared about their mission and what their actual charter intended—these were important differences.

"The Council didn't know what to do at first. They'd just been through war and seen the chaos that followed. Somehow, they couldn't bring themselves to start yet another fight. There'd been enough violence already. Instead, they sought compromise. Cooperation was seen as the best way to contain unintended harm the scientists might do."

Phoebe still hadn't connected with him, but she couldn't help sensing the feelings that came through. Father James was being truthful, and he was still broadcasting this bewildering fatherly feeling toward her.

"Tell me about the Order and its charter," she said.

"The Order wasn't really so very different from the Council. They were organized in much the same way, and were almost as secretive. They were determined to keep the most dangerous knowledge contained. Their charter charged them to choose which knowledge should be shared, and which should not. They wanted to bring the benefits of the most advanced things from the past, but only share the core knowledge of the things they considered safe. This caution on their part soothed the Council's fears, and formed the basis of cooperation. Compromise allowed the Order to do exactly what they wanted: bring many of the benefits of modern technology, and to share limited knowledge with the people. That's what sold the Council."

"What kinds of things did they withhold?"

"The Order didn't want to release its core secrets—nuclear and weapons technologies, for example, and some of their more advanced materials and electronics knowledge. They were as distrustful of raw power as the Council. So together, the two organizations created The Balance. It codified the vital importance of spiritual life, ensuring that the Council would always retain political leadership. In return, the Order was given an important place at the table, and allowed to govern its own people, independently."

"And then the Purge happened?"

"Trouble started long before the Purge. About ninety years ago, one of the leaders of the Order, a man named Alexander Martin, publicly said something that alarmed everyone, not just the Council. He stated that one of his own goals was to eliminate the need for faith—referring to it as superstition. His speech should have been made in a closed meeting, but representatives from the Council were present, too. He predicted a future where they would be able to manipulate the very design of humans to create beings with supernatural powers, and that these 'superior humans' would have no need of a God.

"We'd been working together so well that even the Council tried to hush up his statements, and they overlooked the comments as arrogant bluster—but the words still troubled them. They'd been given a glimpse into a darker side of the Order. Somehow, the transcript of his speech got out and angered the public, but the disquiet faded after a few years."

"I never heard about that," Phoebe said.

"Repeating it wouldn't have helped anything. I suspect all organizations have these kinds of secrets, but you can imagine how his words affected the Council. The seeds of distrust had been planted. Seventy years later we all learned that what he'd been predicting wasn't just bluster, but fact, and based on work already done."

"What do you mean?"

"We learned about the genetics programs and how they were all wrapped up into a project called Future Man, a long-term plan to surreptitiously manipulate the DNA of everyone, ultimately implanting their own human blueprint into the population—playing God."

"Holy cra..." Phoebe didn't finish. Father James smiled and pretended she hadn't said anything.

"The revelations about Future Man couldn't have come at a worse time. It coincided with the death of the old Supreme Elder—a man of impeccable judgment, and someone you could trust to do the right thing, especially when the pressure was on. A combination of events threw the Council into turmoil. The Bishops at the time were frightened by what they'd heard of the genetics programs, and they went along with recommendations from the more extreme elements within the Council.

"Here, sitting on this path tonight, I'll tell you that while the Council speaks with one voice, our thinking isn't unanimous. You spoke about our organization. Yes, technically, that's how we are organized, but things are a bit more subtle than that."

"What do you mean, subtle?"

"There have always been two main factions within the Council, and they've often battled. I'm head of one of the three spiritual branches. By tradition we three Bishops are drawn from long-time leaders within the three founding faiths, and together we select the Supreme Elder. The combination of the Bishops, and the Supreme Elder, hold ultimate power. Theoretically, we set policy together. But His Holiness *can* override our judgment and propose alternative recommendations, if he chooses. And if he's supported by the other four Elders—those who lead the Curiae—then we lose control.

"Only an overwhelming majority of the Council can override either the Supreme Elder, or the three Bishops. There must be at least five total votes to do that, and we only hold three. Of the four Curiae—Truth, Justice, Law, and Economics—the only other leader who's shown a willingness to listen, is the one leading the Curia of Law, but he's never voted with us."

"I didn't know that." Phoebe was learning more about the inner workings of the Council than most people knew.

"Getting back to what we were discussing, in addition to the troubling revelations about the Future Man genetics programs, Council members at the time received a warning. It seems that some within the Order, a rogue faction no doubt, planned to infiltrate the Council and, ultimately, take over. The information hinted that some of the enhanced beings created under Future Man were involved, and that Council members themselves would be altered somehow. The Inner Circle took a unanimous hard line when they heard this.

"The new Supreme Elder was, and is, a much different person than his predecessor. He'd been heavily influenced by the scholars I discussed before. I might even go so far as to say he is a disciple of that branch of theology. From the time he took control, the Council has increasingly become more harsh in its policies and approach. That doesn't mean that his motives are so very different from my own, but his concept of appropriate methods is much different. We spiritual leaders do what we can to soften things in little ways. The Supreme Guardian for Islam, the Elder Kohen of the Jewish faith, and myself are all in basic agreement, but we're isolated."

"What happened?"

"So, what happened was the Purge. People were killed. The Council loosed the Penitents on the Order and did terrible things in the name of God. They almost lost control of the Penitents. We've created a world that, I think, could be much better—I don't believe that modern science and the benefits it brings are evil, and I wish the Council had moved more slowly. People die of disease that we could prevent, and the people of the Land are denied the ability to use conveniences that would make their lives better. But we're locked into this unhealthy pattern. And I wish I could offer you a good reason for what happened to your mother, too."

Phoebe's mouth opened, as if to say something, but stopped, wondering why Rebecca had come up.

"I'll tell you why I am being so open with you. I knew your mother." Father James let out a long sigh. Phoebe looked around to make sure no one was listening.

"You knew my mother?"

"Yes, and you look just like her, Phoebe. I couldn't believe my eyes when I first saw you tonight—and that dress. I knew Rebecca very well, a good person and, believe it or not, one of the faithful." He gave her a wry smile.

"How did you meet her?"

"Remember, I was born here. My first assignment was as parish priest, but I stayed on to work for the Council as its local representative. I'd been marked for promotion when I was quite young, so it was not unusual for your mother and I to attend the same functions. I've even seen her wearing that dress."

"Do you know what happened to her?" Father James took a deep breath and let it out.

"Yes. The night she died—a terrible night—I tried to catch up with the mob to stop them. But they weren't listening, and there was no denying them." A haunted look entered his eyes, and Phoebe sensed the deep sense of guilt that he still felt for what happened to her. Then she froze. Father James—this Council Elder—knew her mother, and he may even have known *what* she was.

"Don't worry," he said, reading her expression. "Your secret's safe with me. It's the least I can do for her. But I'd advise against wearing that dress, or anything else that belonged to her. Like I said, the two of you look a lot alike, and there may well be other people who remember Rebecca. I probably wouldn't be able to protect you if you were discovered.

"Another thing—a warning. Be careful around some of the people at the dinner tonight. Elizabeth's brother, Ian, works for the Curia of Truth. Stay away from him. I've heard stories...he's young and ambitious—some might say ruthless. Finding you would bring him a lot of prestige." With that, the Bishop put an arm around Phoebe's shoulders and gave her a hug, then got up to walk back toward the house.

CHAPTER 28

Threat

CALEB WAS BACK BY THE time Phoebe returned from speaking with Father James. He seemed happy and, at first, didn't notice how pale Phoebe had become.

"I showed Ian and Liz the family wine collection. Ian's something of an amateur sommelier. When you're an Addison—especially first born," he said, ceremonially bowing, "you're expected to lay down several pipes of wine for future generations. It's a tradition that's been going on for…well, a long time. Of course, some of us Addisons drink more than others, and for several generations we've had comparative teetotalers, but they still did their duty. There's quite a collection downstairs, and some of the vintages are pretty old. Would you like to see?"

Phoebe wanted alone time with Caleb, but didn't want to risk a musty basement in her mother's gown. The conversation with Father James had made her uneasy.

Mary, Ian, and Liz were huddled against the far wall, glowering at her. Phoebe turned away, looking around the room to note the older guests while also trying to hide how exposed she felt. "No thanks. I believe you, but I don't know anything about wine. What's a pipe?"

"Are you all right?" he asked. "You don't look so good." Her shoulders sagged and her hands dropped to her sides and she looked at him, as if hurt. "Uh, what I mean is you look great, of course, but you also look like you don't feel so well," he amended.

"I'm fine," she said with crossed arms, lifting her chin. "A pipe?" she prodded.

"Uh—it's a little over six hundred bottles," he said, scratching the side of his face. "Are you sure you're okay? Would you like to sit down?"

"No. But I'd like to go somewhere else—anywhere. Maybe a walk?" Phoebe looked around again to see if anyone else was looking at her.

It had been a mistake to wear Rebecca's things tonight. Phoebe spent her whole life hiding who and what she was by blending in, but all that had been stripped away by Father James' memory of Rebecca. Who else at the dinner might have known, or just seen photographs of her? Pictures of Rebecca had to exist in the Council's archives, and it would be easy to link them to her if the wrong person was curious. *I shouldn't have come.*

"Okay. Let's go to our bench. It's Saturday—the park's open late," Caleb suggested. Phoebe took a breath, nodding. "Okay, I'll let my dad know we're leaving."

While he went to let his father know what he was doing, Phoebe caught her own father's eye from across the room.

Dad, I'm going for a walk with Caleb. I won't be too late, but don't wait up.

Okay, Princess. Is everything okay?

I'm fine. Don't eat too much, and…well…do you think you can take a piece of cake home for me? The caterers were rolling out dessert trays, and she'd seen a double-chocolate cake passing by. It almost made her decide to stay.

A few minutes later, Caleb returned and they headed toward the door.

"Hey. Where are you guys going?" Mary had overheard Caleb talking to his father and caught up with them just inside the main entrance.

"We decided to skip dessert and go for a walk instead—I'm fat enough." But the lighthearted tone didn't match his expression. Mary must have guessed that Phoebe wanted to be alone with him.

"That sounds great!" she said with an overly enthusiastic grin. "I'll grab Ian and Liz. We can play hooky together." Her grin changed into a frown when Caleb didn't agree right away. He was looking at Phoebe, checking to see if it was all right with her. When she didn't answer quickly enough, Mary stepped in, close to her, and whispered, "Is there a problem?"

Objecting looked like it would only make matters worse, so she acquiesced. "No problem."

"Great," Caleb added without enthusiasm. "We'll wait outside."

While Mary was collecting her friends, they stepped out the door. He shrugged, "We almost made it—sorry."

"It's okay."

Within a few minutes, everyone was ready to set out. Phoebe and Caleb walked a little behind the others, creating enough space to talk without being overheard.

"I can't tell you what it means that you came tonight." Caleb took her hand, and the simple touch brought a connection with it. She could feel contentment flowing up through her arm, and told herself that she could probably put up with a thousand hypothetical Marys for just that feeling. *Of course, the actual Mary's a real pain.*

They reached the park in just a few minutes. It dominated the downtown area, occupying the equivalent of ten square blocks—almost fifty acres. Its grounds were circular and protected by a tall iron fence. The Central Ring Road circled the park's perimeter, and major north-south and east-west streets intersected with it. There were four primary entrances to the park, one in each of the cardinal directions. They entered through the south gate.

Inside, a serpentine path wound its way through the trees and around ponds. The largest was almost a small lake and shaped like a hand, with finger-like appendages extending in different directions.

The gas lamps were still lit since it was a weekend, but spaced out far enough apart so that they could still see the stars. Even in this muted light, Phoebe could tell that the leaves had begun to change. She couldn't make out individual colors but knew that, before long, fall would strip them all from the trees.

They neared the park's center, and crossed a wooden bridge that spanned one of the pond's fingers. Just on the other side was a memorial, built in memory of those lost when the comet fell, and nearby was their favorite bench. Phoebe and Caleb stopped to stand in front of it, looking around the park. Mary and her friends walked a little farther long the path.

"It looks so much different at night, doesn't it?" Phoebe nodded but didn't say anything. Mary's group had turned around and was getting close; they could just begin to hear their voices.

"Did I tell you how...how, well, how beautiful you look tonight?" he said. Phoebe could feel his heart pounding through her fingers. He'd said something like this earlier, but it was different this time. She looked down and took a breath before answering.

"Just a few times, but don't let that stop you." Caleb chuckled. "And did I tell you how truly beautiful *you* look tonight?" she asked. He laughed harder, squeezing her hand.

The others were close enough to hear them now, hanging just outside the edge of the light, still talking among themselves. After a minute or two they approached. Ian and Elizabeth had decided to leave, and would walk directly home. They wanted to say good-bye.

"It was nice to see you again," Elizabeth said unconvincingly. Phoebe returned the cold formality with equal politeness. Her brother took a small bow, and seemed amused by something. He touched Mary's shoulder lightly, giving her a private look, and then followed his sister to the east.

Phoebe's feeling of well-being was evaporating. She'd have to deal with Mary now, and wondered sourly why *she* hadn't gone with her friends. *There must be some dirt to talk about . . . somewhere else.*

They started a walk around the largest portion of the sprawling pond, intending to circle back to the south gate, and then on to Caleb's home. Phoebe dodged a group of younger children, playing. It was late, but there weren't many warm days left, so parents were lenient on Saturdays. The mixture of light and shadows made their game more interesting at night.

Mary stopped, settling onto a bench that was under one of the gas lamps, and not far from the south gate.

"Caleb, I need to sit down a moment, but I'm beginning to regret skipping dessert. There's a shop open till midnight just outside," she said, pointing south through the iron fence. "Could you get me a little ice cream? It would give me the energy to walk home and save my poor feet a few steps." She lifted one of her high heels for emphasis.

Caleb paused, and looked at Phoebe. She tilted her head to the side and shrugged, as if to say that sooner or later this was going to happen.

"No problem. Would you like something, too?" Phoebe shook her head and took a breath to get ready. "I'll be right back," he added.

"He's a great guy, isn't he?" Mary said as they watched him fade into the darkness. Phoebe nodded. "This is the first time we've been alone, isn't it?" She paused to let Phoebe say something, but the question didn't really need an answer. Mary sighed. "I wanted us to have a little chat."

"Sure, what would you like to talk about." *Here it comes*, she thought, shifting her weight to her other foot.

"You may not know it, but Caleb is…well, he's involved with Elizabeth."

"I hadn't noticed a particular attachment," she observed. "Of course, he's free to do as he wants, and with whomever he chooses," she added.

"I don't think you understand." Mary scowled. "Maybe I'm not being clear…I was hoping to avoid unpleasantness, but I guess sometimes it's necessary to be brutally honest about things."

Phoebe translated Mary's expression in her head. 'Brutally honest' usually meant: I'm going to be brutal to you—honestly.

"I'm sure you're a nice girl and all, but Caleb needs to be with…he needs to associate with the right kinds of people—people with connections, who can help him up in the world. Not with someone with a questionable family past. I can see he likes you, but I also know that you're not the right person for him."

Phoebe stared at Mary, unable to think of anything useful to say. Her face had gotten hot as Mary talked, but she didn't see a point in responding right now, and decided this 'little chat' was over. It seemed better to stop, before her temper flared—better than anything else she could think of doing. She turned to step away from the bench, but Mary wasn't finished being brutal yet, and grabbed her arm.

"Where do you think you're going?"

Phoebe closed her eyes. A primitive, dangerous anger was beginning to rise up inside of her, and Mary's grip only made matters worse. Her hand brought a connection that she couldn't completely block. Hostility, contempt, and—most strongly—a sense of insecurity were all coming from Mary. *Calm down*, she thought, *take deep breaths.*

"Caleb needs to stay close to the Council. Your adopted father is what, a defender?" she sneered. "He helps criminals get away with flaunting the law—even overt acts against the Council."

Phoebe was starting to lose the battle with her anger. Bringing her father into the conversation wasn't going to help Mary's case. But she held back, for Caleb. *If I'm not careful, I'm going to do something we'll both regret,* she thought, taking another breath, and willing herself to stay calm.

"Your mother's family obviously must have had some money. Assuming that hand-me-down dress and the jewels are real, they're probably worth more than your father will make in his entire lifetime. Doesn't it seem strange—even irresponsible—for him to have kept them, and for what? Who was your mother, anyway? If she was from a family wealthy enough to buy expensive baubles like that, then why aren't you with *them?* What's the matter with you—or, maybe, with her?

"I asked Ian to take a look into your past, just after the funeral. He works for the Curia of Truth—you do know what that is, right?" Phoebe glared at Mary, grinding her teeth at the implied threat. "He has access to records, you know." Mary was likely mistaking Phoebe's reaction for fear, because she continued to push. "Apparently, at one time, your father was considered an Order sympathizer—that would hardly be good for Caleb. Most of the records for your father's case are sealed and require a Council

Elder's approval to open, but Ian knows people . . . the right kind of people.

"Look, Phoebe, I can't risk having Caleb get mixed up with someone who might threaten his future. You seem like a sweet girl, but you know a nice dress can't make up for everything. I'm going to do what I can to keep him from making a mistake. Your father's records will be opened and, if necessary, more action will be taken."

Mary's a threat, Phoebe thought, *to me and to Dad.* Her blood should have been boiling, but instead her insides had quickly turned to ice. The sensation she'd first felt on the cliffs during the dream was back again—and this time her mother wasn't here to stop her.

Everything she saw became sharp and clear, and it seemed as though she could look right through Mary's flesh. A jolt of energy ran through her body from deep, deep inside, and spread through her limbs—she half expected to see sparks dancing along her arms. But there was no pain this time, just an overwhelming sense of power.

She knew, instinctively, what to do and, without consciously deciding, penetrated her mind, exploring every lobe, cortex, and synapse with a kind of savage joy she'd never felt before. Time in the park stood still, as she explored every part of Mary's memory. She knew exactly what threats the girl posed, and automatically mapped out the location of every thought she'd ever had about her or her father. In just a second or two, she'd learned everything Mary knew that concerned her, and much more.

Her sick relationship with Ian had changed her, twisting her personality and blinding her to what she'd become. But *why* didn't matter now. Still, Phoebe was more than just a cold, calculating machine. She was pissed off, too.

"Maybe you should take a look at yourself, Mary. Your problem isn't really me—it's your so-called 'relationship' with Ian." Mary frowned and let go of her arm. "Does he pay any attention to you at all, other than for sex? And does he treat you like a girlfriend, or just a toy? What you have with him is hardly *normal*. He gives the signal—as he did a little while ago—and it's just like whistling for one of his dogs. Is Ian your idea of the 'right kind of people'? How do you think Liz dating Caleb would ever change that? As long as you're with Ian, you'll always just be one of his bitches—at least until he gets tired of you."

Mary was shaking now. The color had drained from her face, and she looked away to avoid Phoebe's gaze. Caleb had walked up during the last part of the exchange. She could feel that he was very close, but couldn't stop now.

Mary had regained a little control of herself. "What? How? What the hell *are* you?" she asked, staring back, wide-eyed. That's when Phoebe wiped her mind.

She was careful, erasing only those memories she'd identified during her exploration: the last few minutes of time, specific thoughts from the past week, and anything that made her suspicious of her or her father. Despite her anger, Phoebe was surgically precise. It took all of her self-control and discipline to keep from erasing more. When it was over, she was almost as surprised by what she'd done as Mary soon would be.

Waves of alarm were rolling off Caleb, and washing over her. Mary's eyes stared straight ahead, wide, vacant, and unseeing. Her mouth was hanging open, and drool was starting to form on her chin. Then awareness returned, and her eyes filled with terror.

"What? Where am I?" A pause. "Caleb? What are we doing here? Where's Ian?" He dropped the ice cream containers and knelt in front of her, taking her shoulders in his hands.

"Mary, what's wrong?" he asked.

"I don't know, I'm…I don't know," she said and then started to cry. It was several minutes before she could speak again. "I remember being at the dinner—I think. And then I was here. Everything else is a blank."

Caleb looked over his shoulder. "Did she fall and hit her head while I was gone? I heard you fighting, did…did you hit her?" Phoebe blinked. "Of course you didn't! I'm sorry. I didn't mean…"

"No. No hitting," she said as an intense wave of fatigue hit. Vast amounts of energy had passed through her—more than she'd ever felt in her life. It had taken enormous power to change Mary's brain that way, even more than it had taken to contact Rebecca, and it felt as though she actually *had* been in a fight. She needed to sit down. Her head and face were hot to the touch, like a rock that's been sitting in the sun all day. Caleb didn't notice her sway—she managed to catch herself on a metal trashcan nearby, to keep from falling, trying to hide how weak she was.

"I'm sorry," he said again. "I know you'd never hit her." Phoebe thought about it. *But I did.* She hadn't hit Mary with her fists. What she'd done was far worse. Regret and guilt were rapidly replacing the anger she'd been feeling, and she'd started to shake from weakness.

When the cold power had first drained away, she'd almost fallen and had been almost too tired to think. But now, all she felt was disgust at what she'd done. This hadn't been a trick, some temporary confusion planted into someone's mind, like déjà vu. She'd permanently wiped out whole parts of Mary's life, and it had felt as natural as breathing.

What kind of monster am I?

She looked around for something to do—some human act to help her deal with a growing sense of revulsion. "Maybe we should walk her back to your house. Your father will know what to do." Caleb nodded.

"Good idea. Can you help me get her up?"

Caleb put his arms around Mary and they helped her stand. He supported her, putting her arm over his shoulders and his own around her waist. She was unstable, and dropped to her knees to throw up after just a few steps. Caleb took his coat off and put it around Mary's shoulders, and then tore off part of his shirt to wipe her face. After a few minutes, she seemed to recover some, but it was a long walk back to the house.

Mary's parents panicked when they heard about her sudden loss of memory, and how sick she'd been. Caleb's dad called for the horse to be hitched and they took Mary to the hospital right away. He assured his brother that the chief neurologist would come in that very night, and asked one of the caterers, still cleaning up from dinner, to go to the doctor's house to rouse him.

"Dad, I'll take Phoebe home and meet you at the hospital. I don't want her walking alone, and there's not enough room for everyone in the carriage, anyway."

"Don't worry, Caleb. We'll take care of Mary—there's nothing more you can do. I'll see you later."

Phoebe's father had already gone, having been assured that Phoebe would be taken home. She desperately wanted to talk to him now and was even tempted to communicate directly, but held back. She'd see him soon enough.

CHAPTER 29

Inexcusable

THE CARRIAGE HAD ALREADY DEPARTED for the hospital, and it was too late to find a taxi, so Caleb and Phoebe started the long walk home. It would take about thirty minutes.

She'd been in Rebecca's heels all day—shoes designed more for appearance than comfort—so she took them off to carry, and sighed with her first step. Caleb worried that she'd step on something and cut her foot, but she assured him she'd be careful. They'd been walking quietly for five minutes when he broke the silence.

"How did you know so much about Mary and Ian?"

Phoebe looked down at the pavement for almost a minute before answering. Stress had been weighing down on her all day, but it wasn't over yet. She'd hoped that the questions about Mary would wait for later.

As she considered what to say, Phoebe felt tears forming. *God, not now!* she thought, making a tight fist until the pain helped her regain control.

"It was inexcusable…what I said to her." This wasn't really an answer, but she'd drawn a blank.

Caleb took charge of the shoes so he could hold her hand, squeezing it tightly, but she could also feel his disquiet through the touch. They crossed a street, walking counterclockwise around the Central Ring to pick up Second Street, north.

"It's my fault," he said a few minutes later. "I knew she wanted to be alone with you, and hoped she'd try to be conciliatory.

Sometimes I'm not so smart. Whatever it was she said, before I got back, must have been awful. I'm sorry.

"I've been pretending, trying not to see how things were between her and Ian all summer. I kept saying to myself that Mary would be fine; she's smart and strong. But I'm not blind. It wasn't very hard to see that he didn't like her as much as she liked him. I guess I hoped she'd figure it out, and get past him." There was bitterness in his voice. She could feel anger building inside of him. It came through her palm and its intensity even hurt a little. When Phoebe still didn't answer, he let out a deep sigh.

"Phoebe," he said, pausing, "I still don't understand. How did you know so much about Ian—the details of how he treated her? I could see someone figuring it out over time, and I should have picked up on it—but you weren't there. I can't begin to guess how you knew." Another long silence followed before Phoebe spoke.

"I can't tell you," she said, giving up. She hated to lie to Caleb, and had been struggling for weeks to avoid putting herself in a position to do so.

"Are you protecting someone?" he asked. His questions weren't getting any easier. Then a new thought came to her. *What if Caleb were to become a threat?* She wouldn't—couldn't—hurt him, but wasn't sure how much actual control she had over that cold machine-like version of herself—how much was deliberate, and how much pure instinct? *If I accidentally hurt him ...* The thought jolted her and made her stop to pull him around. It felt like she should warn him somehow, to protect him. *How do I do that without telling him everything?*

She struggled for a while. "In a way, yes," she admitted, deliberately being vague, still trying to buy time to think. Caleb frowned more deeply, but nodded. It was an acceptance of sorts, and they started walking again. She knew this was only a temporary reprieve, and not the last time they'd talk about it. He didn't say anything for another two blocks, still mulling over what she'd said.

"I trust you," he said, pulling her to a stop and kissing her. Phoebe wasn't sure that she deserved his trust—or his affection. *Sooner or later he'll start to connect the dots. He may even begin to hate me.* After a moment she wondered if that might be a good thing—for his sake.

When they reached home, he kissed her again. She stood on the first step to make it easier. This wasn't the blazing fire that last Saturday night's kiss had been, but was warm and deep, like heat from a stone hearth when a fire has been burning in it all night long. When it was over, he stared into her face. The questions in his eyes made her nervous. *This may be the last time we kiss.*

"Good night, Phoebe," he said, turning to walk back home.

♎

Her father was still up, waiting.

"How was the date?" he asked. When she didn't look directly at him, he put down the book he'd been reading and stood up.

"Something happened in the park, something bad." She felt guilty for bringing this up now. Her father didn't deserve a crisis, but he needed to know everything. So she took a deep breath and explained, as calmly as she could, what had occurred.

"Did she suffer brain damage?" Phoebe heard the concern in his voice, but knew that he'd have other questions, too.

"No. And before you ask, she won't remember anything either. I could tell that what I was doing was permanent, like erasing parts of a blackboard. I didn't damage her brain, but the memories she had from before are gone forever." She didn't mention the darker thoughts she'd had about herself. He seemed to sense that she was holding something back, but didn't press.

"It'll be okay, kiddo. Do you think Caleb suspects anything?"

"I'm sure he does, but I think his feelings for me may blind him to..." She couldn't finish what she wanted to say and had to make fists with both hands to go on. "I think his feelings are blinding him to what a monster I am." Even with the pain, her voice broke, and she couldn't look at him.

"Phoebe, damn it, you're not a monster! You defended yourself, and protected me—and, by the way, you didn't really hurt her. That's not how a bad person acts."

He'd crossed the room to hug her tightly. "You'll see. Everything will work out." She put her head into his chest.

Maybe I should stay away from Caleb, she thought. *I love him.* She'd never said it before, even to herself, but knew it was true.

Her father let go and she closed her eyes, keeping very still, trying to calm down. There was an exercise she'd often used before— when she was much younger. It came to her almost unconsciously: *Three calming breaths, and release the last one slowly.* It had always helped, at least a little, but wasn't working tonight.

"Caleb and I are going sailing next weekend with your grandfather. It's an overnight trip. You're invited, too, but...well, no one really expects you to come. I'm sorry for taking him away so soon, but I should probably get to know him better—and sooner would be better than later. Do you mind?"

Phoebe forced a half smile, and shook her head again—still trying to decide about Caleb. But there was no need to make up her mind tonight.

"Let's see what happens Monday, after he thinks some more." She'd never felt this way about someone before and she was starting to have more sympathy for how Mary felt.

"Be good. And be careful this week," her father said. *Ugh! School,* she thought.

"Okay, I have a huge headache, and I'm really tired. I doubt I can sleep, but I'm going to try. Good night."

"Good night, Princess."

♎

Caleb headed toward the hospital slowly, needing more time to think. So many things had happened, and walking always helped. The stars were clear and bright tonight, even under the lights. He turned east, deciding to walk along the harbor. There were fewer lamps near the water, and he'd have more time. The enormity of the Milky Way spilled across the sky. Its sight had always affected him. His own problems seemed to shrink to insignificance when he imagined how many other people, or beings, might be out there looking up, each struggling with their own issues.

Chief among his worries was Mary: was she going to be okay? Then there was the ugly truth about her 'relationship' with Ian—what Phoebe had said was obviously true—it had all been so clear on Mary's face. He was fighting the urge to go find Ian now, but realized that, while beating Ian senseless would feel good, it wouldn't solve anything, and would only put poor Mary through more pain.

And what about Phoebe? The last thing Mary had said was 'What are you?' just before the episode hit her. *What did that mean?*

Caleb had been so proud of Phoebe tonight: so beautiful, intelligent, and mature, all at the same time. She'd been under pressure all night, but held her own. In just a little over a month Phoebe had become the most important part of his life, and he couldn't imagine not being with her. Still, there was always something that didn't quite make sense—inconsistencies in her personality that didn't fit. They added up to something…He knew that he needed to find out the truth. *But not tonight.*

"I'll worry about Mary this weekend," he said aloud. "One thing at a time." The lights of the hospital were in sight. The mystery of Phoebe would have to wait for next week.

CHAPTER 30

Suspicion

"**W**HAT ARE YOU LOOKING AT?**"** Her father glanced up, putting his notes away.

"Caleb's downstairs." She peered over her shoulder to see his reaction.

"Well, let him in."

Phoebe stopped by the bathroom mirror to check her hair before going downstairs. Her hand was on the ground-floor doorknob, when she stopped to take a breath. Outside, Caleb was leaning against the handrail at the top of the stoop, he looked up, and the fears from Saturday night seemed less important.

"Hey," he said.

"Hey yourself. Come on in. You can have coffee while I finish getting ready."

"Thanks, I'll pass—had tons of it already. I've been up a long time—couldn't sleep."

"Hmm, Mary?" she asked.

Caleb frowned. "Yeah. She's doing better, but still can't even remember going to the park—at least she feels better. Sorry I didn't come by yesterday, but I needed to spend time with her, and my Uncle John."

"What did you talk about?"

"Ian."

"Oh." People were walking by the building. Some long-time neighbors were staring at her. "I guess that wasn't very pleasant."

"Yeah. But I think she's coming around, at least about him. Whatever happened Saturday night really jolted her. It seems to have triggered something inside of her, at least about him." Phoebe looked away to hide her expression.

"I feel like such a bitch," she said as they climbed the stairs.

"Don't worry about it," Caleb said. They nearly bumped into her father as he was leaving the apartment.

"Phoebe not worry? That'll be the day," he said. "Hello, Caleb. It's good to see you again. Maybe you can convince her to get up a little earlier. I gave up years ago." Daniel smiled at her. "You do know you're late, right?"

"Yeah, I know. Is there any coffee left?"

"Of course. See you tonight. Caleb, you still up for this weekend?"

"You bet," he replied. Her father nodded and left.

"Make yourself comfortable," she said once they were inside the apartment. "I'll just be a minute."

A little later, she emerged from her room in her school uniform and spun in a circle. "How's this? Is it as good as what I was wearing Saturday?" she asked.

"On you, it's perfect," but his smile seemed forced. She looked down, frowning, and pretended to check that her shoes were tied.

"You ready?" he asked.

"Almost." Phoebe went to the kitchen and quickly drank a half cup of coffee. "Gotta get my fix—or else…" she explained.

They held hands all the way to school. She shut her senses off to avoid feeling the conflicting emotions coming from him. They'd probably draw looks from the others when they arrived, but she didn't care today.

The weather had turned cooler on Sunday. A front had moved through without raining, but left air behind that was almost crisp.

"Dad tells me you're going fishing with him next weekend."

"Yeah, sailing *and* fishing—what could be better? I think your dad wants to look me over some more. I hope he doesn't look too hard."

"Hmmm," Phoebe said. "It's more likely he'll be making sure I'm good enough for *you*." Caleb laughed and things between them seemed almost normal again. "Better take a heavy jacket. It gets mighty windy out there this time of year," she warned.

They walked the rest of the way without talking. It seemed like Caleb wanted to say something, but was having a hard time figuring out how to start. She wondered what to say if he asked the same questions as Saturday. They were almost to the school when he finally spoke.

"Phoebe."

"Uh-huh?"

"If you aren't busy this afternoon, I'd like us to hike up into the hills, maybe watch the sun set—assuming it stays clear." He wanted to say more—there was that hesitation in his voice. This wasn't a casual date. She fought the temptation to connect with him. *No!*

"Sure," she said. "No problem. I mean: that'd be great." She couldn't believe how casual her voice sounded, but was certain he'd noticed the pause. "Any reason?"

"We need to talk, and I don't want to be interrupted by...anyone. Are you sure you don't mind?"

"It's fine," she said, but a cold feeling of dread was running through her midsection.

They were on the school grounds before Phoebe let go of his hand. Some of the kids from their class were watching them, but she was only concerned about the mistresses.

"I'll see you in art class," he said. "I'm interested in what you've been working on lately."

"See ya." She'd be late if she didn't hurry.

Ω

During class, Phoebe managed to set aside her misgivings and focused on a sketch she'd wanted to do for weeks: a perspective from the cliff, just before she jumped. She'd also wanted to make a painting, hoping to infuse it with subtle elements that brought out how she'd felt that night.

"Beautiful!" Caleb said, looking over her shoulder. Grace was passing by and looked, too.

"He's right," she said, "but that's not going to get his drawing done, is it, Mr. Addison?" She winked at him, but also pointed at his chair. "Get to work, Caleb. Phoebe, what are you going to do with this? It looks done. Where is this from?"

"I dreamed about this place, a while back—guess it stuck in my head. I was thinking about a painting."

"But it's so dark. There isn't much color to play with. Are you imagining a full moon?"

"No, but there was color in my dream—you know how strange things can be when you're sleeping." Phoebe realized that she'd probably said too much.

Grace frowned, still trying to visualize what the painting would look like, but shook her head and shrugged. "Okay, it's your picture. If you have time, later, I'd like to show you something another student did. His technique reminds me of a drawing you did last year."

"Sure," Phoebe said, rethinking her decision to do the painting at school.

♎

Lunch with Caleb was exactly what she needed after the morning. But he wanted to hear more about the dream.

"Well, there was kind of a red light—a glow touching the waves when they broke on the rocks, and it was strong enough to make me cast a shadow. It was all kinda eerie. I'd like to show that creepy feeling, but now I'm starting to think it's a stupid idea."

"When did you dream this?"

"Uh…weeks ago. Remember when Sarah asked me to eat at your table?" she said, smiling. He nodded. "The night before."

"Wow, some memory!"

"I guess."

They talked about where to go after school. He had an idea but wanted to surprise her, and still wouldn't say what he wanted to talk about.

"Let's meet at my place. I'll change first," she said.

"Good idea. I'll stop by my house to pick up a few things first."

♎

At home, Phoebe undressed, trying not to think about why they were meeting. She was imagining what was going through his head. Where would their relationship go after today? She was finding it hard to see a good outcome. She didn't know what to do if it went really badly, and bit her lip, trying not to think about it. Caleb had a tendency to confront things he didn't understand, or which bothered him, and by now, he had more than enough reason to think there was something odd about her.

Maybe it would be better if we broke up today, she thought. *I'm too dangerous for him—and to his future. Mary was right: I'm not the best person for him.* If the Council were to find out what she was, then his career, and maybe even his life, would be at risk. *I love him, so I should do what's best for him.*

That thought had been in her mind since he'd walked her home Saturday night. But it brought up feelings of guilt. *Wouldn't I be doing the same thing Rebecca did to Dad?* "Crap!" she said aloud. "I don't know what to do."

Phoebe didn't know how to break things off without hurting him, and making him feel as though he'd been abandoned. *He should have a say in this.* The beginning of an idea was coming to her. *Maybe there's some way he can choose—but how?* She didn't know yet, but felt that, one way or another, he should be given a choice—he deserved that much.

Phoebe put on her hiking pants—the ones her grandfather had originally given her for sailing—and the long-sleeved blouse that went with them. They were both made of waxed canvas, durable material to survive if she tripped, and water-resistant in case it rained. She grabbed a light jacket and put on the boots her father bought last summer, and was ready—physically.

Caleb mentioned they'd be going into the northern hills—the same general area as in the dream. She wondered if everything still looked the same as it had back when Rebecca jumped. Before leaving the house, she left a note for her father, telling him where she would be, and with whom.

Caleb had a small pack that he used on weekends slung over one shoulder. It had a strap to go across his chest, so that his hands would be free for climbing. They set out north, and were out of town, climbing, in less than an hour.

The first slopes weren't all that steep, but the trail constantly climbed, just like in the dream. It followed the contours of the mountain, going east, out along the peninsula. Before long Phoebe was breathing heavily, yet it looked as though Caleb was just out for an afternoon stroll around town. He didn't seem to notice the slope at all, but slowed to accommodate her. They held hands when possible, and stopped for a rest halfway up the hill.

"How are you doing?" he asked.

"Great!" she said, panting. He turned his head to hide a grin. "Okay. So I'm not an athlete, big shot!"

Caleb shook his head, still smiling. "As disciplined as you are, you could be world class in no time."

What the hell was that supposed to mean? she wondered. It was getting harder to *not* probe his mind.

The town looked small from out here, halfway along the peninsula. Tiny people were walking along the waterfront—men and women with ordinary problems. It was an oddly comforting thought for her. Caleb pointed out places he recognized. They could even tell where the park was by where the tall trees grew, but neither mentioned it. He showed her places across the harbor, on the southern cliffs. They looked much more dangerous than where they were, but that's where he liked to go, and he traced a few of the faces he'd scaled in the past. They couldn't see much at this distance, but even from here, she could tell how hard it would be to climb.

"Why do you do that?" she asked. "Why take so many risks?"

"I'm not sure how to tell you in just a few words. I suppose I do it for the challenge, but there's more to it than that. I feel driven to compete against…against…me, I guess. It's almost like I *have* to do it—I have to push myself so I can get stronger and better. Every time I go out I have a new goal. I want to be able to climb something I wouldn't have even thought of trying just a year before. You have to work hard to get ready, to make yourself strong enough, until you're *almost* sure you *can* do it. But when you finally make it, you feel wonderful.

"Making a new ascent is like doing anything else that's worthwhile—drawing, painting, whatever. You have to think and plan and practice. But there's a more important element, too—you have to actually *do something*, not just talk about it. You need to take risks, but they're calculated risks, and it's up to you to prepare. If you succeed, or even if you fail, there's no one else to blame. There's nothing quite like it. And then you get to do it all over again next time!"

Phoebe compared Caleb to other people she'd touched before— there'd been thousands of them, but he was unique. She was proud that he wanted to be with her. Caleb was creating his own path in life; he wasn't just a passive observer. And when he chose that path, it was the difficult one, precisely because it *was* difficult. She wished she could somehow capture that spirit in a drawing or painting, but realized she didn't need to. He already was that work of art—a living one at that, and the artist, as well. *The self-rendered person, what a beautiful concept.*

"Shall we go on?" he asked. Phoebe nodded. The rest of the climb was much steeper, but eventually they made it to the top.

The view was spectacular, exactly as she remembered. They were on the very same shelf from her dream, overlooking the sea. She recognized the rock formations.

"It's the same place, isn't it?" Caleb asked. His face had become hard to read now, and his eyes held a detached look—the look of a stranger.

"The same place?" she asked.

"Your drawing. I thought it looked familiar, but I heard you tell Grace that it was from a dream." Phoebe nodded, speechless.

His choice.

"Have you ever actually been here before?" he asked.

"Not really. I walked partway up with my dad, and I knew where the trail went—he'd told me. But we never came up all the way. I was too young and..." She didn't finish. Phoebe might have lied now, but she'd decided not to do that anymore. She knew now why her father had never finished the hike. This is where he thought Rebecca had died.

"I don't see how you do it. How can someone draw this place so accurately when they've never been here? Look at that shoulder of rock, and the shoals. The perspective here is pretty unique, and yet you drew it perfectly. Phoebe, I don't understand you sometimes." She couldn't speak, and her knees had started to shake. Caleb must have seen something in her expression because he took her hand and looked into her eyes—a gentle look.

This is it, she thought, trying to decide what to say, and how to say it. A faint chill, like the last time she was here, threatened to erupt from her core. There was just a twinge of ice forming in her stomach now—the monster was waking up. *Never!* she thought, pushing back on that part of herself. *Not ever!* Phoebe closed her eyes, struggling hard to regain control.

"I don't know what you're hiding, or who you're protecting. I could take a guess but, honestly, I don't want to. A lot of things about you don't seem to add up. It's an understatement, but you're probably the smartest person I've ever known, and yet you pretend to be slow most of the time. Why? How did you know so much about Mary, you'd only met her a few times?"

"Caleb." She paused. "I'm protecting more than just myself."

"I would never deliberately do anything to hurt you." The intensity in his eyes and the certainty in his voice helped, but she'd reached an impasse. "What are you hiding from me?" Her legs had become too weak to stand, so she sank to her knees, still struggling about what to say. Finally, she gave up.

"I'm a freak!" she said. "A leftover, a mistake left behind by the Order. I'm not sure what I'm supposed to be or what I'm supposed to do, but I'm *definitely* not normal, and probably not even completely human."

"Come on, Phoebe, you're not a freak, and you seem pretty human to me. I don't care about the Order, or any of that other stuff. I just need to know more about the girl I love." His face had turned pink.

Wow! Phoebe thought, clenching one hand into a tight fist until she felt the pain and wetness, doing everything she could to keep from crying. She couldn't talk. He knelt down and put both arms around her, and she held onto him, too, with all her strength. "I love you," she said.

"The Order, huh? I can only imagine what that must be like— constantly being afraid." She nodded, the top of her head rubbed against his chest.

"I have to tell you everything. And you may not want to be around me afterward, but I can't be with you unless you know exactly what you're getting into. If you decide—afterward—not to see me, I'll understand—I'm not sure how *I'd* react."

"What are you talking about? Does it have anything to do with what happened to Mary?"

"Yeah, that, too, but there's more to it."

"All right, I'm listening, but nothing you say is going to change anything for me."

"We'll see." Phoebe found a rock to sit on, thinking that they might be there a while. Caleb sat cross-legged on the ground in front of her.

CHAPTER 31

Confession

"I'M NOT SURE WHERE TO start," Phoebe said.

Caleb shrugged.

"Okay," she continued. "I was born almost as the comet hit. My mother was with the Order, and already in hiding at the time. The Purge had gotten very violent, so she left me with my dad, promising to return when things got better."

"Even though he wasn't really your father," Caleb added.

"He's real enough. I have no idea who my *biological* father was, and to be honest, I doubt my mother knew for sure." Caleb was trying not to react, but she saw confusion in his eyes.

"My mother came from the notorious genetic engineering programs. It's not exactly romantic when some scientist decides which genes to mix. I learned that they did other things to us while we were still in the womb, but I don't understand it yet. My mom and me, both started out that way. At least that's what my dad says. The point is that my conception and birth weren't any more normal than I am, and—for all I know—I may even have had more than one father. The important part is how it affected me." Phoebe took a deep breath before going on. "I'm a very strange girl, Caleb," she said, staring into his eyes. She was waiting for signs of alarm, but then he *was* a fairly tough guy—it would take a little more to make him scream.

"How did it affect you?" he asked.

"Remember when I told you I was homeschooled, and that I had a problem?" Caleb nodded. "Well the problem never did go away, I just got a little stronger—strong enough to hide most of the signs, anyway."

"What problems do you mean? What's the matter with you?"

"I hear things…No. That's not the best way to tell it. Let me start a different way. I'm what the Order used to call a Sensitive. When I look at the world through my eyes, I see things pretty much the same way everyone else does, maybe a little better, but more or less the same. An important difference is that I have a second way of seeing the world, and it doesn't depend on the normal senses. I have this other sense, a sense for life."

"What does that mean? What do you see?"

"If I close my eyes, the physical world around me gets dark, just as it does for you. But I see more than just the darkness. I see the sparks of life all around me. Everyone has a spark, and each one is different. When I reach out to touch a spark, mentally, I'm really touching someone's mind. I told you that every spark is different, unique. For me, that spark is how I really know someone. Each one feels different, and I associate that feeling with a person. I can even find them in a crowd, assuming that I've touched that person this way before."

"What does it feel like, what would you compare it with?"

"It's a lot like a flavor…I don't know how else to explain it to you in terms that make sense. Everyone's mental flavor is unmistakable, and it never changes—ever. For me, this aspect of a person is far more intense than, say, how they look, or what their voice sounds like. It's the very essence of who they are, and it can't be masked, altered, or hidden."

"Weird. Not you! Just the concept," he said. "Is there more to it?"

"Oh yeah—lots more. When I just touch the surface of a person—let's say to sample their flavor—I'm really touching their thoughts and emotions. Even without going further than that, I can tell if that person is having a good day or a bad day. Sometimes I absorb their feelings, too, and it can make me feel warm and comfortable, or terrible—even painful." She looked at him again, to see how he was managing everything. His smile was gone, but it didn't look like he was going to panic just yet.

"Okay, here's where it gets really strange," she said, smiling. "If I open my mind up a little, I receive that person's thoughts. People unconsciously broadcast what they think, and I hear it. But it doesn't stop there."

"You read minds?" Caleb frowned, but he still looked okay.

"Uh, kind of—yeah." She decided to take a slightly different tack. "People put thoughts out in the air, I just pick them up, I'm a thought receiver—a very sensitive one. But let's reverse this a little. Imagine that instead of being a passive receiver of your thoughts, I actively seek to find out more about you. That would be more like my entering someone's mind rather than just sitting outside, listening. It'll be a little easier to explain the rest this way."

"Okaaay," he said, shifting.

"Once I enter into a person, it's like swimming in a pool or the ocean. There are layers to consciousness. I can swim just on the surface and hear what they're thinking, or I can go underwater to connect with them more fully. Just below the surface is where the senses feed your mind, the five senses: vision, hearing, taste, and so forth. If I go just a little below the surface I can share what these senses are providing, but I can also dive even deeper. The next layer holds the memories that a person can easily access, people you've met, things you've experienced and can remember. But that's not where it ends," she said. "Are you still okay?" she asked.

"I'm fine. Don't you already know?"

Phoebe grinned at him. "I'll tell you in a little while.

"Anyway, beyond the ordinary memories things get *really* weird. The deepest parts of a person's mind hold echoes of events that they don't remember, but they're available to me, since I see everything. But my deep diving expedition can go farther than that, too. At the limits of my journey, I almost become the person I'm sensing. In the past I'd sometimes lose myself inside of someone, and I couldn't get out.

"Joining with someone can be pleasant or painful, but this ability—or curse—is so tightly wound inside of me that it's part of who and what I am. It's what I was made to do." Caleb hadn't moved for a while, and she desperately wanted to touch him, to know what he was thinking, but bit her lip and held back.

"What was different when you were younger?"

"Well, when I was little, I didn't have very much control over these senses—actually, none. I connected with people all the time, at random, and without meaning to. Half the time, I didn't know who I was, or if the things I was experiencing were coming from my own regular senses, or someone else's.

"Sleep always terrified me. I'd leave my body and wander around the neighborhood, pulled to the brightest sparks, and the strongest feelings. Unfortunately these often come from people who are going through unpleasant things: nightmares, or horrible real experiences. I've been beaten, drowned, abandoned, and…" Phoebe stopped for a moment to take a deep breath. "Other things." She let the breath out, and wiped her eyes.

"You said it used to be like that," Caleb noted. "How did it change?"

"I got stronger, older, and then I started learning how to block other thoughts out. But it's only been recently that I've managed to stop everything completely." She smiled at Caleb.

"Recently?"

"I don't know how, exactly, but you helped."

"Are my thoughts that bad?"

Phoebe laughed and touched a hand to his face. "No, silly, I stopped worrying about it. I stopped trying to block the whole world out and, instead, I started worrying more about you. You did that, and you can't imagine how much it changed me."

"What about Mary?"

Phoebe stopped smiling and bit her lip. She had to tell him everything.

His choice.

"I knew Mary didn't like me, even more than she let on. But that wouldn't have mattered. The real problem was that she was threatening to have Ian dig into my past—and into my father's past. I couldn't let her do that."

"What did you do?" he asked.

"Well, these senses I have work both ways—when I want them to. I can go inside of someone, and read about who they are, but I can also *write* things into their minds, too. What I did to Mary was actually pretty hard to do. I told you I can 'see' everything someone remembers, right?" Phoebe saw Caleb nod. "Well, I learned I can also take those memories away, too, and even erase specific ones. That's what I did to Mary. I only took selected memories from her. That was the first time I ever tried to do that, and it took a lot out of me. I almost fainted in the park.

"I was scared. I love my dad, and I could never let anyone hurt him. It's true, I was mad enough to do almost anything that night, but I promise that I did my absolute best to be gentle with her, and I didn't damage her brain."

Caleb's mouth was a tight line as he thought everything through. Phoebe waited, terrified of what he might think of her.

"I'll understand if you want to stay away from me," she said. "It could be dangerous for you to be near me. But no matter what you decide, please-please don't say anything—I could never hurt you." The tears had started flowing while she talked, but she ignored them.

"So, can you hear what I'm thinking now?" Caleb asked.

"If I want to," she admitted. "If I allow it. But I don't listen to you. Or, to be honest, I've only listened to you a couple of times, and just the bits near the surface. I didn't want to intrude. But I know what you feel like. That flavor I talked about earlier is how I found you when your grandmother was in the hospital. I was so worried when you weren't in school that week." Caleb's face changed at the reminder of his recent loss. "I found you that Friday and then pressured Dad into finding a way for me to be in the hospital. He wasn't happy about it, but he agreed to help." His eyes were softer now.

"I can't imagine what you've been through," he said, standing and stretching his hand out toward her. Phoebe hesitated.

"You're not really listening. It's probably not a good idea to be around me. I'm not one hundred percent sure of what might happen. Sometimes I wonder what I might have become if someone besides my dad had raised me. I won't ever deliberately harm you, but I've just glimpsed what can happen when I panic, and it scared me. After Saturday, I started to think that the Council was right in calling us demons—and I still have doubts about myself. But just being whatever it is that I am . . . I don't think that makes me a monster. Believe me, I know. There are plenty of real monsters walking around out there in the world. They *look* respectable, but can't hide who they are from me. Real monsters hurt people for pleasure, or for no reason at all—they're just not as well armed as I am.

"I feel horrible about what I had to do to Mary, but you should know that if someone were to threaten a person I love, I *would* protect them. If possible, I'll be gentle, but I have my priorities." Caleb was grinning, and so she reached out to meet his hand, and let him pull her up for a kiss.

"I guess I can't complain," he said, "I'm one of the protected ones now." Phoebe laughed. The sense of relief and happiness was beyond anything she'd felt before.

"Okay, there's one good thing about being with a demon," she said. Caleb winced at the word, but she laughed again. Nothing could bring her down now. "Think something *at* me." Caleb frowned, shaking his head. "Pretend you want to tell me something, but don't vocalize it, just think it at me, but think hard—louder than normal. Imagine that you want to think hard enough so that I hear you. You can look at me if it helps, but you don't need to."

What should I say? he thought.

Anything you like. Caleb jumped when he heard her voice in his mind.

"But you said you weren't listening to me."

"I'm not, and I don't. I choose not to listen to you, and everyone for that matter. I keep a kind of protection up around my mind— it's like a wall. The wall doesn't normally let other thoughts through, but remember, I don't choose to listen—I choose to *not* listen. It takes an effort on my part to keep the thoughts out, and no effort at all to hear them. When you think *at* me, it's as if you are yelling louder than the wall I created was designed to stop. I leave the barrier a little thin, and easier to penetrate, at least for thoughts from certain sparks I love." She grinned at him. "I want people who are special to me to be able to get my attention. Until today only one other person had that privilege."

"But I heard you, too," he pointed out.

"I told you, this thing works both ways. I can put thoughts into your head, not just erase them. Putting things in is a *lot* easier than wiping them out. Remember? Freak," she said, raising her free hand. "But I try to be a good freak."

Caleb laughed at her and had trouble stopping. "Okay, okay," he said at last. "How far away can we talk this way?"

"I'm not sure," she said, vaguely. "I don't know my absolute range yet, maybe someday I'll know for sure." She didn't tell him about the long distance exchange with her mother. No one else knew that Becky was still alive.

"Wow! Or should I say..." *Wow!*

"It's useful if you really need to tell me something or to get my attention, but I prefer to use more traditional methods of communication. It's good discipline and, to be honest, it makes me feel a little more normal. If I could get rid of these extra features, I would."

Caleb heard sadness in her voice and hugged her more tightly. "You seem normal enough to me, but I wouldn't bring that drawing of yours to school again," he added.

"Okay," she said.

"Let's go back," he said. "It'll be dark before long." The sun was almost touching the mountains to the southwest. Phoebe wondered if it would take as long going down the hill as it had coming up.

"Crap!" she said. "I forgot to think of something to feed Dad. And I'm late."

The trip back downhill was much easier. Just before they reached the edge of town, Caleb pulled her to a stop.

"There's something I really wanted to do today." He leaned toward her, slowly, allowing her time to adjust, and they kissed. Phoebe wasn't sure how long it lasted, but she was careful not to let the intensity of what she was feeling go into him.

"I'm glad you remembered," she said breathlessly.

They walked back to her home holding hands. Caleb left her at the foot of the stairs with just a brief good-night kiss.

"I'll see you tomorrow," he promised.

"Have a good night," she said.

Phoebe climbed to the apartment, hardly feeling the steps now. Daniel had come home, found her note, and gone to a hot-table vendor, a business that offered freshly cooked foods by weight.

"Thanks," she said.

"So, tell me. Should we be packing to run?" but he was smiling—Phoebe's mood was easy to read tonight.

She told him everything that happened, minus the kissing.

"I knew this day would come eventually. But now I think it's even more important that I spend Saturday and Sunday with him. Not that I don't trust your judgment, Phoebe. I do."

After eating, she excused herself early and went to bed.

"Good night, Princess."

"Good night, Dad."

CHAPTER 32

Tea Party

A SECOND, MORE SEVERE FRONT MOVED in overnight. Phoebe could hear the wind gusting as it rattled her window. Later, heavy rain hammering the side of the building woke her up.

Caleb was outside again, sitting on the steps, waiting. She raised an eyebrow under the raincoat's hood, and wondered if this was going to be a new habit—he laughed at her.

"I was up early," he explained, "but got tired of waiting around the house. Don't worry," he added, "I'm not the clingy type," he sighed, "hanging around, and hoping for a kiss." Phoebe rolled her eyes and kissed him anyway. It wasn't one of her best, but she meant it. "I'd like to try something…a little later, but I didn't want to surprise you."

"What did you have in mind?" she asked, grinning.

"Well, I don't want to violate your rules or anything, but I thought we could try connecting once or twice during school. Would that be all right? Or is it too distracting? This is all pretty new to me, but it's nice to know that we can be together anytime we want." Phoebe nodded.

$$\Omega$$

It turned out that sharing thoughts was a pleasant way to break up the day. For Phoebe, it was a relief to finally be able to touch him this way, and to know that he was aware of her. She didn't want to overdo it—and certainly not at school—but this kind of closeness was something she'd always dreamed about. The first time it happened was during history.

Phoebe?

Hey, what class are you in?

Math. I really liked that sketch of the kids playing. Were there really that many of them?

Uh-huh, an even dozen.

Damn!

What? There was a delay before he answered.

She noticed I wasn't paying attention and asked a question. Sorry.

Caleb had family obligations during the afternoon, so Phoebe walked home alone—it was still raining.

Her father came home early, and was in a good mood. They played chess after dinner. He was a good player, and usually beat her these days. His overall record had improved quite a bit after she'd stopped cheating.

It was too wet to go out after the match, but that didn't keep her from reaching out to Caleb.

Hey, what are you up to?

Family stuff, how 'bout you?

I'm at home, hanging out—you know.

Dad and I have been with Mary ever since I got home. We've been pretty blunt with her about Ian, now that she's feeling better. It's been an emotional evening—she's upset. Sorry, I need to concentrate. Do you mind?

No, no. Go.

Afterward, she and her father played another game—and he beat her again. She was distracted thinking about Caleb and Mary, and told him that the last game shouldn't count. They'd been keeping a tally of wins and losses since they first started playing, although her father had wanted to reset everything after she stopped peeking in his head, but she didn't agree.

"What's a grown man doing playing hard against a kid anyway?" she'd asked him at the time, so they left the record as it was.

Late that night Caleb called to her again. She'd already gone to bed, but was still awake.

Phoebe, you still up?

Zzzzzzzz.

Huh?

I was pretending to be asleep.

Oh.

How did it go with Mary?

Okay, sort of. Well, not so much. She still has to work through everything herself, but for now I think she mostly needs to be around us—people she trusts.

Phoebe paused, thinking about something she'd been wanting to try, ever since the dream.

Caleb?

Yeah?

Would you like to see something?

Uh...see? What do you mean?

Now don't get crazy on me—words aren't the only thing I can put into your head, but I don't want to scare you.

Really? What else can you do?

Get ready. It would be better if you got into bed, so you don't fall down. Are you there? she asked. He paused a few moments.

Okay. I'm ready.

Phoebe entered his mind, just below the surface, and deliberately ignored anything that might be private, while also refraining from looking through his eyes. Then she gave him an experience, something from a memory.

♎

Caleb was standing at the precipice. He could hear the waves breaking against the cliff walls below, and feel their rumble through his feet. He turned and saw a canopy of clouds glowing red over the Land. The damp wind was behind him now, but all he could look at were the pillars of smoke and the fires. They filled the valley, and were even visible, rising up beyond the first ring of mountains in the distance. The town lay across the water from him. This was how he'd always imagined a besieged city would look, surrounded by fire and desolation.

♎

Phoebe wanted him to know what it had been like. She suppressed some of the more unpleasant things from that night, the odor of the fish, and the mob. This was a night of firsts for her: the first time she'd ever created a full world for someone else, and allowed that person the freedom to choose what to do; and it was the first time she'd ever tried to alter a memory from the past. It was much harder to do than she'd thought it would be.

She put Caleb into Rebecca's experience, changing it just enough to make him feel safe. Phoebe wondered how far she could take this new art form, imagining the new worlds she would create some day. As time passed, she added new things to the experience, creating textures on the surfaces of the rocks, and unusual sounds from wind blowing over the edges of the cliff.

Do you see it? Do you feel it? Do you hear it? she asked, feeling almost as excited as he did.

Holy crap! This is incredible! So...so beautiful. It's real and surreal at the same time. Was this your dream? It's like I'm there.

Uh-huh.

I love it!

Hmmm. Well, this is the nicer part of that particular dream. Someday, I'll tell you about the rest.

She shut the stream off to avoid accidentally letting some of the bad things through. The effort had made her tired, more than expected. In fact, ever since she'd felt the strong burst of energy that first time, she'd felt more tired. *It's probably the stress,* she thought.

Good night, Caleb. I love you.

Good night, Phoebe. Love you, too.

Ω

Wednesday, and Caleb was in front of her building again. He'd brought an umbrella this time. She was happy to see him, of course, but worried that he might start feeling that meeting her was a chore. His eyes didn't look right today—troubled—he was frowning. He didn't say what was on his mind until they were halfway to school.

"I've…actually, we've had some pretty intense sessions with Mary these past couple days. She was crying most of last night, again. I hope we aren't being too tough on her. Dad had a talk with Ian, and that didn't go well at all."

Phoebe felt sorry for Mary, but wondered what this had to do with her.

"We've been working pretty hard to make sure she won't try to get back together with him. She's been a little insane ever since seeing that jerk. You can imagine how embarrassed she is—especially since he's being such a jackass, even bragging to his friends."

I'd crawl into a hole and never come out, Phoebe thought.

"Mary's finally seeing him for what he is, and herself, too. She realizes now how much she changed. Believe me, Phoebe, you've never met the real Mary." Caleb wasn't looking directly at her, but had glanced her way from the corner of his eye now and then. "She's been a big help over the years—always there when Dad was brooding over Mom. There was a pretty dark period in our lives after Mom died—it went on for years. Anyway, I mentioned you to her, and how she'd been treating you. Maybe I should have kept my mouth shut, but sometimes I can't help myself. I left out the details from Saturday night, but she's almost as embarrassed by her behavior as she is about Ian."

Suspicious now, Phoebe was waiting for him to get to the point.

"It's hard having the two people closest to me unable to be around each other, but you don't have to do this if you don't want to."

"Do what?" Phoebe asked, a sick feeling churning in her stomach, but her sigh was silent, to encourage him.

"If you don't mind too much, would you be willing to meet us at Owen's Tavern today—for tea? Say around four o'clock? It's just north of the hospital."

She could tell how hard this was for him. "Of course, I'll go home first to change out of my lovely uniform, if you don't mind. I may be a few minutes late." Caleb hugged her, and that made the prospect of tea with Mary worth it—almost.

♎

After school, Phoebe changed into a casual but nice dress. The weather was cool and it was still raining, so she took her raincoat. It was coming down harder now. *Better take the trolley,* she thought.

She got off near the hospital and, after a two-block walk, arrived at Owen's Tavern. Although cloudy outside, the sky was much brighter than the lighting inside. It was hard to see at first, but as her eyes adapted, the room gradually took shape.

A long wooden bar ran the entire length of the room on the right; its surface gleamed, as though recently polished, reflecting light from oil lamps suspended from the ceiling. The bar curved around and met the wall near the entrance. The tavern was mostly empty—it was too early for the drinking crowd.

A man was washing glasses and hanging them upside down from wooden racks over the bar. There were many different types and Phoebe tried to guess which one was used for which drink.

Tables filled up most of the room. The small square ones were scattered in the middle, with larger tables against the walls. The largest one was along the back wall, where a group of old men had gathered. They seemed to be permanent fixtures, a part of the tavern.

Halfway across the room, an arm was waving back and forth—probably for her. As she drew closer to the arm, Caleb's face appeared under it, and some of her nervousness faded. Then she saw Mary. Once at the table, she stood uncomfortably behind one of the unused chairs, wondering how to start.

"Please sit," Mary said. The timid smile she was trying to offer contrasted with her eyes, but before Phoebe could slide a chair back, Caleb jumped up to help.

"Thank you," she said, softly touching the back of his arm, which radiated nervousness through her fingers.

Two half-empty cups were on the table, along with a pot of tea. There was also a plate of pastries, but none were missing. A hostess approached and asked what she wanted to drink, and she requested another cup. When it arrived, Mary poured for her.

"How have you been, Phoebe?"

"Well, thank you. And you?" Phoebe answered stiffly, trying to dredge up something interesting to say.

"Well, thank you," Mary echoed.

"Guys," Caleb began, "I thought it was important we get together. I think you two may have gotten off on the wrong foot."

No kidding! Phoebe thought, drinking the tea, just to be doing something. A long silence followed. She loved Caleb, and was willing to do almost anything for him, but pretending enthusiasm when she didn't feel it wasn't her strong suit. Finally, Mary said something.

"Phoebe, I'm sorry I was such a bitch before. There's really no excuse. I still don't remember what happened in the park, but I can guess. I wasn't very fair to you in the past. Ian and I..." She stopped and looked down. It was almost a minute before she continued. "Well, I guess I knew there was something not right about us. And pretending really changed my perspective on what was important," she said, still looking down. She could feel Mary fighting to hold her emotions back, but she started sobbing anyway, and then put her face onto her arms. Phoebe couldn't stop herself. She shifted the chair over and put an arm around Mary's shoulders. Caleb's face didn't look any better—he was frozen in place, staring through the table. The past days had obviously been hard on both of them.

"Don't worry," she said. "Let's forget everything and start over, okay?"

Mary looked up, her eyes red and her breathing uneven, but she almost managed to smile and even put one hand on top of Phoebe's.

"I know how Caleb feels about you and, God, you must feel the same way about him, or why in the world would you have come today?" Mary took a few moments before going on. "He's always been more like a brother than a cousin, and I *really* want him to be happy." This was not the same Mary she'd met in the hospital.

"How about some more tea?" she asked. Mary tried smiling again, and pushed her cup forward.

The three of them spent the next hour talking. Mary almost seemed to forget her problems for a while, and even laughed, as she entertained Phoebe with stories about Caleb as a young boy. They talked about the difficult times Caleb had gone through with his father—back when they were young. Although they hadn't understood everything at the time, she and Caleb recognized his father's pain. They had both helped him through the grieving and the bouts of depression, just by being around and acting as though everything was normal. Dr. Addison had always managed to hide how much he was suffering from the other doctors at work, and even from his own brother. But the children saw him when he didn't know he was being watched.

Phoebe understood now why Caleb felt the way he did about Mary. She might never be best buddies with her, but at least, for now, they weren't enemies. Over time, they might even become friends.

Phoebe stayed until it was past time to start dinner. "Mary," she offered, "you should come with us some weekend. We could try some of the crazy things Caleb likes to do—dangerous, and probably sweaty, too. Who knows, it might actually be, almost…Well, I was going to say fun, but let's be realistic."

Mary grinned at her. "That would be great. I know he'd make sure we were safe—and take it easy on us," she added, giving him a fierce look. They all laughed. Phoebe left the tavern by herself, so that Caleb could walk Mary home.

Ω

The next day she arranged to meet Caleb at the halfway point to school so they could walk together a little.

"How's Mary?" she asked.

"Better. She really appreciated you coming yesterday, but it's going to be a while before she gets over him."

"Where is Mary?"

"She's at home, too embarrassed to leave the house alone. Ian isn't exactly being a gentleman, and that makes everything harder. My dad's trying to talk her into going out of town to study, maybe at the University in Central City, or one of the schools in the south. She doesn't seem to want to do anything."

Phoebe tried to put herself in Mary's position. *I'd definitely leave. Caleb's dad is right: she should go somewhere else—at least for a while.* There were schools other than Central City University in the Land. The southern ports had large populations, and there was an important school in the colonies.

"What she needs is to start over," she said. "But she needs you guys, too—that makes it hard to decide."

Caleb nodded.

They were close to the school now, and only a few students were outside, since it was continuing to drizzle.

Phoebe gave him a quick kiss. "See ya in art."

♎

The weather cleared Friday night, and Saturday looked promising, although the wind would probably still be blowing hard. The trip was on. *Great! I can't go, not unless I want him to see me throwing up all day.* She grimaced. *He'll probably decide I really am a demon.* There was no way she was going to risk that much reality this early in their relationship, so she'd sit this one out. Saturday dawned clear and warm. There was enough wind to really make sailing interesting. 'Interesting sailing' wasn't for her—it would make her seasickness worse, but her dad loved it.

Caleb came over for breakfast, and he'd brought pastries—a few even had chocolate! Her hands were full when he entered, but she watched the platter to make sure they didn't eat hers.

They both kissed her before leaving to meet her grandfather at the boat. Caleb's was just a peck on the cheek, but she didn't want to complain and embarrass him. She waved them off, and, later, took a walk around the harbor, before going to the market. Their cupboard had been looking pretty bare lately.

CHAPTER 33

Followed

REBECCA AND GABRIEL WERE FOLLOWING a game trail northeast through a valley that paralleled the third and fourth ridges of the Ring Mountains. They planned to meet the Scouts from North Star Sanctuary at the Sisters' Eyes. The plan was for Rebecca to stay at the watch house while most of the Scouts went into town to retrieve Phoebe and Daniel. Before that, she'd be given three days to get them ready to leave.

They'd been traveling for three days, and moving as fast as Rebecca could manage. The evening was drawing near, but they planned to keep going for several more hours, walking in single file along the path. A front had been rolling in all day, and the ceiling of clouds had gradually dropped and changed from wispy cirrus to dark cumulonimbus—cloud formations associated with storms. The wind swirled around the hills and through the valley, and a biting chill was penetrating their clothing. The trees were swaying back and forth, but they both were anxious to put as many kilometers behind them as possible, afraid of being too late. A little after dark it began to rain.

A sense of dread had been growing inside of Rebecca all day, something was terribly wrong. She began to sense the presence of others nearby. Rather than trying to yell over the wind, she sped up to touch Gabriel on the sleeve.

"There are others in the valley—looking for us."

The Scout was instantly alert, and scanned the terrain, looking for any sign of movement. He put his mouth near her ear, "Do you have a sense of where they are, and how many?"

She closed her eyes and tilted her head, first one way and then another. Gabriel stood very still, trying not to distract her.

"There are twelve people—I sense twelve minds. There!" she said, pointing to the west. "I think they're between four and five kilometers away, and getting closer. I don't recognize any of them, but they're Keepers. I could probe more deeply now, but that'll take time, and they'll keep getting closer."

Gabriel nodded and changed their direction, heading more to the east, and angling toward a large hill in the distance. It looked as though the trees and shrubs were denser in this direction. If necessary, they would provide a tactical advantage. He pointed where to walk and followed behind, unslinging his weapon to check its action.

It was an ancient large-caliber rifle—a short-barreled carbine, sometimes referred to as a Guide Gun, and it had been in his family for generations. The weapon was designed for medium-range targets and large game. It was loud, but an effective killing tool.

This direction offered better cover, but that also meant they'd be moving more slowly. The increased vegetation would also make it harder to hide their trail, but at least the Keepers wouldn't be able to see them from a distance.

Rebecca kept track of the others as she walked. Their distance was constant now. She couldn't connect deeply without stumbling, but still managed to form little connections now and then to learn more. It was easy to keep track of their sparks. A sinking feeling came over her when she realized that one of their pursuers was a Sensitive. Rebecca was sure that she hadn't detected them directly yet, but her presence increased their danger significantly—it would only be a matter of time before she and Gabriel were within her range.

The timing is too perfect, she thought, and sensed that Gabriel was thinking along these same lines, too. Who had betrayed them?

"There's a Sensitive with them," she said. "A woman—it always is."

"Why?"

"The active ability is a sex-linked gene. If they get too close or catch us, you'll have to kill her in order to get away. She's not as sensitive as I am—probably stage two or, more likely, the natural offspring of a Sensitive. The abilities fade after a generation or two. I doubt her range will be more than a few hundred meters, but we won't be able to hide and hope that they pass us by."

He gave her a dark look. "We aren't caught yet, Becky," he reminded her. "Let's drop some weight and step up the pace." They paused to transfer food from Rebecca's pack to his, and hid their spare clothing and other nonessentials just off the trail. Gabriel marked the spot with several narrow cuts on the north side of a tree. Unless someone knew to look, their things would be difficult to find. "Now we can go faster."

They moved through the brush, alternating between a fast walk and slow jog. Rebecca had always been athletic, and had kept in reasonable condition, but she hadn't trained hard for a long time. They kept on moving throughout the night. The increased pace opened up the distance from their pursuers, but the Keepers followed them, even in the dark.

"One of them is skilled at tracking, and they have something to help them see in the dark," she told him.

Gabriel changed direction several times, trying to see if he could make them miss a turn. It worked—at least for a while.

She watched the Keepers' sparks move farther away from them, still traveling along the direction they'd been heading before, but she was getting very tired. The detour to escape was also taking them farther away from their destination.

Gabriel didn't seem tired at all. It looked as though he might be able to keep going for days, but they both knew that she couldn't. He stopped and took something from a pouch at his waist, handing her a water skin and two pills.

"Take these," he ordered. "They'll keep you awake and give you an energy boost."

"Amphetamines?"

"Some, but the main drug blocks chemicals in the brain that make you sleepy and fool your brain into thinking you've just slept. I didn't want to use this yet, but I had a suspicion we'd need them this trip. Don't worry, I have plenty."

Rebecca swallowed the drug and within minutes was no longer as tired as before. Since they had already stopped, Gabriel indicated that they should eat, too. He handed her traveling rations, an energy-dense food he made himself, and then started walking. The pace quickened again.

Some of the Keepers were getting closer—maybe six. Gabriel guessed that they'd split up into two teams, each taking parallel paths, and hoping to squeeze them in the middle. This was a tactic taught by the Guard to counter a weaving target, and it's what he would have done in their place.

The pursuers were also moving fast. Rebecca sensed that they were young and well trained. *Even the Sensitive,* she thought. *She's very young, an older teen.* Her throat tightened when she thought about what they would probably have to do. *The girl wasn't engineered—she's the daughter of a captured Sensitive, about Phoebe's age.*

Rebecca was able to shield her mind from the young sensitive, although not her presence. But the Scout was totally defenseless. If he were captured, or if he even got too close to the girl, she'd learn about Phoebe. As difficult as it was to ponder, she'd have to be killed.

♎

They half ran, half walked through the night, and then a good part of the next day. It was still raining, but beginning to slow, as was Rebecca. Her strength was fading again. The Keepers were outpacing them, so she made a decision.

Rebecca stopped to let Gabriel catch up, and then touched his arm, as she had before. "They'll catch us," she said. "I'm not strong enough to get away, but you are."

"I'm not leaving you," he said with a voice like iron. She closed both eyes briefly and wiped her face to mask the tears that were forming.

"Listen!" she said, staring directly at him. "I can protect my mind—I can protect Phoebe—but the Sensitive will get what they want from you, and you won't even know. You-can-not-be-caught! In fact, you can't even let her get close to you. Leave now, go get help and then intercept us on our way to town. They plan to go to the Harbor. Don't worry, I'm too valuable for them to kill right away. But if she gets close, they'll learn about Phoebe and Daniel—then they're as good as dead.

"There's more. I'm not sure you can get far enough away before she senses your presence, so I have to ask you to do something—something terrible." She paused to taste his mood. "You have to kill her," she said. Gabriel froze, and stared at her, then nodded.

"She's only a teenager," Rebecca warned, still staring into his eyes, and sensing him bridle at the thought of killing a child in cold blood. Killing a young girl like that would challenge everything he thought was right—and how he thought about himself. But she couldn't let up. "If you don't stop her now, they'll follow you. There may even be others I haven't sensed yet. I know how difficult this is, but it's got to be done." Her voice broke on the last word.

That'll be hard to live with, he thought, still not completely committed.

"Her range is less than I thought before, probably two hundred meters at most. I know it's a horrible thing, but we have to do everything possible to protect my daughter. I'm not as important as Phoebe will be to the Order. She's already more powerful than me, and we can't let her fall into the Council's hands—the Order needs her." She felt him accept the task—Gabriel trusted her.

"I'll stop here and let them catch up, while you get far enough ahead to make a run for it—afterward. Without her they won't have an advantage, and they won't be eager to chase after you. They'll have me, but I'll be a burden and slow them down, while you get help. When we get closer to town, I'll lead you in," she promised.

"I've never abandoned anyone like this," he said.

"Don't think of it that way. This is a tactical move, no more. I'm counting on you." He nodded, and then took her hand in the fashion of Guard members, at the forearm. "Whatever happens, I'm proud to have traveled with you, Becky. You're as brave as anyone in the Guard. I promise, I'll do everything I can for you and for Phoebe."

She couldn't say anything right away, but nodded. Then she stared into his eyes one more time. "Go," she said. "The girl cannot live!" The look in her eyes made him shiver, and then he steeled himself for what he was about to do.

Rebecca watched Gabriel jog along the path. *It'll be hard on him*, she thought. She could see that he planned to gather the Watchers from the Sisters' Eyes and then backtrack to intercept them. It seemed like a reasonable plan, and with her help, they'd be able to surprise the Keepers.

There was an overhang, under a large rock beside the trail. It seemed like a good place to rest while she waited—at least she could get out of the rain. Gray light was filtering through the trees. It was still overcast, but most of the wind had died down and the rain was just a constant drizzle now. The Keepers were getting close, she peered more deeply into their minds to learn what she could, and was shocked to discover that they knew what she was—they were to capture the Sensitive.

Someone with the Order had leaked that she was coming this way—they even knew Gabriel's name. Thankfully, they still didn't know the purpose of her trip, or even her name, but then she saw how they'd gotten the information. Rebecca's eyes opened wide, afraid now. They were very close—she could feel the girl trying to enter her mind, probing for weakness. Julia. That was her name. She told the others that they'd found the Sensitive and where she was.

Footsteps sounded along the path and then a gunshot rang out from ahead. Something hit the ground, just meters from where Rebecca was hiding, and Julia's spark vanished. A barrage of shooting followed, and Gabriel returned fire. She had to warn him who the traitor was, and tried connecting with him directly, but he was fighting and not listening. In desperation she stood up, stepped out from under the overhang, and waved her arms to get his attention. He paused long enough to hear her warning.

The Watchers betrayed us!

Surprise and anger flared in his thoughts, but then something hit her from behind, and everything went dark.

CHAPTER 34

The Call

SATURDAY, PHOEBE WANDERED ALONG THE waterfront and through town, looking at the city she thought she knew so well—the buildings and streets and shops and...the park. She'd walked on virtually every road over the years, and had memorized almost every part of the harbor town. She knew what kind of stone covered the exterior of the buildings, and where every tree, lamp, and trolley stop was. But today, it was as though she'd never seen the town before. But it wasn't the *place* that had changed.

Sunday dawned bright and clear. Phoebe took a sketchpad and blanket downtown to the park, wanting to find a nice spot on the lawn to draw. It was time to work out a first sketch of the idea she'd had during her hike into the hills with Caleb. Eventually, it would become a painting. She'd just begun working out some initial outlines when a voice came to her. It was faint and weak, as though the person calling to her was either very tired, or very ill.

Phoebe...Phoebe...Phoebe...Can you hear me?...Phoebe...

Rebecca? She started to say something, but then pain ripped through her. It was sharp and piercing, as though a hot knife had been stuck through her shoulder. *Are you hurt?*

Thank God! I didn't think I'd find you in time.

In time? Time for what?

You need to run before they come for you. The Keepers have me— they've had me for days now...I think. I wake up now and then. It's hard to know how much time has passed.

253

What's happened?

They shot me, but the important thing is, I'm afraid of what I'll say…later.

Shot? Where—where are you?

Rather than wait for her mother to figure everything out, she followed her own sense of their connection and found Rebecca nearby. *You're here. In town!*

Maybe. Listen. You need to forget about me and get away. Do it now. There's a man coming for you. His name is Gabriel, and he can protect you. I'm going to share my impression of him. Please, take this memory from me. He can take you someplace safe.

Information flowed in, containing the flavor of the man known as Gabriel, as well as some of her mother's memories of him. Phoebe had never thought of using a connection this way.

You're in danger. We were coming to get you—to take you away. Look for Gabriel, trust him, and get ready to leave. Take as little as possible—but hurry, you need to go before…before…

We won't leave you, Phoebe said. *Maybe Gabriel can help.*

*Never mind me, baby. It's too late for me. But I want you to know that I always loved you and your father—I'm sorry I left. I'll…I'll do my best, but I don't know how long I can…*Rebecca stopped. Phoebe knew that she intended to kill herself when she got a chance. For now she was afraid and very weak.

Can you contact someone for me—I know you can do it. This person. Rebecca sent another stream of information to her, another man, Matthew. *He'll probably be where I was before. Do you remember the place?*

Yes.

Tell him what happened. And tell him…tell him the Watchers at the Sisters' Eyes betrayed us. They're here! I love you, Phoebe.

Rebecca released control of the connection, but now Phoebe knew where she was, and opened up her senses to probe the people nearby. There were four: a physician, a nurse, and two Keepers. Rebecca needed surgery to remove a bullet from her shoulder, but she'd lost a lot of blood—they wanted to give her a transfusion first. The injury was serious, but not immediately life-threatening.

Afterward, they planned to keep her unconscious until someone from the Council arrived.

She was tempted to let her mother know that she'd be safe for a while, but of course her mother could probe their minds as well as she, and contacting her again would just make her worry. Phoebe set a portion of herself to watch over her mother and packed up her things to go home.

The cold angry chill, which she'd begun to think of as a call to action, was starting to rise up from inside again. It felt as though she should be doing something to save her mother, but she didn't know what. So she mastered it before it could overwhelm her. Rebecca needed treatment first. *They'd better not do anything to her,* she thought, marking the people around her, *or I'll let the monster loose.*

Throughout the rest of the morning and early afternoon, she kept tabs on Rebecca's status, peering through the eyes of the doctors, nurses, and those guarding her. Phoebe was coming to understand that whenever the need arose, she'd discover a new way to channel her abilities.

At home, she went to her room to sit in the rocking chair, orienting her body to the west, closing her eyes, and spreading her arms out wide. Rebecca's home took only a moment to find this time. She scanned through fifty or so different sparks until she found the one matching Matthew. He wasn't a Sensitive, but his mind felt strange—definitely not normal.

Matthew!...Matthew, she repeated his name a number of times, feeling his confusion. It wasn't that he couldn't hear her, he just wasn't answering. *To hell with this.* She stood, dialing up the power on the connection. *MATTHEW, ANSWER ME!*

Who is this? I don't recognize you.

I'm Phoebe, Rebecca's daughter.

Where are you?

New Bright Sea Harbor.

But the distance—how is that possible?

She chose not to answer. *My mother asked me to contact you. She's been captured, and she's wounded. They've taken her to the hospital here in town. Can you get her out?*

What about Gabriel?

Rebecca says he'll be here soon, she said.

Any new help I send will take days, maybe a week to get there, but others are already on their way—they should arrive any day. There's nothing you can do. Go with Gabriel. I can protect you here, and I'll send more help for your mother today.

I'm not leaving without her. Then Phoebe told him about the traitors, ignoring his continued protests for her to leave. *How many people can you protect?* she asked. *I have family.*

I'll help whomever you bring, Matthew promised. *But please don't try to rescue Rebecca on your own. I can't see what will happen.*

Phoebe didn't argue with him. The last part of what he'd said confused her, but it didn't matter.

Be careful! Matthew warned just before Phoebe closed the connection.

She still wasn't sure what to think of this guy. He wasn't easy to read at all. There was a strangeness about him, it kept her from even *wanting* to look more deeply into his mind. Now that she'd done what Rebecca asked, she needed to speak with her father.

Later that afternoon, her mother was moved into surgery. The wound looked horrible, but as long as the Council was treating her rather than torturing her, Phoebe stayed calm. She was worried about what this would do to her father, more so than for herself—her own feelings toward her mother remained ambivalent. When she vowed that Rebecca wouldn't be left behind, it was mostly for his sake. He'd never leave her and, if forced to, would never get over it.

She tried connecting with Rebecca's mind again, but the drug they'd given her made Phoebe groggy. She had to pull back quickly to clear her head. *Wow! Okay, now I know: don't connect with people on drugs.*

She thought about Caleb. *I can't do this to him. I can't put him in even more danger, and tear him away, too.* Phoebe started to sob, knowing what she had to do.

CHAPTER 35

Choices

PHOEBE'S FATHER AND CALEB WERE back, tired but happy—and her grandfather was with them. *Great, an audience!* she complained. She'd planned to start an argument with Caleb sometime during the evening, but was having second thoughts with so many people being there. *It's probably better if I wait until we're alone.* She'd pretend everything was normal for tonight. Breaking up could wait a day, and that would give her more time to prepare.

The guys had obviously bonded over the weekend. She noted little signs in the way they treated each other. And they'd brought her a fish. Apparently everyone had forgotten that she'd promised to have dinner ready when they got home.

"Okay, guys," she said with forced enthusiasm. "Let's put the fish away for now, okay? And there might even be enough time before we eat to get close to the soap and water." She wrinkled her nose for effect.

Caleb, quicker than most, shambled toward the bathroom while her family looked at their hands and then each other. Phoebe leaned over to her grandfather and whispered, "Don't worry, I got you covered—land food." He winked at her.

Her father had been watching her, frowning, and his eyes narrowed. "You looked kind of upset when we walked in." He always was just a little *too* observant. She needed to be more careful around him.

"I'm fine," she said. "You know women; one minute we're crying, the next…who knows?" His frown deepened, but that's when Caleb slapped him on the back, telling him it was his turn to wash up. Phoebe took a breath, trying to calm down, even if only for a couple of hours. *Don't try so hard,* she told herself.

A much cleaner Caleb surprised her with a kiss, and right in front of her grandfather. As impressed as she was, that wasn't going to help. Her grandfather put a hand on Caleb's shoulder, grinning. *What the hell happened out there?* she wondered.

"I guess I have to send you out fishing more often," but the tone in her voice didn't sound right, even to her, and they looked at her funny.

Her dad came out, and his eyes focused on her face. She ignored the look and stared at her grandfather's retreating back and then at him, raising an eyebrow. It wasn't that she didn't want to see her grandfather, but they had always been careful when he was around.

One side of her father's mouth turned up, an apologetic smile. *He overheard us talking about you, and I decided it was better to let him know the truth—sorry.*

"Oh," she said aloud.

"What did I miss?" her granddad said, having just returned.

"I was just telling Phoebe that we discussed her gifts this weekend."

Phoebe scowled.

"Come on. It isn't fair to keep him in the dark, especially now that Caleb knows."

"I don't have a problem with him knowing, it was the word 'gifts' that annoyed me."

"Just like Becky," he said. "Having to deal with the senses made her strong, but they cost her a lot, too."

A sense of family and closeness was filling the room, radiating from the people around her. It created warmth inside—unwelcome feelings tonight. Every time her father said Becky's name his voice took on a deeper tone, and that glazed, almost haunted look passed across his face. She took another breath, this time trying not to show how upset she was, but now everyone was staring at her.

"What?" she asked.

"I was about to ask you the same thing. What's the matter, Princess?"

She turned her head coughing, an excuse to wipe her eyes. "I think I forgot to wash my hands after chopping the onions," she said.

"Something's wrong, that's for sure," Caleb said.

"Yeah," her father sighed. *Okay, what aren't you telling us? What happened?*

She looked at him for several seconds before answering. *I'm not sure how to tell you,* she said. *And I don't want to get Caleb mixed up in this—it's ...it's dangerous.*

What's dangerous?

We're out of time—we need to start packing...tonight.

She didn't want to tell him about Rebecca in front of everyone. He'd be crushed. She was waiting for a sense of alarm from him, but instead her father's shoulders seemed to sag and his face grew pale. The look reminded her of the way she'd sometimes feel when she was ready to give up. But he'd always been the strong one, the one she could lean on, the only one who could pull her out of depression. Maybe it was just one time too many. *It's my turn*, she thought.

"What's going on?" Caleb asked, looking back and forth between them. "Is something happening?"

Daniel thought about what she'd just said. The reference to packing had always been their code for 'time to run'. But he sensed there was something more, something she was afraid to say. He looked at Caleb, seeing an echo of himself, from years before. It was obvious that she planned to disappear on him, too. *I suppose it's the correct thing to do,* he thought, *but that doesn't mean it's the right thing to do.* Daniel held his breath, weighing the situation.

Phoebe, Caleb really does love you. I can tell. Do you want to throw that away without thinking about it? He stared into her eyes. *I don't want you to make the same mistake your mother and I made. Even with the risk, we should have stayed together. You're much younger than we were at the time, but not where it counts.*

Phoebe froze and they all stared, waiting for her to say something. Jacob shifted from foot to foot, uneasy with the silence.

"Please say something," Caleb pleaded.

Jacob hadn't wanted to say anything, but the look on Phoebe's face reminded him of her visit several weeks before, she'd had that same look. "I don't know what's happening here, or what's wrong, but whatever it is we're better off facing it together. I kept my word to you and didn't tell your dad about the visit when we talked about Becky, but I have to ask now. You said you thought you'd heard her voice before. What did you mean by that?"

Phoebe frowned, momentarily irritated, but then she thought it over. *This might be a good way to start.* She'd been teetering on the edge of telling them about Rebecca.

"Phoebe," Daniel said aloud, either not hearing or not understanding the implication of her grandfather's question. "Don't do it. Who knows what might happen? Becky didn't know she'd never make it back. Isn't one time enough?"

Phoebe closed her eyes for a moment and then opened them. "I need to tell you something. I should have told you before, but I didn't know how."

"What is it?" he asked. The room was silent again. Caleb and her grandfather looked at each other and shrugged.

"Maybe you should sit down first," she suggested.

"Say what you need to." He didn't sit, but put a hand on the back of a chair.

"Becky's alive." The words came out flat, without a hint of inflection.

"How do you know?"

"I talked to her—twice now." Her father swayed, but then seemed to steady himself. She started to reach toward him, but her arm dropped back to her side. Jacob fell into a chair.

"Where?" Daniel wanted to know.

"She was…a long way from here, that first time."

"And the second time?"

"Yeah. That's what I need to talk to you about. We connected again today."

Hurt passed across his face before he could hide it, and her grandfather was rubbing the back of his neck. She turned to him, wanting to answer his question first.

"Just after school started, I heard a voice in my dreams. It happened two nights in a row, although I didn't know that it was her voice at the time. The first night was that time you slept in my room," she said looking at her dad.

"I didn't know who she was until I heard her voice on the recording in your house." Everyone looked at Jacob, and he nodded. "But I still wasn't absolutely sure—a voice is…just a voice, it's not as certain as how a person feels. Then, one morning, not too long ago, I woke up and couldn't get back to sleep." Phoebe looked at Caleb and then her father. "I used the feel from the woman in the dreams to look for her. I wanted to make sure it actually was Becky before I said something to you." Her father changed his mind and pulled the chair out to sit down. "And I found her. She was…well, she was living west of here, quite a distance away. We connected, and I asked if she was my mother. She said yes. I wanted to talk to her some more, to ask why she didn't come back, but the timing was bad. Later, I got distracted."

"You said you spoke with her today."

"She connected with me this time, and she's here in town." Her father's mouth opened and he turned his head, as if expecting to see Becky walk into the room.

"Where?"

"I'm getting there." Phoebe sighed. "She's in the hospital."

"Why the hospital?" her father asked.

"She was captured a few days ago, but she needed a doctor, so they brought her here." Phoebe didn't want to say the word 'shot' just yet.

"What was wrong with her?" His voice was shaking now. "Is she injured?"

"Her shoulder's hurt." She decided it was time to stop being vague. "Dad, they shot her, but she's going to be okay."

"Shot her? How do you know she'll be okay?"

"I know," she said, looking at him steadily. "I connected with the doctor."

"Maybe we can go see her," Caleb suggested, thinking that his father might be able to get them in.

"No. They've got her drugged up, and won't let her wake up for now. She's under guard. No one's allowed in—they won't even admit that they have her."

"That's why we have to run?" her dad said.

"She told us to run. She said she'd hold out as long as possible, but they're all waiting for the Inquisitor. He's not supposed to be here for several days, so we may have a little time.

"She was coming to get us out of here—her and a man from the Order, a man named Gabriel." A wild look entered her father's eyes. "I know," she added. "We need to get her out, but we should wait for this guy to come first. He's a kind of soldier, sent here to protect us. Dad, I told her we wouldn't leave her, and I meant it."

Her father blinked. "How sure are you about all of this?"

"I'm absolutely certain. Don't forget what I am."

"Run? Were you planning to leave me without saying anything?" Caleb asked.

Phoebe couldn't answer right away. She closed her eyes, and made fists with both hands. She needed the pain, or something, more than ever before.

"How badly is Becky hurt?" her grandfather asked.

It was a few moments before she could say anything. "The bullet's out, her shoulder's bandaged, and the doctor thinks she'll recover."

"Were you leaving me?" Caleb asked again.

Phoebe took another breath before answering. "I was, but now I'm not so sure." Tears were already running down her face. "For your sake, I wish I could, but I can't just do that to you. I think my mother left to protect us, and that's the same reason why I wanted to leave, too, but now I think she was wrong not to give my father a say in the matter.

"Dad," she continued, "she really was coming to get us. This guy, Gabriel, was coming to help. She told me quite a bit about him. We can ask him what happened when he gets here."

"Phoebe," Caleb began, but then stopped and shook his head, not sure what to say. She reached over and took one of his hands, feeling the turmoil flowing through her palm.

Her grandfather spoke up. "Obviously, we have to decide what to do, but I don't think we're ready yet. I remember how it was during the Purge, when we were all afraid and wondering what to do. It was a terrible time, and we all had to make choices of one kind or another. But we don't have to decide right this minute. What helped us in the past was going through with the things we did every day—living. It puts things into perspective and gives you time to think everything over with a clearer head.

"I know your father appreciates the fact that you're willing to try to rescue Rebecca. We all want to do that, but I'm not sure how. You say this Gabriel is coming, and he sounds like the kind of man who might have experience with this sort of thing.

"Since there's nothing we can do right now, I suggest two things: First, let's get on with what we would have done tonight if none of this had come up. I'm not really hungry, but I think we should try to eat. I know you've gone to the trouble of making dinner. Sitting down and eating together is just the sort of thing that helps. Second, it seems clear that we have to leave. Since we have a few days, we should probably think about where we'll go and then start gathering the things we want to take."

"Good idea," her father said.

Ω

After dinner, her dad told her that he would wash the dishes and clean up. She looked at the chaos she'd left behind with a guilty expression, but accepted his offer. Caleb would want to talk with her alone.

"Let's go for a walk," she suggested.

"We'll wait up for you," her grandfather said. Phoebe relaxed a little knowing that her father wouldn't be alone.

They left the apartment and walked toward the waterfront. Caleb waited until they were near the harbor before speaking.

"Phoebe, were you really planning to leave without saying anything at all?"

"You make it sound so easy. It's not. I didn't want to leave you," she said, "and I'm sorry—I was wrong. But I'm afraid for you. I've lived this way most of my life. We never knew when the Keepers might come. Can't you see how hard it would be for me to do that to you?" She stopped and pulled him around to face her. They were under one of the few lights along the water.

"I don't worry so much about myself now. I worry about what might happen to the people close to me." She took a breath. "Especially someone I love this much. I didn't *want* to leave you, but how can I ask you to give up everything for life as a fugitive? Imagine how your dad and Mary will feel. And then imagine what it would do to me if something were to happen to you." Her voice broke, and she buried her face into his shoulder. He hugged her and kissed her hair.

"It's not up to just you, Phoebe. I have a say in this, too, and I've already decided. I'm never leaving you."

She looked up into his eyes, and then hesitatingly touched his mind, wanting to know how he felt for sure. This was far too important a choice to make casually. After a minute, they started walking again.

"All right," she said, squeezing his hand as tightly as she could.

"We'd better go back to the house before your father and Jacob start worrying." Phoebe's heart was lighter, but as they approached her home, she sensed a new presence inside.

"He's here," she said.

"Who?"

"A friend."

CHAPTER 36

A Visitor

THREE PEOPLE WERE SEATED AT the table when they entered. Gabriel stood to greet her. A look of recognition flashed across his eyes, but disappeared as quickly as it had come. He was about the same height as her father, dark skinned, and every part of his clothing was covered with what looked like dried mud. But it was his eyes that drew her attention, serious eyes, resolute. This was not a person with whom to trifle.

"You must be Phoebe," he said.

She nodded, staring. "And you must be Gabriel." He tilted his head, a single nod.

"I've heard you knew I was coming." One corner of his mouth turned up.

Her father interrupted. "He just arrived a few minutes ago. We haven't had much time to talk." Silently, he added, *He was surprised we expected him and that we knew about Becky.*

"I haven't had a chance to go over what happened yet." The Scout looked between Phoebe and her father, an inscrutable expression.

"Please sit down. I'm sure you're tired. Why not be more comfortable?" she offered, pointing to the stuffed chairs.

He looked toward the sitting area and then his own clothing. "Thanks, it's tempting, but it's been a long time since I've had a chance to clean up."

They all sat around the table. Caleb retrieved one of the extra chairs from Phoebe's desk by the window.

Gabriel told her that she looked a lot like her mother, and she smiled. "Yeah, I've heard that. By the way, this is Caleb." The Scout and he briefly clasped hands. Gabriel scanned everyone, looking uncomfortable. He seemed reluctant to speak openly.

"Everyone in this room can be trusted," she said looking him in the eye. "As you heard, we learned a little about what happened to my mother," Phoebe began. "She connected with me today, just before they sedated her." She closed her eyes for a moment, and then opened them again. "She's sleeping now, and the staff at the hospital has orders to keep her that way. They aren't sure who she is, exactly, but one of the Keepers on guard knows a little about her."

Even without probing, Phoebe sensed Gabriel's confusion. "Obviously, I'm like my mother in more than just appearance. I can see through the eyes of the people around her." His expression changed, and a look she'd come to associate with hope filled his eyes.

"I'm willing to risk a lot to save her," he said. "What can you tell me about their security?"

"Probably everything, but that doesn't mean it'll be easy to get her out. She's been hurt pretty badly. They operated on her late this afternoon and she'll need some time to heal, at least a few days. Even if she weren't being guarded, it would be hard to move her quickly or very far. And where would we take her? Do you have a plan?"

Phoebe softly touched his mind, as he thought about her questions. A rescue would conflict with his primary objective. He was here to get her and her father to safety, but torn. He really wanted to rescue her mother, and felt a strong sense of loyalty to her personally. She had to let go of his thoughts before they affected her.

"My father's the director of the hospital," Caleb offered. "Maybe he can help us find a way in." Gabriel's eyes narrowed when he looked at Caleb—he was naturally suspicious of people close to the Council.

"Caleb is just trying to help. He's with us," she said, firmly.

The Scout nodded. "All right. But I'll need everything you know: her exact location, what the security around her is like, and the physical layout of the building. You'll have to keep track of her condition, so we know as soon as she can be moved. We have"—he paused a moment—"we have a long way to go, and it won't be easy. I'd hate to rescue her and then watch her bleed out in the wild. If she's too weak, we'll need to find another way. How long did the doctor believe it would be before she could walk?"

"It didn't come up, he was mainly trying to stabilize her."

Her father interrupted. "Gabriel, can you tell us what happened, and why you were coming in the first place? I'm sure Phoebe can get what you need."

The Scout nodded and recounted the story of their trip. He looked at Phoebe now and then to help him remember small details.

"As for why, Rebecca and I were coming here to get you two out. This town has become too dangerous for you. Our leader—we call him the Guide—is a little like your mother, gifted, but in a different way. He can see into the future." Her father frowned and started to say something, but Phoebe held up a finger, asking him to let the Scout finish his story first.

"Months ago, he saw a danger to you, Phoebe, and warned us that your life was at risk if we didn't intervene." She felt Caleb squeeze her hand.

"How soon?" her father wanted to know. "Do you know what the danger is?"

"I don't know the nature of the threat. He said it was difficult, even for him, to see exactly what was happening, but he was sure— and I believe him. I've known the Guide for years, and he never gets these things wrong."

Her father nodded.

"Toward the end of August, Rebecca and I traveled to a safe house nearby. The Guide asked her to come and had me protect her. At that time, your mother connected with you on two separate nights. Do you remember unusual dreams around the end of August or the beginning of September?"

Phoebe nodded; the final piece of the puzzle had finally fallen into place. She'd wondered why the connections had suddenly come and then stopped just as abruptly.

"The Guide needed her to help with a test. It was intended to see if there was a chance to save you. He thought you'd be safe for several months—long enough for us to set up a plan that would both get you out and protect other people who know about you. Operations like this go wrong all the time, even seemingly easy ones, especially when you're in a hurry. He thought it better—safer—for you and the people around you, if we took more time and planned."

Phoebe saw Gabriel's eyes flicker toward Caleb again.

"Now I wish we'd acted right away. I can take you to a safe place, called a Sanctuary."

"When you talk about the Guide, you mean Matthew, right?" Phoebe asked.

The Scout frowned, but then nodded. "How did you know?"

"My mother asked me to connect with him. He knows what happened now, and told me more help was on the way."

"Is he here?" Gabriel asked, confused again.

"No. He's at the Sanctuary."

Gabriel shook his head. "I don't understand…"

"I'm like my mother, but a little different, too," she said.

The Scout's eyes grew wide, and his mouth opened. She touched his mind again, curious. He was wondering how much her abilities played into Matthew's insistence on helping her. It made her uncomfortable, but she pushed her doubts aside for now and urged him to continue.

"We were headed to the same safe house we'd used before. There were two agents here—local recruits, really. Their job was to keep watch on the area, and render aid when necessary. As you say, there are more people coming from the north—a backup team— and it looks like we're going to need them. They're more heavily armed than me." The Scout looked at Caleb and her grandfather, probably wondering what their roles were.

"This is my family," she said. "Wherever I go, they go." Gabriel clearly wasn't looking for an argument. He simply seemed to want a better grasp of the situation.

"These others, the 'help' you described, are supposed to get here in the next day or two," Gabriel said. "Matthew sent them some time ago, but they were farther away. Before Rebecca connected with you this summer, we didn't know exactly what your condition might be. He's been watching over you for years—at Rebecca's request—so we knew you were safe, but not much more than that. A long time ago, she asked us to stay away from you, not wanting to draw the Council's attention your way. I guess she thought you were safer here in town.

"Unfortunately, when we ran into the Keepers, there was another Sensitive with them. They knew who we were and where we were going."

Phoebe didn't interrupt him, but Rebecca's warning about the traitors came back to her.

"Since we couldn't outrun them, your mother insisted we split up. She was afraid the Sensitive would learn about you from me, and she was too exhausted to go on. It seemed a reasonable plan to let her be captured—temporarily—while I went to get help. I was going to take her back along the way, with help from the local agents. To be safe, and to give us a chance to retake her, I killed the Sensitive before I ran." He stopped talking for a moment.

Phoebe saw that his jaw muscles were clenched. She reached into his thoughts again and experienced what happened, gasping. The others looked at her, but she shook her head.

"It was Rebecca's plan. I didn't like it, but I didn't have a better one.

"I killed that girl." The Scout stopped speaking and was shaking his head. "I've never done that to someone so young, let alone a girl, but we couldn't have rescued Rebecca with her around, and if she'd learned about Phoebe..." His voice broke and he coughed. "Afterward, I fired a few shots to make them keep their heads down. They shot back, but erratically.

"I thought I heard your mother—inside my head, you know. I really should have been listening better, but was too distracted. To get my attention, she stepped into the open and raised her arms. It looked like she was surrendering, and that's when I heard her. She told me the local agents, the Watchers, had sold us out. Unfortunately, the Keepers kept on shooting and I saw her go down. I didn't know for sure if she was dead or alive, but I had to run.

"My orders are to get you out, but I'm going to do what I can for her first. We'll have some reinforcements pretty soon, but we need a plan."

Phoebe sensed the pain he felt about the young girl. The killing would haunt him for the rest of his life, and she knew now that he'd done it for her. The thought made her swallow hard, and she put a hand on his arm. "I'm sorry," she said, feeling tears and a guilt that she shared with him. Gabriel took a breath, and nodded.

"I took care of the traitors." A murderous look entered his eyes when he said that, a look she hoped never to see again. "I'll spare you the details," he said in a voice hard and cold. There was no hint of remorse in him now.

It was Phoebe's turn to talk. She related her conversations with Rebecca and Matthew.

"I told her that we wouldn't leave her, and that upset her." Phoebe looked at her father. "She was pretty determined that we run. I think she's afraid of what she might say under the drugs, or under…well, later. She'll kill herself if she gets a chance, so it's probably a good thing they're keeping her sedated."

"Phoebe, how's she doing now?" her father asked.

"Her shoulder is heavily bandaged. It looked pretty ugly before. I've never shot anything, but would guess that it took a big gun to do that to her. The nurses don't seem to be concerned about her condition. I take that as a good sign."

"The Keepers use standard-issue weapons," Gabriel said, "not a large caliber, but they have a high muzzle velocity. It's the energy that does the damage. It sounds like the surgery went fairly well."

"Yeah, the doctor was pleased, and she looked a lot better after the bullet was out." The Scout nodded. "I doubt she'll be able to walk. She'll be weak, and under the effects of the drugs. They're guarding the door to her room and the hallway outside of it, but they leave her alone most of the time. Someone from Central City is on the way to question her."

"Where is the room? Is there a back entrance or an adjoining room? What about windows?" Gabriel had a hundred questions. Both her father and Caleb started describing the hospital to him.

"They aren't using the regular security rooms on the ground floor," Phoebe said, interrupting them. "She's in a separate wing, in the basement. It's at the bottom of a stairway that starts near the receptionist's desk. There's an armed guard at the bottom of the stairs and another one just outside her room, plus three more Keepers who move around. They're afraid someone might mount a rescue. The Keepers who brought her here are still in town, too, and the entire Keeper force is on alert. The Council Inquisitor is coming with even more Keepers. We have a week—at most." That quieted the room.

"I can see if my father can help," Caleb offered again. Both Gabriel and her father shook their heads, obviously not comfortable with the idea. "Or maybe I could just get the information we need by myself."

"If you could get ahold of an architectural drawing, or even a floor plan that showed where the stairs, windows, and other features are, it would help a lot."

Her grandfather spoke up. "If we get her out of the hospital, I can get us all out of town on the Molly. Becky probably won't be able to go very far on foot. Sorry, Phoebe," he added. "Anyway, it'll buy more time for her to heal before she has to walk. We can meet up with your people anywhere that's convenient—or disappear until we think of something else."

"You know, maybe Rebecca can walk after all," Phoebe said, with a grim smile. Her father told Gabriel about Phoebe's aversion to the sea.

"For tonight, you can stay with one of us," her dad offered.

"It's probably best if you stay with me," her grandfather said. "I have more space, and you can pretend to be someone I hired for maintenance. Plus, my place is isolated."

"Fair enough. Still," he said, "I need to make sure Phoebe's safe."

"Okay, okay," she said. "Poor little Phoebe's not totally helpless, you know." Caleb snorted.

"You're not helpless, but we still worry," her father said.

"All right, Jacob, I accept your offer," Gabriel said. "Phoebe, let me know if anything changes. I suggest everyone start packing. Use a backpack if you have one, and be ready to leave at a moment's notice."

Her grandfather left with Gabriel.

"I think I'd better get home, too," Caleb said, "but I'll be back tomorrow evening." He looked at Phoebe.

She walked him to the door and kissed him good night.

After Caleb had gone, she faced her father. "All right, you've been wanting to say something all night."

"Yes, at first, but not anymore. You and Caleb seemed to be moving fast, but life has a funny way of changing things."

"You were right before—about me leaving him. I know this is awfully fast, but in a funny way Caleb's a lot like me, an old soul stuck in a young body. We'll be fine together."

"Sometimes I forget," he said.

CHAPTER 37

Visions

MATTHEW STRODE TOWARD SECURITY, HARDLY noticing the people he passed in the corridor. The exchange with Phoebe had allowed him to understand the enigma he'd been wrestling with for months—the strange out-of-focus visions, futures that seemed to suddenly shift on their own, and his own intuitive sense that some momentous change was on the way. It was all clear now.

He'd been looking at the future the wrong way. Phoebe didn't fit the pattern of a linear movement through time, and she was not part of a larger trend—Phoebe was pure chaos. The blurred imagery and shadowy alternate futures alone should have made that obvious. No thread for her would ever be absolute, and all of them could change without warning. She wasn't an incremental evolution within the Sensitives' program plan, she was something else altogether. *Why didn't I see this before?*

Jürgen was in the office, waiting.

"I need to get a message to Samuel right away, and could you contact Lake John? Tell them to get the Duck ready."

Matthew spoke without greeting or preamble, but Jürgen was familiar with how he worked and didn't take offense. Everyone understood that when he acted this way it was because something urgent was happening, and his mind was in high gear—it was just part of his nature.

"Do you know where the North Star team is?" Jürgen shook his head. "The Watchers at the Sisters' Eyes have turned on us.

Rebecca's been taken prisoner, and I'm pretty sure Phoebe's going to try to rescue her. She's certainly determined enough, but I can't see a good outcome. I feel blind. At least I can look for the Scout Team, but once they're with her it'll be hard to predict anything."

Jürgen paled. He knew all too well the short, painful future Rebecca faced as a 'guest' of the Council. "The team of three should get there soon. Unfortunately, the closest terminal is in Bardon, and there's no reason for them to check in. Do you think the Watchers will attack?"

"No," Matthew said as he encoded a message for Samuel. "By now they're dead, but the cabin's been compromised." His vision was clearing. Several alternative futures were emerging, very fuzzy, but almost readable. There were no less than five high-probability fatal threads, and just one improbable possibility of survival—but not for everyone. Chances were that Phoebe's future would end soon, but if—by some miracle—she managed to survive, she'd need Samuel.

"I'll rest for a few hours, then I'm off to the lake. Wake me if you hear from Samuel's team."

"Will do."

The many-layered fluid of time still swirled in his head, most of the images were changing faster than he could focus. He saw boats filled with Keepers, a storm, and death. The threads of her future were so tightly bound with those of the people around her that their fates were indistinguishable. Along almost all of them he saw her corpse. Matthew took a deep breath, trying to prepare for the worst. It was likely he would lose both Rebecca and Phoebe. *If we lose her now, we lose our best chance, and without Becky...* he didn't even want to think about it. He estimated their chance of survival at less than 2 percent.

It was after midnight when he left for Lake John, still not having heard back from Samuel. As a precaution, he took one of the Corbin physicians with him. There was an 85-percent chance the Healer would make it in time, but 85 percent wasn't 100 percent.

CHAPTER 38

The Plan

O VER THE NEXT SEVERAL DAYS, Rebecca slept in her dungeon-like room, while Caleb collected information on the hospital's layout. He'd managed to secure a key to the door that accessed the basement from inside the loading dock. It opened onto a back stairway that descended into what used to be refrigerated storage, just adjacent to the wing where Rebecca was being held. There would be one remaining physical obstacle standing in the rescue team's way: a heavy iron security door. It wouldn't be easy to breach, but it did offer a slightly less dangerous way in and out.

Phoebe had seen one side of this door through the eyes of a Keeper in the underground security wing. Although close to her room, it was around a bend at the end of the hallway and wasn't visible from the Keeper's station. In order to see it, a person would need to walk all the way to the end of the hallway and look around the corner, but it was rusted in place, and hadn't been opened for years.

Six rooms opened off of the basement hallway. Rebecca's was the last one on the left, as seen from the Keeper's station. The other rooms were empty. In order to get to her, the team would need to enter the hospital grounds from the rear, break into the loading dock, go down the rear stairs to the abandoned storage area, and then break through the iron door.

Five Keepers were stationed at the hospital, and several members of the nursing staff also regularly visited her room.

Breaking through the door would be noisy—there was no avoiding that. The team needed to be ready to fight their way through the Keepers, or to draw them off first. Either way, they'd have to move fast, before more Keepers came from the barracks—four Scouts couldn't take on a whole platoon.

Gabriel used the time to plan and to prepare rations, just in case they had to escape on foot. These were the same compact, high-energy bars that he and Rebecca used during their travels. After tasting one, Phoebe almost hoped that they wouldn't have to walk. Surely, her grandfather would have better food than that, assuming she could keep it down.

$$\Omega$$

Jacob had officially ended the fishing season and released his crew for the winter. He pretended he was performing off-season maintenance on the Molly. In fact, he was stocking it with the supplies and equipment needed for an indefinite journey. He'd also quietly wrapped up his business affairs in town, since he'd never be back.

$$\Omega$$

Daniel surreptitiously checked into what was happening with the Keepers, always being careful not to seem overly interested. The head of the Curia of Truth was rumored to be coming for a visit, and the local prosecutor was nervously fretting over what he should do. The Council Elder usually traveled with an extensive retinue, and word had come down that they would need a lot of office space.

$$\Omega$$

Caleb and Phoebe found time to be together, both during and after school, although very little of that was alone. She went to his home

Wednesday evening, and spent time with his father and Mary. Dr. Addison insisted that she call him George. He seemed so enthusiastic that Caleb had found such a nice girlfriend. *If he only knew what was about to happen, he wouldn't be quite so friendly,* she thought. Mary was quiet all night, her mind obviously somewhere else, but she probably didn't want to be alone. Phoebe felt guilty for planning to take Caleb away from them.

Every day, it was harder for Phoebe to say good night to him. They connected frequently, but it wasn't the same as being able to touch each other physically. She made time to watch over Rebecca, to monitor the Keepers guarding her, the doctors and nurses treating her, and anyone else who got close. But Caleb took a lot of her attention, too. She was afraid that she might accidentally tell one of the Keepers that she loved him by mistake.

♎

Gabriel watched out for the other Scouts. He'd hiked up to the Sisters' Eyes early Monday morning to leave a note asking them to set up a signal to let him know when they arrived. He borrowed Jacob's binoculars and looked for the sign. Tuesday morning, he saw what he was looking for and went to meet them.

The Scout and Jacob also spent time fashioning a tool to pry open the iron door. It had been made to keep people locked into the prison wing, rather than out of it, so its hinges were accessible from the storage area where they would be. According to the plans Caleb had 'borrowed', this was the best way to open the door, but nothing was certain. The newly arrived Scouts had brought equipment with them: weapons and ammunition, explosive material, detonators, and several remote transmitters. They all got to work, fashioning weapons from the explosives, using metal parts they scavenged from Jacob's workshop. By Wednesday night, everything was ready. Gabriel wanted to wait as long as possible to allow Rebecca time to heal.

♎

It was Thursday when Daniel's voice interrupted her.

Phoebe?

Dad! What is it?

The Keepers say the Inquisitor will be here tomorrow morning. We go tonight. Let Caleb know and tell the teacher you feel sick. Get them to contact me. She felt a brief moment of panic, but took a breath and pushed her fears aside.

After passing the message on to Caleb, she told her teacher she was sick. The school sent a messenger to the defender's office and, in less than a half hour, she was with her father and on her way home.

Everyone met at Jacob's house for a quick update, and to go over the plan. The three new Scouts had been staying out of sight, or helping on the Molly, but everyone was in Jacob's living room now.

Gabriel drew a map to show where each person was expected to be as they went through the phases of the plan. They would all wait in Jacob's house until after ten o'clock, and then move into position. The operation would begin at ten forty-five. Phoebe would be on lookout from a safe distance outside of the hospital. The four Scouts, including Gabriel, would infiltrate the hospital through the loading dock at the rear of the hospital, and then work their way down to the iron door in the basement.

An explosive device was already in place outside the front of the hospital, near the street. This would create a diversion to draw the Keepers away from Rebecca's room. A second, smaller explosive could be used on the iron door should the pry tool fail to open it. Gabriel would set off the explosion outside to mask the sound of them tearing the hinges off of the door. Their weapons were equipped with sound suppressors and capable of full automatic fire should a fight be necessary.

Phoebe's father wanted to go, too. "Someone needs to look after Becky, especially if there's fighting."

"Dad, you're not a member of the Guard. You've never even fired a gun before. You might get hurt, even killed!" She understood how he felt, but...

"There are only four Scouts, Princess, and you said she's unconscious most of the time," he pointed out. "They'll be busy enough. Who's going to look after Becky?"

"Then I should go, too," her grandfather said. "It'll take two people to carry her, especially since she's wounded."

Phoebe shook her head. "We can't send everyone—why are you all being so reckless?"

"I'll go with you," Caleb said. "Jacob should stay with the Molly."

An icy feeling hit Phoebe, and she wondered if she might lose everyone she loved in one night.

Caleb put an arm around her. "Don't worry, your dad and I aren't going to fight."

"Jacob," Gabriel said, "I think Caleb's right. You should stay with the boat. We won't have time to get her ready if we're on the run. But if you don't see us by midnight, take her out anyway. We'll arrange to meet somewhere else. Phoebe can help.

"Caleb and Daniel, you're right. If this turns into a fight, we'll need you to look after Rebecca. I don't like it any more than Phoebe does, but I haven't liked a lot of the choices I've had lately." Gabriel took a breath and looked into her eyes—a hard look to let her know that the decision had been made.

He conferred with the rest of the Scouts. Mark was older than the rest and looked as though he'd seen as many operations as Gabriel. The other two were young, and looked alike. Phoebe had learned that they were brothers, Julian and David. Julian was a little older.

Mark had hidden the explosive near the front of the hospital, just behind a wall that surrounded the grounds out front. Gabriel planned to detonate it at 11:00 p.m. using one of the transmitters.

Phoebe would watch the hospital from across and down the street to keep Gabriel posted on what was happening outside. She was also responsible for making sure the area around the explosive was clear before he detonated it. Then she'd look out for reinforcements. More Keepers would surely come when they heard the explosion, but the barracks were south of town and it should take them at least twenty minutes to respond.

Mark had picked out a safe spot for her. It was protected by another wall that surrounded the town marketplace. He'd also sabotaged the streetlights nearby, to keep her in the shadows.

If everything worked out, most of the Keepers would go check on the explosion. Rebecca's room was close to where the team would enter, and they planned to take her back through the storage area, up the stairs, and out the loading dock to a gate in the hospital's back fence.

If the iron door didn't open right away, they'd blow it using the smaller charge. The team would rush in and wound or kill any Keepers that remained. The sound-suppressed guns would help them maintain surprise should additional Keepers come early.

Caleb and Daniel were responsible for retrieving and carrying Rebecca to the back gate. A narrow service road ran behind the hospital, and they'd use a handcart that Jacob provided to transport Rebecca to the port.

Everyone would rendezvous at the Molly, unless Phoebe warned them away. The backup plan called for them to go by foot over the pass between the Sisters, but—as a last resort—they'd hide everyone in an empty house Julian had located earlier that day. They'd stay put until the initial ruckus subsided, or until more help arrived. Gabriel warned everyone that no plan ever went exactly as expected.

Phoebe didn't like it. She wouldn't be close enough to Caleb and her dad to protect them, and her offensive abilities had only worked close up. She sulked for a while, but then realized that she was wasting valuable time—time she could be spending with Caleb. Mercifully, her father and Gabriel let them go out alone.

They walked through town visiting some of their favorite places for the last time, and found a secluded spot to be alone for a while. Both knew this might be the last time they were together, but neither mentioned it. Later, they walked back to Jacob's house in time to grab some of the last food her grandfather would cook in his house.

CHAPTER 39

First Contact

T HE HOSPITAL WAS SET WELL back from Main Street. Its grounds were surrounded by stone wall in front and an iron fence out back. An alley paralleled Main Street behind the hospital, and a gate in the fence was left open during the day to accept deliveries. Carts arriving with supplies used a circular drive to reach a loading dock at the rear of the building. Here, various goods were delivered and moved into a receiving area protected by a set of double doors, kept locked at night.

The building itself had two aboveground levels and a subterranean basement. The upper levels were each bisected by a main east-west hallway that ran from the Main Street side of the building to the back. Two north-south corridors further divided each level into more or less equal sections; smaller hallways opened off of these. The ground floor had four units: a surgical ward, convalescent rooms for critical care, lab spaces, and a security wing in the southeast corner of the building. The second level housed additional patient rooms as well as administrative offices.

The basement had originally been the same size as the ground floor, however, the north side, which housed mechanical and generator machinery, had been emptied and sealed off. The remaining space could be accessed using a stairway located where the main corridor intersected with the first north-south hallway. There was a door at the bottom of the stairs, which opened into a hall that led away and provided access to the high-security rooms, several on either side. At its end, the hall took a ninety-degree right turn and ended in a heavy iron door. Beyond this was a large unfinished area, and directly across this room, the hallway continued on past a smaller room that had once been refrigerated, and was off to the left. The hall ended at a second stairway going up to the delivery area at the back of the hospital, and just inside the loading dock.

The Scouts planned to break in through the hospital's rear gate, and enter through the loading dock doors. They'd leave a handcart outside the rear gate to help transport Rebecca to the Molly.

Ω

Phoebe watched the clock march forward with a growing sense of dread. No amount of willpower on her part could slow its hands, and it was almost time to say good-bye. She tried to distract herself by doing unnecessary housework. Caleb watched her repeatedly fold and unfold a napkin. She stopped when he pointed out that what she was doing could be considered torture.

Activity at the hospital was much the same as it had been for the past few days, and the Keepers had settled into a routine.

The last shift change had been at six o'clock that evening and this crew would be on duty until two. There were five Keepers assigned to the shift, most were armed with handguns.

The shift boss occupied a desk near the door at the bottom of the stairs. Two more Keepers were assigned to be downstairs, one stayed near Rebecca's door at the end of the hallway, and the other spent most of his time talking with his boss, or wandering down the hallway to speak with the other Keeper. Phoebe noticed that he sometimes peered around the corner at the iron door—its presence bothered him. A fourth Keeper, armed with an automatic weapon, was near the top of the stairs along the main hallway. The last Keeper acted as a kind of floater, roaming throughout the hospital, and checking exterior windows and doors from time to time. This guy worried Phoebe the most, since he didn't have a set routine and it was hard to predict where he'd be. She'd already seen him go into the receiving area twice tonight. Each night the Keepers would rotate assignments to help relieve boredom.

There were a total of four nurses assigned to Rebecca; one was on the shift tonight. He had visited Phoebe's mother two times since six o'clock, but had other duties on the first floor as well. There was no obvious pattern or schedule that Phoebe had been able to detect. Rebecca had remained in her drug-induced sleep all week, only waking for brief periods now and then.

Phoebe warned Gabriel about the nurse and the roaming Keeper for what seemed the hundredth time. He gave her a patient look and nodded with a slight smile.

"Don't worry, Phoebe," he said. "We'll watch out for your family."

As time to get into position drew near, she could hear her heart pounding so hard that she couldn't understand why everyone else didn't hear it, too. At a quarter to ten Gabriel gathered everyone together in the living room for a last review. He wanted to make sure that each person knew their assignment, and what to do if something went wrong. Afterward, he looked at Phoebe, and her stomach dropped through the floor.

"Okay," he said, "time to get into position."

I'm ready, she lied silently.

Gabriel smiled at the tone of her internal voice. "Let me know when you're there."

Phoebe tried to stand up but her legs were weak, and she had to use her arms to push up from the sofa. Her father rested his forehead against hers. *Don't worry, kiddo; we'll be all right. These guys know what they're doing.* She wanted to smile, but couldn't.

Next she wrapped her arms around Caleb as though she'd never let go. He grinned at the strength she was using, and kissed her. *Be careful!* she told him.

"I'll see you in about an hour and a half. *You* be careful," he added, and then leaned in close to whisper "I love you" into her ear.

"I love you, Caleb," she said aloud, staring into his eyes for several seconds before closing them to leave.

♎︎

Phoebe made her way to the hospital on foot, not really paying attention to where she was. Everything felt so unreal tonight—remote, as though it wasn't really happening. Her nervousness faded as she approached the assigned position. Having something to do helped.

It was already late and a weeknight, so the streets were almost empty and nearby businesses were all closed. Her post was on Main Street, a little behind a half wall that surrounded the market, just across the street from the southeast corner of the hospital. A large evergreen shrub shaded her from background light, and the nearest gas lamp was dark. Even if someone were looking for her, Phoebe doubted they'd be able to see her here. The main entrance to the hospital was across the street and to her right. She told Gabriel she was in place and then sent him a quick update on what the Keepers were doing.

Understood, he said, *we're moving out now. I told everyone to leave you alone tonight so you can concentrate on keeping me informed of anything you see—anything you think I need to know,* he amended.

Got it. The Keepers are at their posts, and the floater is talking to the guy at the top of the stairs.

The Scouts left Jacob's house one at a time rather than as a group. Each chose a different route that would put him near the back of the hospital around ten forty-five. Only Daniel and Caleb walked together. She watched their progress through town. Everyone made it to the rendezvous point on time, and without incident.

Phoebe warned Gabriel that the Keeper with the automatic weapon had stepped outside and was walking around the front lawn. He paused where the explosive was, but then moved on, circling the grounds to reenter the building. The Scout used information she provided about each Keeper's whereabouts to time the crossing of the back property. Mark picked the lock on the double doors and they made it into the receiving area without being seen. Thirty seconds after reaching the building, they were all inside, and Caleb's key had been used to open the door to the rear stairway.

We're making our way to the basement now. Any change? Gabriel asked.

Phoebe quickly scanned through the eyes of the Keepers. Two were near the hospital's front entrance, the boss was at his desk, and the other two were standing outside Rebecca's room. She started providing him updates every time someone changed position. It was close to eleven o'clock now.

A couple came out of the hospital—probably late visitors. They were walking in the direction of the bomb. Hearing this, Gabriel held up his hand, for everyone to freeze.

I'm ready with the detonator. Let me know when it's clear.

She watched the man and woman amble along the sidewalk. They stopped to talk at the corner. She hugged herself, digging her fingernails into her upper arms, wondering what to do.

They're standing exactly where the bomb is, and it doesn't look like they're leaving right away, she warned. The words poured into the Scout's mind rapidly, and he sensed how stressed she was feeling.

Phoebe, we can wait a little while—there's no rush here. Keep me posted. She tried to absorb his feeling of calmness.

♎

Caleb and Daniel stood side-by-side, leaning against the east wall in a small room, just off the hallway at the bottom of the stairs. Their backs were against a concrete wall and toward the iron door. The wall would protect them if the Scouts needed to use an explosive to breach the door, or should bullets start flying through the door's opening. Caleb could see Julian's arm through the opening to the hallway. He was guarding the stairs against surprise from behind.

Mark and Gabriel were like statues on either side of the iron door. They'd already fitted the pry-bar tool onto the door's hinges, and were ready to tear them off as soon as the bomb outside detonated. They'd leave the door in place for a ten count as a shield, in case they'd been heard. David was behind them and outside the opening to the room where Caleb and Daniel were. He was facing the door with his weapon drawn, and seemed more nervous than the others. Caleb guessed that this was his first live mission. It was eleven o'clock when Gabriel gave the signal to freeze.

"What is it?" David asked in a whisper. The Scout looked over his shoulder to give him a cold look. The younger Scout fidgeted with his weapon, nervously rechecking the ammunition. He made a slight noise, which prompted Gabriel to glare at him again.

Flustered, his hands shaking, David dropped a spare ammo clip and it hit the concrete floor sounding like a gunshot in the silence of the room. Both Daniel and Caleb flinched at the noise, and Gabriel mentally swore to himself, glaring at the young Scout for a full five seconds this time. He listened at the door for any sign of movement from the other side.

♎

Phoebe heard Gabriel swearing. *What is it?* she asked.

Just a little accident—what's going on downstairs in the ward right now? The urgent tone of his voice frightened her.

She looked in horror and saw that the two Keepers on the other side of the door had both drawn their weapons, and their boss was headed up the front stairs.

The couple? Gabriel wanted to know. She heard him thinking that the diversion might reduce the number of people they'd need to face, but that they'd lost the element of surprise.

Still there! she said.

Get them out, now! And then you get out, too. Let me know when you're clear. Phoebe felt his patience evaporate.

She jumped over the half wall and ran down the street to confront the couple. "You've got to get out of here—now! A bomb's about to go off—right here! Run!"

They looked at her as though she were crazy, so she ran forward and pushed against them, yelling and cursing. They finally seemed to get the message and retreated down the street, looking back at her over their shoulders as they hurried away.

Phoebe was in a hurry, too. *The guys need this now!* She ran back toward her corner, furious at how slow she was. When she was a little more than halfway back to her hiding place, she gave Gabriel the all-clear.

Phoebe had no experience with explosives, or she might have waited a little longer. The bomb went off while she was running and something struck her from behind. Her right leg was suddenly numb, and then a pressure wave from the explosion hit her, knocking her down hard. Loud ringing filled her ears, and for several moments she wasn't sure where she was.

Reason returned slowly, but when she realized what had happened, panic started to overcome her. Another sound made its way through the ringing, a howling noise was coming from the hospital—the alarm.

Unable to get up, Phoebe crawled the rest of the way to the wall and lay under a different shrub. She wasn't as protected as before, but it would still be hard to see her in the dark. Muffled gunfire came from the building, although the ringing made it hard for her to be sure—she feared the worst. Her leg was bleeding badly and blood was pooling around her. She couldn't feel the leg and was afraid that it might be broken.

♎

David grimaced when the clip fell. Gabriel still had his hand up for silence and leaned over to whisper a command. Mark went back to warn Julian that someone might be coming from behind now, and then returned to Gabriel's side.

David had a wild look in his eyes. Daniel could see the panic growing in him and wanted to do something to help, but he knew better than to move or say anything. He wondered what they were waiting for and counted the passing seconds. Finally, he heard the bomb go off.

The explosion resonated through the building. Mark and Gabriel ripped the door's hinges off, leaving it in the frame. They waited on either side, as Gabriel did a countdown with his fingers. The explosion had masked the noise of the hinges breaking, but they knew the Keepers were alert.

♎

Phoebe gritted her teeth and passed word to Gabriel that the head Keeper from the basement and the one with the automatic weapon had both come outside to investigate the explosion. One of the basement Keepers was at the iron door with his weapon drawn, while the other had retreated down the hallway to the desk near the front door. The floater was upstairs, sounding the alarm.

Gabriel looked at Mark and shrugged. He signaled for everyone to take cover and then the two of them stepped back from the opening, sliding the heavy iron door with them, and using it as a shield. Bullets flew through the open doorway, as the Keeper on the other side fired blindly into the darkness. When he paused to reload, Gabriel stepped into the opening and killed him with three quick bursts to the chest, and the rescue team swept into the secure area. Another burst of suppressed gunfire sounded when Mark killed the other Keeper downstairs.

Caleb and Daniel headed straight for Rebecca's room, and found her half awake—the explosion had partially brought her out of it.

"Becky," Daniel said, "we're going to get you out of here. This is Caleb. We're going to carry you."

Rebecca winced when they moved her. They picked her up, using her blanket as a sling, and carried her out of the room, then turned left to reenter the storage area. More shooting came from behind while they retreated. It was Gabriel killing the Keeper with the automatic weapon, who'd come down the front stairs.

The alarm was fading now, which meant the floater, who'd been turning the alarm's handle, would be coming soon. Caleb stepped over a body in the hallway—David. He was able to stoop over just far enough to retrieve his gun and put its sling over his head, before following Daniel up the back stairs.

They climbed with Rebecca between them. The stairway was too narrow to walk abreast, so Daniel went up first, twisting so that he didn't have to walk backward. Caleb looked up the stairs and saw Julian framed in the doorway above. The Scout turned and fired a quiet burst from his weapon, killing the roving Keeper who'd come to check the back entrance.

They moved as quickly as possible, up and out the loading dock, with Julian weaving a path ahead, scanning for signs of movement. Mark followed them up the stairs and out the back doors, then they all headed toward the back gate.

♎

Gabriel stayed in the basement, waiting for the Sergeant of the Keepers to return, and dispatched him as he came down the stairs. He was sure the alarm and the explosion would bring more Keepers before long, but they should have at least ten minutes to get away.

Phoebe, what's happening outside? Gabriel asked. He heard the strain in her thoughts as she answered, and realized she'd been hurt—probably by the explosion. He ground his teeth at their luck, knowing that he'd need to go get her. An old expression ran through his head: "No plan survives first contact with the enemy."

Then more bad news came: Phoebe told him they didn't have ten or even five minutes—more Keepers were arriving now, at least a dozen were swarming across the front grounds. Gabriel swore again, thinking quickly. *Tell Mark what's happening,* he said. He decided it would probably be best to take the first wave of reinforcements in the basement.

CHAPTER 40

No Good Choices

PHOEBE LOOKED THROUGH THE EYES of the Keeper in the basement in disbelief. He was shooting through the opening, to where Daniel and Caleb were hiding. She felt David die, and the trauma of his death made her mind go blank for a while.

Phoebe, what's happening outside? Gabriel asked.

No change yet, she answered tersely, not wanting to distract him with her own problems.

She managed to remove her belt and wound it around her leg above the wound to help slow the bleeding. It wasn't easy since the injury was so high up, but then a surrealistic calm took over—keeping everyone safe was her job; she had to keep it together.

Phoebe nervously felt for everyone's spark, afraid of what she might find, but only David had been hurt so far—her father and Caleb were with Rebecca now; the three of them were already up the back stairs. The sound of running footfalls drew her attention. More Keepers were passing her as they rushed toward the hospital's entrance. She lay very still, hoping they wouldn't notice her.

Gabriel, there are at least a dozen more Keepers coming, she said.

Tell Mark what's happening. His voice was cool and even.

Mark received the information from her with a simple *Okay.*

Phoebe saw that he and Julian were both with her family, already out of the hospital and partway to the back gate. Several of the newly arrived Keepers ran around the building toward the rear of the hospital while the rest went in through the main door. She wasn't sure that they'd get away in time, and focused her attention on her family, ready to help if she could.

Mark, there are four guards heading around the building from the north, she said.

He acknowledged her message, but she was beginning to doubt that he'd be able to protect everyone. Just then she heard Gabriel tell her that he was coming. Somehow he'd guessed that she'd been hurt.

♎︎

A large group of the reinforcements rushed into the hospital's security wing and down the stairs, firing as they descended. Gabriel had moved past the opening where the iron door had been, and into the room where Daniel and Caleb had hidden. As he'd retreated, Gabriel dropped a number of objects on the floor. Guns were being fired into the basement. He knew they'd be coming down the front steps and through the empty ward in a matter of seconds. Footsteps echoed through the long hallway, when he sprang the trap, detonating the antipersonnel devices that Julian and David had made that week. The explosive material wrapped in layer after layer of metal wire and cable created a deadly spray of shrapnel that tore through the men in the hallway—they died quickly.

Gabriel went back into the security ward and moved toward the front entrance, stepping over bodies and body parts in the hall. The lamps in the hall had been blown out, but there was still light from Rebecca's room. One of the uniform cloaks looked less damaged than most, so he threw it over his shoulders, and grabbed a clean uniform cap from the desk. He walked up the front stairway, his own silenced weapon ready. At the top of the stairs he surprised two more Keepers, killing them before they realized who he was. The cloak had confused them just long enough to slow their reactions. Then he put his head down, pulled the cap forward on his head, and walked out the front door.

Phoebe lay on the ground across the street, just a little to the south. From the amount of blood on the ground, he could tell that her injury was serious, but the makeshift tourniquet reassured him that she was alive. He bent over and helped her up to a standing position, then put her over his shoulder before vanishing into the shadows down a side street.

"Tell Mark we'll meet him at the boat," he said aloud. A few seconds later he heard Phoebe scream. Her body tensed up and grew very hot in his arms, even through the clothing.

♎

Phoebe had watched the Keepers moving toward the back of the hospital, still keeping track of her family. She was trying to see if they would be able to get away—it was still too close to call. The ringing in her ears had partially faded, and she could hear shooting again.

Another explosion came from the hospital, but she couldn't let herself be distracted now.

Mark and Julian were spread out to either side of Caleb and Daniel as they moved. Phoebe warned Mark that the guards were coming from his right, meaning right with respect to their direction of travel. For some inexplicable reason he looked left and didn't see them in time—they killed him. Partially dazed from his death, Phoebe looked through the Keepers' eyes. Just then, Gabriel bent over her. He was wearing a bloody Keeper's uniform, but she paid him little attention. He lifted her up onto one leg and then slung her painfully over his shoulder—the leg was no longer numb, and she clamped her teeth together to keep from screaming. He said something, but she didn't listen.

The four Keepers behind the hospital had found her family and were pointing rifles at Caleb and Daniel—they'd be dead in seconds. "No!" she yelled. The icy feeling she'd first felt on the cliffs in Rebecca's dream tore through her body—its power amplified thousands of times. She reached out in a panic, savagely spearing into the minds of all four Keepers simultaneously. Anxiety had freed her of all restraint—she didn't dare take time to be gentle, and frantically shredded their minds. All four dropped to the ground at the same time, their life forces were fading fast. She could see that two were dead, and when she looked again a third spark had gone out. Then a weakness greater than anything she'd ever felt before hit. The energy she'd used was more than her body could handle, but somehow she still managed to hold onto consciousness—her family might still need her.

"What happened?" Gabriel asked. They were a block east of the hospital now.

Phoebe was slow to answer, and almost too weak to talk. Thoughts from other people around them were starting to intrude—hundreds, maybe thousands of them were in the buildings nearby. Then she remembered Gabriel's question. "Mark's dead," she said in a voice like a thread. "I'll tell Caleb where to go," she added. It was all she could do to speak, but her family was still in danger and she had to reach him.

Caleb, head for the boat! I'm with Gabriel! Phoebe put every bit of force remaining in her body into the command.

Phoebe, what happened? She could barely hear him over the din from the other voices.

Please go, she pleaded, but wasn't sure he'd heard her this time. The voices were getting louder, and then her vision faded into a dark tunnel.

♎

When she regained consciousness, Jacob was helping Gabriel carry her below the deck of the Molly, one was on either side of her. They helped her onto a bunk, setting her facedown.

The Scout cut the leg off of her pants, revealing an ugly wound on the back of her leg, high up on the thigh. She didn't want to see it, but images from him came through uninvited.

"I don't think it's broken," he said, "but there are pieces of something, maybe rock, embedded in the muscle. We have to remove them so she can heal. Do you have any alcohol?"

"I'm way ahead of you," Jacob said, handing him a bottle.

"I'm going to need a small, sharp knife, some clean bandages, and, if you have it, a needle and thread. Also, can you get me a pair of narrow pliers or forceps, and a piece of rubber or soft cloth—something that gives."

"Uh-oh, that doesn't sound good," Phoebe said. Gabriel didn't say anything.

"This is going to hurt, sweetheart," he warned.

"Ugh, what doesn't? Go ahead," she said, tensing up.

He used the alcohol first, trying to clean the area around the wound. Phoebe thought that this burning pain was about all she could bear, which only proved she lacked imagination. He handed her a rolled up piece of material, torn from a raincoat, and told her to bite down on it.

"It's so you don't hurt yourself," he advised. It tasted like old fish.

"Yuk!" she complained, spitting out some of the flavor.

Later, she realized that by 'remove' Gabriel meant that he was going to dig a hole into her leg—punishment for making him detonate the explosive too soon. Sometime during the excavation she lost consciousness again.

CHAPTER 41

Molly

REBECCA LAY ON THE BUNK, staring at her daughter for the first time in almost eighteen years, trying not to think about what had almost happened. Her shoulder hurt, but at the moment she welcomed the pain as a distraction. Phoebe was still asleep on the bunk across the passageway from her. Her leg was bandaged and most of the blood had been cleaned up, but Rebecca shivered anyway.

It was so tempting to reach across and touch her, just once, to know for sure that she was really there. But she hesitated to do it—Phoebe might not like that. She didn't yet know how things stood between them.

When she'd awakened in the hospital room, Rebecca's first notion was that she was dead. After all, she'd been shot and the last thing she remembered was someone giving her an injection. She'd stared into Daniel's eyes, only partially hearing what he said. Maybe she really *was* dead. It seemed a reasonable hypothesis, considering what was happening—but the pain of being moved quickly dispelled that theory. It was as though a hot knife had gone through her shoulder. It almost sent her back into the darkness again.

There were bright lights in a hallway and then semi-darkness in a humid place. She remembered an uncomfortable trip up some stairs—Daniel was above her, climbing—and then fresh air hit her face; its coolness revived her a little, even more than the pain.

Two people were carrying her, one was a young man—the name Caleb came to her mind, but she wasn't sure why. Had Daniel told her that, or had she unconsciously connected with him? Suddenly everyone was frozen. Tension and fear emanated from the people around her. *Keepers,* someone thought, and she sensed four hostile sparks to their right. They carried guns and were determined to kill them. Then she felt it, an explosion of power passed through the Keepers—more power than Rebecca thought was possible, and all concentrated into the four hostile minds. A blistering heat radiated from them—painful, even to her—and then the sparks were gone.

Rebecca seemed to float the rest of the way to the boat. There were a number of discontinuities in her awareness, but the cool air continued to work its magic. The escape from the hospital still seemed more like a dream than anything else, and she wondered again what had really happened.

Jacob had welcomed her with the same lopsided grin she remembered from her youth, but there was a tightness to his eyes that she didn't remember being there before. Everyone's face seemed older, more care-lined and worried. The men exuded tension, although they tried to hide it. She wondered why until she saw Phoebe.

There was a large jagged gap in the back of her leg, and the bed—the floor—the whole cabin, was swimming in blood. It was everywhere. That had been the worst moment of her life, even worse than that night she'd run from the Penitents and jumped to what she'd assumed was her death.

Gabriel was just finishing his surgery and tried to explain that the wound looked much worse than it was. Phoebe would recover, but Rebecca couldn't help sobbing. The Scout blamed himself.

"I should have emphasized how dangerous it was—anything to do with explosives is risky." After sewing the wound and bandaging her leg, he looked down at Phoebe with more emotion on his face than Rebecca remembered seeing before, and put a hand on her shoulder before cleaning up and leaving them alone.

What the hell have I done? Rebecca thought.

Ω

The boat was underway when Daniel stepped through the hatch to sit beside her. The stress of the night was on his face, worry and fatigue—but there was hope in his eyes.

"How are you feeling?" he asked, his tone a little stiff.

"Guilty, terrified, grateful, and embarrassed—take your pick." Rebecca's eyes felt swollen from crying, but she managed a faint smile.

They both looked at Phoebe, and an uncomfortable silence filled the cabin. She'd dreamed of this moment a thousand times, and had played out what she would say in her head repeatedly. But she'd never really allowed herself to believe they'd see each other again, and none of the things she'd thought to say before made sense now.

"Sorry doesn't begin—" Becky started, but he interrupted her, shaking his head.

"We can talk later. I just wanted to check on the two of you, but I have to go above for a little while longer," he sighed. "My father needs help, at least till we clear the harbor." He took her good hand and squeezed it before leaving.

$$\Omega$$

On deck, Daniel passed Caleb, who was reefing the mainsail to decrease its power. Jacob was maneuvering the Molly around some of the more dangerous rocks in the dark and they needed to keep the speed down. Gabriel was on deck, too.

"She's doing pretty well," he said, "I think I got the stones out of her leg, but she'll probably have a decent scar. Hope you don't mind," Gabriel added with a twisted grin.

Caleb closed his eyes briefly, relief clear on his face. Earlier, he'd walked in carrying Rebecca, and had almost collapsed. Daniel made him leave the cabin, so he wouldn't distract Gabriel while he worked. He was obviously anxious to go below again to see her.

$$\Omega$$

Phoebe's leg was throbbing and she had a massive headache. Across the cabin, on the opposite bunk, Rebecca was looking at her. Thoughts, like voices, drifted in from the people above, but they were subdued now and she could ignore what they were thinking.

Her mother sighed, and she looked at her.

"Hello, Rebecca," Phoebe said coolly, and saw the hurt in her mother's eyes—there was a change in their focus and she looked away. It was still hard for Phoebe to feel much sympathy. She knew Rebecca had stayed away from them for their own good, but that didn't change the fact that she'd been abandoned, and left to deal with the curse of her senses all alone. And tonight she'd had to do something truly awful, something she didn't want to think about yet. Phoebe closed her eyes and took several deep breaths, trying to push the guilt and anger away for now.

"Did you meet Caleb?" she asked, trying to sound friendly.

"After a fashion," Rebecca said. There was a cautious note in her mother's voice. "We were introduced for about three seconds—I think—he helped carry me out of the hospital. I'm afraid I wasn't completely coherent until we reached the boat. Is he your boyfriend?"

Phoebe stared at her mother for a full ten seconds before answering. "He's more than that," she said. "I don't think I ever *could* leave him." But even as she said it, Phoebe knew she wasn't being fair.

Rebecca was quiet again, thinking, but she spoke after a few moments. "I guess I deserve that. But I hope you'll let me try to explain why...It wasn't because I didn't love you, and it wasn't because I didn't want to be there for you."

"I'm listening," Phoebe said. Her voice still sounded a little hostile, even in her own ears. "Sorry," she added. "I'm not exactly in the best mood tonight." Just then, her father returned with a big grin on his face.

"Hello, Princess," he said. "You know you scared the crap out of me, don't you?"

"Guess I forgot to duck."

He rolled his eyes and shook his head. Phoebe noticed that he'd been doing that a lot lately, usually it was because of something she'd done.

He sat on the bed beside Rebecca, and gently took her hand. "So, are you going to stay awake this time?"

Her mother caught her eye with a look that said they'd talk later. And then she looked at her father. Phoebe could see right away that he'd always be her mother's Caleb—it was so obvious. But what she couldn't understand was how her mother could have left him, and then stayed away from the one person who could make her feel that way. It gave her a new appreciation for what she'd given up for them. *Maybe I'm not being fair,* she thought. Phoebe caught her mother's eye again and smiled. It was all she could manage for now.

Caleb finally made it down, and he leaned on the edge of the bunk to hug her. Nothing else seemed to matter all that much when he was around.

"Hey, Phoebe, how ya doing?" He was smiling, but there was still an echo of worry on his face.

"I'm good."

He sighed, but she sensed that something else was bothering him, too. There was a tension flowing in through her arms.

"What is it?" she asked. "Were you hurt?"

"No, I'm just worried about Dad and Mary. You know...what might happen to them?"

"Don't worry, Caleb," her father said. "They didn't know anything, and the Council will see that. They're tyrants, but not completely unreasonable."

Phoebe leaned against Caleb's shoulder. It was finally sinking in that they were free and together for good. She shifted over to make space for him on the bunk, and they lay beside each other holding hands until they fell asleep.

CHAPTER 42

Long Shot

HAMMERING ON THE FRONT DOOR awakened the desk clerk. It was four in the morning.

He didn't like the look of the man outside. It appeared as though he'd ridden through the night and through a light snow that had been falling off and on since sunset—his horse looked as though it was about ready to fall over. *What's so important that it couldn't wait till dawn?* he wondered.

Next, the man demanded immediate access to certain guests, a group of young seminary students traveling together. At first the clerk refused, but the look on the rider's face convinced him otherwise. He insisted on at least awakening the guests himself. Now three people, including the messenger, were sitting around a table in the dining room, speaking in urgent, hushed voices. The clerk assumed it was Council business, and kept his distance—but he still didn't like it.

Samuel was surprised at how fast Matthew was moving. It was a haste that spoke volumes about the urgency of the mission. They were staying in a town in the foothills of the Western Mountains, having just attended to a patient nearby. The message from Matthew had come to a security station just twelve hours earlier. As promised, Samuel had kept the Guard informed of his itinerary, but it was just blind luck that he'd stayed in this town an extra day. The note said that Rebecca's daughter was gravely ill and injured. Rebecca was wounded, too, and they were fleeing from the Keepers. There was no time to lose.

It would take at least a day to reach the rendezvous point, so he looked at Jonathan and nodded, telling him it was time to get ready, and then he headed upstairs to pack.

♎︎

It was an ancient aircraft, originally manufactured more than three hundred years before. Probably none of the original parts remained—maybe a bolt…somewhere. The aircraft, and others like it, had been purchased by the Order from museums just prior to the war, relics of the past even then. Mechanics had been forced to completely rebuild them and to fabricate all new parts to substitute for obsolete components.

It was amphibious and could take off and land on either water or land. The Duck was an ideal vehicle for an organization like the Order, unsure of what infrastructure might remain after the war. But it had always been a backup measure. The Order possessed far more sophisticated, modern aircraft—vehicles that didn't need runways at all. But these ancient airplanes had become the mainstay of the Order's fleet following the Purge. They couldn't risk having their modern machines fall into the hands of the Council.

The Ducks had all been converted to run on compressed natural gas, which was readily available in the Land. Prior to the war, vast gas reserves in the Northern Province had been tapped from shale formations deep below ground. The wells had the capacity to supply energy to a billion people for over a decade, and would supply the Land's needs for more than a thousand years.

♎︎

Matthew received a message from Jürgen, providing the time and location of where he could meet Samuel. They'd fly to a lake in a sparsely populated area near the mountains, between the Western Highway and Sangre River, where they could pick him up without being seen. The Duck would fly low and skirt populated areas to avoid being detected.

After dark, Matthew and the two pilots climbed into the Duck, essentially an oversized canoe with wings and retractable wheels. It was kept in a camouflaged structure, built on Lake John. Its name had been inspired by the graceful way it took off and landed. The Duck lifted off from the lake after full dark.

Their route took them over the low hills bordering the eastern edge of the Central Plains, across the north-south highway, and on to the edge of the Western Mountains before turning north to search for the lake where they'd meet Samuel's team. The pilot, Margaret, had flown Matthew on numerous missions, and he was comfortable with her skill. She and the copilot were flying on instruments, although they had visual aids for landing. These consisted of low-light intensified goggles, and a mid-wave infrared camera that was mounted in the nose of the aircraft.

The copilot helped Margaret find the lake using an old map. They wanted to land quickly to avoid potentially drawing unwanted attention, so Margaret took the aircraft directly in on the first pass. A few minutes after landing Matthew saw a light flash three times—Jonathan's signal. He opened the cabin hatch and lowered an inflatable raft into the water to go retrieve the team.

Ω

Samuel settled into the seat across a narrow aisle from him, he looked tired. Matthew thought it better to let the Healer sleep for now. The return flight was uneventful and they were soon back at the Lake John facility, sitting in the lodge.

"What do you see?" Samuel asked. It was a more direct question than Matthew was used to answering, but this was his friend.

"Aside from a tangled mess? I see her wounds, and an illness that hasn't fully manifested yet. The odds don't look good, but her potential is worth almost any risk." Tightness in his voice carried a conviction the Healer had rarely heard from him. "If they survive, if they can escape, if they aren't killed by the Keepers or the storm, and if we can find them in time, Phoebe's going to need you. Becky was wounded, too, but her fate's so tightly bound with Phoebe's that I can't see how seriously she's been injured."

"What is the girl?"

"Something…something new. She's an incredibly powerful Sensitive—that much is certain—but I think there's more to her."

"You see her as a weapon, then." It wasn't a question. A look, almost anger, crossed Samuel's face. He'd never liked it when Matthew manipulated people. It went against his nature, and his personal philosophy.

"I understand your reservations, but yes. If she decides to help us then she'd be a fearsome inducement for the Council to be more reasonable."

"If *she* decides," Samuel said.

"Yes. I promise you that; it'll be up to her."

"Of course I'll help. I told you that before. I'd do it no matter what. But you should understand that I *will* hold you to your word."

Matthew nodded.

"And now?" Samuel wanted to know.

"Now we wait," Matthew said.

"Do they really have a chance?" Samuel asked, looking at Matthew's face.

The Guide glanced down a moment, and the stress he rarely allowed to show openly surfaced. "It's a long shot, but we have to try."

CHAPTER 43

Remorse

T HEIR FIRST FULL DAY AT sea dawned with a cloudless sky and fair winds. The water was smooth. Phoebe had been worried about a rough sea, but for now her stomach was holding out. Her grandfather had fashioned a crutch for her from an old oar, and it helped to get around without feeling like a burden. The others heard her clomping about the deck all afternoon, up and down, waiting to watch the sun set on her first full day of freedom, and life as a refugee.

Phoebe still hadn't spoken about what she'd done, nor had she come to terms with it, but knew exactly what had happened. *I killed four people,* she thought staring out over the water.

The sun was about one hand's width above the horizon—an hour till sunset. She'd been desperately clinging to the thought that she'd had no choice, and that keeping Julian and her family alive had forced her to act, but it sounded hollow today. *I'm a monster,* she thought.

Because of her, four Keepers were dead—or worse. If any actually *had* survived, they'd live a miserable shell of a life, barely able to function. The breeze was from behind, blowing her hair forward and across her face. Her grandfather was sailing the Molly north with the wind a quarter behind the port beam, but she didn't notice the hair, or much of anything that was happening around her. She'd just been staring at the horizon all afternoon, and at light rippling on the small waves.

I was too quick—careless. She couldn't help second-guessing her actions. *Did I really have to kill them?* She'd been telling herself that there'd been no real choice, but she still didn't know for sure.

Other things haunted her, too. What if they had families—people who loved them the same way she loved Caleb and her father? Maybe they were husbands, fathers, and brothers, ordered into the fight but not really sure why. Now four families were destroyed, and she'd done it. Phoebe found a crate on which to perch, with one foot up on the crate and her head resting on her good knee. The guilt had been eating away at her all day, and it didn't seem to be getting any better.

At first, she'd been so thankful her family had survived, that everything else seemed unimportant. But the more she thought about it, the worse everything felt. She looked down, putting her forehead on her knee, and started to cry. She tried to be quiet, but couldn't stop. Her hands were gripped into fists as tightly as she could manage. Pain had always been a reliable friend—it helped her suppress strong feelings, and brought her back to the present. But today it wasn't enough.

Did they deserve to die? How come I get to live? She wondered how many people she might have massacred in anger and grief had Caleb or her father been killed last night. Her foot dropped back onto the deck and she looked at the horizon, releasing the control she'd been keeping over her memory. She was back at the hospital again.

It was dark. Gabriel had just lifted her up, and she was watching the last moments of the escape. She knew this was a memory now and pushed back against the raw explosion of power as the scene unfolded. She played it over and over, looking through the Keepers' eyes and seeing her family about to die. She kept enough awareness of where she really was to stifle the scream that would follow, but a small noise escaped her anyway.

"What's the matter, Phoebe?" Caleb asked, bringing her all the way back to the present. "Does your leg hurt?"

She didn't speak right away, and he squatted down on the deck beside her, trying to take her hand. Phoebe didn't think she deserved his touch and pulled her hand back. She couldn't help imagining some other woman or girl sitting in a darkened room beside the person she loved at this very moment, holding on to a cold, dead hand.

"Caleb," Gabriel's voice drifted across the deck, "do you mind if I speak with Phoebe for a while?"

"Do you know what's wrong with her—why she's crying?" Caleb asked. He shifted to one knee, to look over his left shoulder at Gabriel.

"I have an idea."

"What is it? What's wrong?"

"It's nothing you can help her with right now. Do you mind?"

"All right." He sighed, hesitating a moment before walking away.

Phoebe and the Scout were alone now. He pulled another crate over to sit next to her. At first he didn't say anything, but followed her gaze to the horizon. She shifted the shortened oar across her legs and started twisting it in both directions at the same time. The pain helped—a little. She noticed in passing that she was tearing the skin of both palms and coating the wood with her blood.

Gabriel had started talking before she noticed, his voice was softer than she remembered. "I killed for the first time when I was even younger than you are. I was fourteen. The Purge was underway and there were a lot of horrible things going on at the time. Some were being burned alive by the mobs, even innocent bystanders got caught up in it—especially once the Penitents were out in force. They'd brutalize people before killing them, and all in the name of their perverted version of faith."

"I've seen some of what you're talking about, but I didn't know you had to start fighting so young," she said.

"I was with my father at the time. We ran away from the AJ's, 'the Arms of Justice'—that's what the Keepers were called at the time— and fought our way through the Penitents to reach the mountains to the north. You can still see the letters 'AJ' embroidered on the lapels of the Keeper uniform. Now they call themselves Justice Keepers, but they still serve the same purpose as they did eighteen years back: protect the Council, and impose its will on others.

"Decades ago, the Council stood for something. They began with a noble purpose, and understood that the ends didn't justify any means. At the same time, the Order did things I wasn't happy about. But ultimately, I made the choice a long time ago."

"I spoke with someone from the Council not long ago," Phoebe said. "He seemed nice—honorable. I think there are some good people in the Council, too."

"I'm sure there are. Unfortunately we have to deal with the ones calling the shots, and right now they're not so nice. But that doesn't change how we feel. I can tell you that it's never easy to kill, not if you're a normal human being, anyway. Maybe they need to administer a test, before arming people. Killing *should* bother you. It's a terrible thing to have to do. But Phoebe, please understand that none of us wanted to be there last night. Those deaths— David, Mark, and the others—and the terrible things that we had to do—are because of the Council. It was by their will that your mother was shot, and it was they who put those men in the line of fire last night—enforcing the Council's version of justice. The same justice that would see your mother executed. The Council labeled her a demon years ago, and they'll do the same to you now, just because you exist."

"How did you know about…what I did?" Phoebe asked.

"I spoke with Julian, and your dad. It wasn't hard to guess that you had something to do with what happened. Make no mistake, if you hadn't stopped them—and stopped them quickly—your family and Julian would be dead now. Instead, those other men would be second-guessing what they'd done last night."

"But I keep thinking that maybe I could have just confused them, or caused them to blink, or…or—I don't know—maybe made them pass out." Phoebe wanted to grab onto what he was offering but, at the same time, she couldn't let go of her guilt so easily.

"Have you had much experience with that sort of thing? I mean, have you ever tried to stop four people from executing your family before? You had, what, less than a second to act, right?"

It wasn't a real question, but she answered anyway. "No. I didn't even know I could do that—affect more than one person at a time that way. And I didn't know, for sure, what I could do from that far away. I just knew I had to stop them. The only other person I ever touched that way was Caleb's cousin, Mary. Even then I didn't know beforehand that I could do what I did to her—it was my first time. But I was so careful with her. The threat wasn't immediate—and, of course, Caleb loves Mary."

"Looking back now, could you have killed the Keepers in the basement, or tried to harm them before we went in?"

"I suspected that I might have been able to…well, at least do something to affect them, but I've been afraid of myself ever since I erased Mary's memory. Now I'm afraid in another way. I'm not sure what I might do if I got really-really mad. Last night I…I hoped you guys could just get in and get out without anyone being hurt. Of course, I knew that someone *could* get hurt."

The Scout smiled at her summary. "Yeah, someone usually gets hurt. I'd hoped to avoid killing, too. But once the Keepers were alert it was too late." He sounded bitter, and Phoebe realized that, even with all of his experience, Gabriel was deeply disturbed by the killing he'd done, too.

"Later, when the second wave of Keepers arrived, could you have done something to them?"

"Now I'm sure I could have, but at the time, I didn't think of it—and I hoped you guys could get away before they reached the basement. But I watched, ready to help if I had to." Phoebe stared back at the horizon again. *I might have been able to stop them,* she realized. *They were so close.* She wondered what her limits were. *How many people can I kill at a time?* she asked herself, but fervently hoped that she'd never need to find out.

"You don't sound bloodthirsty to me, Phoebe. You provided me with perfect intelligence, and even ran across the street to save those innocent people—and got injured in the process. By the way, why didn't you wait until you were behind the wall before giving me the signal?" This had obviously been bothering him, too. She didn't want him to bear the burden of her own stupidity.

"I was afraid that every second I waited made things more dangerous. The Keepers were already suspicious, and I thought that, if I waited too long, you guys might be killed. I was stupid. A few more seconds probably wouldn't have mattered. But for me, the lives of my family are too important. You *know* it was my fault, right? Not yours. I took the chance."

"So you risked your own life to save us."

Phoebe nodded. "What's your point?"

"You remind me more and more of your mother. You know, Matthew warned her that she might not live if she came to get you. The danger was real, but she knew waiting increased the risk for you. We may never know what might have happened if she hadn't come, but—for Rebecca—none of that mattered. You're much more important to her than her own life. I thought you should hear that." Gabriel stood to go.

Phoebe knew she'd have more tears for the people she'd killed, but felt a little better now. Before he could leave, she put a hand on his arm.

"Thank you," she said. "For now, for last night, and for the horrible thing you had to do to protect me…before." He closed his eyes and nodded before walking off. Phoebe doubted he'd ever get over killing the young Sensitive. She knew how he felt. *Maybe it's good we feel this way.* At least she knew *why* she'd killed last night.

She took a handkerchief from her pocket and blew her nose before looking around. Caleb was watching her. She held her arms out toward him for a hug, trying unsuccessfully to smile. Relief replaced the worry on his face—and that made her feel a little better, too.

CHAPTER 44

Pursued

Ω

FOR THREE DAYS JACOB SAILED the Molly north, following the coast while he considered where to go ashore. The sea had been gentle thus far—no seasickness complaints from Phoebe yet—but she wasn't looking good.

♎

Pain in her leg woke Phoebe in the middle of the night, and it took a while for her to remember where she was. While the discussion with Gabriel had helped, she wasn't quite ready to throw a party. The combination of her aching leg and guilty conscience had been robbing her of sleep and it was taking its toll.

She and Caleb shared the Captain's cabin with Daniel and Rebecca. There'd been some initial resistance to her sleeping with Caleb, but she'd put her good foot down. "Look, it isn't like we're having orgies over here." There'd been a fierce look on her face when she said this, but then she closed her eyes and added, "Yet," trying to smile. Her father thought it over for a minute and then gave in.

Her parents were asleep just across the aisle; she could hear her father's familiar snore. Caleb's arm was draped over her and, except for the pain, she'd have been content to doze back off, but her leg had other ideas. It felt swollen and had begun to throb. The cabin was stuffy, too, and she wondered if she could get Caleb to crack open the tiny portal above their bunk without waking the others. A little cool air would make her feel a lot better, but she hated to disturb him.

"Phoebe, what's the matter?" her father whispered. She hadn't noticed his breathing change, and when she moved, Caleb woke up, too. He leaned up on an elbow to look at her then put a hand on the side of her face.

"She's a bit warm, and damp," he said.

"It's nothing, really. My leg hurts a little, and it's kind of hot in here," she said in a hushed voice.

"Do you have a fever?" Rebecca asked.

"Great! Now everyone's awake." Phoebe just hoped her voice hadn't carried into the main cabin.

Becky clumsily disentangled herself from Daniel to sit up on the edge of the bunk, difficult with just one good arm—she half fell, half slid onto her feet. The bunks here were taller than normal beds; they had locking drawers for storage underneath. Her mother's bad arm was in a sling, but she'd been getting about on deck the past two days.

Rebecca leaned over to feel her head and face. "You *do* feel warm. We should look at your leg."

"I'm okay, it doesn't hurt that much," Phoebe protested. Her mother didn't look convinced. "All right, it hurts," she admitted. "And it might be a little swollen—but that's normal, right?"

"Lie on your stomach so I can have a look. It's almost time to change the dressing anyway."

Phoebe felt the pressure loosen and then air on her wound.

"Should it be that red?" Caleb asked.

"Hmm, I think it might be a bit infected," Rebecca observed. Phoebe couldn't see what they were looking at, but her father's face looked worried from across the cabin.

There'd been a change in him these past few days. He was different now, happy. He and Becky had spent a lot of time together, talking. They seemed to have come to terms with what happened, although—sometimes—she noticed they were overly polite with each other. *They just need time,* she thought.

"I'm sure it'll clear up," Phoebe said, although her voice didn't sound confident.

"It should," her mother said. "But I'll ask Gabriel to have a look anyway. He'll have a better idea—he's seen a lot of wounds. I wish we had antibiotics. Julian said they'd brought drugs, but David was carrying the medkit. Still, I wouldn't be too worried just yet. You're a strong girl."

Caleb twisted around to open the portal on his other side, and Phoebe sighed when the cool night air came in. Rebecca asked Caleb to replace the dressing, since she wasn't used to working with just one arm yet. She started to lean down, but stopped.

It looked as though she was going to kiss Phoebe on the forehead, but wasn't sure if that would be okay, so she reached up and squeezed her mother's good hand. "Thanks," she said. Things between them were better, although not completely comfortable. That would take time, too. After the new bandage was on, she felt a lot better. It was still dark outside, so they all tried to go back to sleep.

The following day, the pain was worse. Phoebe didn't complain right away, but everyone noticed she wasn't eating. Caleb insisted she needed food to heal, but she shook her head. Rebecca didn't say anything, but looked at her funny. She could feel her mother measuring the strength of her defenses, and knew she wasn't happy.

♎

Phoebe lay on the bunk her grandfather normally used, watching the oil lamp on the wall. It was mounted with a swivel to stay upright when the boat swayed. She'd been using this to gauge the strength of the sea from the way it moved. The cabin was just long enough for the two parallel bunks, each no wider than a normal single bed—cozy enough if you were with the right person.

The overhead was painted an off-white to match the cabin walls, and there were pictures attached to the bulkheads: a photo of her with her father when she was very young, and two of Phoebe's drawings. Seeing them there had made her feel good, but there'd always been a blank spot on one side. The paint was a little darker there. She'd often wondered what had hung there before, but it wasn't empty now. An old photograph fit the space perfectly. It was of a much younger Rebecca and her father together. She gazed at their expressions for several minutes. They seemed so happy, so full of life. And there was a sense of hope in their eyes, too, so strong that it made her want to cry. Just then her father stepped into the cabin and noticed where she was looking.

"I remember when that was taken," he said, putting a hand on the top of her head. He noticed that her eyes were wet. "What's the matter, Princess? Does your leg hurt?"

"No. I was just thinking. About the good things we have to look forward to, and how much we missed."

He ruffled her hair then left without saying more. After a few minutes, she tried to get up, but dizziness made her sway and she caught herself on the bed. Rebecca saw her teetering through the hatch and came in to help her back into the bed.

"Feeling dizzy?"

"A little."

Rebecca perched on the opposite bunk, looking at her. "I used to sleep in that bunk. In fact…" She paused to lift a corner of the covers, checking for something. "Well, what do you know! You were born in that bunk."

"Oh God!" Phoebe said. "And now I sleep here with Caleb. Doesn't look like I've made much progress, does it?" They both laughed.

"Actually, I'm amazed at how strong you are. Even this last summer, when I contacted you that very first time."

"The dream. So, did all that really happen?"

Her mother closed her eyes, nodding. "It was horrible. But I knew I couldn't let them get me. If they didn't kill me right away, the Inquisition would have found you and your father."

Phoebe caught her breath, thinking about how close they'd all come. She'd jumped, too, but in her case it was just to avoid what the mob would have done to her. Her mother's admission made her swallow.

"Can we talk about something else from that night?" Phoebe wanted to know.

"Anything."

"Do you remember a surge of energy, just before I jumped?"

"Yes." There was a cautious look in her mother's eyes, as if she'd been expecting a different question. "I don't know what that was. I've felt similar things before, but much less intense. It usually meant something inside of me was changing, but I never felt anything that—that powerful."

"The strange thing is that it's happened to me more than once. It seems to come whenever I'm in danger—when I need to do something to protect myself, or someone I care about."

"Maybe it comes from the other bloodline," Rebecca said, almost to herself. "When you were conceived, they crossed two different genetic strains. Or maybe it's just you, something new."

"What else did they do to us?" Phoebe asked.

Rebecca took a deep breath. This was obviously an uncomfortable subject. "Phoebe." She paused to think about what to say. "Phoebe, both of us were…altered, while we were in the womb. Our basic gifts are natural; they come from who and what we are. But to increase the power of our connections, they needed to do more." She stopped again. She looked upset. "I'm sorry I let them do that to you. I should have known better. There's no good excuse, but you need to understand…I *really* trusted them. They raised me. They were my family. Before I met your father, the program team was the center of my life." Rebecca bit her lip. Phoebe waited for her to calm down before pushing.

"What *exactly* did they do to us?" she asked.

"Your dad said he'd explained a lot. He mentioned that other things were done to you—things he didn't really understand." Phoebe nodded, watching as her mother made fists with both hands.

"After I found my way back to the Order, I had a chance to speak with one of the program scientists. I'd always been curious about the details of their treatments, but they weren't open to questions at the time. Since the programs were dead, and the data lost, he was more talkative.

"He said the genes were just the beginning. At some point, they realized that genetic manipulation could only take them so far. I think the program team had already gone beyond the Order's original intent. They were no longer just nurturing basic characteristics, but were trying to see how far they could push things.

"Characteristics like sensitivity to other people are a part of our DNA, although they've been enhanced over many generations. In your case, no model could predict exactly what would happen by crossing the bloodlines, but since the precursor programs had been a success, they didn't think there was much to lose."

"So they were willing to just throw the dice with me," Phoebe said—angry.

"I don't know if it's quite that simple. Let's say they thought they could take more risk with you. I know they always tried to be kind to us, but I think they sometimes thought of us as experiments more than people.

"But let's get back to what I learned. Being able to connect with other minds wasn't the only thing engineered into us. They had to enhance portions of our brains—especially those parts linked to ordinary senses. I think that's why we perceive things so much more clearly than most people. We need to be able to interpret other people's senses, too. But for you and me, they went much further. Without a way to amplify the signals our brains generate, we'd probably never be able to reach out more than a couple hundred meters. Plus, we needed something they called 'the programming', so we could integrate with other minds more easily, and understand what's happening in the deeper layers of a person's brain. I was a part of the first group to receive these enhancements. They called them stage-three enhancements, and that's why I'm called a stage-three Sensitive."

"How did they do that?" Phoebe asked.

"They controlled the way parts of our brain grew, and how it developed over time, forcing portions to grow in patterns that aren't natural. But they didn't limit themselves to just our brains. They also grew a network of neurological cells throughout our bodies, called 'enhanced pathways'. These are self-replicating, self-repairing strands that run through us and turn our limbs into antennae, so we can focus the energy we generate. I suspect you have a lot more of these pathways than I do, and that your brain was enhanced more, too. Although the scientist I spoke with didn't work on your case directly, he may be able to find out more, and you can talk to him when we get back home."

"So I have a freaky brain—I knew that much—but what did the changes do to me?"

"They make our brains generate and channel more energy. It's as if they grew biological machines in our heads. You can't see them in a scan, but they act like electronic circuits, and they're structured to act in small groups, or all together at once. They channel energy more efficiently, and help us control where we want the energy to go. For you, they probably supercharged everything, but I still think that some of your strength comes from the merging of the bloodlines.

"I don't think they ever intended to make you into a weapon— that goes against the very purpose of the Order. It may be that you went beyond what they intended."

"You said 'the programming' before—what does that mean?"

"When I said that they controlled how our tissue grows, I was mainly talking about how they built in biological amplifiers for power-handling, but they also grew other kinds of circuits that help us process information and enhance memory, too. The programming contains information, knowledge about how to use our senses and about how a brain works. It's why some things seem to come so intuitively. But, of course, we learn from experience, too. The scientists didn't really know how to be a Sensitive, but they did know how brains function, and how to manipulate information."

"Why do I feel so weak after I've done something that takes a lot of energy?"

"The energy you use is thousands of times what I channel. I suppose that could drain you."

"But I'm still tired. I don't have the energy I had that night at the hospital. I feel weak inside."

Rebecca frowned. "That's not normal. That's something else. Maybe it's because of your leg, or…"

"Or what?"

"I don't know for sure. Matthew said that you might be getting sick. This could have something to do with that."

Phoebe shrugged. "I felt okay before, just weak now and then."

"Phoebe," Rebecca said, "I'm sorry I did this to you. I don't think about things the same way now that I did when I was younger. Back then, I wanted the very best for you and I've always been proud of what I could do—at least once I got past the insane period. Of course I had help with that. The Order always paired us with an older Sensitive once we started developing. That's how they've done it for generations, but I wasn't there for you." Rebecca stopped.

She reached for her hand and her mother moved across the cabin to be closer. "That's all behind us now," Phoebe said. "I know you risked your life for me. Gabriel told me about what happened when you were shot. I've been thinking for a while—there's not much else to do down here—and I see things differently now."

Becky put her arm around her daughter, and she hugged her back. "It's going to be okay."

♎︎

During the night, the sea grew in strength, and the lamp on the bulkhead often tilted far over.

"Storm's coming." Her grandfather's voice drifted through the open porthole. Phoebe was tired of moping around and, ignoring the fatigue, managed to make it onto the deck. She wanted to see her enemy firsthand—to look at its clouds forming, and to feel its wind blow through her hair. She didn't see an organized storm yet, but the waves were bigger than before and she was starting to feel a little queasy. Her grandfather suggested she lie down, saying that it helped with seasickness.

Throughout the rest of the day the waves grew larger, lifting, tilting, and sometimes dropping the boat. It put even more of a damper on her appetite than before.

Caleb scowled when she refused her lunch again, and she scowled back. *I love him, I'd do almost anything for him, but I know what's going to happen. No food!*

"Daniel, look at those clouds. It's a big storm." Her grandfather's voice had an edge to it. She could feel the tension rising from everyone aboard. Her defenses were weaker, so she had to work harder to not hear their thoughts.

"I see. How long do you think?" her father asked.

"Less than a day—and it'll be wicked. We're going to take a pounding."

They were paralleling the coast still far out from land. Jacob planned to linger in the waters in the north for a while, and then to turn back, southwest, to make landfall somewhere north of New Bright Sea. He wanted to stay well away from Chooser territory to the north, and stay within the Eastern Province. Gabriel told him there was an Order outpost not far from Bardon. He didn't know its exact location, but did know how to get in touch with someone who did.

Later that afternoon her grandfather stuck his head into the cabin and asked Gabriel to join him on deck. She could tell he was trying to hide how worried he was. Gabriel was visiting her and giving Rebecca his opinion on her leg at the time. Her mother had taken charge of her care since their talk.

The Scout looked at Phoebe, shrugging. What did he know about boats and the sea? Rebecca trailed after him. When they came back, she could tell how nervous they all were.

"What's up?" she asked, fighting the urge to listen directly.

Rebecca paused before speaking. "There are two boats on the horizon. Still pretty far out, just their sails are visible. They may be following us. I can tell there are a lot of people aboard, but not much more than that." She looked at her.

"Which way?" Phoebe asked. Her mother pointed just to port of the stern. She opened her senses, spreading her arms out slightly.

"Uh-oh," she said after a few moments. "Yeah, two large boats, each with more than twenty Keepers aboard, and there's a Council member on one."

"Who is he? Someone from the Inner Circle?" her father asked, leaning in through the hatch.

"Uh—yeah. His name is Ambrose Fletcher."

"I thought so—head of the Curia of Truth."

"They're after us," Gabriel said.

"Yep," Phoebe said.

"To capture or kill?" Rebecca asked.

"They plan to kill everyone but you, Mom." This was the first time Phoebe had ever called her that, and her mother blinked in surprise.

"Jacob, how do their boats compare with yours?" Gabriel asked.

"Well, this is a fishing boat, not a racing yacht. I'd bet they're using light transports. They'll be much faster, especially into the wind—and they'll eventually catch us." He held up a hand when everyone started to talk. "Let me finish. The Molly was built for heavy seas and theirs for speed. There's a storm coming from the southeast, and it's moving in fast. We might be able to take advantage of it to get away."

"How?" Gabriel and Phoebe both asked at the same time.

"If we turn into the path of the storm, we'll be able to weather it better than they can. We may even be able to lose them. If I can circle the eye and get in behind the storm, we can follow it up north, maybe even past the Northern Wilderness. They'll probably flee to the west. Or, we could just keep going south and decide what to do later. If we do nothing, they'll catch us in eight or nine hours, not long after dark, or they might wait till sunrise." Everyone looked at him and then at each other. No one spoke. The idea of going into the worst part of the storm seemed reckless, and sounded crazy, but what choice did they have?

Her grandfather continued. "If I turn now, during the daylight, they'll see what we're up to and cut us off in about half the time. In that case they'll reach us by sundown. But if we wait until dark, and assume they can't see when we turn east, they should keep on going north. We'll need to make sure the Molly is dark, no lights of any kind. If you're the praying type, now would be a good time to start. We need all the luck we can get.

"If we do lose them, they'll probably head west to a safe harbor. Their boats are fast, but fragile. With a big-shot official like a Council Elder aboard, I'm guessing they'll run for it as soon as they lose sight of us."

"I can keep track of them, and monitor what they do," Phoebe said.

"Can you do more—confuse them?" Gabriel wanted to know.

"Even if I had my full strength, they're too far away. That kind of thing—manipulating brains that way—takes a lot of energy. As it is, I'm not sure I could do much of anything, even if they were standing right in front of me. I'm very weak, but I can still listen."

"I'll help track them," her mother said. "Phoebe's more sensitive than me, but I can already detect their minds. We'll take shifts," she added, winking at Phoebe.

"Okay," Jacob said. "Remember, no lights. There's a gibbous moon, but the clouds will take care of that. Right now, we need to start getting ready for the storm. All of the things on deck need to be stowed, the hatches locked down, and anything that's loose put away. Let's get started."

He looked at Phoebe. "Sorry, honey, looks like it's going to be a rough night."

CHAPTER 45

The Storm

EVERYBODY PITCHED IN TO GET the Molly ready—
everyone but Rebecca and Phoebe. They were forbidden from
working. Most small things were stowed in cabinets, with the
doors latched closed, and larger items were tied down to cleats.
There were covers for the hatches, covers for the portals, and canvas
tarps to cover and protect the crates. Separate hatches in the deck
provided access to watertight storage compartments. This is where
the fish were normally put on ice, but Jacob had filled them with
supplies. Their openings were sealed using strong lids, held in place
by sturdy handles that locked when twisted.

Jacob had brought extra supplies—enough to feed everyone
aboard for more than a year if necessary. There were dry and
canned foods, kegs of fresh water, lamp oil, tools, rope—all the
essentials of life. Each compartment was checked and double-
checked, and its contents braced with timber so that things
wouldn't suddenly shift around and cause damage. The crates
on deck were triple-tested to make sure they wouldn't fly off and
injure someone.

By the time it was dark, the Molly was ready, and the people
aboard were buzzing with tension now that there was nothing left
to do. They gathered in the main cabin, just aft of where Phoebe
and her family slept. The space contained fold-down bunks, a table,
and a kitchen. It was here that Jacob's crew spent most of their off-
hours, when fishing.

Gabriel and Julian were at the table, cleaning and loading their weapons. They showed Caleb how to use and maintain David's gun. If the Molly couldn't elude the pursuers, they'd have to fight. No one expected to win.

Phoebe wondered how she could help if it came to that. She no longer had strength, but was determined not to go down without a fight. As the last of the sunlight faded, the boat's lamps were extinguished and everything made as dark as possible.

Jacob had fashioned harnesses from rope and canvas. These would keep the people on deck from being washed overboard when the waves hit. He was going to need help handling old Molly through the storm. The winds would be chaotic, changing in direction and speed. The crew would need to work in shifts to avoid the mistakes caused by being overly fatigued. Daniel, Jacob, Julian, and Caleb would all rotate in teams of two or three, as needed— each had experience sailing. Gabriel was not a waterman, but was willing to help.

A half hour after dark, Phoebe felt the boat turn; she noted the change in the cadence as her grandfather tacked into the wind, and could hear him softly calling out commands. The wind had been off the starboard beam most of the day, but now they were sailing almost directly into it, as close as the Molly could go.

Later, when they approached the center of the storm, the winds would swirl, and waves would hit with incredible power. It was already becoming rough, and occasionally a wave made the boat tilt up and then dive down. Her grandfather did his best to compensate as he tacked back and forth across the wind. Their path would eventually take them close to the very heart of the storm.

If the Council sailors had noticed the turn, this would be their best chance to catch them. Their boats were designed for speed and able to sail much closer to the wind than the Molly—fewer turns and a straighter line doubled their speed advantage. Rebecca and Phoebe both kept watch, listening to thoughts of the Council pilots.

With every passing minute, the sea grew in strength. Storms create massive waves that can easily swamp a boat like the Molly— or even swallow it whole. Jacob wasn't sure how large or strong this storm would be, and he was gambling that the Molly could survive. As a last resort, he'd try to turn and run with the wind. A maneuver like that brought its own risks, so he hoped it wouldn't be necessary.

Two hours after the course change, the Molly was being pounded by waves. She often tilted far over on her side. Once a wave made the boat spin and drop at the same time, and the next wave washed over her deck—some of the water found its way below.

Phoebe was seasick. Whenever he was below, Caleb did his best to distract her. They were lying in their bunk with Phoebe curled up on her side with her head across Caleb's chest. He prattled on about anything he could think of to take her mind off her stomach.

"When we find a place we like, maybe we can build a little house, and grow our own food in the summer. Julian's parents have a house, and he said he'd help us build one of our own."

Phoebe checked the Council boats again—they'd lost sight of the Molly not long after dark—none of their crew suspected that they'd be crazy enough to turn into the storm. After four hours, it was clear they'd gotten away, and everyone relaxed—just a little bit.

Phoebe's stomach had tolerated the rising sea for an hour, and lying down did make things better, but eventually nothing helped. She hated throwing up, and hated Caleb watching her throw up even more. Soon, a pattern emerged. The nausea would gradually increase and then, after the eruption, she'd feel almost human for a little while—a little weaker, maybe, but better. Then it would start all over again.

Caleb helped when he was present, holding her hair back as she vomited and then wiping her face with a wet towel. She was embarrassed at first, but after a while she stopped worrying about much of anything.

"How can you even look at me?" she asked after a bout of sickness.

He gave her a half smile, but didn't say anything.

"You're never going to want to kiss me again," she complained.

"Well," he said, "maybe not just this minute."

Phoebe hit him on the leg as he was laughing.

The boat's motion didn't seem to bother most people, which made her feel like a wimp, until she heard that Gabriel wasn't doing any better. She didn't wish this sickness on anyone, but having someone like him in the same condition made her feel—well, not better exactly, but less bad.

Phoebe's leg was bothering her, too. The pain had been getting worse for days, but with the constant threat of death, the frequent bouts of vomiting, and the weakness, she'd managed to forget it for a while. Phoebe was hot, too, much more than before, and it was becoming increasingly difficult for her to stay focused on where and when she was.

Her family had begun using wet cloths to help keep her temperature down, and they changed her dressing several times that night, even while the boat was being thrown around.

Phoebe drifted in and out of consciousness, and when she was awake, the inner voices from people nearby kept coming through. Most of what she heard was worry—worry about her leg, worry about her fever, and worry about surviving.

The storm's violence continued to grow throughout the night. Scary sounds, popping and groaning and sharp creaking noises, all came from the Molly's hull and rigging. Both she and her mother looked up, white-eyed, expecting the worst to happen.

As the night progressed, Phoebe was aware less of the time. During a last lucid moment, she asked her mother what life as a normal girl might have been like. Phoebe doubted that such a thing as 'normal' really existed. *It's a myth—a bedtime story for little girls who don't pay attention when they're riding dreams. What the hell does that mean?* she wondered, struggling to stay awake.

"I have to throw up!" she blurted out, reaching for the bucket. Her mother was there this time.

Afterward, she heard Becky say her name, "Phoebe, Phoebe." She wanted to answer. She tried very hard, but wasn't sure if actual words came out. That was the last thing she remembered.

Ω

"Uh-huh," Phoebe muttered in response to Rebecca's calls.

"I'm afraid it's too much for her—she's burning up. We've been fooling ourselves; she's not getting any better. I don't know what to do!" Rebecca looked around, as if she'd find an answer in the cabin.

Gabriel leaned in heavily through the hatch, pale and miserable. He'd heard the panic in Rebecca's voice. "We'll head in soon," he said. "She'll have to hang in there. I tried to get the wound as clean as I could, but the pieces from that wall hit her pretty hard. I must have missed something, but she's tough. Keep her temperature down as much as you can—keep her wet." Then he rushed away to vomit.

After the sickness, Gabriel decided it would be better to be above deck. *Keep busy,* he told himself. On deck, he relieved Caleb, telling him that Rebecca needed someone to be with her. He repeated the advice to keep Phoebe cool, and warned him not to alarm Rebecca too much. Caleb descended the short stairway, looking soaked and exhausted. Gabriel doubted they'd be able to get help for the girl in time. It would be close to a week before they could find a doctor who could help.

The storm had reached a critical point, and Jacob was seriously considering coming about to run before the wind. The Molly was a two-masted schooner; the mainmast—aft—was taller than the foremast. Daniel and Gabriel were each secured to one—Daniel to the mainmast and Gabriel the foremast. Jacob had harnessed himself at the stern, near the wheel. He steered using one hand, his leg, and shoulder, while pointing out commands with his other hand. It was impossible to hear over the wind.

All the sails, except for a storm jib, had been reefed, or they'd have been torn to shreds, but Jacob still needed power for the rudder to maintain a degree of control. As he was directing them, using signals, a rogue wave slapped the stern from the starboard side, and the boat pirouetted sideways, leaving them at the mercy of the sea.

A monster wave engulfed the Molly from the port side, nearly capsizing her. Jacob heard popping noises as shrouds and stays parted, and then a thunderous crack when the foremast snapped off at the deck and was swept overboard. It was still attached to the Molly by two shrouds that had twisted together. The mast was partially caught under the boat near the bow, and was being sucked down, pulling the Molly over.

Gabriel's harness had barely enough play to keep him aboard, and there were just a few seconds to act before the Molly capsized. He knew what he had to do. Gabriel leapt over the mangled wreckage on deck, his knife clearing its sheath while he was in the air, and he hacked through the last two shrouds, freeing the mast. It went down under the Molly quickly and the boat righted itself, but the Scout—still tied to the mast—was dragged under, too. Daniel saw it happen, but everything moved so fast that he didn't have time to react. Gabriel was gone.

Jacob tried desperately to get the Molly back onto a safe line. The aft-mast was all they had now, but it would have to do. He pointed at the sails, sharply signaling Daniel to let out an edge to give the rudder some bite. As he worked, the end of the foremast came back up and slammed into the Molly, opening a breach in the starboard side of the hull before disappearing again. They were taking on water, and the storm wasn't finished yet.

When the Molly keeled over, people below deck were thrown across the cabin, and water started coming in through a hole in the hull—Rebecca was sure they were about to die.

Caleb and Julian managed to fight their way onto the deck. They freed the sail chest and cut a piece of canvas from the spare sail, and then used the material and wood hacked from the chest to fashion a temporary patch for the hull. Jacob leaned into the wheel, trying to keep the boat steady as they climbed out, far over the side, to plug the hole. Caleb lost his hammer before he could spike his part of the patch in place—his hands were slippery and cold. Julian finished his part and handed the other hammer to Caleb. Once the cover was in place, Julian told Daniel to go below and deal with the water. He and Caleb would stay on deck to help Jacob.

Below, Daniel started the hand-operated pump, trying to keep up with the water still coming in. The patch had slowed the inflow, but a lot of water was already aboard and more was coming through. Rebecca secured Phoebe to her bunk and then went to help Daniel—even with one hand she could take turns on the pump. Everyone was fighting as hard as they could, but things didn't look good.

CHAPTER 46

His Holiness

H E WAS DRESSED ALL IN black. The simplicity of his suit and its understated appearance belied the power and wealth the man controlled, but it was made from the highest quality fabrics. The only adornment he permitted was the ornate signet ring on his hand. While it was no longer used to authenticate messages, it was still a symbol of the power he held: the Supreme Elder, head of the Council of God—His Holiness.

The Elder stood with his back to the room, looking out the window of his modestly furnished working office. He had a formal office, too, where he received important visitors, and it was far more opulent, but he preferred this one. Extravagance was one of the trappings of power, not power itself, and accumulating real power was how he protected the Council. "In absolute power," he'd often say, "is absolute security."

"What did you learn?" His voice was calm but direct.

A second man, dressed in the scarlet robes of the Inner Circle, rose from one knee. He was careful to keep his voice level, and worked hard to suppress the agitation he felt. The Elder was not known to tolerate fear in his subordinates.

"There was no sign of them, we lost them in the storm. Some of the sailors say they must have turned directly into its path to avoid capture, and they believe the boat perished, but I'll believe it when I see the wreckage and their bodies. Until then I'll assume they've escaped to rejoin the remnants of the Order." Ambrose paused to allow the Elder an opportunity to speak, but he only nodded to continue.

"The woman *was* the Sensitive Rebecca. I compared photos taken in the hospital with those from our archive. She's the same one who disappeared after the great revelation. We assumed she'd died when she jumped from the cliffs. Unfortunately, the informers who let us know she was going to the harbor were both martyred—undoubtedly murdered by one of the Order's trained killers.

"Several other people disappeared at the same time she escaped. I don't believe the boat was stolen. Its owner, his son, and an adopted daughter are all missing, too, and there was a boy with them—a young man from a respectable family. Caleb Addison is the son of Dr. George Addison, director of the hospital. He seems to have been involved with the adopted daughter. Caleb was a top student and marked as one who would do well within the Council's circle of friends—before all this happened, of course."

"Did George Addison aid the escape?"

"No, Your Holiness, I don't believe he was involved. I...tested him, and other members of his family as well. While I think his devotion to the Council is, perhaps, less enthusiastic than we might expect, I don't think he had knowledge of the plot. My theory is that the son helped somehow, maybe by using his own knowledge of the hospital, or he may have stolen the facility's plans. They would have helped to identify vulnerabilities in our security."

"What about the Keepers, the ones who died with no apparent wounds?"

Ambrose wondered if he'd imagined a hint of concern in the Elder's voice.

"That's been the most vexing mystery of all. It's the first time we've seen anything like this. As you said, there were no marks on the Keepers. Three of them died immediately, and the fourth is completely mindless, and unlikely to recover. He can't speak, or eat, or even control the most basic bodily functions. I doubt he even realizes we're around him. Naturally, we'll take care of him and I'll pray for his recovery.

"The cause of his affliction, and the deaths of the other Keepers, was undoubtedly some kind of demonic act. It was done so rapidly that the men fell in their tracks during combat. At first, I attributed it to the Rebecca creature. She's reputedly the strongest of the surviving mind demons, but why didn't she do the same thing to avoid capture? Plus, she was under heavy sedation at the time, a precaution to prevent her from exercising her powers. I doubt she did this."

"Then who did?"

"I think I know. Let me explain how. This issue disturbed me so much that I broadened the investigation. I wanted to look at who else may have been involved."

The Supreme Elder nodded.

"I started with the family that fled with the creature. The older man is a fisherman, and his son a defender in the Council Court. There was nothing special about them, although the younger man had lived with Rebecca in the past. Then there's the adopted daughter. That's where my research yielded some interesting results. We traced her origin to a birth certificate and a certificate of adoption. Both seemed to have been forged—they both pointed to a nonexistent birth family. This made me suspect that the girl might have been Rebecca's offspring.

"Next, I interviewed the girl's schoolmates. The girl appears to have been rather unremarkable—quiet to the point of being inarticulate, and purportedly a slow learner. But closer inspection of her record shows something else, and I had to conclude that her slowness was a feint. Her test scores were erratic, easy questions were answered incorrectly, while more complex ones with surprising skill. Then there's her artwork. For such a slow learner, she's a remarkable artist, and her memory for detail is astounding. She's anything but ordinary.

"There are other factors, too. She first appeared around the time of the Purge, about the same time the Rebecca creature disappeared. I had an artist draw pictures of her, using descriptions from the people at school. No recent photographs of her were available, and she seems to have been conveniently absent every time the school photos were taken. We compared the drawings of her with the likenesses of Rebecca—both the recent photos taken at the hospital and photos from the archives. The resemblance between the two is striking. They confirm that she's the spawn of Rebecca, and possibly more potent.

"With this in mind, I re-interviewed people who had interacted with her recently, looking for signs of the unexplained: the cousin and friends of the Addison boy. Many commented that the girl had displayed evidence of surprising wealth at a recent dinner party at George Addison's house. The clothing and jewelry she wore couldn't be explained by her adopted father's position. Curiously, the cousin of the boy, a young woman named Mary, recently experienced a sudden loss of memory while with her. This is probably the most direct evidence of an aggressive ability. I suspect the mystery girl acted on Miss Addison somehow—possibly to conceal something. The boy may well be under her spell, too.

"All of this is outlined in the report. But I've concluded that she's a powerful demon, perhaps a new variation of the Sensitive, and seemingly a weapon. She may well be the most dangerous creature we've ever faced, and able to kill multiple people with a single thought."

"What is this creature's name?" the Elder asked.

"Phoebe, an aggressive dark mind demon, one I think we need to find and kill quickly."

The Supreme Elder frowned at the rising tone in his voice. "We are nothing if not patient, Ambrose. It's only a matter of time before we get her."

The Elder continued, "What of the infiltrator, the one who led us to the two martyred agents? He promised to find out more. Has he located their Sanctuaries yet? That's where they'll shelter this Phoebe. Didn't the infiltrator tell you that he thought one of their Sanctuaries was not far from this very city? Wouldn't it be logical to base a new weapon near their enemy?"

"The infiltrator has not yet discovered the location of their Sanctuaries. However, we recently captured a new hostage, one who is dear to an important member of their own inner circle. I plan to leak this information to the Order through our informer. It might cause them to make a mistake, or at least to trust more in our informer. If we can get their location, we can flood the area with Keepers, more than any one demon could possibly handle."

The Supreme Elder nodded. The use of hostages had been common since the Purge, and was effective. The three Bishops disapproved, but they were outnumbered in the Council.

"About George Addison: Because his family has been loyal, we'll forgive him, but he's never to be trusted again, and he should be *encouraged* to retire. For the rest, keep me informed but don't take direct action without consulting with me first."

"Of course, Your Holiness."

"Now, I have some good news for *you*," the Supreme Elder said. "The workers made good progress on our new home, and they even installed the reactor we found—it still works. You should make arrangements for your people to move in soon, but keep it very quiet."

"Thank you, Your Holiness. God's Will be done."

"God's Will be done, Ambrose."

CHAPTER 47

Infection

SOMETIME DURING THE DARK OF the morning, the worst of the storm faded. Daniel and Rebecca were still at the pump, and Jacob, Caleb, and Julian fought the storm above, on deck. They couldn't relax just yet, but the waves and wind were diminishing, and the storm's center had passed them by.

Deep lines were etched in Jacob's face, and they told the story of his long battle at the helm. The storm was still moving northwest, so he turned south to get farther from it. An hour later, the sun rose and Jacob steered the Molly west, toward land. They could see the massive storm still churning to the north, its fury unabated, but they were still days from getting help for Phoebe.

Below deck, she'd been delirious and talking in her sleep for hours. Rebecca had removed most of her outer clothing and covered her with a light sheet, which she kept damp. Caleb sat on the bunk now, holding her hand and talking to her softly. Meanwhile, Daniel and Julian removed the hatch covers, and opened portals to let fresh air in. The storm was over, but the race to save Phoebe was just beginning.

Jacob inspected the hastily made patch and added additional layers of canvas to further slow the leak. Water was still coming in, but slowly.

Rebecca had long since made up her mind that she trusted Caleb. It was clear he loved Phoebe, and she watched helplessly as he spoke, pleading with her to hold on. She compared him with Daniel, noting how similar they were.

Throughout the day, Rebecca and Caleb kept Phoebe as cool as possible. She was having terrible nightmares, so Rebecca tried putting calming thoughts and images into her mind, anything to replace the terrible visions she was having. The fever, seasickness, and pain of her wound had sapped most of Phoebe's strength, and were still pulling her down into her own personal hell. Everyone else was exhausted from the storm, too. Rebecca saw Daniel fall asleep while talking to Julian at the table.

The next day was pretty much the same for Phoebe. She half woke up now and then, just long enough to take in a little water—but the fever had her in its grip. Rebecca and Daniel tried to get Caleb to take a break. He needed sleep, but wouldn't leave Phoebe. Finally, Julian convinced him that it wouldn't help if he got sick, too.

"She's going to need you even more when she wakes up," he said. Rebecca didn't think Julian believed she would recover, but it worked, and Caleb agreed to take a break on deck. Rebecca found him asleep in the sun, and left him be.

Jacob was steering the Molly directly west. He'd added as much sail as he could onto the remaining mast. There was no specific destination in his mind yet. "Maybe one of the more isolated villages," he told Daniel. There'd been no sign of the Council boats.

It was during the afternoon of the second day following the storm when Rebecca heard Daniel call her onto the deck, and then he waved her over to the bow.

She moved slowly, feeling the accumulated stress and fatigue of the past several days. The sky was cloudless and blue, and there was a fresh breeze stirring across the deck. It lightened the atmosphere—a different world than the gloom below the deck, but she wouldn't stay away from Phoebe for long.

Daniel took her good hand and gently put an arm around her, asking how they were doing.

"About the same," she said, soaking in his quiet presence. Then she asked why he'd called.

"I wanted you to look at something. There," he indicated, pointing.

A small speck, more of a smudge in the distance, marred the blue of the horizon. It didn't appear to be moving.

"What is it?" she asked. New signs of worry creased her forehead. "A bird?"

"No, too far away. It'd have to be an awfully big bird at this range. If I didn't know better, I'd guess it was an airplane. Dad, can I use your binoculars?"

"Sure," Jacob said, retrieving them from the main cabin.

Daniel focused on the object, staring for a whole minute, and then let out a sigh. Jacob and Rebecca looked at each other, both frowning.

"It sure looks like an airplane," he said. There was no way to run from it. Rebecca and Jacob each took a turn looking through the binoculars.

"Is it the Council?" Jacob wanted to know. Rebecca shrugged.

"I haven't seen anything like it in years, not since the Purge," Jacob said.

"I have," Rebecca said. "The Order has a few, but they don't use them very often."

"Where do they get their fuel?" Daniel asked.

"From the Council of God," she said, smiling. "They converted the entire fleet to run on natural gas, which they steal from the Council's pipelines." It was possible this was an Order aircraft, but she didn't want to get her hopes up yet.

"The Council has them, too," Julian said from behind.

"We'll know soon enough," Rebecca said. The plane was getting closer. It would be within her range before long. *Friend or enemy?* she wondered.

"How will it land?" Daniel wanted to know.

"Almost all of the aircraft we use are amphibious," Julian said.

The plane continued its approach and Rebecca began to sense familiar patterns within. Tears ran down her face when she recognized who was aboard, and she sank to the deck, her legs giving way.

"What is it, Becky?" Daniel asked, kneeling down beside her.

"They're friends." It was all she could manage.

CHAPTER 48

Flight of the Duck

SOON, EVERYONE COULD HEAR THE twin engines as the plane started its descent. The pilot circled once, to let Jacob know that she intended to land. He'd already dropped the sails when Rebecca said the aircraft was friendly, and had just finished letting out a sea anchor. The Molly moved differently without forward motion, tilting from side to side with every small wave.

Rebecca went below to check on Phoebe and to let Caleb come up for the airplane's landing. At first he refused, but she insisted he go up. She wanted to be alone with Phoebe, and with her own feelings for a little while.

♎

On deck, Daniel put an arm around his shoulders. Caleb sensed the radical shift in everyone's mood and, for the first time in days, started to believe they might actually make it.

"Rebecca told me everything will be all right now," Daniel said. "There's a doctor on the airplane—she said he can handle anything."

Caleb closed his eyes, finally ready to let go. Only the most intense force of will had kept him going. Neither of them had spoken about Gabriel, yet. The pain was still too fresh. So many things had happened in the past few days that he wondered if he was really awake now.

"You know, I'd give her my own leg," Caleb said.

336

"That won't be necessary, you know." Daniel was grinning. "I don't worry as much now about who'll look after her."

They watched the plane settle onto the surface of the water and move toward them. Jacob started to lower the dinghy then saw it wouldn't be necessary. The airplane had stopped, far enough away to avoid contact, and someone had opened a side hatch and was lowering an inflatable raft. Three men climbed down into it and one of them rowed.

Jacob and Daniel met and helped the three men onto the deck. One man was tall—well over two meters—with bushy dark hair and dark piercing eyes. The second looked more like a boy, close to Caleb's age—maybe even a bit younger—while the third man appeared to be in his mid-twenties. He had the look of a Scout.

Daniel shook hands with the tall man first—he acted like the leader.

"I can't tell you how relieved we are to see you. I'm Daniel Lambert."

The man laughed. "I'm Matthew Martin," he said. "I can't tell *you* how glad I am we found you. I was sure you wouldn't make it. But I picked out the most optimistic path possible anyway—the only thread where anyone lived—and here we are. Sometimes you need to trust to luck."

Daniel wasn't sure he'd heard the man right, and didn't completely understand the context of what he'd said, but smiled anyway. "Can I ask if there's a doctor with you? My little girl's very sick."

"I'm the Healer," the young boy said. Daniel looked at him more closely, noticing for the first time that his eyes didn't match the boy's youthful appearance. This inconsistency reminded him a little bit of Phoebe, but the contrast here was more pronounced.

"Please don't think me rude, but could you have a look at her now? We're all very worried."

"You're not being rude at all. That's why I came," the boy said.

"How did you find us?" Daniel asked, as he led him down the short companionway below. "I'm sorry, I didn't ask your name."

"I'm Samuel, Healer for the Order. Matthew is the one who found you—he's pretty good at that sort of thing."

As soon as they entered the cabin, the fragile facade that Rebecca had so carefully prepared melted away and she started to sob. She had wanted to remain calm, but the sudden relief of seeing Samuel made that impossible. After a short pause, she threw her arms around him. "Thank God you're here. I couldn't believe it when I felt you coming—I won't ask how you found us. This is my daughter, Phoebe."

Samuel didn't say anything. This was someone who needed him. He looked at her closely and asked for privacy, but changed his mind, requesting that Rebecca stay.

Once Daniel left, he examined Phoebe thoroughly. The wound was horribly infected. There had been some less-than-professional surgery done to her leg, but he could fix that. There was something more wrong with her. He smelled her breath and sampled a miniscule quantity of her blood.

He was beginning to understand why Matthew thought the girl was in danger. She had a deeper problem—it felt like a genetic flaw of some sort. Although less urgent than the infection, it was probably fatal. In all likelihood—assuming his guess was right— Phoebe would have succumbed within a year.

He removed various instruments from his bag, and laid them out on the empty bunk: the blood-transfusion kit, a scalpel, a suture kit, and some of the drugs he'd been given by the physician from Corbin. After drawing a unit of blood from Phoebe, he started transfusing it into his own body. The portable kit allowed Samuel to keep on working even as he received her blood.

"I'll use a broad spectrum antibiotic," he said, forgetting that he hadn't actually spoken to Rebecca yet.

"What's this genetic flaw you think you see?" she asked.

"Ah, a Sensitive. I forgot for a moment."

"Sorry," she said.

"It's okay. I understand. Let me treat the wound first, then we'll talk."

Samuel gave Phoebe a local anesthetic. Although unconscious, he didn't want to cause her unnecessary pain. Next, he used the scalpel to reopen the wound, discarding the crude stitches and allowing the infection to drain. He probed deeply into the muscle, removing tiny bits of stone, and then washed the area with water before inspecting the wound's edges.

"What I am about to do will look a little strange," he said. "But my saliva contains healing elements that will help clean and prepare the injury. Remember I was engineered to do this, and I use more than just blood when I work."

Rebecca nodded. She watched him clean the wound and, amazingly, the tissue was already starting to look better. Afterward he drew some blood from himself and allowed it to enter and coat the wound directly. Then he sewed the tissue back together again.

"There'll always be a scar, but my saliva and blood will help her heal better. I think the scar will fade, but it'll take a long time."

What wonderful gifts, Rebecca thought.

Finally, Samuel gave Phoebe an injection.

"Now we wait. My body needs time to adapt to her infection, and to create the needed antibodies to help her. The antibiotic I gave her will work to reduce the infection, but I think her immune system's been compromised by this other issue. My blood will lend her strength for now. I'll give her half a unit before we leave and another when we get to Lake John.

"Rebecca. The problem you heard me thinking about is deeper—too deep for me to treat quickly. It isn't an issue within her tissues. I believe it's a problem in her immune system. I'll treat her as I would anyone else—and that will help—but in this case I'll just be treating the symptoms and not the root cause. My blood can't stop the progression of the deterioration. For that, I'll need to give her bone-marrow transplants, and I'll implant certain stem cells. We'll create a new immune system for her.

"If I'm right, she has a genetic condition that's been lying dormant for years. Something triggered it within the past year. Do you know if she's been feeling weak lately? I mean, before she was injured."

"She talked about a lingering weakness, especially after she exerts herself."

"That would be consistent with my theory. I think it's a flaw linked with what she is, probably an unintended consequence of the crossed bloodlines. We aren't equipped to treat her here. I'll need Corbin for that. But don't worry, there's no immediate danger to her, and my blood can protect her for many months."

Rebecca frowned. "Is this what Matthew saw earlier?"

"Probably, but even he isn't certain. This issue would have manifested itself in a matter of months, but he seemed to believe that she was developing Council problems, too. Either way, it's a good thing we got her out."

"All I managed to do was to get myself captured and other people killed," Rebecca said.

"What you did had to be done. Don't blame yourself. And you did a good job taking care of her, especially by keeping her temperature down." He covered Phoebe again and wet the sheet to keep her cool. "She looks a lot like you, especially when you first came to Corbin. I think you were a little older at the time."

"Phoebe is prettier than I was. She's certainly a lot stronger Sensitive than I'll ever be."

"Now," he said, "let me look at your shoulder." Rebecca protested that she felt fine, but he was determined. After the examination he told her that the doctor in the hospital had done a good job treating her.

"I could probably reduce the scarring a little, but why inflict more pain and trauma, as long as it doesn't bother you."

"I don't mind. And I'm sure Daniel won't mind either," she added.

He laughed. "Well, you're finally together with your family again, and I know how much this means to you." She put her arms around him again.

"Thank you, Samuel."

"A thought." There was a pained expression on his face, as if he were conflicted about something.

"What is it?"

"Be careful at Corbin. Some in that place may have their own agenda, and that may not always be in Phoebe's best interest." Rebecca's eyebrows went up, but she stopped herself from probing his mind. "You've done a lot for the Order," he added, "maybe it's time you thought of yourself for a while—it's not too late, you know, for you and for Phoebe. Think about it."

Samuel looked back at his own life, a life dedicated to healing—there'd been no real choice for him. He often wondered how much of what he did was governed by his DNA, and how much by choice—not that it made any difference. In some ways Rebecca and he shared a compulsion to help, but she had more of a choice, and she had a family.

Reducing the infection helped Phoebe rest, and her fever started to come down. They kept her cool, waiting for the next phase of the treatment.

"Was anyone else injured?" Samuel asked.

"Not that I know of," Rebecca said, "but we're dealing with a fairly stoic group, so they might be hiding anything."

"I'll go on deck and ask around," he said. "We'll move her this evening." Rebecca's eyebrows went up. "Don't worry, everything will be all right. Matthew's watching out for us." Then he laughed. "That sounded like a prayer, didn't it?"

On deck, Jacob was expressing concern about abandoning the Molly. "It's not that I can't leave her, but it's such a waste. She's still got a lot of life left in her."

Matthew stared at the horizon for a moment. "You're right. There's no reason why the Molly can't be repaired. From what I saw, the Council boats gave up the chase. They'll be heading back south in the next couple of days. After that you can move toward land. We have a secure spot for her, it's a little south of your old home port. Jonathan, are you familiar with the Rocky Point grotto?"

"I am. We stayed there last year—but my place is with Samuel. I'm his protector."

"You're right, and you'll continue to be his protector in the future, but first I need you and Julian to help Jacob hide the boat at Rocky Point. I'll take responsibility for Samuel until you're back. Don't worry. We'll meet at Corbin before long," he added.

"Jacob, I'd like you to join us once you've secured the Molly. Jonathan will bring you in along a different route than the one we're taking. The boat will remain yours, although we may ask to borrow it from time to time. For now, we'll protect all of you as welcome guests. I think we might even be able to manage new port documents. Obviously, you'll need to stay away from New Bright Sea Harbor for the rest of your life."

He looked at Daniel. "I need you and your family to get ready to leave this evening. Bring everything you'll need—within reason."

Daniel nodded.

Samuel interrupted, "I've begun treatment, but will need to do more before we leave." He turned to Daniel. "By the time we reach Corbin, she'll feel a lot better. The wound is clean and it'll heal now, but I'm still in the midst of treating the infection. Don't worry, she'll be her old self in a couple of days. The scars will fade after a few months, but she'll always carry a little reminder of that night." Daniel and Caleb couldn't thank him enough.

♎

Samuel sat on the deck watching the sun dip toward the horizon. After an hour he went below and started the transfusion into Phoebe. He would have liked more time to concentrate his antibodies, but there'd be an additional treatment soon enough.

At dusk, Caleb and Daniel moved Phoebe to the dinghy. Most of their things had already been transferred to the strange-looking aircraft. They said farewell to Jacob, knowing they'd see each other soon.

Phoebe woke up just after they transferred her into the dinghy. She was between Daniel and Rebecca while Caleb rowed.

"Mom? Where are we going?"

"We're taking you home. I know you'll like it there."

"I had such horrible dreams. I dreamed I was pulled into the sea and drowned."

"Don't worry, kiddo," Daniel said, closing his eyes. "It was just a dream. We're all together now. How do you feel?"

"Strange. I feel a lot better but..."

"But what?" Caleb asked.

"I don't know, it's like something or someone is missing."

"Go back to sleep, sweetheart," her mother suggested. "We'll be on land in a couple of hours." Phoebe didn't argue, and closed her eyes and drifted back into a more restful sleep.

Caleb returned from the Duck for the rest of the people. Matthew gave last-minute instructions to Jonathan before climbing in. Samuel and he were the last to leave the Molly.

Margaret had stayed aboard the Duck to make sure it didn't drift too close to the Molly, and now she started the twin engines. The thunderous roar startled those who'd never heard the engines up close before. They waved good-bye to Jacob and the others through the windows as she turned the aircraft into the wind for takeoff.

Rebecca peered out when she felt the sudden lift, and watched as the Molly dropped away from them, until she looked just like a bit of debris floating in the endless sea. Seconds later, the last of the sun's rays disappeared and everyone settled back into their seats for the flight to their new home.

CHAPTER 49

The Message

The Following Spring

THE PACKAGE WAS POSTMARKED NEW Bright Sea Harbor, but there was no return address, but the sender's name ensured that it received attention. It read: "From Phoebe Lambert, care of Matthew Martin." The package had been inspected for dangerous contents before being allowed through to the Supreme Elder's office. It was open, but no one would have dared read the documents inside.

The Elder had been meeting with his most trusted advisors over the past three days, and, when informed of the package, asked that they remain to help him interpret the message. They all surrounded the conference table and leaned forward to see what it contained.

Inside was a handwritten note, a photograph, and a large drawing. The drawing was beautifully rendered and contained multiple elements. At its center was a precise plan and map of their new secret headquarters—perfect in every detail. Surrounding this were lifelike representations of the five of them, along with drawings of their closest friends and family members. They stared at the drawing, each absorbing its significance as their hearts beat in the silence of the room. The photograph was a postmortem snapshot of the Council's infiltrator. The note was short, and written in a flowing but firm hand:

Wishing you and your family a healthy future on the occasion of the opening of your new home.

With Love,

Phoebe

Epilogue

THE STORM THAT HAD BEGUN so early that morning had long since passed. The old woman eased an ache in her leg and put a hand on Becky's shoulder to let her know that their time for the day was drawing to a close. The girl looked tired. Phoebe could feel her exhaustion through their light touch, remembering what it was like to experience things this way for the very first time. But Becky wouldn't be going through this alone. The pairing of the old with the young was one of the best ideas of the Order, and Phoebe made sure it was kept alive.

"What happened next?" the girl asked.

"We escaped from the Council and tried to start a new life at Corbin. We all hoped that we could live together in peace—Jacob, my father, my mother, Caleb, and myself.

"But it's late. I'm sure you're tired and I know you'll want to talk with your mother. She'll be here in a few minutes. When you come back tomorrow, I'll show you how life at Corbin didn't work out for us, and why we had to leave the Land altogether. Then you'll see some of the incredible places we'd never planned to go. Tell your mother about what we shared today—she'll remember from when she was a little girl."

Becky looked at her grandmother and closed her eyes to concentrate on asking one last question.

"No," Phoebe said. "That happened later."

ABOUT THE COVER IMAGES

The front cover shows the faces of Phoebe and Rebecca, with each looking in a different direction, representative of different choices made in life.

The scale is the classical symbol for truth and justice, and is also used as the symbol for Libra. Currently justice is out of balance as is the political balance of power in the Land. Themis was the Greek Titan of justice and truth and she is represented in modern times by the symbol of a blindfolded woman: Justice holding the scales of truth. On the cover, her hand has been replaced by the masculine fist that seized power in the Land, and which has displaced the hand of Justice. Libra has an additional and more subtle meaning: the ruling planet for Libra is Venus, and this hints at a potential change in power for the future.

The back cover shows an ideal balance between the Council and the Order. The Libra symbol serves as the scale here, and the Council is represented by a circle enclosing a symbol for its three founding faiths. The Order is represented by the symbol of the Philosopher's Stone, since the organization was founded at a time when its members were delving into the mysteries of alchemy.